Kate Chopin

A SHAMEFUL AFFAIR
and other stories

Selected and edited by Janet Beer

PHŒNIX

This edition first published by Phoenix Paperbacks, 1998
Selection, Introduction and other critical apparatus

copyright © Phoenix paperbacks, 1998

Phoenix paperbacks
Orion Publishing Group
Orion House
5 Upper Saint Martin's Lane
London
WC2H 9EA

Typeset by Deltatype Ltd, Birkenhead, Merseyside
Printed in Great Britain by
The Guernsey Press Co. Ltd, Guernsey, C.I.

British Library Cataloguing-in-Publication
Data is available on request.

ISBN 0 75380 524 3

Contents

Note on the Author

KATHERINE O'FLAHERTY, who would grow up to be the writer Kate Chopin, was born in St Louis, Missouri, in 1850. She received a full, if somewhat intermittent, education at the Sacred Heart Academy between 1855 and 1868 and met her husband, Oscar Chopin, during the following year. They were married in 1870, honeymooned in Europe and on their return went to live in Oscar Chopin's home state of Louisiana, first in New Orleans, then in Cloutierville in Natchitoches Parish, where, by 1880, they had a family of five sons and a daughter. After Oscar Chopin's death from swamp fever in 1882 his widow remained in Louisiana for two years before returning to St Louis, where she lived until her death in 1904. She began writing for publication after her return to St Louis but the landscape, people and customs which are depicted in the majority of her novels and short stories are those of Louisiana, the scene of her brief married life. She wrote approximately one hundred short stories as well as poetry, articles and reviews; she published two novels, *At Fault* (1890), and *The Awakening* (1899). Chopin was well known to her contemporaries as a regional writer but her fiction, and in particular *The Awakening*, is more highly esteemed in modern critical opinion than it was during her lifetime.

Introduction

Kate Chopin, born in St Louis, Missouri, in 1850 to a Creole mother and an Irish father, grew up in a society which was more French than American. She moved with ease between the English and French languages, whether formal French or the Creole patois spoken in her own and in her husband's Louisianan family. This linguistic flexibility and verve is put to good use in her fiction, for example, in the story 'La Belle Zoraïde', where Chopin makes the Creole language contextualize and frame the standard English of the narrative for her north American audience. In terms of her background and education Kate Chopin was a citizen of a world set apart from conventional late nineteenth-century American culture, a culture dominated by Protestant New England or New York traditions and values. Her social and literary tastes were formed outside the mainstream and although she was best known in her lifetime as a writer of regional or local colour tales, her fiction is not narrowly focused – it is cosmopolitan not provincial, sophisticated not naïve in its form, structure and content.

Chopin's work is, quite properly, read in the broader context of European as well as American literature. From the time of its publication in 1899, her novel, *The Awakening*, was described as the American *Madame Bovary*, treating as it does the controversial matter of the married, middle-class woman attempting to break free from convention. The first commentator to make the comparison, interestingly enough, was another writer of fiction, Willa Cather, reviewing the novel for the *Pittsburgh Leader*. The direct connection between her work and French literature is one that Chopin herself made; she paid sincere homage to Guy de Maupassant and attributed her own artistic awakening to his example and influence – 'It was at this period of my emerging from the vast solitude in which I had been making my own acquaintance, that I stumbled upon Maupassant'. Although she was not in any way a slavish imitator of Maupassant her writing owes debts of style and structure to his work; stories like

'Désirée's Baby' and 'The Story of an Hour' rely partly for their effects on the Maupassantian twist at the end of the tale, but they go beyond the showy cleverness of the narrative design to illustrate profound truths about the terms and conditions of existence for women in the nineteenth century.

Chopin's fictional subjects were often daring and iconoclastic; in her early novel, *At Fault*, she experimented with unconventional themes and characters: one of the central players is a female alcoholic, while matters at issue include divorce and remarriage, law and order, racial tension and contrasting attitudes between north and south, subjects Chopin would revisit in her short stories. Her intentions in her work, however, were not polemical; unlike her contemporary Charlotte Perkins Gilman, an ardent social reformer, Chopin had no ambition to bring about social change. She wrote to reflect the world around her, seeking to portray 'human existence in its subtle, complex, true meaning, stripped of the veil with which ethical and conventional standards have draped it', as she described the proper province of fiction in a review article. Notwithstanding, she knew that the constraints of the marketplace were such that she could not afford to be too transparent in the depiction of either race or sex in her work: both were controversial subjects in post-Civil-War America. Fortunately for the modern reader, her stories only require close reading to yield meaning and signification vastly beyond the initial impression which is created. Chopin's contemporaries expected scenes of local colour from her pen and she satisfied their expectations whilst embedding a complex arabesque of artistry and signification in the text. The vignette, 'Boulôt and Boulotte', at first sight a coy and somewhat cloying piece of whimsy about the foolish notions acted upon by children, becomes, at a second reading, a tale depicting rites of passage, a tale which describes gendered lives, the growth in continued physical freedom for the male and the imminence of physical constraint for the woman. Chopin's stories make no absolute judgements, however; she is careful to write good and bad, weakness and strength into both black and white, male and female, transcending the limits of her age in the depiction of race as well as sexual relations. Her last story, 'The Godmother', illustrates beautifully the oblique manner in which she explored –

and subtly undermined – dominant social attitudes towards slavery, Christian morality and the limits of sexual conduct.

Kate Chopin was very prolific during the last fifteen years of her comparatively short life. Her first printed story, 'A Point at Issue!', appeared in the *St. Louis Post-Dispatch* in October 1889; she subsequently wrote for many of the prestigious journals of her age – *Century*, *Atlantic*, *Harper's* and *Vogue* among them – and her last published piece, 'Polly', featured in *Youth's Companion* in July 1902. The fiction produced in this period reflects the fact that Chopin developed or changed many of her opinions during her adult life; she questioned the value of marriage, she lost – or mislaid – her religion, she became more broad-minded about sexual expression and speculated endlessly in her fiction upon the anarchic nature of sexual attraction. She became in every way more liberal and her freedom from inhibition is reflected in both the content and the increasing sophistication of her writing. Her choice of subject matter, however, sometimes meant that her work could not reach its audience: the story, 'Two Portraits', which poses alternative adult lives for the same child, one as a nun and one as a prostitute, was refused by every publisher to whom she sent it; 'The Storm', a depiction of an adulterous encounter narrated without the merest hint of a moral judgement, was never submitted to any editor, so certain was Chopin of its unpublishability. *The Awakening* caused a storm of adverse criticism, chiefly because Chopin had, as the reviewers described it, failed to condemn the immoral behaviour of her chief protagonist, Edna Pontellier.

Chopin was a complex and skilful technician in the medium of the short story and her refusal to compromise her art by moralizing, whilst marking her as distinct and sometimes dangerous to an audience at the turn of the nineteenth into the twentieth century, makes her a writer of enduring and exciting possibility for the twenty-first.

Janet Beer, London 1998

A SHAMEFUL AFFAIR
and other stories

Emancipation. A Life Fable

There was once an animal born into this world, and opening his eyes upon Life, he saw above and about him confining walls, and before him were bars of iron through which came air and light from without; this animal was born in a cage.

Here he grew, and throve in strength and beauty under care of an invisible protecting hand. Hungering, food was ever at hand. When he thirsted water was brought, and when he felt the need of rest, there was provided a bed of straw upon which to lie: and here he found it good, licking his handsome flanks, to bask in the sun beam that he thought existed but to lighten his home.

Awaking one day from his slothful rest, lo! the door of his cage stood open: accident had opened it. In the corner he crouched, wondering and fearingly. Then slowly did he approach the door, dreading the unaccustomed, and would have closed it, but for such a task his limbs were purposeless. So out the opening he thrust his head, to see the canopy of the sky grow broader, and the world waxing wider.

Back to his corner but not to rest, for the spell of the Unknown was over him, and again and again he goes to the open door, seeing each time more Light.

Then one time standing in the flood of it; a deep in-drawn breath – a bracing of strong limbs, and with a bound he was gone.

On he rushes, in his mad flight, heedless that he is wounding and tearing his sleek sides – seeing, smelling, touching of all things; even stopping to put his lips to the noxious pool, thinking it may be sweet.

Hungering there is no food but such as he must seek and ofttimes fight for; and his limbs are weighted before he reaches the water that is good to his thirsting throat.

So does he live, seeking, finding, joying and suffering. The door which accident had opened is open still, but the cage remains forever empty!

A No-Account Creole

I

One agreeable afternoon in late autumn two young men stood together on Canal Street, closing a conversation that had evidently begun within the club-house which they had just quitted.

'There's big money in it, Offdean,' said the elder of the two. 'I would n't have you touch it if there was n't. Why, they tell me Patchly's pulled a hundred thousand out of the concern a'ready.'

'That may be,' replied Offdean, who had been politely attentive to the words addressed to him, but whose face bore a look indicating that he was closed to conviction. He leaned back upon the clumsy stick which he carried, and continued: 'It's all true, I dare say, Fitch; but a decision of that sort would mean more to me than you'd believe if I were to tell you. The beggarly twenty-five thousand's all I have, and I want to sleep with it under my pillow a couple of months at least before I drop it into a slot.'

'You'll drop it into Harding & Offdean's mill to grind out the pitiful two and a half per cent commission racket; that's what you 'll do in the end, old fellow – see if you don't.'

'Perhaps I shall; but it's more than likely I shan't. We'll talk about it when I get back. You know I 'm off to north Louisiana in the morning'—

'No! What the deuce'—

'Oh, business of the firm.'

'Write me from Shreveport, then; or wherever it is.'

'Not so far as that. But don't expect to hear from me till you see me. I can't say when that will be.'

Then they shook hands and parted. The rather portly Fitch boarded a Prytania Street car, and Mr. Wallace Offdean hurried to the bank in order to replenish his portemonnaie, which had been materially lightened at the club through the medium of unpropitious jack-pots and bobtail flushes.

He was a sure-footed fellow, this young Offdean, despite an occasional fall in slippery places. What he wanted, now that he had reached his twenty-sixth year and his inheritance, was to get his feet well planted on solid ground, and to keep his head cool and clear.

With his early youth he had had certain shadowy intentions of shaping his life on intellectual lines. That is, he wanted to; and he meant to use his faculties intelligently, which means more than is at once apparent. Above all, he would keep clear of the maelstroms of sordid work and senseless pleasure in which the average American business man may be said alternately to exist, and which reduce him, naturally, to a rather ragged condition of soul.

Offdean had done, in a temperate way, the usual things which young men do who happen to belong to good society, and are possessed of moderate means and healthy instincts. He had gone to college, had traveled a little at home and abroad, had frequented society and the clubs, and had worked in his uncle's commission-house; in all of which employments he had expended much time and a modicum of energy.

But he felt all through that he was simply in a preliminary stage of being, one that would develop later into something tangible and intelligent, as he liked to tell himself. With his patrimony of twenty-five thousand dollars came what he felt to be the turning-point in his life, – the time when it behooved him to choose a course, and to get himself into proper trim to follow it manfully and consistently.

When Messrs. Harding & Offdean determined to have some one look after what they called 'a troublesome piece of land on Red River,' Wallace Offdean requested to be intrusted with that special commission of land-inspector.

A shadowy, ill-defined piece of land in an unfamiliar part of his native State, might, he hoped, prove a sort of closet into which he could retire and take counsel with his inner and better self.

II

What Harding & Offdean had called a piece of land on Red River was better known to the people of Natchitoches* parish as 'the old Santien place.'

In the days of Lucien Santien and his hundred slaves, it had been very splendid in the wealth of its thousand acres. But the war did its work, of course. Then Jules Santien was not the man to mend such damage as the war had left. His three sons were even less able than he had been to bear the weighty inheritance of debt that came to them with the dismantled plantation; so it was a deliverance to all when Harding & Offdean, the New Orleans creditors, relieved them of the place with the responsibility and indebtedness which its ownership had entailed.

Hector, the eldest, and Grégoire, the youngest of these Santien boys, had gone each his way. Placide alone tried to keep a desultory foothold upon the land which had been his and his forefathers'. But he too was given to wandering – within a radius, however, which rarely took him so far that he could not reach the old place in an afternoon of travel, when he felt so inclined.

There were acres of open land cultivated in a slovenly fashion, but so rich that cotton and corn and weed and 'cocoa-grass' grew rampant if they had only the semblance of a chance. The negro quarters were at the far end of this open stretch, and consisted of a long row of old and very crippled cabins. Directly back of these a dense wood grew, and held much mystery, and witchery of sound and shadow, and strange lights when the sun shone. Of a gin-house there was left scarcely a trace; only so much as could serve as inadequate shelter to the miserable dozen cattle that huddled within it in winter-time.

A dozen rods or more from the Red River bank stood the dwelling-house, and nowhere upon the plantation had time touched so sadly as here. The steep, black, moss-covered roof sat like an extinguisher above the eight large rooms that it covered, and had come to do its office so poorly that not more than half of these were habitable when the rain fell. Perhaps the live-oaks made too thick and close a shelter about it. The verandas were long and broad and inviting; but it was well to know that the brick pillar was crumbling away under one corner, that the railing was insecure at another, and that still another had long ago been condemned as unsafe. But that, of course, was not the

* Prounounced Nack-e-tosh.

corner in which Wallace Offdean sat the day following his arrival at the Santien place. This one was comparatively secure. A gloire-de-Dijon, thick-leaved and charged with huge creamy blossoms, grew and spread here like a hardy vine upon the wires that stretched from post to post. The scent of the blossoms was delicious; and the stillness that surrounded Offdean agreeably fitted his humor that asked for rest. His old host, Pierre Manton, the manager of the place, sat talking to him in a soft, rhythmic monotone; but his speech was hardly more of an interruption than the hum of the bees among the roses. He was saying:—

'If it would been me myse'f, I would nevair grumb'. W'en a chimbly breck, I take one, two de boys; we patch 'im up bes' we know how. We keep on men' de fence', firs' one place, anudder; an' if it would n' be fer dem mule' of Lacroix – *tonnerre!* I don' wan' to talk 'bout dem mule'. But me, I would n' grumb'. It 's Euphrasie, hair. She say dat's all fool nonsense fer rich man lack Hardin'-Offde'n to let a piece o' lan' goin' lack dat.'

'Euphrasie?' questioned Offdean, in some surprise; for he had not yet heard of any such person.

'Euphrasie, my li'le chile. Escuse me one minute,' Pierre added, remembering that he was in his shirt-sleeves, and rising to reach for his coat, which hung upon a peg near by. He was a small, square man, with mild, kindly face, brown and roughened from healthy exposure. His hair hung gray and long beneath the soft felt hat that he wore. When he had seated himself, Offdean asked:—

'Where is your little child? I have n't seen her,' inwardly marveling that a little child should have uttered such words of wisdom as those recorded of her.

'She yonder to Mme. Duplan on Cane River. I been kine espectin' hair sence yistiday – hair an' Placide,' casting an unconscious glance down the long plantation road. 'But Mme. Duplan she nevair want to let Euphrasie go. You know it's hair raise' Euphrasie sence hair po' ma die', Mr. Offde'n. She teck dat li'le chile, an' raise it, sem lack she raisin' Ninette. But it 's mo' 'an a year now Euphrasie say dat 's all fool nonsense to leave me livin' 'lone lack dat, wid nuttin' 'cep' dem nigger' – an' Placide once a w'ile. An' she came yair bossin'! My goodness!' The old man chuckled, 'Dat 's hair been writin' all dem letter' to Hardin'-Offde'n. If it would been me myse'f'—

III

Placide seemed to have had a foreboding of ill from the start when he found that Euphrasie began to interest herself in the condition of the plantation. This ill feeling voiced itself partly when he told her it was none of her lookout if the place went to the dogs. 'It 's good enough for Joe Duplan to run things *en grand seigneur*, Euphrasie; that 's w'at 's spoiled you.'

Placide might have done much single-handed to keep the old place in better trim, if he had wished. For there was no one more clever than he to do a hand's turn at any and every thing. He could mend a saddle or bridle while he stood whistling a tune. If a wagon required a brace or a bolt, it was nothing for him to step into a shop and turn out one as deftly as the most skilled blacksmith. Any one seeing him at work with plane and rule and chisel would have declared him a born carpenter. And as for mixing paints, and giving a fine and lasting coat to the side of a house or barn, he had not his equal in the country.

This last talent he exercised little in his native parish. It was in a neighboring one, where he spent the greater part of his time, that his fame as a painter was established. There, in the village of Orville, he owned a little shell of a house, and during odd times it was Placide's great delight to tinker at this small home, inventing daily new beauties and conveniences to add to it. Lately it had become a precious possession to him, for in the spring he was to bring Euphrasie there as his wife.

Maybe it was because of his talent, and his indifference in turning it to good, that he was often called 'a no-account creole' by thriftier souls than himself. But no-account creole or not, painter, carpenter, blacksmith, and whatever else he might be at times, he was a Santien always, with the best blood in the country running in his veins. And many thought his choice had fallen in very low places when he engaged himself to marry little Euphrasie, the daughter of old Pierre Manton and a problematic mother a good deal less than nobody.

Placide might have married almost any one, too; for it was the easiest thing in the world for a girl to fall in love with him, – sometimes the hardest thing in the world not to, he was such a splendid fellow, such a careless, happy, handsome fellow. And he did not seem to mind in the least that young men who had grown up with him were lawyers now, and planters, and members of Shakespeare clubs in town. No one ever expected anything quite so humdrum as that of the Santien boys. As youngsters, all three had been the despair of the country schoolmaster; then of the private tutor who had come to shackle them; and had failed in his design. And the state of mutiny and revolt that they had brought about at the college of Grand Coteau when their father, in a moment of weak concession to prejudice, had sent them there, is a thing yet remembered in Natchitoches.

And now Placide was going to marry Euphrasie. He could not recall the time when he had not loved her. Somehow he felt that it began the day when he was six years old, and Pierre, his father's overseer, had called him from play to come and make her acquaintance. He was permitted to hold her in his arms a moment, and it was with silent awe that he did so. She was the first whitefaced baby he remembered having seen, and he straightway believed she had been sent to him as a birthday gift to be his little playmate and friend. If he loved her, there was no great wonder; every one did, from the time she took her first dainty step, which was a brave one, too.

She was the gentlest little lady ever born in old Natchitoches parish, and the happiest and merriest. She never cried or whimpered for a hurt. Placide never did, why should she? When she wept, it was when she did what was wrong, or when he did; for that was to be a coward, she felt. When she was ten, and her mother was dead, Mme. Duplan, the Lady Bountiful of the parish, had driven across from her plantation, Les Chêniers, to old Pierre's very door, and there had gathered up this precious little maid, and carried her away, to do with as she would.

And she did with the child much as she herself had been done by. Euphrasie went to the convent soon, and was taught all gentle things, the pretty arts of manner and speech that the ladies of the 'Sacred Heart' can teach so well. When she quitted them, she left a trail of love behind her; she always did.

Placide continued to see her at intervals, and to love her always. One day he told her so; he could not help it. She stood under one of the big oaks at Les Chêniers. It was midsummer time, and the tangled sunbeams had enmeshed her in a golden fretwork. When he saw her standing there in the sun's glamour, which was like a glory upon her, he trembled. He seemed to see

her for the first time. He could only look at her, and wonder why
her hair gleamed so, as it fell in those thick chestnut waves about
her ears and neck. He had looked a thousand times into her eyes
before; was it only to-day they held that sleepy, wistful light in
them that invites love? How had he not seen it before? Why had
he not known before that her lips were red, and cut in fine,
strong curves? that her flesh was like cream? How had he not
seen that she was beautiful? 'Euphrasie,' he said, taking her
hands, – 'Euphrasie, I love you!'

She looked at him with a little astonishment. 'Yes; I know,
Placide.' She spoke with the soft intonation of the creole.

'No, you don't, Euphrasie. I did n' know myse'f how much tell
jus' now.'

Perhaps he did only what was natural when he asked her next
if she loved him. He still held her hands. She looked thoughtfully
away, unready to answer.

'Do you love anybody better?' he asked jealously. 'Any one jus'
as well as me?'

'You know I love papa better, Placide, an' Maman Duplan jus'
as well.'

Yet she saw no reason why she should not be his wife when he
asked her to.

Only a few months before this, Euphrasie had returned to live
with her father. The step had cut her off from everything that
girls of eighteen call pleasure. If it cost her one regret, no one
could have guessed it. She went often to visit the Duplans,
however; and Placide had gone to bring her home from Les
Chêniers the very day of Offdean's arrival at the plantation.

They had traveled by rail to Natchitoches, where they found
Pierre's no-top buggy awaiting them, for there was a drive of five
miles to be made through the pine woods before the plantation
was reached. When they were at their journey's end, and had
driven some distance up the long plantation road that led to the
house in the rear, Euphrasie exclaimed:—

'W'y, there's some one on the gall'ry with papa, Placide!'

'Yes; I see.'

'It looks like some one f'om town. It mus' be Mr. Gus Adams;
but I don' see his horse.'

''T ain't no one f'om town that I know. It 's boun' to be some
one f'om the city.'

'Oh, Placide, I should n' wonder if Harding & Offdean have sent some one to look after the place at las',' she exclaimed a little excitedly.

They were near enough to see that the stranger was a young man of very pleasing appearance. Without apparent reason, a chilly depression took hold of Placide.

'I tole you it was n' yo' lookout f'om the firs', Euphrasie,' he said to her.

IV

Wallace Offdean remembered Euphrasie at once as a young person whom he had assisted to a very high perch on his clubhouse balcony the previous Mardi Gras night. He had thought her pretty and attractive then, and for the space of a day or two wondered who she might be. But he had not made even so fleeting an impression upon her; seeing which, he did not refer to any former meeting when Pierre introduced them.

She took the chair which he offered her, and asked him very simply when he had come, if his journey had been pleasant, and if he had not found the road from Natchitoches in very good condition.

'Mr. Offde'n only come sence yistiday, Euphrasie,' interposed Pierre. 'We been talk' plenty 'bout de place, him an' me. I been tole 'im all 'bout it – va! An' if Mr. Offde'n want to escuse me now, I b'lieve I go he'p Placide wid dat hoss an' buggy;' and he descended the steps slowly, and walked lazily with his bent figure in the direction of the shed beneath which Placide had driven, after depositing Euphrasie at the door.

'I dare say you find it strange,' began Offdean, 'that the owners of this place have neglected it so long and shamefully. But you see,' he added, smiling, 'the management of a plantation does n't enter into the routine of a commission merchant's business. The place has already cost them more than they hope to get from it, and naturally they have n't the wish to sink further money in it.' He did not know why he was saying these things to a mere girl, but he went on: 'I'm authorized to sell the plantation if I can get anything like a reasonable price for it.' Euphrasie laughed in a way that made him uncomfortable, and he thought he would say no more at present, – not till he knew her better, anyhow.

'Well,' she said in a very decided fashion, 'I know you 'll fin' one or two persons in town who 'll begin by running down the lan' till you would n' want it as a gif', Mr. Offdean; and who will en' by offering to take it off yo' han's for the promise of a song, with the lan' as security again.'

They both laughed, and Placide, who was approaching, scowled. But before he reached the steps his instinctive sense of the courtesy due to a stranger had banished the look of ill humor. His bearing was so frank and graceful, and his face such a marvel of beauty, with its dark, rich coloring and soft lines, that the well-clipped and groomed Offdean felt his astonishment to be more than half admiration when they shook hands. He knew that the Santiens had been the former owners of this plantation which he had come to look after, and naturally he expected some sort of co-operation or direct assistance from Placide in his efforts at reconstruction. But Placide proved non-committal, and exhibited an indifference and ignorance concerning the condition of affairs that savored surprisingly of affectation.

He had positively nothing to say so long as the talk touched upon matters concerning Offdean's business there. He was only a little less taciturn when more general topics were approached, and directly after supper he saddled his horse and went away. He would not wait until morning, for the moon would be rising about midnight, and he knew the road as well by night as by day. He knew just where the best fords were across the bayous, and the safest paths across the hills. He knew for a certainty whose plantations he might traverse, and whose fences he might derail. But, for that matter, he would derail what he liked, and cross where he pleased.

Euphrasie walked with him to the shed when he went for his horse. She was bewildered at his sudden determination, and wanted it explained.

'I don' like that man,' he admitted frankly; 'I can't stan' him. Sen' me word w'en he 's gone, Euphrasie.'

She was patting and rubbing the pony, which knew her well. Only their dim outlines were discernible in the thick darkness.

'You are foolish, Placide,' she replied in French. 'You would do better to stay and help him. No one knows the place so well as you'—

'The place is n't mine, and it 's nothing to me,' he answered bitterly. He took her hands and kissed them passionately, but stooping, she pressed her lips upon his forehead.

'Oh!' he exclaimed rapturously, 'you do love me, Euphrasie?' His arms were holding her, and his lips brushing her hair and cheeks as they eagerly but ineffectually sought hers.

'Of co'se I love you, Placide. Ain't I going to marry you nex' spring? You foolish boy!' she replied, disengaging herself from his clasp.

When he was mounted, he stooped to say, 'See yere, Euphrasie, don't have too much to do with that d—Yankee.'

'But, Placide, he is n't a – a – "d—Yankee;" he 's a Southerner, like you, – a New Orleans man.'

'Oh, well, he looks like a Yankee.' But Placide laughed, for he was happy since Euphrasie had kissed him, and he whistled softly as he urged his horse to a canter and disappeared in the darkness.

The girl stood awhile with clasped hands, trying to understand a little sigh that rose in her throat, and that was not one of regret. When she regained the house, she went directly to her room, and left her father talking to Offdean in the quiet and perfumed night.

V

When two weeks had passed, Offdean felt very much at home with old Pierre and his daughter, and found the business that had called him to the country so engrossing that he had given no thought to those personal questions he had hoped to solve in going there.

The old man had driven him around in the no-top buggy to show him how dismantled the fences and barns were. He could see for himself that the house was a constant menace to human life. In the evenings the three would sit out on the gallery and talk of the land and its strong points and its weak ones, till he came to know it as if it had been his own.

Of the rickety condition of the cabins he got a fair notion, for he and Euphrasie passed them almost daily on horseback, on their way to the woods. It was seldom that their appearance together did not rouse comment among the darkies who happened to be loitering about.

La Chatte, a broad black woman with ends of white wool sticking out from under her *tignon*, stood with arms akimbo watching them as they disappeared one day. Then she turned and said to a young woman who sat in the cabin door:—

'Dat young man, ef he want to listen to me, he gwine quit dat ar caperin' roun' Miss 'Phrasie.'

The young woman in the doorway laughed, and showed her white teeth, and tossed her head, and fingered the blue beads at her throat, in a way to indicate that she was in hearty sympathy with any question that touched upon gallantry.

'Law! La Chatte, you ain' gwine hinder a gemman f'om payin' intentions to a young lady w'en he a mine to.'

'Dat all I got to say,' returned La Chatte, seating herself lazily and heavily on the doorstep. 'Nobody don' know dem Sanchun boys bettah 'an I does. Did n' I done part raise 'em? W'at you reckon my ha'r all tu'n plumb w'ite dat-a-way ef it warn't dat Placide w'at done it?'

'How come he make yo' ha'r tu'n w'ite, La Chatte?'

'Dev'ment, pu' dev'ment, Rose. Did n' he come in dat same cabin one day, w'en he warn't no bigga 'an dat Pres'dent Hayes w'at you sees gwine 'long de road wid dat cotton sack 'crost 'im? He come an' sets down by de do', on dat same t'ree-laigged stool w'at you's a-settin' on now, wid his gun in his han', an' he say: "La Chatte, I wants some croquignoles, an' I wants 'em quick, too." I 'low: "G' 'way f'om dah, boy. Don' you see I's flutin' yo' ma's petticoat?" He say: "La Chatte, put 'side dat ar flutin'-i'on an' dat ar petticoat;" an' he cock dat gun an' p'int it to my head. "Dar de ba'el," he say; "git out dat flour, git out dat butta an' dat aigs; step roun' dah, ole 'oman. Dis heah gun don' quit yo' head tell dem croquignoles is on de table, wid a w'ite tableclof an' a cup o' coffee." Ef I goes to de ba'el, de gun's a-p'intin'. Ef I goes to de fiah, de gun's a-p'intin'. W'en I rolls out de dough, de gun 's a-p'intin'; an' him neva say nuttin', an' me a-trim'lin' like ole Uncle Noah w'en de mis'ry strike 'im.'

'Lordy! w'at you reckon he do ef he tu'n roun' an' git mad wid dat young gemman f'om de city?'

'I don' reckon nuttin'; I knows w'at he gwine do, – same w'at his pa done.'

'W'at his pa done, La Chatte?'

'G' 'long 'bout yo' business; you 's axin' too many questions.'

And La Chatte arose slowly and went to gather her party-colored wash that hung drying on the jagged and irregular points of a dilapidated picket-fence.

But the darkies were mistaken in supposing that Offdean was paying attention to Euphrasie. Those little jaunts in the wood were purely of a business character. Offdean had made a contract with a neighboring mill for fencing, in exchange for a certain amount of uncut timber. He had made it his work – with the assistance of Euphrasie – to decide upon what trees he wanted felled, and to mark such for the woodman's axe.

If they sometimes forgot what they had gone into the woods for, it was because there was so much to talk about and to laugh about. Often, when Offdean had blazed a tree with the sharp hatchet which he carried at his pommel, and had further discharged his duty by calling it 'a fine piece of timber,' they would sit upon some fallen and decaying trunk, maybe to listen to a chorus of mocking-birds above their heads, or to exchange confidences, as young people will.

Euphrasie thought she had never heard any one talk quite so pleasantly as Offdean did. She could not decide whether it was his manner or the tone of his voice, or the earnest glance of his dark and deep-set blue eyes, that gave such meaning to everything he said; for she found herself afterward thinking of his every word.

One afternoon it rained in torrents, and Rose was forced to drag buckets and tubs into Offdean's room to catch the streams that threatened to flood it. Euphrasie said she was glad of it; now he could see for himself.

And when he had seen for himself, he went to join her out on a corner of the gallery, where she stood with a cloak around her, close up against the house. He leaned against the house, too, and they stood thus together, gazing upon as desolate a scene as it is easy to imagine.

The whole landscape was gray, seen through the driving rain. Far away the dreary cabins seemed to sink and sink to earth in abject misery. Above their heads the live-oak branches were beating with sad monotony against the blackened roof. Great pools of water had formed in the yard, which was deserted by every living thing; for the little darkies had scampered away to their cabins, the dogs had run to their kennels, and the hens were puffing big with wretchedness under the scanty shelter of a fallen wagon-body.

Certainly a situation to make a young man groan with ennui, if he is used to his daily stroll on Canal Street, and pleasant afternoons at the club. But Offdean thought it delightful. He only wondered that he had never known, or some one had never told him, how charming a place an old, dismantled plantation can be – when it rains. But as well as he liked it, he could not linger there forever. Business called him back to New Orleans, and after a few days he went away.

The interest which he felt in the improvement of this plantation was of so deep a nature, however, that he found himself thinking of it constantly. He wondered if the timber had all been felled, and how the fencing was coming on. So great was his desire to know such things that much correspondence was required between himself and Euphrasie, and he watched eagerly for those letters that told him of her trials and vexations with carpenters, bricklayers, and shingle-bearers. But in the midst of it, Offdean suddenly lost interest in the progress of work on the plantation. Singularly enough, it happened simultaneously with the arrival of a letter from Euphrasie which announced in a modest postscript that she was going down to the city with the Duplans for Mardi Gras.

VI

When Offdean learned that Euphrasie was coming to New Orleans, he was delighted to think he would have an opportunity to make some return for the hospitality which he had received from her father. He decided at once that she must see everything: day processions and night parades, balls and tableaux, operas and plays. He would arrange for it all, and he went to the length of begging to be relieved of certain duties that had been assigned him at the club, in order that he might feel himself perfectly free to do so.

The evening following Euphrasie's arrival, Offdean hastened to call upon her, away down on Esplanade Street. She and the Duplans were staying there with old Mme. Carantelle, Mrs. Duplan's mother, a delightfully conservative old lady who had not 'crossed Canal Street' for many years.

He found a number of people gathered in the long high-ceiled drawing-room, – young people and old people, all talking French, and some talking louder than they would have done if Madame Carantelle had not been so very deaf.

When Offdean entered, the old lady was greeting some one who had come in just before him. It was Placide, and she was calling him Grégoire, and wanting to know how the crops were up on Red River. She met every one from the country with this stereotyped inquiry, which placed her at once on the agreeable and easy footing she liked.

Somehow Offdean had not counted on finding Euphrasie so well provided with entertainment, and he spent much of the evening in trying to persuade himself that the fact was a pleasing one in itself. But he wondered why Placide was with her, and sat so persistently beside her, and danced so repeatedly with her when Mrs. Duplan played upon the piano. Then he could not see by what right these young creoles had already arranged for the Proteus ball, and every other entertainment that he had meant to provide for her.

He went away without having had a word alone with the girl whom he had gone to see. The evening had proved a failure. He did not go to the club as usual, but went to his rooms in a mood which inclined him to read a few pages from a stoic philosopher whom he sometimes affected. But the words of wisdom that had often before helped him over disagreeable places left no impress tonight. They were powerless to banish from his thoughts the look of a pair of brown eyes, or to drown the tones of a girl's voice that kept singing in his soul.

Placide was not very well acquainted with the city; but that made no difference to him so long as he was at Euphrasie's side. His brother Hector, who lived in some obscure corner of the town, would willingly have made his knowledge a more intimate one; but Placide did not choose to learn the lessons that Hector was ready to teach. He asked nothing better than to walk with Euphrasie along the streets, holding her parasol at an agreeable angle over her pretty head, or to sit beside her in the evening at the play, sharing her frank delight.

When the night of the Mardi Gras ball came, he felt like a lost spirit during the hours he was forced to remain away from her. He stood in the dense crowd on the street gazing up at her, where she sat on the clubhouse balcony amid a bevy of gayly dressed women. It was not easy to distinguish her, but he could think of no more agreeable occupation than to stand down there on the street trying to do so.

She seemed during all this pleasant time to be entirely his own, too. It made him very fierce to think of the possibility of her not being entirely his own. But he had no cause whatever to think this. She had grown conscious and thoughtful of late about him and their relationship. She often communed with herself, and as a result tried to act toward him as an engaged girl would toward her *fiancé*. Yet a wistful look came sometimes into the brown eyes when she walked the streets with Placide, and eagerly scanned the faces of passers-by.

Offdean had written her a note, very studied, very formal, asking to see her a certain day and hour, to consult about matters on the plantation, saying he had found it so difficult to obtain a word with her, that he was forced to adopt this means, which he trusted would not be offensive.

This seemed perfectly right to Euphrasie. She agreed to see him one afternoon – the day before leaving town – in the long, stately drawing-room, quite alone.

It was a sleepy day, too warm for the season. Gusts of moist air were sweeping lazily through the long corridors, rattling the slats of the half-closed green shutters, and bringing a delicious perfume from the courtyard where old Charlot was watering the spreading palms and brilliant parterres. A group of little children had stood awhile quarreling noisily under the windows, but had moved on down the street and left quietness reigning.

Offdean had not long to wait before Euphrasie came to him. She had lost some of that ease which had marked her manner during their first acquaintance. Now, when she seated herself before him, she showed a disposition to plunge at once into the subject that had brought him there. He was willing enough that it should play some rôle, since it had been his pretext for coming; but he soon dismissed it, and with it much restraint that had held him till now. He simply looked into her eyes, with a gaze that made her shiver a little, and began to complain because she was going away next day and he had seen nothing of her; because he had wanted to do so many things when she came – why had she not let him?

'You fo'get I'm no stranger here,' she told him. 'I know many people. I've been coming so often with Mme. Duplan. I wanted to see mo' of you, Mr. Offdean'—

'Then you ought to have managed it; you could have done so. It 's – it 's aggravating,' he said, far more bitterly than the subject warranted, 'when a man has so set his heart upon something.'

'But it was n' anything ver' important,' she interposed; and they both laughed, and got safely over a situation that would soon have been strained, if not critical.

Waves of happiness were sweeping through the soul and body of the girl as she sat there in the drowsy afternoon near the man whom she loved. It mattered not what they talked about, or whether they talked at all. They were both scintillant with feeling. If Offdean had taken Euphrasie's hands in his and leaned forward and kissed her lips, it would have seemed to both only the rational outcome of things that stirred them. But he did not do this. He knew now that overwhelming passion was taking possession of him. He had not to heap more coals upon the fire; on the contrary, it was a moment to put on the brakes, and he was a young gentleman able to do this when circumstances required.

However, he held her hand longer than he needed to when he bade her good-by. For he got entangled in explaining why he should have to go back to the plantation to see how matters stood there, and he dropped her hand only when the rambling speech was ended.

He left her sitting by the window in a big brocaded armchair. She drew the lace curtain aside to watch him pass in the street. He lifted his hat and smiled when he saw her. Any other man she knew would have done the same thing, but this simple act caused the blood to surge to her cheeks. She let the curtain drop, and sat there like one dreaming. Her eyes, intense with the unnatural light that glowed in them, looked steadily into vacancy, and her lips stayed parted in the half-smile that did not want to leave them.

Placide found her thus, a good while afterward, when he came in, full of bustle, with theatre tickets in his pocket for the last night. She started up, and went eagerly to meet him.

'W'ere have you been, Placide?' she asked with unsteady voice, placing her hands on his shoulders with a freedom that was new and strange to him.

He appeared to her suddenly as a refuge from something, she did not know what, and she rested her hot cheek against his breast. This made him mad, and he lifted her face and kissed her passionately upon the lips.

She crept from his arms after that, and went away to her room, and locked herself in. Her poor little inexperienced soul was torn and sore. She knelt down beside her bed, and sobbed a little and prayed a little. She felt that she had sinned, she did not know exactly in what; but a fine nature warned her that it was in Placide's kiss.

VII

The spring came early in Orville, and so subtly that no one could tell exactly when it began. But one morning the roses were so luscious in Placide's sunny parterres, the peas and bean-vines and borders of strawberries so rank in his trim vegetable patches, that he called out lustily, 'No mo' winta, Judge!' to the staid Judge Blount, who went ambling by on his gray pony.

'There 's right smart o' folks don't know it, Santien,' responded the judge, with occult meaning that might be applied to certain indebted clients back on the bayou who had not broken land yet. Ten minutes later the judge observed sententiously, and apropos of nothing, to a group that stood waiting for the post-office to open:—

'I see Santien 's got that noo fence o' his painted. And a pretty piece o' work it is,' he added reflectively.

'Look lack Placide goin' pent mo' 'an de fence,' sagaciously snickered 'Tit-Edouard, a strolling *maigre-échine* of indefinite occupation. 'I seen 'im, me, pesterin' wid all kine o' pent on a piece o' bo'd yistiday.'

'I knows he gwine paint mo' 'an de fence,' emphatically announced Uncle Abner, in a tone that carried conviction. 'He gwine paint de house; dat what he gwine do. Did n' Marse Luke Williams orda de paints? An' did n' I done kyar' 'em up dah myse'f?'

Seeing the deference with which this positive piece of knowledge was received, the judge coolly changed the subject by announcing that Luke Williams's Durham bull had broken a leg the night before in Luke's new pasture ditch, – a piece of news that fell among his hearers with telling, if paralytic effect.

But most people wanted to see for themselves these astonishing things that Placide was doing. And the young ladies of the village strolled slowly by of afternoons in couples and arm in arm. If Placide happened to see them, he would leave his work to hand them a fine rose or a bunch of geraniums over the dazzling white fence. But if it chanced to be 'Tit Edouard or Luke Williams, or any of the young men of Orville, he pretended not to see them, or to hear the ingratiating cough that accompanied their lingering footsteps.

In his eagerness to have his home sweet and attractive for Euphrasie's coming, Placide had gone less frequently than ever before up to Natchitoches. He worked and whistled and sang until the yearning for the girl's presence became a driving need; then he would put away his tools and mount his horse as the day was closing, and away he would go across bayous and hills and fields until he was with her again. She had never seemed to Placide so lovable as she was then. She had grown more womanly and thoughtful. Her cheek had lost much of its color, and the light in her eyes flashed less often. But her manner had gained a something of pathetic tenderness toward her lover that moved him with an intoxicating happiness. He could hardly wait with patience for that day in early April which would see the fulfillment of his lifelong hopes.

After Euphrasie's departure from New Orleans, Offdean told himself honestly that he loved the girl. But being yet unsettled in life, he felt it was no time to think of marrying, and, like the worldly-wise young gentleman that he was, resolved to forget the little Natchitoches girl. He knew it would be an affair of some difficulty, but not an impossible thing, so he set about forgetting her.

The effort made him singularly irascible. At the office he was gloomy and taciturn; at the club he was a bear. A few young ladies whom he called upon were astonished and distressed at the cynical views of life which he had so suddenly adopted.

When he had endured a week or more of such humor, and inflicted it upon others, he abruptly changed his tactics. He decided not to fight against his love for Euphrasie. He would not marry her, – certainly not; but he would let himself love her to his heart's bent, until that love should die a natural death, and not a violent one as he had designed. He abandoned himself completely to his passion, and dreamed of the girl by day and thought of her by night. How delicious had been the scent of her hair, the warmth of her breath, the nearness of her body, that rainy day when they stood close together upon the veranda! He recalled the glance of her honest, beautiful eyes, that told him things which made his heart beat fast now when he thought of them. And then her voice! Was there another like it when she laughed or when she talked! Was there another woman in the world possessed of so alluring a charm as this one he loved!

He was not bearish now, with these sweet thoughts crowding his brain and thrilling his blood; but he sighed deeply, and worked languidly, and enjoyed himself listlessly.

One day he sat in his room puffing the air thick with sighs and smoke, when a thought came suddenly to him – an inspiration, a very message from heaven, to judge from the cry of joy with which he greeted it. He sent his cigar whirling through the window, over the stone paving of the street, and he let his head fall down upon his arms, folded upon the table.

It had happened to him, as it does to many, that the solution of a vexed question flashed upon him when he was hoping least for it. He positively laughed aloud, and somewhat hysterically. In the space of a moment he saw the whole delicious future which a kind fate had mapped out for him: those rich acres upon the Red River his own, bought and embellished with his inheritance; and Euphrasie, whom he loved, his wife and companion throughout a life such as he knew now he had craved for, – a life that, imposing bodily activity, admits the intellectual repose in which thought unfolds.

Wallace Offdean was like one to whom a divinity had revealed his vocation in life, – no less a divinity because it was love. If doubts assailed him of Euphrasie's consent, they were soon stilled. For had they not spoken over and over to each other the mute and subtile language of reciprocal love – out under the forest trees, and in the quiet night-time on the plantation when the stars shone? And never so plainly as in the stately old drawing-room down on Esplanade Street. Surely no other speech was needed then, save such as their eyes told. Oh, he knew that she loved him; he was sure of it! The knowledge made him all the more eager now to hasten to her, to tell her that he wanted her for his very own.

VIII

If Offdean had stopped in Natchitoches on his way to the plantation, he would have heard something there to astonish him, to say the very least; for the whole town was talking of Euphrasie's wedding, which was to take place in a few days. But he did not linger. After securing a horse at the stable, he pushed on with all the speed of which the animal was capable, and only in such company as his eager thoughts afforded him.

The plantation was very quiet, with that stillness which broods over broad, clean acres that furnish no refuge for so much as a bird that sings. The negroes were scattered about the fields at work, with hoe and plow, under the sun, and old Pierre, on his horse, was far off in the midst of them.

Placide had arrived in the morning, after traveling all night, and had gone to his room for an hour or two of rest. He had drawn the lounge close up to the window to get what air he might through the closed shutters. He was just beginning to doze when he heard Euphrasie's light footsteps approaching. She stopped and seated herself so near that he could have touched her if he had but reached out his hand. Her nearness banished all desire to sleep, and he lay there content to rest his limbs and think of her.

The portion of the gallery on which Euphrasie sat was facing the river, and away from the road by which Offdean had reached the house. After fastening his horse, he mounted the steps, and traversed the broad hall that intersected the house from end to end, and that was open wide. He found Euphrasie engaged upon a piece of sewing. She was hardly aware of his presence before he had seated himself beside her.

She could not speak. She only looked at him with frightened eyes, as if his presence were that of some disembodied spirit.

'Are you not glad that I have come?' he asked her. 'Have I made a mistake in coming?' He was gazing into her eyes, seeking to read the meaning of their new and strange expression.

'Am I glad?' she faltered. 'I don' know. W'at has that to do?

You 've come to see the work, of co'se. It 's – it 's only half done, Mr. Offdean. They would n' listen to me or to papa, an' you did n' seem to care.'

'I have n't come to see the work,' he said, with a smile of love and confidence. 'I am here only to see you, – to say how much I want you, and need you – to tell you how I love you.'

She rose, half choking with words she could not utter. But he seized her hands and held her there.

'The plantation is mine, Euphrasie, – or it will be when you say that you will be my wife,' he went on excitedly. 'I know that you love me'—

'I do not!' she exclaimed wildly. 'W'at do you mean? How do you dare,' she gasped, 'to say such things w'en you know that in two days I shall be married to Placide?' The last was said in a whisper; it was like a wail.

'Married to Placide!' he echoed, as if striving to understand, – to grasp some part of his own stupendous folly and blindness. 'I knew nothing of it,' he said hoarsely. 'Married to Placide! I would never have spoken to you as I did, if I had known. You believe me, I hope? Please say that you forgive me.'

He spoke with long silences between his utterances.

'Oh, there is n' anything to fo'give. You 've only made a mistake. Please leave me, Mr. Offdean. Papa is out in the fiel', I think, if you would like to speak with him. Placide is somew'ere on the place.'

'I shall mount my horse and go see what work has been done,' said Offdean, rising. An unusual pallor had overspread his face, and his mouth was drawn with suppressed pain. 'I must turn my fool's errand to some practical good,' he added, with a sad attempt at playfulness; and with no further word he walked quickly away.

She listened to his going. Then all the wretchedness of the past months, together with the sharp distress of the moment, voiced itself in a sob: 'O God – O my God, he'p me!'

But she could not stay out there in the broad day for any chance comer to look upon her uncovered sorrow.

Placide heard her rise and go to her room. When he had heard the key turn in the lock, he got up, and with quiet deliberation prepared to go out. He drew on his boots, then his coat. He took his pistol from the dressing-bureau, where he had placed it a while before, and after examining its chambers carefully, thrust it into his pocket. He had certain work to do with the weapon before night. But for Euphrasie's presence he might have accomplished it very surely a moment ago, when the hound – as he called him – stood outside his window. He did not wish her to know anything of his movements, and he left his room as quietly as possible, and mounted his horse, as Offdean had done.

'La Chatte,' called Placide to the old woman, who stood in her yard at the washtub, 'w'ich way did that man go?'

'W'at man dat? I is n' studyin' 'bout no mans; I got 'nough to do wid dis heah washin'. 'Fo' God, I don' know w'at man you 's talkin' 'bout'—

'La Chatte, w'ich way did that man go? Quick, now!' with the deliberate tone and glance that had always quelled her.

'Ef you 's talkin' 'bout dat Noo Orleans man, I could 'a' tole you dat. He done tuck de road to de cocoa-patch,' plunging her black arms into the tub with unnecessary energy and disturbance.

'That 's enough. I know now he 's gone into the woods. You always was a liar, La Chatte.'

'Dat his own lookout, de smoove-tongue' raskil,' soliloquized the woman a moment later. 'I done said he did n' have no call to come heah, caperin' roun' Miss 'Phrasie.'

Placide was possessed by only one thought, which was a want as well, – to put an end to this man who had come between him and his love. It was the same brute passion that drives the beast to slay when he sees the object of his own desire laid hold of by another.

He had heard Euphrasie tell the man she did not love him, but what of that? Had he not heard her sobs, and guessed what her distress was? It needed no very flexible mind to guess as much, when a hundred signs besides, unheeded before, came surging to his memory. Jealousy held him, and rage and despair.

Offdean, as he rode along under the trees in apathetic despondency, heard some one approaching him on horseback, and turned aside to make room in the narrow pathway.

It was not a moment for punctilious scruples, and Placide had not been hindered by such from sending a bullet into the back of his rival. The only thing that stayed him was that Offdean must know why he had to die.

'Mr. Offdean,' Placide said, reining his horse with one hand, while he held his pistol openly in the other, 'I was in my room 'w'ile ago, and yeared w'at you said to Euphrasie. I would 'a' killed you then if she had n' been 'longside o' you. I could 'a' killed you jus' now w'en I come up behine you.'

'Well, why did n't you?' asked Offdean, meanwhile gathering his faculties to think how he had best deal with this madman.

'Because I wanted you to know who done it, an' w'at he done it for.'

'Mr. Santien, I suppose to a person in your frame of mind it will make no difference to know that I'm unarmed. But if you make any attempt upon my life, I shall certainly defend myself as best I can.'

'Defen' yo'se'f, then.'

'You must be mad,' said Offdean, quickly, and looking straight into Placide's eyes, 'to want to soil your happiness with murder. I thought a creole knew better than that how to love a woman.'

'By——! are you goin' to learn me how to love a woman?'

'No, Placide,' said Offdean eagerly, as they rode slowly along; 'your own honor is going to tell you that. The way to love a woman is to think first of her happiness. If you love Euphrasie, you must go to her clean. I love her myself enough to want you to do that. I shall leave this place tomorrow; you will never see me again if I can help it. Is n't that enough for you? I 'm going to turn here and leave you. Shoot me in the back if you like; but I know you won't.' And Offdean held out his hand.

'I don' want to shake han's with you,' said Placide sulkily. 'Go 'way f'om me.'

He stayed motionless watching Offdean ride away. He looked at the pistol in his hand, and replaced it slowly in his pocket; then he removed the broad felt hat which he wore, and wiped away the moisture that had gathered upon his forehead.

Offdean's words had touched some chord within him and made it vibrant; but they made him hate the man no less.

'The way to love a woman is to think firs' of her happiness,' he muttered reflectively. 'He thought a creole knew how to love. Does he reckon he 's goin' to learn a creole how to love?'

His face was white and set with despair now. The rage had all left it as he rode deeper on into the wood.

IX

Offdean rose early, wishing to take the morning train to the city. But he was not before Euphrasie, whom he found in the large hall arranging the breakfast-table. Old Pierre was there too, walking slowly about with hands folded behind him, and with bowed head.

A restraint hung upon all of them, and the girl turned to her father and asked him if Placide were up, seemingly for want of something to say. The old man fell heavily into a chair, and gazed upon her in the deepest distress.

'Oh, my po' li'le Euphrasie! my po' li'le chile! Mr. Offde'n, you ain't no stranger.'

'*Bon Dieu!* Papa!' cried the girl sharply, seized with a vague terror. She quitted her occupation at the table, and stood in nervous apprehension of what might follow.

'I yaired people say Placide was one no-'count creole. I nevair want to believe dat, me. Now I know dat 's true. Mr. Offde'n, you ain't no stranger, you.'

Offdean was gazing upon the old man in amazement.

'In de night,' Pierre continued, 'I yaired some noise on de winder. I go open, an' dere Placide, standin' wid his big boot' on, an' his w'ip w'at he knocked wid on de winder, an' his hoss all saddle'. Oh, my po' li'le chile! He say, "Pierre, I yaired say Mr. Luke William' want his house pent down in Orville. I reckon I go git de job befo' somebody else teck it." I say, "You come straight back, Placide?" He say, "Don' look fer me." An w'en I ax 'im w'at I goin' tell to my li'le chile, he say, "Tell Euphrasie Placide know better 'an anybody livin' w'at goin' make her happy." An' he start 'way; den he come back an' say, "Tell dat man" – I don' know who he was talk' 'bout – "tell 'im he ain't goin' learn nuttin' to a creole." *Mon Dieu! Mon Dieu!* I don' know w'at all dat mean.'

He was holding the half-fainting Euphrasie in his arms, and stroking her hair.

'I always yaired say he was one no-'count creole. I nevair want to believe dat.'

'Don't – don't say that again, papa,' she whisperingly entreated, speaking in French. 'Placide has saved me!'

'He has save' you f'om w'at, Euphrasie?' asked her father, in dazed astonishment.

'From sin,' she replied to him under her breath.

'I don' know w'at all dat mean,' the old man muttered, bewildered, as he arose and walked out on the gallery.

Offdean had taken coffee in his room, and would not wait for breakfast. When he went to bid Euphrasie good-by, she sat beside the table with her head bowed upon her arm.

He took her hand and said good-by to her, but she did not look up.

'Euphrasie,' he asked eagerly, 'I may come back? Say that I may – after a while.'

She gave him no answer, and he leaned down and pressed his cheek caressingly and entreatingly against her soft thick hair.

'May I, Euphrasie?' he begged. 'So long as you do not tell me no, I shall come back, dearest one.'

She still made him no reply, but she did not tell him no.

So he kissed her hand and her cheek, – what he could touch of it, that peeped out from her folded arm, – and went away.

An hour later, when Offdean passed through Natchitoches, the old town was already ringing with the startling news that Placide had been dismissed by his *fiancée*, and the wedding was off, information which the young creole was taking the trouble to scatter broadcast as he went.

A Shameful Affair

I

Mildred Orme, seated in the snuggest corner of the big front porch of the Kraummer farmhouse, was as content as a girl need hope to be.

This was no such farm as one reads about in humorous fiction. Here were swelling acres where the undulating wheat gleamed in the sun like a golden sea. For silver there was the Meramec — or, better, it was pure crystal, for here and there one might look clean through it down to where the pebbles lay like green and yellow gems. Along the river's edge trees were growing to the very water, and in it, sweeping it when they were willows.

The house itself was big and broad, as country houses should be. The master was big and broad, too. The mistress was small and thin, and it was always she who went out at noon to pull the great clanging bell that called the farmhands in to dinner.

From her agreeable corner where she lounged with her Browning or her Ibsen, Mildred watched the woman do this every day. Yet when the clumsy farmhands all came tramping up the steps and crossed the porch in going to their meal that was served within, she never looked at them. Why should she? Farmhands are not so very nice to look at, and she was nothing of an anthropologist. But once when the half dozen men came along, a paper which she had laid carelessly upon the railing was blown across their path. One of them picked it up, and when he had mounted the steps restored it to her. He was young, and brown, of course, as the sun had made him. He had nice blue eyes. His fair hair was dishevelled. His shoulders were broad and square and his limbs strong and clean. A not unpicturesque figure in the rough attire that bared his throat to view and gave perfect freedom to his every motion.

Mildred did not make these several observations in the half second that she looked at him in courteous acknowledgment. It took her as many days to note them all. For she signaled him out each time that he passed her, meaning to give him a condescending little smile, as she knew how. But he never looked at her. To be sure, clever young women of twenty, who are handsome, besides, who have refused their half dozen offers and are settling down to the conviction that life is a tedious affair, are not going to care a straw whether farmhands look at them or not. And Mildred did not care, and the thing would not have occupied her a moment if Satan had not intervened, in offering the employment which natural conditions had failed to supply. It was summer time; she was idle; she was piqued, and that was the beginning of the shameful affair.

'Who are these men, Mrs. Kraummer, that work for you? Where do you pick them up?'

'Oh, ve picks 'em up everyvere. Some is neighbors, some is tramps, and so.'

'And that broad-shouldered young fellow – is he a neighbor? The one who handed me my paper the other day – you remember?'

'Gott, no! You might yust as well say he vas a tramp. Aber he vorks like a steam ingine.'

'Well, he's an extremely disagreeable-looking man. I should think you'd be afraid to have him about, not knowing him.'

'Vat you vant to be 'fraid for?' laughed the little woman. 'He don't talk no more un ven he vas deef und dumb. I didn't t'ought you vas sooch a baby.'

'But, Mrs. Kraummer, I don't want you to think I'm a baby, as you say – a coward, as you mean. Ask the man if he will drive me to church to-morrow. You see, I'm not so very much afraid of him,' she added with a smile.

The answer which this unmannerly farmhand returned to Mildred's request was simply a refusal. He could not drive her to church because he was going fishing.

'Aber,' offered good Mrs. Kraummer, 'Hans Platzfeldt will drive you to church, oder vereever you vants. He vas a goot boy vat you can trust, dat Hans.'

'Oh, thank him very much. But I find I have so many letters to write to-morrow, and it promises to be hot, too. I shan't care to go to church after all.'

She could have cried for vexation. Snubbed by a farmhand! a tramp, perhaps. She, Mildred Orme, who ought really to have been with the rest of the family at Narragansett – who had come to seek in this retired spot the repose that would enable her to follow exalted lines of thought. She marvelled at the problematic nature of farmhands.

After sending her the uncivil message already recorded, and as he passed beneath the porch where she sat, he did look at her finally, in a way to make her positively gasp at the sudden effrontery of the man.

But the inexplicable look stayed with her. She could not banish it.

II

It was not so very hot after all, the next day, when Mildred walked down the long narrow footpath that led through the bending wheat to the river. High above her waist reached the yellow grain. Mildred's brown eyes filled with a reflected golden light as they caught the glint of it, as she heard the trill that it answered to the gentle breeze. Anyone who has walked through the wheat in midsummer-time knows that sound.

In the woods it was sweet and solemn and cool. And there beside the river was the wretch who had annoyed her, first, with his indifference, then with the sudden boldness of his glance.

'Are you fishing?' she asked politely and with kindly dignity, which she supposed would define her position toward him. The inquiry lacked not pertinence, seeing that he sat motionless, with a pole in his hand and his eyes fixed on a cork that bobbed aimlessly on the water.

'Yes, madam,' was his brief reply.

'It won't disturb you if I stand here a moment, to see what success you will have?'

'No, madam.'

She stood very still, holding tight to the book she had brought with her. Her straw hat had slipped disreputably to one side, over the wavy bronze-brown bang that half covered her forehead. Her cheeks were ripe with color that the sun had coaxed there; so were her lips.

All the other farmhands had gone forth in Sunday attire. Perhaps this one had none better than these working clothes that he wore. A feminine commiseration swept her at the thought. He spoke never a word. She wondered how many hours he could sit there, so patiently waiting for fish to come to his hook. For her part, the situation began to pall, and she wanted to change it at last.

'Let me try a moment, please? I have an idea—'

'Yes, madam.'

'The man is surely an idiot, with his monosyllables,' she commented inwardly. But she remembered that monosyllables belong to a boor's equipment.

She laid her book carefully down and took the pole gingerly that he came to place in her hands. Then it was his turn to stand back and look respectfully and silently on at the absorbing performance.

'Oh!' cried the girl, suddenly, seized with excitement upon seeing the line dragged deep in the water.

'Wait, wait! Not yet.'

He sprang to her side. With his eyes eagerly fastened on the tense line, he grasped the pole to prevent her drawing it, as her intention seemed to be. That is, he meant to grasp the pole, but instead, his brown hand came down upon Mildred's white one.

He started violently at finding himself so close to a bronze-brown tangle that almost swept his chin – to a hot cheek only a few inches away from his shoulder, to a pair of young, dark eyes that gleamed for an instant unconscious things into his own.

Then, why ever it happened, or how ever it happened, his arms were holding Mildred and he kissed her lips. She did not know if it was ten times or only once.

She looked around – her face milk-white – to see him disappear with rapid strides through the path that had brought her there. Then she was alone.

Only the birds had seen, and she could count on their discretion. She was not wildly indignant, as many would have been. Shame stunned her. But through it she gropingly wondered if she should tell the Kraummers that her chaste lips had been rifled of their innocence. Publish her own confusion? No! Once in her room she would give calm thought to the situation, and determine then how to act. The secret must remain her own: a hateful burden to bear alone until she could forget it.

III

And because she feared not to forget it, Mildred wept that night. All day long a hideous truth had been thrusting itself upon her that made her ask herself if she could be mad. She feared it. Else why was that kiss the most delicious thing she had known in her twenty years of life? The sting of it had never left her lips since it was pressed into them. The sweet trouble of it banished sleep from her pillow.

But Mildred would not bend the outward conditions of her life to serve any shameful whim that chanced to visit her soul, like an ugly dream. She would avoid nothing. She would go and come as always.

In the morning she found in her chair upon the porch the book she had left by the river. A fresh indignity! But she came and went as she intended to, and sat as usual upon the porch amid her familiar surroundings. When the Offender passed her by she knew it, though her eyes were never lifted. Are there only sight and sound to tell such things? She discerned it by a wave that swept her with confusion and she knew not what besides.

She watched him furtively, one day, when he talked with Farmer Kraummer out in the open. When he walked away she remained like one who has drunk much wine. Then unhesitatingly she turned and began her preparations to leave the Kraummer farmhouse.

When the afternoon was far spent they brought letters to her. One of them read like this:

'My Mildred, deary! I am only now at Narragansett, and so broke up not to find you. So you are down at that Kraummer farm, on the Iron Mountain. Well! What do you think of that delicious crank, Fred Evelyn? For a man must be a crank who does such things. Only fancy! Last year he chose to drive an engine back and forth across the plains. This year he tills the soil with laborers. Next year it will be something else as insane – because he likes to live more lives than one kind, and other Quixotic reasons. We are great chums. He writes me he's grown as strong as an ox. But he hasn't mentioned that you are there. I know you don't get on with him, for he isn't a bit intellectual – detests Ibsen and abuses Tolstoi. He doesn't read "in books" – says they are spectacles for the short-sighted to look at life through. Don't snub him, dear, or be too hard on him; he has a heart of gold, if he is the first crank in America.'

Mildred tried to think – to feel that the intelligence which this letter brought to her would take somewhat of the sting from the shame that tortured her. But it did not. She knew that it could not.

In the gathering twilight she walked again through the wheat that was heavy and fragrant with dew. The path was very long and very narrow. When she was midway she saw the Offender coming toward her. What could she do? Turn and run, as a little child might? Spring into the wheat, as some frightened four-footed creature would? There was nothing but to pass him with the dignity which the occasion clearly demanded.

But he did not let her pass. He stood squarely in the pathway before her, hat in hand, a perturbed look upon his face.

'Miss Orme,' he said, 'I have wanted to say to you, every hour of the past week, that I am the most consummate hound that walks the earth.'

She made no protest. Her whole bearing seemed to indicate that her opinion coincided with his own.

'If you have a father, or brother, or any one, in short, to whom you may say such things—'

'I think you aggravate the offense, sir, by speaking of it. I shall ask you never to mention it again. I want to forget that it ever happened. Will you kindly let me by.'

'Oh,' he ventured eagerly, 'you want to forget it! Then, maybe, since you are willing to forget, you will be generous enough to forgive the offender some day?'

'Some day,' she repeated, almost inaudibly, looking seemingly through him, but not at him – 'some day – perhaps; when I shall have forgiven myself.'

He stood motionless, watching her slim, straight figure lessening by degrees as she walked slowly away from him. He was wondering what she meant. Then a sudden, quick wave came beating into his brown throat and staining it crimson, when he guessed what it might be.

A Harbinger

Bruno did very nice work in black and white; sometimes in green and yellow and red. But he never did anything quite so clever as during that summer he spent in the hills.

The spring-time freshness had stayed, some way. And then there was the gentle Diantha, with hair the color of ripe wheat, who posed for him when he wanted. She was as beautiful as a flower, crisp with morning dew. Her violet eyes were baby-eyes – when he first came. When he went away he kissed her, and she turned red and white and trembled. As quick as thought the baby look went out of her eyes and another flashed into them.

Bruno sighed a good deal over his work that winter. The women he painted were all like mountain-flowers. The big city seemed too desolate for endurance often. He tried not to think of sweet-eyed Diantha. But there was nothing to keep him from remembering the hills; the whirr of the summer breeze through delicate-leafed maples; the bird-notes that used to break clear and sharp into the stillness when he and Diantha were together on the wooded hillside.

So when summer came again, Bruno gathered his bags, his brushes and colors and things. He whistled soft low tunes as he did so. He sang even, when he was not lost in wondering if the sunlight would fall just as it did last June, aslant the green slopes; and if – and if Diantha would quiver red and white again when he called her his sweet own Diantha, as he meant to.

Bruno had made his way through a tangle of underbrush; but before he came quite to the wood's edge, he halted: for there about the little church that gleamed white in the sun, people were gathered – old and young. He thought Diantha might be among them, and strained his eyes to see if she were. But she was not. He did see her though – when the doors of the rustic temple swung open – like a white-robed lily now.

There was a man beside her – it mattered not who; enough that it was one who had gathered this wild flower for his own, while Bruno was dreaming. Foolish Bruno! to have been only love's harbinger after all! He turned away. With hurried strides he descended the hill again, to wait by the big water-tank for a train to come along.

Doctor Chevalier's Lie

The quick report of a pistol rang through the quiet autumn night. It was no unusual sound in the unsavory quarter where Dr. Chevalier had his office. Screams commonly went with it. This time there had been none.

Midnight had already rung in the old cathedral tower.

The doctor closed the book over which he had lingered so late, and awaited the summons that was almost sure to come.

As he entered the house to which he had been called he could not but note the ghastly sameness of detail that accompanied these oft-recurring events. The same scurrying; the same groups of tawdry, frightened women bending over banisters – hysterical, some of them; morbidly curious, others; and not a few shedding womanly tears; with a dead girl stretched somewhere, as this one was.

And yet it was not the same. Certainly she was dead: there was the hole in the temple where she had sent the bullet through. Yet it was different. Other such faces had been unfamiliar to him, except so far as they bore the common stamp of death. This one was not.

Like a flash he saw it again amid other surroundings. The time was little more than a year ago. The place, a homely cabin down in Arkansas, in which he and a friend had found shelter and hospitality during a hunting expedition.

There were others beside. A little sister or two; a father and mother – coarse, and bent with toil, but proud as archangels of their handsome girl, who was too clever to stay in an Arkansas cabin, and who was going away to seek her fortune in the big city.

'The girl is dead,' said Doctor Chevalier. 'I knew her well, and charge myself with her remains and decent burial.'

The following day he wrote a letter. One, doubtless, to carry sorrow, but no shame to the cabin down there in the forest.

It told that the girl had sickened and died. A lock of hair was sent and other trifles with it. Tender last words were even invented.

Of course it was noised about that Doctor Chevalier had cared for the remains of a woman of doubtful repute.

Shoulders were shrugged. Society thought of cutting him. Society did not, for some reason or other, so the affair blew over.

A Very Fine Fiddle

When the half dozen little ones were hungry, old Cléophas would take the fiddle from its flannel bag and play a tune upon it. Perhaps it was to drown their cries, or their hunger, or his conscience, or all three. One day Fifine, in a rage, stamped her small foot and clinched her little hands, and declared:

'It 's no two way'! I 'm goin' smash it, dat fiddle, some day in a t'ousan' piece'!'

'You mus' n' do dat, Fifine,' expostulated her father. 'Dat fiddle been ol'er 'an you an' me t'ree time' put togedder. You done yaird me tell often 'nough 'bout dat *Italien* w'at give it to me w'en he die, 'long yonder befo' de war. An' he say, "Cléophas, dat fiddle – dat one part my life – w'at goin' live w'en I be dead – *Dieu merci!*" You talkin' too fas', Fifine.'

'Well, I'm goin' do some'in' wid dat fiddle, *va!*' returned the daughter, only half mollified. 'Mine w'at I say.'

So once when there were great carryings-on up at the big plantation – no end of ladies and gentlemen from the city, riding, driving, dancing, and making music upon all manner of instruments – Fifine, with the fiddle in its flannel bag, stole away and up to the big house where these festivities were in progress.

No one noticed at first the little barefoot girl seated upon a step of the veranda and watching, lynx-eyed, for her opportunity.

'It's one fiddle I got for sell,' she announced, resolutely, to the first who questioned her.

It was very funny to have a shabby little girl sitting there wanting to sell a fiddle, and the child was soon surrounded.

The lustreless instrument was brought forth and examined, first with amusement, but soon very seriously, especially by three gentlemen: one with very long hair that hung down, another with equally long hair that stood up, the third with no hair worth mentioning.

These three turned the fiddle upside down and almost inside out. They thumped upon it, and listened. They scraped upon it, and listened. They walked into the house with it, and out of the house with it, and into remote corners with it. All this with much putting of heads together, and talking together in familiar and unfamiliar languages. And, finally, they sent Fifine away with a fiddle twice as beautiful as the one she had brought, and a roll of money besides!

The child was dumb with astonishment, and away she flew. But when she stopped beneath a big chinaberry-tree, to further scan the roll of money, her wonder was redoubled. There was far more than she could count, more than she had ever dreamed of possessing. Certainly enough to top the old cabin with new shingles; to put shoes on all the little bare feet and food into the hungry mouths. Maybe enough – and Fifine's heart fairly jumped into her throat at the vision – maybe enough to buy Blanchette and her tiny calf that Unc' Siméon wanted to sell!'

'It 's jis like you say, Fifine,' murmured old Cléophas, huskily, when he had played upon the new fiddle that night. 'It 's one fine fiddle; an' like you say, it shine' like satin. But some way or udder, 't ain' de same. Yair, Fifine, take it – put it 'side. I b'lieve, me, I ain' goin' play de fiddle no mo'.'

Boulôt and Boulotte

When Boulôt and Boulotte, the little piny-wood twins, had reached the dignified age of twelve, it was decided in family council that the time had come for them to put their little naked feet into shoes. They were two brown-skinned, black-eyed 'Cadian roly-polies, who lived with father and mother and a troop of brothers and sisters halfway up the hill, in a neat log cabin that had a substantial mud chimney at one end. They could well afford shoes now, for they had saved many a picayune through their industry of selling wild grapes, blackberries, and 'socoes' to ladies in the village who 'put up' such things.

Boulôt and Boulotte were to buy the shoes themselves, and they selected a Saturday afternoon for the important transaction, for that is the great shopping time in Natchitoches Parish. So upon a bright Saturday afternoon Boulôt and Boulotte, hand in hand, with their quarters, their dimes, and their picayunes tied carefully in a Sunday handkerchief, descended the hill, and disappeared from the gaze of the eager group that had assembled to see them go.

Long before it was time for their return, this same small band, with ten year old Seraphine at their head, holding a tiny Seraphin in her arms, had stationed themselves in a row before the cabin at a convenient point from which to make quick and careful observation.

Even before the two could be caught sight of, their chattering voices were heard down by the spring, where they had doubtless stopped to drink. The voices grew more and more audible. Then, through the branches of the young pines, Boulotte's blue sun-bonnet appeared, and Boulôt's straw hat. Finally the twins, hand in hand, stepped into the clearing in full view.

Consternation seized the band.

'You bof crazy *donc*, Boulôt an' Boulotte,' screamed Seraphine. 'You go buy shoes, an' come home barefeet like you was go!'

Boulôt flushed crimson. He silently hung his head, and looked sheepishly down at his bare feet, then at the fine stout brogans that he carried in his hand. He had not thought of it.

Boulotte also carried shoes, but of the glossiest, with the highest of heels and brightest of buttons. But she was not one to be disconcerted or to look sheepish; far from it.

'You 'spec' Boulôt an' me we got money fur was'e – us?' she retorted, with withering condescension. 'You think we go buy shoes fur ruin it in de dus'? *Comment!'*

And they all walked into the house crestfallen; all but Boulotte, who was mistress of the situation, and Seraphin, who did not care one way or the other.

Beyond the Bayou

The bayou curved like a crescent around the point of land on which La Folle's cabin stood. Between the stream and the hut lay a big abandoned field, where cattle were pastured when the bayou supplied them with water enough. Through the woods that spread back into unknown regions the woman had drawn an imaginary line, and past this circle she never stepped. This was the form of her only mania.

She was now a large, gaunt black woman, past thirty-five. Her real name was Jacqueline, but every one on the plantation called her La Folle, because in childhood she had been frightened literally 'out of her senses,' and had never wholly regained them.

It was when there had been skirmishing and sharpshooting all day in the woods. Evening was near when P'tit Maître, black with powder and crimson with blood, had staggered into the cabin of Jacqueline's mother, his pursuers close at his heels. The sight had stunned her childish reason.

She dwelt alone in her solitary cabin, for the rest of the quarters had long since been removed beyond her sight and knowledge. She had more physical strength than most men, and made her patch of cotton and corn and tobacco like the best of them. But of the world beyond the bayou she had long known nothing, save what her morbid fancy conceived.

People at Bellissime had grown used to her and her way, and they thought nothing of it. Even when 'Old Mis" died, they did not wonder that La Folle had not crossed the bayou, but had stood upon her side of it, wailing and lamenting.

P'tit Maître was now the owner of Bellissime. He was a middle-aged man, with a family of beautiful daughters about him, and a little son whom La Folle loved as if he had been her own. She called him Chéri, and so did every one else because she did.

None of the girls had ever been to her what Chéri was. They had each and all loved to be with her, and to listen to her wondrous stories of things that always happened 'yonda, beyon' de bayou.'

But none of them had stroked her black hand quite as Chéri did, nor rested their heads against her knee so confidingly, nor fallen asleep in her arms as he used to do. For Chéri hardly did such things now, since he had become the proud possessor of a gun, and had had his black curls cut off.

That summer – the summer Chéri gave La Folle two black curls tied with a knot of red ribbon – the water ran so low in the bayou that even the little children at Bellissime were able to cross it on foot, and the cattle were sent to pasture down by the river. La Folle was sorry when they were gone, for she loved these dumb companions well, and liked to feel that they were there, and to hear them browsing by night up to her own inclosure.

It was Saturday afternoon, when the fields were deserted. The men had flocked to a neighboring village to do their week's trading, and the women were occupied with household affairs, – La Folle as well as the others. It was then she mended and washed her handful of clothes, scoured her house, and did her baking.

In this last employment she never forgot Chéri. To-day she had fashioned croquignoles of the most fantastic and alluring shapes for him. So when she saw the boy come trudging across the old field with his gleaming little new rifle on his shoulder, she called out gayly to him, 'Chéri! Chéri!'

But Chéri did not need the summons, for he was coming straight to her. His pockets all bulged out with almonds and raisins and an orange that he had secured for her from the very fine dinner which had been given that day up at his father's house.

He was a sunny-faced youngster of ten. When he had emptied his pockets, La Folle patted his round red cheek, wiped his soiled hands on her apron, and smoothed his hair. Then she watched him as, with his cakes in his hand, he crossed her strip of cotton back of the cabin, and disappeared into the wood.

He had boasted of the things he was going to do with his gun out there.

'You think they got plenty deer in the wood, La Folle?' he had inquired, with the calculating air of an experienced hunter.

'Non, non!' the woman laughed. 'Don't you look fo' no deer, Chéri. Dat 's too big. But you bring La Folle one good fat squirrel fo' her dinner to-morrow, an' she goin' be satisfi'.'

'One squirrel ain't a bite. I'll bring you mo' 'an one, La Folle,' he had boasted pompously as he went away.

When the woman, an hour later, heard the report of the boy's rifle close to the wood's edge, she would have thought nothing of it if a sharp cry of distress had not followed the sound.

She withdrew her arms from the tub of suds in which they had been plunged, dried them upon her apron, and as quickly as her trembling limbs would bear her, hurried to the spot whence the ominous report had come.

It was as she feared. There she found Chéri stretched upon the ground, with his rifle beside him. He moaned piteously:—

'I'm dead, La Folle! I'm dead! I'm gone!'

'Non, non!' she exclaimed resolutely, as she knelt beside him. 'Put you' arm 'roun' La Folle's nake, Chéri. Dat 's nuttin'; dat goin' be nuttin'.' She lifted him in her powerful arms.

Chéri had carried his gun muzzle-downward. He had stumbled, – he did not know how. He only knew that he had a ball lodged somewhere in his leg, and he thought that his end was at hand. Now, with his head upon the woman's shoulder, he moaned and wept with pain and fright.

'Oh, La Folle! La Folle! it hurt so bad! I can' stan' it, La Folle!'

'Don't cry, mon bébé, mon bébé, mon Chéri!' the woman spoke soothingly as she covered the ground with long strides. 'La Folle goin' mine you; Doctor Bonfils goin' come make mon Chéri well agin.'

She had reached the abandoned field. As she crossed it with her precious burden, she looked constantly and restlessly from side to side. A terrible fear was upon her, – the fear of the world beyond the bayou, the morbid and insane dread she had been under since childhood.

When she was at the bayou's edge she stood there, and shouted for help as if a life depended upon it:—

'Oh, P'tit Maître! P'tit Maître! Venez donc! Au secours! Au secours!'

No voice responded. Chéri's hot tears were scalding her neck. She called for each and every one upon the place, and still no answer came.

She shouted, she wailed; but whether her voice remained unheard or unheeded, no reply came to her frenzied cries. And all the while Chéri moaned and wept and entreated to be taken home to his mother.

La Folle gave a last despairing look around her. Extreme terror was upon her. She clasped the child close against her breast, where he could feel her heart beat like a muffled hammer. Then shutting her eyes, she ran suddenly down the shallow bank of the bayou, and never stopped till she had climbed the opposite shore.

She stood there quivering an instant as she opened her eyes. Then she plunged into the footpath through the trees.

She spoke no more to Chéri, but muttered constantly, 'Bon Dieu, ayez pitié La Folle! Bon Dieu, ayez pitié moi!'

Instinct seemed to guide her. When the pathway spread clear and smooth enough before her, she again closed her eyes tightly against the sight of that unknown and terrifying world.

A child, playing in some weeds, caught sight of her as she neared the quarters. The little one uttered a cry of dismay.

'La Folle!' she screamed, in her piercing treble. 'La Folle done cross de bayer!'

Quickly the cry passed down the line of cabins.

'Yonda, La Folle done cross de bayou!'

Children, old men, old women, young ones with infants in their arms, flocked to doors and windows to see this awe-inspiring spectacle. Most of them shuddered with superstitious dread of what it might portend. 'She totin' Chéri!' some of them shouted.

Some of the more daring gathered about her, and followed at her heels, only to fall back with new terror when she turned her distorted face upon them. Her eyes were bloodshot and the saliva had gathered in a white foam on her black lips.

Some one had run ahead of her to where P'tit Maître sat with his family and guests upon the gallery.

'P'tit Maître! La Folle done cross de bayou! Look her! Look her yonda totin' Chéri!' This startling intimation was the first which they had of the woman's approach.

She was now near at hand. She walked with long strides. Her eyes were fixed desperately before her, and she breathed heavily, as a tired ox.

At the foot of the stairway, which she could not have mounted, she laid the boy in his father's arms. Then the world that had looked red to La Folle suddenly turned black, – like that day she had seen powder and blood.

She reeled for an instant. Before a sustaining arm could reach her, she fell heavily to the ground.

When La Folle regained consciousness, she was at home again, in her own cabin and upon her own bed. The moon rays, streaming in through the open door and windows, gave what light was needed to the old black mammy who stood at the table concocting a tisane of fragrant herbs. It was very late.

Others who had come, and found that the stupor clung to her, had gone again. P'tit Maître had been there, and with him Doctor Bonfils, who said that La Folle might die.

But death had passed her by. The voice was very clear and steady with which she spoke to Tante Lizette, brewing her tisane there in a corner.

'Ef you will give me one good drink tisane, Tante Lizette, I b'lieve I'm goin' sleep, me.'

And she did sleep; so soundly, so healthfully, that old Lizette without compunction stole softly away, to creep back through the moonlit fields to her own cabin in the new quarters.

The first touch of the cool gray morning awoke La Folle. She arose, calmly, as if no tempest had shaken and threatened her existence but yesterday.

She donned her new blue cottonade and white apron, for she remembered that this was Sunday. When she had made for herself a cup of strong black coffee, and drunk it with relish, she quitted the cabin and walked across the old familiar field to the bayou's edge again.

She did not stop there as she had always done before, but crossed with a long, steady stride as if she had done this all her life.

When she had made her way through the brush and scrub cottonwood-trees that lined the opposite bank, she found herself upon the border of a field where the white, bursting cotton, with the dew upon it, gleamed for acres and acres like frosted silver in the early dawn.

La Folle drew a long, deep breath as she gazed across the country. She walked slowly and uncertainly, like one who hardly knows how, looking about her as she went.

The cabins, that yesterday had sent a clamor of voices to

pursue her, were quiet now. No one was yet astir at Bellissime. Only the birds that darted here and there from hedges were awake, and singing their matins.

When La Folle came to the broad stretch of velvety lawn that surrounded the house, she moved slowly and with delight over the springy turf, that was delicious beneath her tread.

She stopped to find whence came those perfumes that were assailing her senses with memories from a time far gone.

There they were, stealing up to her from the thousand blue violets that peeped out from green, luxuriant beds. There they were, showering down from the big waxen bells of the magnolias far above her head, and from the jessamine clumps around her.

There were roses, too, without number. To right and left palms spread in broad and graceful curves. It all looked like enchantment beneath the sparkling sheen of dew.

When La Folle had slowly and cautiously mounted the many steps that led up to the veranda, she turned to look back at the perilous ascent she had made. Then she caught sight of the river, bending like a silver bow at the foot of Bellissime. Exultation possessed her soul.

La Folle rapped softly upon a door near at hand. Chéri's mother soon cautiously opened it. Quickly and cleverly she dissembled the astonishment she felt at seeing La Folle.

'Ah, La Folle! Is it you, so early?'

'*Oui*, madame. I come ax how my po' li'le Chéri to, 's mo'nin'.'

'He is feeling easier, thank you, La Folle. Dr. Bonfils says it will be nothing serious. He's sleeping now. Will you come back when he awakes?'

'*Non*, madame. I'm goin' wait yair tell Chéri wake up.' La Folle seated herself upon the topmost step of the veranda.

A look of wonder and deep content crept into her face as she watched for the first time the sun rise upon the new, the beautiful world beyond the bayou.

The Bênitous' Slave

Old Uncle Oswald believed he belonged to the Bênitous, and there was no getting the notion out of his head. Monsieur tried every way, for there was no sense in it. Why, it must have been fifty years since the Bênitous owned him. He had belonged to others since, and had later been freed. Beside, there was not a Bênitou left in the parish now, except one rather delicate woman, who lived with her little daughter in a corner of Natchitoches town, and constructed 'fashionable millinery.' The family had dispersed, and almost vanished, and the plantation as well had lost its identity.

But that made no difference to Uncle Oswald. He was always running away from Monsieur – who kept him out of pure kindness – and trying to get back to those Bênitous.

More than that, he was constantly getting injured in such attempts. Once he fell into the bayou and was nearly drowned. Again he barely escaped being run down by an engine. But another time, when he had been lost two days, and finally discovered in an unconscious and half-dead condition in the woods, Monsieur and Doctor Bonfils reluctantly decided that it was time to 'do something' with the old man.

So, one sunny spring morning, Monsieur took Uncle Oswald in the buggy, and drove over to Natchitoches with him, intending to take the evening train for the institution in which the poor creature was to be cared for.

It was quite early in the afternoon when they reached town, and Monsieur found himself with several hours to dispose of before train-time. He tied his horses in front of the hotel – the quaintest old stuccoed house, too absurdly unlike a 'hotel' for anything – and entered. But he left Uncle Oswald seated upon a shaded bench just within the yard.

There were people occasionally coming in and going out; but no one took the smallest notice of the old negro drowsing over the cane that he held between his knees. The sight was common in Natchitoches.

One who passed in was a little girl about twelve, with dark, kind eyes, and daintily carrying a parcel. She was dressed in blue calico, and wore a stiff white sun-bonnet, extinguisher fashion, over her brown curls.

Just as she passed Uncle Oswald again, on her way out, the old man, half asleep, let fall his cane. She picked it up and handed it back to him, as any nice child would have done.

'Oh, thankee, thankee, missy,' stammered Uncle Oswald, all confused at being waited upon by this little lady. 'You is a putty li'le gal. W'at 's yo' name, honey?'

'My name 's Susanne; Susanne Bênitou,' replied the girl.

Instantly the old negro stumbled to his feet. Without a moment's hesitancy he followed the little one out through the gate, down the street, and around the corner.

It was an hour later that Monsieur, after a distracted search, found him standing upon the gallery of the tiny house in which Madame Bênitou kept 'fashionable millinery.'

Mother and daughter were sorely perplexed to comprehend the intentions of the venerable servitor, who stood, hat in hand, persistently awaiting their orders.

Monsieur understood and appreciated the situation at once, and he has prevailed upon Madame Bênitou to accept the gratuitous services of Uncle Oswald for the sake of the old darky's own safety and happiness.

Uncle Oswald never tries to run away now. He chops wood and hauls water. He cheerfully and faithfully bears the parcels that Susanne used to carry; and makes an excellent cup of black coffee.

I met the old man the other day in Natchitoches, contentedly stumbling down St. Denis street with a basket of figs that some one was sending to his mistress. I asked him his name.

'My name 's Oswal', Madam; Oswal' – dat's my name. I b'longs to de Bênitous,' and some one told me his story then.

A Turkey Hunt

Three of Madame's finest bronze turkeys were missing from the brood. It was nearing Christmas, and that was the reason, perhaps, that even Monsieur grew agitated when the discovery was made. The news was brought to the house by Sévérin's boy, who had seen the troop at noon a half mile up the bayou three short. Others reported the deficiency as even greater. So, at about two in the afternoon, though a cold drizzle had begun to fall, popular feeling in the matter was so strong that all the household forces turned out to search for the missing gobblers.

Alice, the housemaid, went down the river, and Polisson, the yard-boy, went up the bayou. Others crossed the fields, and Artemise was rather vaguely instructed to 'go look too.'

Artemise is in some respects an extraordinary person. In age she is anywhere between ten and fifteen, with a head not unlike in shape and appearance to a dark chocolate-colored Easter-egg. She talks almost wholly in monosyllables, and has big round glassy eyes, which she fixes upon one with the placid gaze of an Egyptian sphinx.

The morning after my arrival at the plantation, I was awakened by the rattling of cups at my bedside. It was Artemise with the early coffee.

'Is it cold out?' I asked, by way of conversation, as I sipped the tiny cup of ink-black coffee.

'Ya, 'm.'

'Where do you sleep, Artemise?' I further inquired, with the same intention as before.

'In uh hole,' was precisely what she said, with a pump-like motion of the arm that she habitually uses to indicate a locality. What she meant was that she slept in the hall.

Again, another time, she came with an armful of wood, and having deposited it upon the hearth, turned to stare fixedly at me, with folded hands.

'Did Madame send you to build a fire, Artemise?' I hastened to ask, feeling uncomfortable under the look.

'Ya, 'm.'

'Very well; make it.'

'Matches!' was all she said.

There happened to be no matches in my room, and she evidently considered that all personal responsibility ceased in face of this first and not very serious obstacle. Pages might be told of her unfathomable ways; but to the turkey hunt.

All afternoon the searching party kept returning, singly and in couples, and in a more or less bedraggled condition. All brought unfavorable reports. Nothing could be seen of the missing fowls. Artemise had been absent probably an hour when she glided into the hall where the family was assembled, and stood with crossed hands and contemplative air beside the fire. We could see by the benign expression of her countenance that she possibly had information to give, if any inducement were offered her in the shape of a question.

'Have you found the turkeys, Artemise?' Madame hastened to ask.

'Ya, 'm.'

'You Artemise!' shouted Aunt Florindy, the cook, who was passing through the hall with a batch of newly baked light bread. 'She 's a-lyin', mist'ess, if dey ever was! *You* foun' dem turkeys?' turning upon the child. 'Whar was you at, de whole blesse' time? Warn't you stan'in' plank up agin de back o' de hen-'ous'? Never budged a inch? Don't jaw me down, gal; don't jaw me!' Artemise was only gazing at Aunt Florindy with unruffled calm. 'I warn't gwine tell on 'er, but arter dat untroof, I boun' to.'

'Let her alone, Aunt Florindy,' Madame interfered. 'Where are the turkeys, Artemise?'

'Yon'a,' she simply articulated, bringing the pump-handle motion of her arm into play.

'Where "yonder"?' Madame demanded, a little impatiently.

'In uh hen-'ous'!'

Sure enough! The three missing turkeys had been accidentally locked up in the morning when the chickens were fed.

Artemise, for some unknown reason, had hidden herself during the search behind the hen-house, and had heard their muffled gobble.

Old Aunt Peggy

When the war was over, old Aunt Peggy went to Monsieur, and said:—

'Massa, I ain't never gwine to quit yer. I'm gittin' ole an' feeble, an' my days is few in dis heah lan' o' sorrow an' sin. All I axes is a li'le co'ner whar I kin set down an' wait peaceful fu de en'.'

Monsieur and Madame were very much touched at this mark of affection and fidelity from Aunt Peggy. So, in the general reconstruction of the plantation which immediately followed the surrender, a nice cabin, pleasantly appointed, was set apart for the old woman. Madame did not even forget the very comfortable rocking-chair in which Aunt Peggy might 'set down,' as she herself feelingly expressed it, 'an' wait fu de en'.'

She has been rocking ever since.

At intervals of about two years Aunt Peggy hobbles up to the house, and delivers the stereotyped address which has become more than familiar:—

'Mist'ess, I 's come to take a las' look at you all. Le' me look at you good. Le' me look at de chillun, – de big chillun an' de li'le chillun. Le' me look at de picters an' de photygraphts an' de pianny, an' eve'ything 'fo' it 's too late. One eye is done gone, an' de udder 's a-gwine fas'. Any mo'nin' yo' po' ole Aunt Peggy gwine wake up an' fin' herse'f stone-bline.'

After such a visit Aunt Peggy invariably returns to her cabin with a generously filled apron.

The scruple which Monsieur one time felt in supporting a woman for so many years in idleness has entirely disappeared. Of late his attitude towards Aunt Peggy is simply one of profound astonishment, – wonder at the surprising age which an old black woman may attain when she sets her mind to it, for Aunt Peggy is a hundred and twenty-five, so she says.

It may not be true, however. Possibly she is older.

The Lilies

That little vagabond Mamouche amused himself one afternoon
by letting down the fence rails that protected Mr. Billy's young
crop of cotton and corn. He had first looked carefully about him
to make sure there was no witness to this piece of rascality. Then
he crossed the lane and did the same with the Widow Angèle's
fence, thereby liberating Toto, the white calf who stood disconso-
lately penned up on the other side.

It was not ten seconds before Toto was frolicking madly in Mr.
Billy's crop, and Mamouche – the young scamp – was running
swiftly down the lane, laughing fiendishly to himself as he went.

He could not at first decide whether there could be more fun in
letting Toto demolish things at his pleasure, or in warning Mr.
Billy of the calf's presence in the field. But the latter course
commended itself as possessing a certain refinement of perfidy.

'Ho, the'a, you!' called out Mamouche to one of Mr. Billy's
hands, when he got around to where the men were at work; 'you
betta go yon'a an' see 'bout that calf o' Ma'me Angèle; he done
broke in the fiel' an' 'bout to finish the crop, him.' Then
Mamouche went and sat behind a big tree, where, unobserved,
he could laugh to his heart's content.

Mr. Billy's fury was unbounded when he learned that Madame
Angèle's calf was eating up and trampling down his corn. At
once he sent a detachment of men and boys to expel the animal
from the field. Others were required to repair the damaged fence;
while he himself, boiling with wrath, rode up the lane on his
wicked black charger.

But merely to look upon the devastation was not enough for
Mr. Billy. He dismounted from his horse, and strode belligerently
up to Madame Angèle's door, upon which he gave, with his
riding-whip, a couple of sharp raps that plainly indicated the
condition of his mind.

Mr. Billy looked taller and broader than ever as he squared
himself on the gallery of Madame Angèle's small and modest
house. She herself half-opened the door, a pale, sweet-looking

woman, somewhat bewildered, and holding a piece of sewing in her hands. Little Marie Louise was beside her, with big, inquiring, frightened eyes.

'Well, Madam!' blustered Mr. Billy, 'this is a pretty piece of work! That young beast of yours is a fence-breaker, Madam, and ought to be shot.'

'Oh, non, non, M'sieur. Toto's too li'le; I'm sho he can't break any fence, him.'

'Don't contradict me, Madam. I say he's a fence-breaker. There's the proof before your eyes. He ought to be shot, I say, and – don't let it occur again, Madam.' And Mr. Billy turned and stamped down the steps with a great clatter of spurs as he went.

Madame Angèle was at the time in desperate haste to finish a young lady's Easter dress, and she could not afford to let Toto's escapade occupy her to any extent, much as she regretted it. But little Marie Louise was greatly impressed by the affair. She went out in the yard to Toto, who was under the fig-tree, looking not half so shamefaced as he ought. The child, with arms clasped around the little fellow's white shaggy neck, scolded him roundly.

'Ain't you shame', Toto, to go eat up Mr. Billy's cotton an' co'n? W'at Mr. Billy ev'a done to you, to go do him that way? If you been hungry, Toto, w'y you did'n' come like always an' put yo' head in the winda? I'm goin' tell yo' maman w'en she come back f'om the woods to 's'evenin', M'sieur.'

Marie Louise only ceased her mild rebuke when she fancied she saw a penitential look in Toto's big soft eyes.

She had a keen instinct of right and justice for so young a little maid. And all the afternoon, and long into the night, she was disturbed by the thought of the unfortunate accident. Of course, there could be no question of repaying Mr. Billy with money; she and her mother had none. Neither had they cotton and corn with which to make good the loss he had sustained through them.

But had they not something far more beautiful and precious than cotton and corn? Marie Louise thought with delight of that row of Easter lilies on their tall green stems, ranged thick along the sunny side of the house.

The assurance that she would, after all, be able to satisfy Mr. Billy's just anger, was a very sweet one. And soothed by it, Marie Louise soon fell asleep and dreamt a grotesque dream: that the lilies were having a stately dance on the green in the moonlight, and were inviting Mr. Billy to join them.

The following day, when it was nearing noon, Marie Louise said to her mamma: 'Maman, can I have some of the Easter lily, to do with like I want?'

Madame Angèle was just then testing the heat of an iron with which to press out the seams in the young lady's Easter dress, and she answered a shade impatiently:

'Yes, yes; va t'en, chérie,' thinking that her little girl wanted to pluck a lily or two.

So the child took a pair of old shears from her mother's basket, and out she went to where the tall, perfumed lilies were nodding, and shaking off from their glistening petals the rain-drops with which a passing cloud had just laughingly pelted them.

Snip, snap, went the shears here and there, and never did Marie Louise stop plying them till scores of those long-stemmed lilies lay upon the ground. There were far more than she could hold in her small hands, so she literally clasped the great bunch in her arms, and staggered to her feet with it.

Marie Louise was intent upon her purpose, and lost no time in its accomplishment. She was soon trudging earnestly down the lane with her sweet burden, never stopping, and only once glancing aside to cast a reproachful look at Toto, whom she had not wholly forgiven.

She did not in the least mind that the dogs barked, or that the darkies laughed at her. She went straight on to Mr. Billy's big house, and right into the dining-room, where Mr. Billy sat eating his dinner all alone.

It was a finely-furnished room, but disorderly – very disorderly, as an old bachelor's personal surroundings sometimes are. A black boy stood waiting upon the table. When little Marie Louise suddenly appeared, with that armful of lilies, Mr. Billy seemed for a moment transfixed at the sight.

'Well – bless – my soul! what's all this? What's all this?' he questioned, with staring eyes.

Marie Louise had already made a little courtesy. Her sunbonnet had fallen back, leaving exposed her pretty round head; and her sweet brown eyes were full of confidence as they looked into Mr. Billy's.

'I'm bring some lilies to pay back fo' yo' cotton an' co'n w'at Toto eat all up, M'sieur.'

Mr. Billy turned savagely upon Pompey. 'What are you laughing at, you black rascal? Leave the room!'

Pompey, who out of mistaken zeal had doubled himself with merriment, was too accustomed to the admonition to heed it literally, and he only made a pretense of withdrawing from Mr. Billy's elbow.

'Lilies! well, upon my – isn't it the little one from across the lane?'

'Dat's who,' affirmed Pompey, cautiously insinuating himself again into favor.

'Lilies! who ever heard the like? Why, the baby's buried under 'em. Set 'em down somewhere, little one; anywhere.' And Marie Louise, glad to be relieved from the weight of the great cluster, dumped them all on the table close to Mr. Billy.

The perfume that came from the damp, massed flowers was heavy and almost sickening in its pungency. Mr. Billy quivered a little, and drew involuntarily back, as if from an unexpected assailant, when the odor reached him. He had been making cotton and corn for so many years, he had forgotten there were such things as lilies in the world.

'Kiar 'em out? fling 'em 'way?' questioned Pompey, who had observed his master cunningly.

'Let 'em alone! Keep your hands off them! Leave the room, you outlandish black scamp! Whar are you standing there for? Can't you set the Mamzelle a place at table, and draw up a chair?'

So Marie Louise – perched upon a fine old-fashioned chair, supplemented by a Webster's Unabridged – sat down to dine with Mr. Billy.

She had never eaten in company with so peculiar a gentleman before; so irascible toward the inoffensive Pompey, and so courteous to herself. But she was not ill at ease, and conducted herself properly as her mamma had taught her how.

Mr. Billy was anxious that she should enjoy her dinner, and began by helping her generously to Jambalaya. When she had tasted it she made no remark, only laid down her fork, and looked composedly before her.

'Why, bless me! what ails the little one? You don't eat your rice.'

'It ain't cook', M'sieur,' replied Marie Louise politely.

Pompey nearly strangled in his attempt to smother an explosion.

'Of course it isn't cooked,' echoed Mr. Billy, excitedly, pushing away his plate. 'What do you mean, setting a mess of that sort before human beings? Do you take us for a couple of – of rice-birds? What are you standing there for; can't you look up some jam or something to keep the young one from starving? Where's all that jam I saw stewing a while back, here?'

Pompey withdrew, and soon returned with a platter of black-looking jam. Mr. Billy ordered cream for it. Pompey reported there was none.

'No cream, with twenty-five cows on the plantation if there's one!' cried Mr. Billy, almost springing from his chair with indignation.

'Aunt Printy 'low she sot de pan o' cream on de winda-sell, suh, an' Unc' Jonah come 'long an' tu'n it cl'ar ova; neva lef' a drap in de pan.'

But evidently the jam, with or without cream, was as distasteful to Marie Louise as the rice was; for after tasting it gingerly she laid away her spoon as she had done before.

'O, no! little one; you don't tell me it isn't cooked this time,' laughed Mr. Billy. 'I saw the thing boiling a day and a half. Wasn't it a day and a half, Pompey? if you know how to tell the truth.'

'Aunt Printy alluz do cooks her p'esarves tell dey plumb done, sho,' agreed Pompey.

'It's burn', M'sieur,' said Marie Louise, politely, but decidedly, to the utter confusion of Mr. Billy, who was as mortified as could be at the failure of his dinner to please his fastidious little visitor.

Well, Mr. Billy thought of Marie Louise a good deal after that; as long as the lilies lasted. And they lasted long, for he had the whole household employed in taking care of them. Often he would chuckle to himself: 'The little rogue, with her black eyes and her lilies! And the rice wasn't cooked, if you please; and the jam was burnt. And the best of it is, she was right.'

But when the lilies withered finally, and had to be thrown away, Mr. Billy donned his best suit, a starched shirt and fine silk necktie. Thus attired, he crossed the lane to carry his somewhat tardy apologies to Madame Angèle and Mamzelle Marie Louise, and to pay them a first visit.

Ripe Figs

Maman-Nainaine said that when the figs were ripe Babette might go to visit her cousins down on the Bayou-Lafourche where the sugar cane grows. Not that the ripening of figs had the least thing to do with it, but that is the way Maman-Nainaine was.

It seemed to Babette a very long time to wait; for the leaves upon the trees were tender yet, and the figs were like little hard, green marbles.

But warm rains came along and plenty of strong sunshine, and though Maman-Nainaine was as patient as the statue of la Madone, and Babette as restless as a humming-bird, the first thing they both knew it was hot summer-time. Every day Babette danced out to where the fig-trees were in a long line against the fence. She walked slowly beneath them, carefully peering between the gnarled, spreading branches. But each time she came disconsolate away again. What she saw there finally was something that made her sing and dance the whole long day.

When Maman-Nainaine sat down in her stately way to breakfast, the following morning, her muslin cap standing like an aureole about her white, placid face, Babette approached. She bore a dainty porcelain platter, which she set down before her godmother. It contained a dozen purple figs, fringed around with their rich, green leaves.

'Ah,' said Maman-Nainaine, arching her eyebrows, 'how early the figs have ripened this year!'

'Oh,' said Babette, 'I think they have ripened very late.'

'Babette,' continued Maman-Nainaine, as she peeled the very plumpest figs with her pointed silver fruit-knife, 'you will carry my love to them all down on Bayou-Lafourche. And tell your Tante Frosine I shall look for her at Toussaint – when the chrysanthemums are in bloom.'

Croque-Mitaine

There was one thing about the nursery-governess from Paris that did not suit P'tit-Paul. It was her constant reference, in a semi-threatening way, to one Croque-Mitaine, a hideous ogre, said to inhabit the strip of wood just beyond the children's playground.

The darkies knew nothing of such an existence; for P'tit-Paul questioned them:

'You neva saw Croque-Mitaine, you, Unc' Juba?'

'No, honey. Don't you listen tu no sich talk. Dat 'ar wood ain't no mo' haunted 'an my ole 'oman's veg'tible patch. W'y dar hain't no buryin'-groun' din fo' mile' o' heah! You knows dat diz uz well uz I does, boy.'

But as Mamzelle's allusions to Croque-Mitaine grew more and more frequent, P'tit-Paul decided to investigate the matter himself, finally.

A favorable occasion soon presented itself. Mamzelle was going to a ball at a neighboring plantation. But before leaving she impressed upon the little ones that they must lie very still and go to sleep, or Croque-Mitaine would stalk from the wood and come to devour them where they lay.

She had hardly gone than P'tit-Paul slipped into his clothes and stole away to go sit at the far end of the play-ground upon a bench there, that commanded a view of the road which was much travelled. It will be seen that beside an inquiring spirit, P'tit-Paul possessed a very courageous one.

The night was beautiful, with a round moon lighting the landscape and a delicious fragrance filling the soft, warm air. Off in the Magnolia-trees the mocking-birds had begun their nightly serenade.

After a half-hour, no one had yet passed by except Uncle Juba who stopped a moment to upbraid the child for 'settin' dis so, in de full o' de moon.'

Then another half-hour went by and P'tit-Paul was growing drowsy, when suddenly the blood chilled in his veins and the hair fairly rose on his head. For, coming towards him from the wood, was an object more horrible than his eyes had ever beheld or his fancy pictured. It bore the grotesque shape of a man, but its head was that of an unfamiliar beast having great horns and wild tremendous eyes. The monster wielded a pitch-fork in his misshapen hand and Paul doubted not that in a few moments he would feel its cruel prongs piercing his own body.

Besides being almost powerless to run, he felt it would be useless, and reasoned confusedly that perhaps Croque-Mitaine might be conciliated, for he was even then flourishing in his paw what seemed to be a flag of truce.

The shape approached nearer and nearer, and Paul shrunk smaller and smaller in the corner of the bench.

Then a most singular thing happened. Croque-Mitaine stood still in the road, rested his pitch-fork, and removing his hideous face, began to mop his head with the flag of truce! Then P'tit-Paul understood!

He hardly remembers how he reached home.

Next morning he confided his discovery to the little brothers and sisters.

When Mamzelle talks of Croque-Mitaine now, they look at each other and smile slyly and very provokingly. For they know that Croque-Mitaine is only Monsieur Alcée going to a masked ball!

A Little Free-Mulatto*

M'sié Jean-Ba' – that was Aurélia's father – was so especially fine
and imposing when he went down to the city, with his glossy
beard, his elegant clothes, and gold watch-chain, that he could
easily have ridden in the car 'For Whites.' No one would ever
have known the difference. But M'sié Jean-Ba' was too proud to
do that. He was very proud. So was Ma'ame Jean-Ba'. And
because of that unyielding pride, little Aurélia's existence was not
altogether a happy one.

She was not permitted to play with the white children up at
the big-house, who would often willingly have had her join their
games. Neither was she allowed to associate in any way with the
little darkies who frolicked all day long as gleefully as kittens
before their cabin doors. There seemed nothing for her to do in
the world but to have her shiny hair plaited, or to sit at her
mother's knee learning to spell or to patch quilt pieces.

It was well enough so long as she was a baby and crawled
about the gallery satisfied to play with a sun-beam. But growing
older she pined for some more real companionship.

'La p'tite, 'pear tu me lack she gittin' po', yere lately,' remarked
M'sié Jean-Ba' solicitously to his wife one day when he noted his
little daughter's drooping mien.

'You right, Jean-Ba'; Aurélia a'n't pick up none, the las' year.'
And they watched the child carefully after that. She seemed to
fade like a flower that wants the sun.

Of course M'sié Jean-Ba' could not stand that. So when
December came, and his contract with the planter had ceased, he
gathered his family and all his belongings and went away to live
– in paradise.

That is, little Aurélia thinks it is paradise, the change is so
wonderful.

There is a constant making and receiving of visits, now. She
trudges off every morning to the convent where numbers of little

* A term still applied in Louisiana to Mulattoes who were never in slavery.

children just like herself are taught by the sisters. Even in the church in which she, her mamma and papa make their Sunday devotions, they breathe an atmosphere which is native to them. And then, such galloping about the country on little creole ponies!

Well, there is no question about it. The happiest little Free-Mulatto in all Louisiana is Aurélia, since her father has moved to 'L'Isle des Mulâtres.'

At the 'Cadian Ball

Bobinôt, that big, brown, good-natured Bobinôt, had no intention of going to the ball, even though he knew Calixta would be there. For what came of those balls but heartache, and a sickening disinclination for work the whole week through, till Saturday night came again and his tortures began afresh? Why could he not love Ozéina, who would marry him tomorrow; or Fronie, or any one of a dozen others, rather than that little Spanish vixen? Calixta's slender foot had never touched Cuban soil; but her mother's had, and the Spanish was in her blood all the same. For that reason the prairie people forgave her much that they would not have overlooked in their own daughters or sisters.

Her eyes, – Bobinôt thought of her eyes, and weakened, – the bluest, the drowsiest, most tantalizing that ever looked into a man's; he thought of her flaxen hair that kinked worse than a mulatto's close to her head; that broad, smiling mouth and tiptilted nose, that full figure; that voice like a rich contralto song, with cadences in it that must have been taught by Satan, for there was no one else to teach her tricks on that 'Cadian prairie. Bobinôt thought of them all as he plowed his rows of cane.

There had even been a breath of scandal whispered about her a year ago, when she went to Assumption, – but why talk of it? No one did now. 'C'est Espagnol, ça,' most of them said with lenient shoulder-shrugs. 'Bon chien tient de race,' the old men mumbled over their pipes, stirred by recollections. Nothing was made of it, except that Fronie threw it up to Calixta when the two quarreled and fought on the church steps after mass one Sunday, about a lover. Calixta swore roundly in fine 'Cadian French and with true Spanish spirit, and slapped Fronie's face. Fronie had slapped her back; 'Tiens, cocotte, va!' 'Espèce de lionèse; prends ça, et ça!' till the curé himself was obliged to hasten and make peace between them. Bobinôt thought of it all, and would not go to the ball.

But in the afternoon, over at Friedheimer's store, where he was buying a trace-chain, he heard some one say that Alcée

Laballière would be there. Then wild horses could not have kept him away. He knew how it would be – or rather he did not know how it would be – if the handsome young planter came over to the ball as he sometimes did. If Alcée happened to be in a serious mood, he might only go to the card-room and play a round or two; or he might stand out on the galleries talking crops and politics with the old people. But there was no telling. A drink or two could put the devil in his head, – that was what Bobinôt said to himself, as he wiped the sweat from his brow with his red bandanna; a gleam from Calixta's eyes, a flash of her ankle, a twirl of her skirts could do the same. Yes, Bobinôt would go to the ball.

That was the year Alcée Laballière put nine hundred acres in rice. It was putting a good deal of money into the ground, but the returns promised to be glorious. Old Madame Laballière, sailing about the spacious galleries in her white *volante*, figured it all out in her head. Clarisse, her goddaughter, helped her a little, and together they built more air-castles than enough. Alcée worked like a mule that time; and if he did not kill himself, it was because his constitution was an iron one. It was an every-day affair for him to come in from the field well-nigh exhausted, and wet to the waist. He did not mind if there were visitors; he left them to his mother and Clarisse. There were often guests: young men and women who came up from the city, which was but a few hours away, to visit his beautiful kinswoman. She was worth going a good deal farther than that to see. Dainty as a lily; hardy as a sunflower; slim, tall, graceful, like one of the reeds that grew in the marsh. Cold and kind and cruel by turn, and everything that was aggravating to Alcée.

He would have liked to sweep the place of those visitors, often. Of the men, above all, with their ways and their manners; their swaying of fans like women, and dandling about hammocks. He could have pitched them over the levee into the river, if it had n't meant murder. That was Alcée. But he must have been crazy the day he came in from the rice-field, and, toil-stained as he was, clasped Clarisse by the arms and panted a volley of hot, blistering love-words into her face. No man had ever spoken love to her like that.

'Monsieur!' she exclaimed, looking him full in the eyes,

without a quiver. Alcée's hands dropped and his glance wavered before the chill of her calm, clear eyes.

'*Par exemple!*' she muttered disdainfully, as she turned from him, deftly adjusting the careful toilet that he had so brutally disarranged.

That happened a day or two before the cyclone came that cut into the rice like fine steel. It was an awful thing, coming so swiftly, without a moment's warning in which to light a holy candle or set a piece of blessed palm burning. Old madame wept openly and said her beads, just as her son Didier, the New Orleans one, would have done. If such a thing had happened to Alphonse, the Laballière planting cotton up in Natchitoches, he would have raved and stormed like a second cyclone, and made his surroundings unbearable for a day or two. But Alcée took the misfortune differently. He looked ill and gray after it, and said nothing. His speechlessness was frightful. Clarisse's heart melted with tenderness; but when she offered her soft, purring words of condolence, he accepted them with mute indifference. Then she and her nénaine wept afresh in each other's arms.

A night or two later, when Clarisse went to her window to kneel there in the moonlight and say her prayers before retiring, she saw that Bruce, Alcée's negro servant, had led his master's saddle-horse noiselessly along the edge of the sward that bordered the gravel-path, and stood holding him near by. Presently, she heard Alcée quit his room, which was beneath her own, and traverse the lower portico. As he emerged from the shadow and crossed the strip of moonlight, she perceived that he carried a pair of well-filled saddle-bags which he at once flung across the animal's back. He then lost no time in mounting, and after a brief exchange of words with Bruce, went cantering away, taking no precaution to avoid the noisy gravel as the negro had done.

Clarisse had never suspected that it might be Alcée's custom to sally forth from the plantation secretly, and at such an hour; for it was nearly midnight. And had it not been for the telltale saddle-bags, she would only have crept to bed, to wonder, to fret and dream unpleasant dreams. But her impatience and anxiety would not be held in check. Hastily unbolting the shutters of her door that opened upon the gallery, she stepped outside and called softly to the old negro.

'Gre't Peter! Miss Clarisse. I was n' sho it was a ghos' o' w'at, stan'in' up dah, plumb in de night, dataway.'

He mounted halfway up the long, broad flight of stairs. She was standing at the top.

'Bruce, w'ere has Monsieur Alcée gone?' she asked.

'W'y, he gone 'bout he business, I reckin,' replied Bruce, striving to be non-committal at the outset.

'W'ere has Monsieur Alcée gone?' she reiterated, stamping her bare foot. 'I won't stan' any nonsense or any lies; mine, Bruce.'

'I don' ric'lic ez I eva tole you lie *yit*, Miss Clarisse. Mista Alcée, he all broke up, sho.'

'W'ere – has – he gone? Ah, Sainte Vierge! faut de la patience! butor, va!'

'W'en I was in he room, a-breshin' off he clo'es to-day,' the darkey began, settling himself against the stair-rail, 'he look dat speechless an' down, I say, "You 'pear to me like some pussun w'at gwine have a spell o' sickness, Mista Alcée." He say, "You reckin?" 'I dat he git up, go look hisse'f stiddy in de glass. Den he go to de chimbly an' jerk up de quinine bottle an' po' a gre't hoss-dose on to he han'. An' he swalla dat mess in a wink, an' wash hit down wid a big dram o' w'iskey w'at he keep in he room, aginst he come all soppin' wet outen de fiel'.

'He 'lows, "No, I ain' gwine be sick, Bruce." Den he square off. He say, "I kin mak out to stan' up an' gi' an' take wid any man I knows, lessen hit 's John L. Sulvun. But w'en God A'mighty an' a 'oman jines fo'ces agin me, dat 's one too many fur me." I tell 'im, "Jis so," whils' I 'se makin' out to bresh a spot off w'at ain' dah, on he coat colla. I tell 'im, "You wants li'le res', suh." He say, "No, I wants li'le fling; dat w'at I wants; an' I gwine git it. Pitch me a fis'ful o' clo'es in dem 'ar saddle-bags." Dat w'at he say. Don't you bodda, missy. He jis' gone a-caperin' yonda to de Cajun ball. Uh – uh – de skeeters is fair' a-swarmin' like bees roun' yo' foots!'

The mosquitoes were indeed attacking Clarisse's white feet savagely. She had unconsciously been alternately rubbing one foot over the other during the darkey's recital.

'The 'Cadian ball,' she repeated contemptuously. 'Humph! *Par exemple!* Nice conduc' for a Laballière. An' he needs a saddle-bag, fill' with clothes, to go to the 'Cadian ball!'

'Oh, Miss Clarisse; you go on to bed, chile; git yo' soun' sleep.

He 'low he come back in couple weeks o' so. I kiarn be repeatin' lot o' truck w'at young mans say, out heah face o' young gal.'

Clarisse said no more, but turned and abruptly reëntered the house.

'You done talk too much wid yo' mouf a'ready, you ole fool nigga, you,' muttered Bruce to himself as he walked away.

Alcée reached the ball very late, of course – too late for the chicken gumbo which had been served at midnight.

The big, low-ceiled room – they called it a hall – was packed with men and women dancing to the music of three fiddles. There were broad galleries all around it. There was a room at one side where sober-faced men were playing cards. Another, in which babies were sleeping, was called *le parc aux petits*. Any one who is white may go to a 'Cadian ball, but he must pay for his lemonade, his coffee and chicken gumbo. And he must behave himself like a 'Cadian. Grosbœuf was giving this ball. He had been giving them since he was a young man, and he was a middle-aged one, now. In that time he could recall but one disturbance, and that was caused by American railroaders, who were not in touch with their surroundings and had no business there. 'Ces maudits gens du raiderode,' Grosbœuf called them.

Alcée Laballière's presence at the ball caused a flutter even among the men, who could not but admire his 'nerve' after such misfortune befalling him. To be sure, they knew the Laballières were rich – that there were resources East, and more again in the city. But they felt it took a *brave homme* to stand a blow like that philosophically. One old gentleman, who was in the habit of reading a Paris newspaper and knew things, chuckled gleefully to everybody that Alcée's conduct was altogether *chic, mais chic*. That he had more *panache* than Boulanger. Well, perhaps he had.

But what he did not show outwardly was that he was in a mood for ugly things to-night. Poor Bobinôt alone felt it vaguely. He discerned a gleam of it in Alcée's handsome eyes, as the young planter stood in the doorway, looking with rather feverish glance upon the assembly, while he laughed and talked with a 'Cadian farmer who was beside him.

Bobinôt himself was dull-looking and clumsy. Most of the men were. But the young women were very beautiful. The eyes that glanced into Alcée's as they passed him were big, dark, soft as those of the young heifers standing out in the cool prairie grass.

But the belle was Calixta. Her white dress was not nearly so handsome or well made as Fronie's (she and Fronie had quite forgotten the battle on the church steps, and were friends again), nor were her slippers so stylish as those of Ozéina; and she fanned herself with a handkerchief, since she had broken her red fan at the last ball, and her aunts and uncles were not willing to give her another. But all the men agreed she was at her best to-night. Such animation! and abandon! such flashes of wit!

'Hé, Bobinôt! *Mais* w'at 's the matta? W'at you standin' *planté là* like ole Ma'ame Tina's cow in the bog, you?'

That was good. That was an excellent thrust at Bobinôt, who had forgotten the figure of the dance with his mind bent on other things, and it started a clamor of laughter at his expense. He joined good-naturedly. It was better to receive even such notice as that from Calixta than none at all. But Madame Suzonne, sitting in a corner, whispered to her neighbor that if Ozéina were to conduct herself in a like manner, she should immediately be taken out to the mule-cart and driven home. The women did not always approve of Calixta.

Now and then were short lulls in the dance, when couples flocked out upon the galleries for a brief respite and fresh air. The moon had gone down pale in the west, and in the east was yet no promise of day. After such an interval, when the dancers again assembled to resume the interrupted quadrille, Calixta was not among them.

She was sitting upon a bench out in the shadow, with Alcée beside her. They were acting like fools. He had attempted to take a little gold ring from her finger; just for the fun of it, for there was nothing he could have done with the ring but replace it again. But she clinched her hand tight. He pretended that it was a very difficult matter to open it. Then he kept the hand in his. They seemed to forget about it. He played with her earring, a thin crescent of gold hanging from her small brown ear. He caught a wisp of the kinky hair that had escaped its fastening, and rubbed the ends of it against his shaven cheek.

'You know, last year in Assumption, Calixta?' They belonged to the younger generation, so preferred to speak English.

'Don't come say Assumption to me, M'sieur Alcée. I done yeard Assumption till I 'm plumb sick.'

'Yes, I know. The idiots! Because you were in Assumption, and

I happened to go to Assumption, they must have it that we went together. But it was nice – *hein*, Calixta? – in Assumption?'

They saw Bobinôt emerge from the hall and stand a moment outside the lighted doorway, peering uneasily and searchingly into the darkness. He did not see them, and went slowly back.

'There is Bobinôt looking for you. You are going to set poor Bobinôt crazy. You 'll marry him some day; *hein*, Calixta?'

'I don't say no, me,' she replied, striving to withdraw her hand, which he held more firmly for the attempt.

'But come, Calixta; you know you said you would go back to Assumption, just to spite them.'

'No, I neva said that, me. You mus' dreamt that.'

'Oh, I thought you did. You know I 'm going down to the city.'

'W'en?'

'To-night.'

'Betta make has'e, then; it 's mos' day.'

'Well, to-morrow 'll do.'

'W'at you goin' do, yonda?'

'I don't know. Drown myself in the lake, maybe; unless you go down there to visit your uncle.'

Calixta's senses were reeling; and they well-nigh left her when she felt Alcée's lips brush her ear like the touch of a rose.

'Mista Alcée! Is dat Mista Alcée?' the thick voice of a negro was asking; he stood on the ground, holding to the banister-rails near which the couple sat.

'W'at do you want now?' cried Alcée impatiently. 'Can't I have a moment of peace?'

'I ben huntin' you high an' low, suh,' answered the man. 'Dey – dey some one in de road, onda de mulbare-tree, want see you a minute.'

'I would n't go out to the road to see the Angel Gabriel. And if you come back here with any more talk, I 'll have to break your neck.' The negro turned mumbling away.

Alcée and Calixta laughed softly about it. Her boisterousness was all gone. They talked low, and laughed softly, as lovers do.

'Alcée! Alcée Laballière!'

It was not the negro's voice this time; but one that went through Alcée's body like an electric shock, bringing him to his feet.

Clarisse was standing there in her riding-habit, where the

negro had stood. For an instant confusion reigned in Alcée's thoughts, as with one who awakes suddenly from a dream. But he felt that something of serious import had brought his cousin to the ball in the dead of night.

'W'at does this mean, Clarisse?' he asked.

'It means something has happen' at home. You mus' come.'

'Happened to maman?' he questioned, in alarm.

'No; nénaine is well, and asleep. It is something else. Not to frighten you. But you mus' come. Come with me, Alcée.'

There was no need for the imploring note. He would have followed the voice anywhere.

She had now recognized the girl sitting back on the bench.

'Ah, c'est vous, Calixta? Comment ça va, mon enfant?'

'Tcha va b'en; et vous, mam'zélle?'

Alcée swung himself over the low rail and started to follow Clarisse, without a word, without a glance back at the girl. He had forgotten he was leaving her there. But Clarisse whispered something to him, and he turned back to say 'Good-night, Calixta,' and offer his hand to press through the railing. She pretended not to see it.

'How come that? You settin' yere by yo'se'f, Calixta?' It was Bobinôt who had found her there alone. The dancers had not yet come out. She looked ghastly in the faint, gray light struggling out of the east.

'Yes, that's me. Go yonda in the *parc aux petits* an' ask Aunt Olisse fu' my hat. She knows w'ere 't is. I want to go home, me.'

'How you came?'

'I come afoot, with the Cateaus. But I 'm goin' now. I ent goin' wait fu' 'em. I 'm plumb wo' out, me.'

'Kin I go with you, Calixta?'

'I don' care.'

They went together across the open prairie and along the edge of the fields, stumbling in the uncertain light. He told her to lift her dress that was getting wet and bedraggled; for she was pulling at the weeds and grasses with her hands.

'I don' care; it 's got to go in the tub, anyway. You been sayin' all along you want to marry me, Bobinôt. Well, if you want, yet, I don' care, me.'

The glow of a sudden and overwhelming happiness shone out

in the brown, rugged face of the young Acadian. He could not speak, for very joy. It choked him.

'Oh well, if you don' want,' snapped Calixta, flippantly, pretending to be piqued at his silence.

'*Bon Dieu!* You know that makes me crazy, w'at you sayin'. You mean that, Calixta? You ent goin' turn roun' agin?'

'I neva tole you that much *yet*, Bobinôt. I mean that. *Tiens*,' and she held out her hand in the business-like manner of a man who clinches a bargain with a hand-clasp. Bobinôt grew bold with happiness and asked Calixta to kiss him. She turned her face, that was almost ugly after the night's dissipation, and looked steadily into his.

'I don' want to kiss you, Bobinôt,' she said, turning away again, 'not to-day. Some other time. *Bonté divine!* ent you satisfy, *yet!*'

'Oh, I 'm satisfy, Calixta,' he said.

Riding through a patch of wood, Clarisse's saddle became ungirted, and she and Alcée dismounted to readjust it.

For the twentieth time he asked her what had happened at home.

'But, Clarisse, w'at is it? Is it a misfortune?'

'Ah Dieu sait! It 's only something that happen' to me.'

'To you!'

'I saw you go away las' night, Alcée, with those saddle-bags,' she said, haltingly, striving to arrange something about the saddle, 'an' I made Bruce tell me. He said you had gone to the ball, an' wouldn' be home for weeks an' weeks. I thought, Alcée – maybe you were going to – to Assumption. I got wild. An' then I knew if you did n't come back, *now*, tonight, I could n't stan' it, – again.'

She had her face hidden in her arm that she was resting against the saddle when she said that.

He began to wonder if this meant love. But she had to tell him so, before he believed it. And when she told him, he thought the face of the Universe was changed – just like Bobinôt. Was it last week the cyclone had well-nigh ruined him? The cyclone seemed a huge joke, now. It was he, then, who, an hour ago was kissing little Calixta's ear and whispering nonsense into it. Calixta was like a myth, now. The one, only, great reality in the world was Clarisse standing before him, telling him that she loved him.

In the distance they heard the rapid discharge of pistol-shots; but it did not disturb them. They knew it was only the negro musicians who had gone into the yard to fire their pistols into the air, as the custom is, and to announce, '*le bal est fini.*'

Désirée's Baby

As the day was pleasant, Madame Valmondé drove over to L'Abri to see Désirée and the baby.

It made her laugh to think of Désirée with a baby. Why, it seemed but yesterday that Désirée was little more than a baby herself; when Monsieur in riding through the gateway of Valmondé had found her lying asleep in the shadow of the big stone pillar.

The little one awoke in his arms and began to cry for 'Dada.' That was as much as she could do or say. Some people thought she might have strayed there of her own accord, for she was of the toddling age. The prevailing belief was that she had been purposely left by a party of Texans, whose canvas-covered wagon, late in the day, had crossed the ferry that Coton Maïs kept, just below the plantation. In time Madame Valmondé abandoned every speculation but the one that Désirée had been sent to her by a beneficent Providence to be the child of her affection, seeing that she was without child of the flesh. For the girl grew to be beautiful and gentle, affectionate and sincere, – the idol of Valmondé.

It was no wonder, when she stood one day against the stone pillar in whose shadow she had lain asleep, eighteen years before, that Armand Aubigny riding by and seeing her there, had fallen in love with her. That was the way all the Aubignys fell in love, as if struck by a pistol shot. The wonder was that he had not loved her before; for he had known her since his father brought him home from Paris, a boy of eight, after his mother died there. The passion that awoke in him that day, when he saw her at the gate, swept along like an avalanche, or like a prairie fire, or like anything that drives headlong over all obstacles.

Monsieur Valmondé grew practical and wanted things well considered: that is, the girl's obscure origin. Armand looked into her eyes and did not care. He was reminded that she was nameless. What did it matter about a name when he could give her one of the oldest and proudest in Louisiana? He ordered the *corbeille* from Paris, and contained himself with what patience he could until it arrived; then they were married.

Madame Valmondé had not seen Désirée and the baby for four weeks. When she reached L'Abri she shuddered at the first sight of it, as she always did. It was a sad looking place, which for many years had not known the gentle presence of a mistress, old Monsieur Aubigny having married and buried his wife in France, and she having loved her own land too well ever to leave it. The roof came down steep and black like a cowl, reaching out beyond the wide galleries that encircled the yellow stuccoed house. Big, solemn oaks grew close to it, and their thick-leaved, far-reaching branches shadowed it like a pall. Young Aubigny's rule was a strict one, too, and under it his negroes had forgotten how to be gay, as they had been during the old master's easy-going and indulgent lifetime.

The young mother was recovering slowly, and lay full length, in her soft white muslins and laces, upon a couch. The baby was beside her, upon her arm, where he had fallen asleep, at her breast. The yellow nurse woman sat beside a window fanning herself.

Madame Valmondé bent her portly figure over Désirée and kissed her, holding her an instant tenderly in her arms. Then she turned to the child.

'This is not the baby!' she exclaimed, in startled tones. French was the language spoken at Valmondé in those days.

'I knew you would be astonished,' laughed Désirée, 'at the way he has grown. The little *cochon de lait!* Look at his legs, mamma, and his hands and fingernails, – real finger-nails. Zandrine had to cut them this morning. Is n't it true, Zandrine?'

The woman bowed her turbaned head majestically, 'Mais si, Madame.'

'And the way he cries,' went on Désirée, 'is deafening. Armand heard him the other day as far away as La Blanche's cabin.'

Madame Valmondé had never removed her eyes from the child. She lifted it and walked with it over to the window that was lightest. She scanned the baby narrowly, then looked as searchingly at Zandrine, whose face was turned to gaze across the fields.

'Yes, the child has grown, has changed,' said Madame

Valmondé, slowly, as she replaced it beside its mother. 'What does Armand say?'

Désirée's face became suffused with a glow that was happiness itself.

'Oh, Armand is the proudest father in the parish, I believe, chiefly because it is a boy, to bear his name; though he says not, – that he would have loved a girl as well. But I know it is n't true. I know he says that to please me. And mamma,' she added, drawing Madame Valmondé's head down to her, and speaking in a whisper, 'he has n't punished one of them – not one of them – since baby is born. Even Négrillon, who pretended to have burnt his leg that he might rest from work – he only laughed, and said Négrillon was a great scamp. Oh, mamma, I 'm so happy; it frightens me.'

What Désirée said was true. Marriage, and later the birth of his son had softened Armand Aubigny's imperious and exacting nature greatly. This was what made the gentle Désirée so happy, for she loved him desperately. When he frowned she trembled, but loved him. When he smiled, she asked no greater blessing of God. But Armand's dark, handsome face had not often been disfigured by frowns since the day he fell in love with her.

When the baby was about three months old, Désirée awoke one day to the conviction that there was something in the air menacing her peace. It was at first too subtle to grasp. It had only been a disquieting suggestion; an air of mystery among the blacks; unexpected visits from far-off neighbors who could hardly account for their coming. Then a strange, an awful change in her husband's manner, which she dared not ask him to explain. When he spoke to her, it was with averted eyes, from which the old love-light seemed to have gone out. He absented himself from home; and when there, avoided her presence and that of her child, without excuse. And the very spirit of Satan seemed suddenly to take hold of him in his dealings with the slaves. Désirée was miserable enough to die.

She sat in her room, one hot afternoon, in her *peignoir*, listlessly drawing through her fingers the strands of her long, silky brown hair that hung about her shoulders. The baby, half naked, lay asleep upon her own great mahogany bed, that was like a sumptuous throne, with its satin-lined half-canopy. One of La Blanche's little quadroon boys – half naked too – stood fanning the child slowly with a fan of peacock feathers. Désirée's eyes had been fixed absently and sadly upon the baby, while she was striving to penetrate the threatening mist that she felt closing about her. She looked from her child to the boy who stood beside him, and back again; over and over. 'Ah!' It was a cry that she could not help; which she was not conscious of having uttered. The blood turned like ice in her veins, and a clammy moisture gathered upon her face.

She tried to speak to the little quadroon boy; but no sound would come, at first. When he heard his name uttered, he looked up, and his mistress was pointing to the door. He laid aside the great, soft fan, and obediently stole away, over the polished floor, on his bare tiptoes.

She stayed motionless, with gaze riveted upon her child, and her face the picture of fright.

Presently her husband entered the room, and without noticing her, went to a table and began to search among some papers which covered it.

'Armand,' she called to him, in a voice which must have stabbed him, if he was human. But he did not notice. 'Armand,' she said again. Then she rose and tottered towards him. 'Armand,' she panted once more, clutching his arm, 'look at our child. What does it mean? tell me.'

He coldly but gently loosened her fingers from about his arm and thrust the hand away from him. 'Tell me what it means!' she cried despairingly.

'It means,' he answered lightly, 'that the child is not white; it means that you are not white.'

A quick conception of all that this accusation meant for her nerved her with unwonted courage to deny it. 'It is a lie; it is not true, I am white! Look at my hair, it is brown; and my eyes are gray, Armand, you know they are gray. And my skin is fair,' seizing his wrist. 'Look at my hand; whiter than yours, Armand,' she laughed hysterically.

'As white as La Blanche's,' he returned cruelly; and went away leaving her alone with their child.

When she could hold a pen in her hand, she sent a despairing letter to Madame Valmondé.

'My mother, they tell me I am not white. Armand has told me I am not white. For God's sake tell them it is not true. You must know it is not true. I shall die. I must die. I cannot be so unhappy, and live.'

The answer that came was as brief:

'My own Désirée: Come home to Valmondé; back to your mother who loves you. Come with your child.'

When the letter reached Désirée she went with it to her husband's study, and laid it open upon the desk before which he sat. She was like a stone image: silent, white, motionless after she placed it there.

In silence he ran his cold eyes over the written words. He said nothing. 'Shall I go, Armand?' she asked in tones sharp with agonized suspense.

'Yes, go.'

'Do you want me to go?'

'Yes, I want you to go.'

He thought Almighty God had dealt cruelly and unjustly with him; and felt, somehow, that he was paying Him back in kind when he stabbed thus into his wife's soul. Moreover he no longer loved her, because of the unconscious injury she had brought upon his home and his name.

She turned away like one stunned by a blow, and walked slowly towards the door, hoping he would call her back.

'Good-by, Armand,' she moaned.

He did not answer her. That was his last blow at fate.

Désirée went in search of her child. Zandrine was pacing the sombre gallery with it. She took the little one from the nurse's arms with no word of explanation, and descending the steps, walked away, under the live-oak branches.

It was an October afternoon; the sun was just sinking. Out in the still fields the negroes were picking cotton.

Désirée had not changed the thin white garment nor the slippers which she wore. Her hair was uncovered and the sun's rays brought a golden gleam from its brown meshes. She did not take the broad, beaten road which led to the far-off plantation of Valmondé. She walked across a deserted field, where the stubble bruised her tender feet, so delicately shod, and tore her thin gown to shreds.

She disappeared among the reeds and willows that grew thick along the banks of the deep, sluggish bayou; and she did not come back again.

Some weeks later there was a curious scene enacted at L'Abri. In the centre of the smoothly swept back yard was a great bonfire. Armand Aubigny sat in the wide hallway that commanded a view of the spectacle; and it was he who dealt out to a half dozen negroes the material which kept this fire ablaze.

A graceful cradle of willow, with all its dainty furbishings, was laid upon the pyre, which had already been fed with the richness of a priceless *layette*. Then there were silk gowns, and velvet and satin ones added to these; laces, too, and embroideries; bonnets and gloves; for the *corbeille* had been of rare quality.

The last thing to go was a tiny bundle of letters; innocent little scribblings that Désirée had sent to him during the days of their espousal. There was the remnant of one back in the drawer from which he took them. But it was not Désirée's; it was part of an old letter from his mother to his father. He read it. She was thanking God for the blessing of her husband's love:—

'But, above all,' she wrote, 'night and day, I thank the good God for having so arranged our lives that our dear Armand will never know that his mother, who adores him, belongs to the race that is cursed with the brand of slavery.'

In and Out of Old Natchitoches

Precisely at eight o'clock every morning except Saturdays and Sundays, Mademoiselle Suzanne St. Denys Godolph would cross the railroad trestle that spanned Bayou Boispourri. She might have crossed in the flat which Mr. Alphonse Laballière kept for his own convenience; but the method was slow and unreliable; so, every morning at eight, Mademoiselle St. Denys Godolph crossed the trestle.

She taught public school in a picturesque little white frame structure that stood upon Mr. Laballière's land, and hung upon the very brink of the bayou.

Laballière himself was comparatively a new-comer in the parish. It was barely six months since he decided one day to leave the sugar and rice to his brother Alcée, who had a talent for their cultivation, and to try his hand at cotton-planting. That was why he was up in Natchitoches parish on a piece of rich, high, Cane River land, knocking into shape a tumbled-down plantation that he had bought for next to nothing.

He had often during his perambulations observed the trim, graceful figure stepping cautiously over the ties, and had sometimes shivered for its safety. He always exchanged a greeting with the girl, and once threw a plank over a muddy pool for her to step upon. He caught but glimpses of her features, for she wore an enormous sun-bonnet to shield her complexion, that seemed marvelously fair; while loosely-fitting leather gloves protected her hands. He knew she was the school-teacher, and also that she was the daughter of that very pig-headed old Madame St. Denys Godolph who was hoarding her barren acres across the bayou as a miser hoards gold. Starving over them, some people said. But that was nonsense; nobody starves on a Louisiana plantation, unless it be with suicidal intent.

These things he knew, but he did not know why Mademoiselle St. Denys Godolph always answered his salutation with an air of chilling hauteur that would easily have paralyzed a less sanguine man.

The reason was that Suzanne, like every one else, had heard the stories that were going the rounds about him. People said he was entirely too much at home with the free mulattoes.* It seems a dreadful thing to say, and it would be a shocking thing to think of a Laballière; but it wasn't true.

When Laballière took possession of his land, he found the plantation-house occupied by one Giestin and his swarming family. It was past reckoning how long the free mulatto and his people had been there. The house was a six-room, long, shambling affair, shrinking together from decrepitude. There was not an entire pane of glass in the structure; and the Turkey-red curtains flapped in and out of the broken apertures. But there is no need to dwell upon details; it was wholly unfit to serve as a civilized human habitation; and Alphonse Laballière would no sooner have disturbed its contented occupants than he would have scattered a family of partridges nesting in a corner of his field. He established himself with a few belongings in the best cabin he could find on the place, and, without further ado, proceeded to supervise the building of house, of gin, of this, that, and the other, and to look into the hundred details that go to set a neglected plantation in good working order. He took his meals at the free mulatto's, quite apart from the family, of course; and they attended, not too skillfully, to his few domestic wants.

Some loafer whom he had snubbed remarked one day in town that Laballière had more use for a free mulatto than he had for a white man. It was a sort of catching thing to say, and suggestive, and was repeated with the inevitable embellishments.

One morning when Laballière sat eating his solitary breakfast, and being waited upon by the queenly Madame Giestin and a brace of her weazened boys, Giestin himself came into the room. He was about half the size of his wife, puny and timid. He stood beside the table, twirling his felt hat aimlessly and balancing himself insecurely on his high-pointed boot-heels.

'Mr. Laballière,' he said, 'I reckon I tell you; it 's betta you git shed o' me en' my fambly. Jis like you want, yas.'

'What in the name of common sense are you talking about?'

* A term still applied in Louisiana to Mulattoes who were never in slavery, and whose families in most instances were themselves slave owners.

asked Laballière, looking up abstractedly from his New Orleans paper. Giestin wriggled uncomfortably.

'It 's heap o' story goin' roun' 'bout you, if you want b'lieve me.' And he snickered and looked at his wife, who thrust the end of her shawl into her mouth and walked from the room with a tread like the Empress Eugenie's, in that elegant woman's palmiest days.

'Stories!' echoed Laballière, his face the picture of astonishment. 'Who – where – what stories?'

'Yon'a in town en' all about. It 's heap o' tale goin' roun', yas. They say how come you mighty fon' o' mulatta. You done shoshiate wid de mulatta down yon'a on de suga plantation, tell you can't res' lessen it 's mulatta roun' you.'

Laballière had a distressingly quick temper. His fist, which was a strong one, came down upon the wobbling table with a crash that sent half of Madame Giestin's crockery bouncing and crashing to the floor. He swore an oath that sent Madame Giestin and her father and grandmother, who were all listening in the next room, into suppressed convulsions of mirth.

'Oh, ho! so I 'm not to associate with whom I please in Natchitoches parish. We 'll see about that. Draw up your chair, Giestin. Call your wife and your grandmother and the rest of the tribe, and we 'll breakfast together. By thunder! if I want to hobnob with mulattoes, or negroes or Choctaw Indians or South Sea savages, whose business is it but my own?'

'I don' know, me. It 's jis like I tell you, Mr. Laballière,' and Giestin selected a huge key from an assortment that hung against the wall, and left the room.

A half hour later, Laballière had not yet recovered his senses. He appeared suddenly at the door of the schoolhouse, holding by the shoulder one of Giestin's boys. Mademoiselle St. Denys Godolph stood at the opposite extremity of the room. Her sunbonnet hung upon the wall, now, so Laballière could have seen how charming she was, had he not at the moment been blinded by stupidity. Her blue eyes that were fringed with dark lashes reflected astonishment at seeing him there. Her hair was dark like her lashes, and waved softly about her smooth, white forehead.

'Mademoiselle,' began Laballière at once, 'I have taken the liberty of bringing a new pupil to you.'

Mademoiselle St. Denys Godolph paled suddenly and her voice was unsteady when she replied:—

'You are too considerate, Monsieur. Will you be so kine to give me the name of the scholar whom you desire to int'oduce into this school?' She knew it as well as he.

'What 's your name, youngster? Out with it!' cried Laballière, striving to shake the little free mulatto into speech; but he stayed as dumb as a mummy.

'His name is André Giestin. You know him. He is the son'—

'Then, Monsieur,' she interrupted, 'permit me to remine you that you have made a se'ious mistake. This is not a school conducted fo' the education of the colored population. You will have to go elsew'ere with yo' protégé.'

'I shall leave my protégé right here, Mademoiselle, and I trust you 'll give him the same kind attention you seem to accord to the others;' saying which Laballière bowed himself out of her presence. The little Giestin, left to his own devices, took only the time to give a quick, wary glance round the room, and the next instant he bounded through the open door, as the nimblest of four-footed creatures might have done.

Mademoiselle St. Denys Godolph conducted school during the hours that remained, with a deliberate calmness that would have seemed ominous to her pupils, had they been better versed in the ways of young women. When the hour for dismissal came, she rapped upon the table to demand attention.

'Chil'ren,' she began, assuming a resigned and dignified mien, 'you all have been witness to-day of the insult that has been offered to yo' teacher by the person upon whose lan' this schoolhouse stan's. I have nothing further to say on that subjec'. I only shall add that to-morrow yo' teacher shall sen' the key of this schoolhouse, together with her resignation, to the gentlemen who compose the school-boa'd.' There followed visible disturbance among the young people.

'I ketch that li'le m'latta, I make 'im see sight', yas,' screamed one.

'Nothing of the kine, Mathurin, you mus' take no such step, if only out of consideration fo' my wishes. The person who has offered the affront I consider beneath my notice. André, on the other han', is a chile of good impulse, an' by no means to blame. As you all perceive, he has shown mo' taste and judgment than those above him, f'om whom we might have espected good breeding, at least.'

She kissed them all, the little boys and the little girls, and had a kind word for each. '*Et toi, mon petit Numa, j'espère qu'un autre*' — She could not finish the sentence, for little Numa, her favorite, to whom she had never been able to impart the first word of English, was blubbering at a turn of affairs which he had only miserably guessed at.

She locked the schoolhouse door and walked away towards the bridge. By the time she reached it, the little 'Cadians had already disappeared like rabbits, down the road and through and over the fences.

Mademoiselle St. Denys Godolph did not cross the trestle the following day, nor the next nor the next. Laballière watched for her; for his big heart was already sore and filled with shame. But more, it stung him with remorse to realize that he had been the stupid instrument in taking the bread, as it were, from the mouth of Mademoiselle St. Denys Godolph.

He recalled how unflinchingly and haughtily her blue eyes had challenged his own. Her sweetness and charm came back to him and he dwelt upon them and exaggerated them, till no Venus, so far unearthed, could in any way approach Mademoiselle St. Denys Godolph. He would have liked to exterminate the Giestin family, from the great-grandmother down to the babe unborn.

Perhaps Giestin suspected this unfavorable attitude, for one morning he piled his whole family and all his effects into wagons, and went away; over into that part of the parish known as *l'Isle des Mulâtres*.

Laballière's really chivalrous nature told him, beside, that he owed an apology, at least, to the young lady who had taken his whim so seriously. So he crossed the bayou one day and penetrated into the wilds where Madame St. Denys Godolph ruled.

An alluring little romance formed in his mind as he went; he fancied how easily it might follow the apology. He was almost in love with Mademoiselle St. Denys Godolph when he quitted his plantation. By the time he had reached hers, he was wholly so.

He was met by Madame mère, a sweet-eyed, faded woman, upon whom old age had fallen too hurriedly to completely efface all traces of youth. But the house was old beyond question; decay had eaten slowly to the heart of it during the hours, the days, and years that it had been standing.

'I have come to see your daughter, Madame,' began Laballière, all too bluntly; for there is no denying he was blunt.

'Mademoiselle St. Denys Godolph is not presently at home, sir,' Madame replied. 'She is at the time in New Orleans. She fills there a place of high trus' an' employment, Monsieur Laballière.'

When Suzanne had ever thought of New Orleans, it was always in connection with Hector Santien, because he was the only soul she knew who dwelt there. He had had no share in obtaining for her the position she had secured with one of the leading dry-goods firms; yet it was to him she addressed herself when her arrangements to leave home were completed.

He did not wait for her train to reach the city, but crossed the river and met her at Gretna. The first thing he did was to kiss her, as he had done eight years before when he left Natchitoches parish. An hour later he would no more have thought of kissing Suzanne than he would have tendered an embrace to the Empress of China. For by that time he had realized that she was no longer twelve nor he twenty-four.

She could hardly believe the man who met her to be the Hector of old. His black hair was dashed with gray on the temples; he wore a short, parted beard and a small moustache that curled. From the crown of his glossy silk hat down to his trimly-gaitered feet, his attire was faultless. Suzanne knew her Natchitoches, and she had been to Shreveport and even penetrated as far as Marshall, Texas, but in all her travels she had never met a man to equal Hector in the elegance of his mien.

They entered a cab, and seemed to drive for an interminable time through the streets, mostly over cobble-stones that rendered conversation difficult. Nevertheless he talked incessantly, while she peered from the windows to catch what glimpses she could, through the night, of that New Orleans of which she had heard so much. The sounds were bewildering; so were the lights, that were uneven, too, serving to make the patches of alternating gloom more mysterious.

She had not thought of asking him where he was taking her. And it was only after they crossed Canal and had penetrated some distance into Royal Street, that he told her. He was taking her to a friend of his, the dearest little woman in town. That was Maman Chavan, who was going to board and lodge her for a ridiculously small consideration.

Maman Chavan lived within comfortable walking distance of Canal Street, on one of those narrow, intersecting streets between Royal and Chartres. Her house was a tiny, single-story one, with overhanging gable, heavily shuttered door and windows and three wooden steps leading down to the banquette. A small garden flanked it on one side, quite screened from outside view by a high fence, over which appeared the tops of orange trees and other luxuriant shrubbery.

She was waiting for them – a lovable, fresh-looking, white-haired, black-eyed, small, fat little body, dressed all in black. She understood no English; which made no difference. Suzanne and Hector spoke but French to each other.

Hector did not tarry a moment longer than was needed to place his young friend and charge in the older woman's care. He would not even stay to take a bite of supper with them. Maman Chavan watched him as he hurried down the steps and out into the gloom. Then she said to Suzanne: 'That man is an angel, Mademoiselle, *un ange du bon Dieu.*'

'Women, my dear Maman Chavan, you know how it is with me in regard to women. I have drawn a circle round my heart, so – at pretty long range, mind you – and there is not one who gets through it, or over it or under it.'

'*Blagueur, va!*' laughed Maman Chavan, replenishing her glass from the bottle of sauterne.

It was Sunday morning. They were breakfasting together on the pleasant side gallery that led by a single step down to the garden. Hector came every Sunday morning, an hour or so before noon, to breakfast with them. He always brought a bottle of sauterne, a paté, or a mess of artichokes or some tempting bit of *charcuterie*. Sometimes he had to wait till the two women returned from hearing mass at the cathedral. He did not go to mass himself. They were both making a Novena on that account, and had even gone to the expense of burning a round dozen of candles before the good St. Joseph, for his conversion. When Hector accidentally discovered the fact, he offered to pay for the candles, and was distressed at not being permitted to do so.

Suzanne had been in the city more than a month. It was already the close of February, and the air was flower-scented, moist, and deliciously mild.

'As I said: women, my dear Maman Chavan'—

'Let us hear no more about women!' cried Suzanne, impatiently. '*Cher Maître!* but Hector can be tiresome when he wants. Talk, talk; to say what in the end?'

'Quite right, my cousin; when I might have been saying how charming you are this morning. But don't think that I have n't noticed it,' and he looked at her with a deliberation that quite unsettled her. She took a letter from her pocket and handed it to him.

'Here, read all the nice things mamma has to say of you, and the love messages she sends to you.' He accepted the several closely written sheets from her and began to look over them.

'*Ah, la bonne tante,*' he laughed, when he came to the tender passages that referred to himself. He had pushed aside the glass of wine that he had only partly filled at the beginning of breakfast and that he had scarcely touched. Maman Chavan again replenished her own. She also lighted a cigarette. So did Suzanne, who was learning to smoke. Hector did not smoke; he did not use tobacco in any form, he always said to those who offered him cigars.

Suzanne rested her elbows on the table, adjusted the ruffles about her wrists, puffed awkwardly at her cigarette that kept going out, and hummed the Kyrie Eleison that she had heard so beautifully rendered an hour before at the Cathedral, while she gazed off into the green depths of the garden. Maman Chavan slipped a little silver medal toward her, accompanying the action with a pantomime that Suzanne readily understood. She, in turn, secretly and adroitly transferred the medal to Hector's coat-pocket. He noticed the action plainly enough, but pretended not to.

'Natchitoches has n't changed,' he commented. 'The everlasting *cancans!* when will they have done with them? This is n't little Athénaïse Miché, getting married! *Sapristi!* but it makes one old! And old Papa Jean-Pierre only dead now? I thought he was out of purgatory five years ago. And who is this Laballière? One of the Laballières of St. James?'

'St. James, *mon cher*. Monsieur Alphonse Laballière; an aristocrat from the "golden coast." But it is a history, if you will believe me. *Figurez vous*, Maman Chavan, – *pensez donc, mon ami'* – And with much dramatic fire, during which the cigarette went irrevocably out, she proceeded to narrate her experiences with Laballière.

'Impossible!' exclaimed Hector when the climax was reached; but his indignation was not so patent as she would have liked it to be.

'And to think of an affront like that going unpunished!' was Maman Chavan's more sympathetic comment.

'Oh, the scholars were only too ready to offer violence to poor little André, but that, you can understand, I would not permit. And now, here is mamma gone completely over to him; entrapped, God only knows how!'

'Yes,' agreed Hector, 'I see he has been sending her tamales and *boudin blanc*.'

'*Boudin blanc*, my friend! If it were only that! But I have a stack of letters, so high, – I could show them to you, – singing of Laballière, Laballière, enough to drive one distracted. He visits her constantly. He is a man of attainment, she says, a man of courage, a man of heart; and the best of company. He has sent her a bunch of fat robins as big as a tub'—

'There is something in that – a good deal in that, mignonne,' piped Maman Chavan, approvingly.

'And now *boudin blanc!* and she tells me it is the duty of a Christian to forgive. Ah, no; it 's no use; mamma's ways are past finding out.'

Suzanne was never in Hector's company elsewhere than at Maman Chavan's. Beside the Sunday visit, he looked in upon them sometimes at dusk, to chat for a moment or two. He often treated them to theatre tickets, and even to the opera, when business was brisk. Business meant a little notebook that he carried in his pocket, in which he sometimes dotted down orders from the country people for wine, that he sold on commission. The women always went together, unaccompanied by any male escort; trotting along, arm in arm, and brimming with enjoyment.

That same Sunday afternoon Hector walked with them a short distance when they were on their way to vespers. The three walking abreast almost occupied the narrow width of the banquette. A gentleman who had just stepped out of the Hotel Royal stood aside to better enable them to pass. He lifted his hat to Suzanne, and cast a quick glance, that pictured stupefaction and wrath, upon Hector.

'It 's he!' exclaimed the girl, melodramatically seizing Maman Chavan's arm.

'Who, he?'

'Laballière!'

'No!'

'Yes!'

'A handsome fellow, all the same,' nodded the little lady, approvingly. Hector thought so too. The conversation again turned upon Laballière, and so continued till they reached the side door of the cathedral, where the young man left his two companions.

In the evening Laballière called upon Suzanne. Maman Chavan closed the front door carefully after he entered the small parlor, and opened the side one that looked into the privacy of the garden. Then she lighted the lamp and retired, just as Suzanne entered.

The girl bowed a little stiffly, if it may be said that she did anything stiffly. 'Monsieur Laballière.' That was all she said.

'Mademoiselle St. Denys Godolph,' and that was all he said. But ceremony did not sit easily upon him.

'Mademoiselle,' he began, as soon as seated, 'I am here as the bearer of a message from your mother. You must understand that otherwise I would not be here.'

'I do understan', sir, that you an' maman have become very warm frien's during my absence,' she returned, in measured, conventional tones.

'It pleases me immensely to hear that from you,' he responded, warmly; 'to believe that Madame St. Denys Godolph is my friend.'

Suzanne coughed more affectedly than was quite nice, and patted her glossy braids. 'The message, if you please, Mr. Laballière.'

'To be sure,' pulling himself together from the momentary abstraction into which he had fallen in contemplating her. 'Well, it 's just this; your mother, you must know, has been good enough to sell me a fine bit of land – a deep strip along the bayou'—

'Impossible! *Mais* w'at sorcery did you use to obtain such a thing of my mother, Mr. Laballière? Lan' that has been in the St. Denys Godolph family since time untole!'

'No sorcery whatever, Mademoiselle, only an appeal to your mother's intelligence and common sense; and she is well supplied with both. She wishes me to say, further, that she desires your presence very urgently and your immediate return home.'

'My mother is unduly impatient, surely,' replied Suzanne, with chilling politeness.

'May I ask, mademoiselle,' he broke in, with an abruptness that was startling, 'the name of the man with whom you were walking this afternoon?'

She looked at him with unaffected astonishment, and told him: 'I hardly understan' yo' question. That gentleman is Mr. Hector Santien, of one of the firs' families of Natchitoches; a warm ole frien' an' far distant relative of mine.'

'Oh, that 's his name, is it, Hector Santien? Well, please don't walk on the New Orleans streets again with Mr. Hector Santien.'

'Yo' remarks would be insulting if they were not so highly amusing, Mr. Laballière.'

'I beg your pardon if I am insulting; and I have no desire to be amusing,' and then Laballière lost his head. 'You are at liberty to walk the streets with whom you please, of course,' he blurted, with ill-suppressed passion, 'but if I encounter Mr. Hector Santien in your company again, in public, I shall wring his neck, then and there, as I would a chicken; I shall break every bone in his body' – Suzanne had arisen.

'You have said enough, sir. I even desire no explanation of yo' words.'

'I did n't intend to explain them,' he retorted, stung by the insinuation.

'You will escuse me further,' she requested icily, motioning to retire.

'Not till – oh, not till you have forgiven me,' he cried impulsively, barring her exit; for repentance had come swiftly this time.

But she did not forgive him. 'I can wait,' she said. Then he stepped aside and she passed by him without a second glance.

She sent word to Hector the following day to come to her. And when he was there, in the late afternoon, they walked together to the end of the vine-sheltered gallery, – where the air was redolent with the odor of spring blossoms.

'Hector,' she began, after a while, 'some one has told me I should not be seen upon the streets of New Orleans with you.'

He was trimming a long rose-stem with his sharp penknife. He did not stop nor start, nor look embarrassed, nor anything of the sort.

'Indeed!' he said.

'But, you know,' she went on, 'if the saints came down from heaven to tell me there was a reason for it, I could n't believe them.'

'You would n't believe them, *ma petite Suzanne?*' He was getting all the thorns off nicely, and stripping away the heavy lower leaves.

'I want you to look me in the face, Hector, and tell me if there is any reason.'

He snapped the knife-blade and replaced the knife in his pocket; then he looked in her eyes, so unflinchingly, that she hoped and believed it presaged a confession of innocence that she would gladly have accepted. But he said indifferently: 'Yes, there are reasons.'

'Then I say there are not,' she exclaimed excitedly; 'you are amusing yourself – laughing at me, as you always do. There are no reasons that I will hear or believe. You will walk the streets with me, will you not, Hector?' she entreated, 'and go to church with me on Sunday; and, and – oh, it 's nonsense, nonsense for you to say things like that!'

He held the rose by its long, hardy stem, and swept it lightly and caressingly across her forehead, along her cheek, and over her pretty mouth and chin, as a lover might have done with his lips. He noticed how the red rose left a crimson stain behind it.

She had been standing, but now she sank upon the bench that was there, and buried her face in her palms. A slight convulsive movement of the muscles indicated a suppressed sob.

'Ah, Suzanne, Suzanne, you are not going to make yourself unhappy about a *bon à rien* like me. Come, look at me; tell me that you are not.' He drew her hands down from her face and held them a while, bidding her good-by. His own face wore the quizzical look it often did, as if he were laughing at her.

'That work at the store is telling on your nerves, *mignonne*. Promise me that you will go back to the country. That will be best.'

'Oh, yes; I am going back home, Hector.'

'That is right, little cousin,' and he patted her hands kindly, and laid them both down gently into her lap.

He did not return; neither during the week nor the following Sunday. Then Suzanne told Maman Chavan she was going home. The girl was not too deeply in love with Hector; but imagination counts for something, and so does youth.

Laballière was on the train with her. She felt, somehow, that he would be. And yet she did not dream that he had watched and waited for her each morning since he parted from her.

He went to her without preliminary of manner or speech, and held out his hand; she extended her own unhesitatingly. She could not understand why, and she was a little too weary to strive to do so. It seemed as though the sheer force of his will would carry him to the goal of his wishes.

He did not weary her with attentions during the time they were together. He sat apart from her, conversing for the most time with friends and acquaintances who belonged in the sugar district through which they traveled in the early part of the day.

She wondered why he had ever left that section to go up into Natchitoches. Then she wondered if he did not mean to speak to her at all. As if he had read the thought, he went and sat down beside her.

He showed her, away off across the country, where his mother lived, and his brother Alcée, and his cousin Clarisse.

On Sunday morning, when Maman Chavan strove to sound the depth of Hector's feeling for Suzanne, he told her again: 'Women, my dear Maman Chavan, you know how it is with me in regard to women,' – and he refilled her glass from the bottle of sauterne.

'*Farceur va!*' and Maman Chavan laughed, and her fat shoulders quivered under the white *volante* she wore.

A day or two later, Hector was walking down Canal Street at

four in the afternoon. He might have posed, as he was, for a fashion-plate. He looked not to the right nor to the left; not even at the women who passed by. Some of them turned to look at him.

When he approached the corner of Royal, a young man who stood there nudged his companion.

'You know who that is?' he said, indicating Hector.

'No; who?'

'Well, you are an innocent. Why, that 's Deroustan, the most notorious gambler in New Orleans.'

A Matter of Prejudice

Madame Carambeau wanted it strictly understood that she was not to be disturbed by Gustave's birthday party. They carried her big rocking-chair from the back gallery, that looked out upon the garden where the children were going to play, around to the front gallery, which closely faced the green levee bank and the Mississippi coursing almost flush with the top of it.

The house – an old Spanish one, broad, low and completely encircled by a wide gallery – was far down in the French quarter of New Orleans. It stood upon a square of ground that was covered thick with a semi-tropical growth of plants and flowers. An impenetrable board fence, edged with a formidable row of iron spikes, shielded the garden from the prying glances of the occasional passer-by.

Madame Carambeau's widowed daughter, Madame Cécile Lalonde, lived with her. This annual party, given to her little son, Gustave, was the one defiant act of Madame Lalonde's existence. She persisted in it, to her own astonishment and the wonder of those who knew her and her mother.

For old Madame Carambeau was a woman of many prejudices – so many, in fact, that it would be difficult to name them all. She detested dogs, cats, organ-grinders, white servants and children's noises. She despised Americans, Germans and all people of a different faith from her own. Anything not French had, in her opinion, little right to existence.

She had not spoken to her son Henri for ten years because he had married an American girl from Prytania street. She would not permit green tea to be introduced into her house, and those who could not or would not drink coffee might drink tisane of *fleur de Laurier* for all she cared.

Nevertheless, the children seemed to be having it all their own way that day, and the organ-grinders were let loose. Old madame, in her retired corner, could hear the screams, the laughter and the music far more distinctly than she liked. She rocked herself noisily, and hummed 'Partant pour la Syrie.'

She was straight and slender. Her hair was white, and she wore it in puffs on the temples. Her skin was fair and her eyes blue and cold.

Suddenly she became aware that footsteps were approaching, and threatening to invade her privacy – not only footsteps, but screams! Then two little children, one in hot pursuit of the other, darted wildly around the corner near which she sat.

The child in advance, a pretty little girl, sprang excitedly into Madame Carambeau's lap, and threw her arms convulsively around the old lady's neck. Her companion lightly struck her a 'last tag,' and ran laughing gleefully away.

The most natural thing for the child to do then would have been to wriggle down from madame's lap, without a 'thank you' or a 'by your leave,' after the manner of small and thoughtless children. But she did not do this. She stayed there, panting and fluttering, like a frightened bird.

Madame was greatly annoyed. She moved as if to put the child away from her, and scolded her sharply for being boisterous and rude. The little one, who did not understand French, was not disturbed by the reprimand, and stayed on in madame's lap. She rested her plump little cheek, that was hot and flushed, against the soft white linen of the old lady's gown.

Her cheek was very hot and very flushed. It was dry, too, and so were her hands. The child's breathing was quick and irregular. Madame was not long in detecting these signs of disturbance.

Though she was a creature of prejudice, she was nevertheless a skillful and accomplished nurse, and a connoisseur in all matters pertaining to health. She prided herself upon this talent, and never lost an opportunity of exercising it. She would have treated an organ-grinder with tender consideration if one had presented himself in the character of an invalid.

Madame's manner toward the little one changed immediately. Her arms and her lap were at once adjusted so as to become the most comfortable of resting places. She rocked very gently to and fro. She fanned the child softly with her palm leaf fan, and sang 'Partant pour la Syrie' in a low and agreeable tone.

The child was perfectly content to lie still and prattle a little in that language which madame thought hideous. But the brown eyes were soon swimming in drowsiness, and the little body grew heavy with sleep in madame's clasp.

When the little girl slept Madame Carambeau arose, and treading carefully and deliberately, entered her room, that opened near at hand upon the gallery. The room was large, airy and inviting, with its cool matting upon the floor, and its heavy, old, polished mahogany furniture. Madame, with the child still in her arms, pulled a bell-cord; then she stood waiting, swaying gently back and forth. Presently an old black woman answered the summons. She wore gold hoops in her ears, and a bright bandanna knotted fantastically on her head.

'Louise, turn down the bed,' commanded madame. 'Place that small, soft pillow below the bolster. Here is a poor little unfortunate creature whom Providence must have driven into my arms.' She laid the child carefully down.

'Ah, those Americans! Do they deserve to have children? Understanding as little as they do how to take care of them!' said madame, while Louise was mumbling an accompanying assent that would have been unintelligible to any one unacquainted with the negro patois.

'There, you see, Louise, she is burning up,' remarked madame; 'she is consumed. Unfasten the little bodice while I lift her. Ah, talk to me of such parents! So stupid as not to perceive a fever like that coming on, but they must dress their child up like a monkey to go play and dance to the music of organ-grinders.'

'Haven't you better sense, Louise, than to take off a child's shoe as if you were removing the boot from the leg of a cavalry officer?' Madame would have required fairy fingers to minister to the sick. 'Now go to Mamzelle Cécile, and tell her to send me one of those old, soft, thin nightgowns that Gustave wore two summers ago.'

When the woman retired, madame busied herself with concocting a cooling pitcher of orange-flower water, and mixing a fresh supply of *eau sédative* with which agreeably to sponge the little invalid.

Madame Lalonde came herself with the old, soft nightgown. She was a pretty, blonde, plump little woman, with the deprecatory air of one whose will has become flaccid from want of use. She was mildly distressed at what her mother had done.

'But, mamma! But, mamma, the child's parents will be sending the carriage for her in a little while. Really, there was no use. Oh dear! oh dear!'

If the bedpost had spoken to Madame Carambeau, she would have paid more attention, for speech from such a source would have been at least surprising if not convincing. Madame Lalonde did not possess the faculty of either surprising or convincing her mother.

'Yes, the little one will be quite comfortable in this,' said the old lady, taking the garment from her daughter's irresolute hands.

'But, mamma! What shall I say, what shall I do when they send? Oh, dear; oh, dear!'

'That is your business,' replied madame, with lofty indifference. 'My concern is solely with a sick child that happens to be under my roof. I think I know my duty at this time of life, Cécile.'

As Madame Lalonde predicted, the carriage soon came, with a stiff English coachman driving it, and a red-cheeked Irish nurse-maid seated inside. Madame would not even permit the maid to see her little charge. She had an original theory that the Irish voice is distressing to the sick.

Madame Lalonde sent the girl away with a long letter of explanation that must have satisfied the parents; for the child was left undisturbed in Madame Carambeau's care. She was a sweet child, gentle and affectionate. And, though she cried and fretted a little throughout the night for her mother, she seemed, after all, to take kindly to madame's gentle nursing. It was not much of a fever that afflicted her, and after two days she was well enough to be sent back to her parents.

Madame, in all her varied experience with the sick, had never before nursed so objectionable a character as an American child. But the trouble was that after the little one went away, she could think of nothing really objectionable against her except the accident of her birth, which was, after all, her misfortune; and her ignorance of the French language, which was not her fault.

But the touch of the caressing baby arms; the pressure of the soft little body in the night; the tones of the voice, and the feeling of the hot lips when the child kissed her, believing herself to be with her mother, were impressions that had sunk through the crust of madame's prejudice and reached her heart.

She often walked the length of the gallery, looking out across the wide, majestic river. Sometimes she trod the mazes of her garden where the solitude was almost that of a tropical jungle. It was during such moments that the seed began to work in her soul – the seed planted by the innocent and undesigning hands of a little child.

The first shoot that it sent forth was Doubt. Madame plucked it away once or twice. But it sprouted again, and with it Mistrust and Dissatisfaction. Then from the heart of the seed, and amid the shoots of Doubt and Misgiving, came the flower of Truth. It was a very beautiful flower, and it bloomed on Christmas morning.

As Madame Carambeau and her daughter were about to enter her carriage on that Christmas morning, to be driven to church, the old lady stopped to give an order to her black coachman, François. François had been driving these ladies every Sunday morning to the French Cathedral for so many years – he had forgotten exactly how many, but ever since he had entered their service, when Madame Lalonde was a little girl. His astonishment may therefore be imagined when Madame Carambeau said to him:

'François, to-day you will drive us to one of the American churches.'

'Plait-il, madame?' the negro stammered, doubting the evidence of his hearing.

'I say, you will drive us to one of the American churches. Any one of them,' she added, with a sweep of her hand. 'I suppose they are all alike,' and she followed her daughter into the carriage.

Madame Lalonde's surprise and agitation were painful to see, and they deprived her of the ability to question, even if she had possessed the courage to do so.

François, left to his fancy, drove them to St. Patrick's Church on Camp street. Madame Lalonde looked and felt like the proverbial fish out of its element as they entered the edifice. Madame Carambeau, on the contrary, looked as if she had been attending St. Patrick's church all her life. She sat with unruffled calm through the long service and through a lengthy English sermon, of which she did not understand a word.

When the mass was ended and they were about to enter the carriage again, Madame Carambeau turned, as she had done before, to the coachman.

'François,' she said, coolly, 'you will now drive us to the residence of my son, M. Henri Carambeau. No doubt Mamzelle

Cécile can inform you where it is,' she added, with a sharply
penetrating glance that caused Madame Lalonde to wince.

Yes, her daughter Cécile knew, and so did François, for that
matter. They drove out St. Charles avenue – very far out. It was
like a strange city to old madame, who had not been in the
American quarter since the town had taken on this new and
splendid growth.

The morning was a delicious one, soft and mild; and the roses
were all in bloom. They were not hidden behind spiked fences.
Madame appeared not to notice them, or the beautiful and
striking residences that lined the avenue along which they drove.
She held a bottle of smelling-salts to her nostrils, as though she
were passing through the most unsavory instead of the most
beautiful quarter of New Orleans.

Henri's house was a very modern and very handsome one,
standing a little distance away from the street. A well-kept lawn,
studded with rare and charming plants, surrounded it. The
ladies, dismounting, rang the bell, and stood out upon the
banquette, waiting for the iron gate to be opened.

A white maid-servant admitted them. Madame did not seem to
mind. She handed her a card with all proper ceremony, and
followed with her daughter to the house.

Not once did she show a sign of weakness; not even when her
son, Henri, came and took her in his arms and sobbed and wept
upon her neck as only a warm-hearted Creole could. He was a
big, good-looking, honest-faced man, with tender brown eyes like
his dead father's and a firm mouth like his mother's.

Young Mrs. Carambeau came, too, her sweet, fresh face
transfigured with happiness. She led by the hand her little
daughter, the 'American child' whom madame had nursed so
tenderly a month before, never suspecting the little one to be
other than an alien to her.

'What a lucky chance was that fever! What a happy accident!'
gurgled Madame Lalonde.

'Cécile, it was no accident, I tell you; it was Providence,' spoke
madame, reprovingly, and no one contradicted her.

They all drove back together to eat Christmas dinner in the old
house by the river. Madame held her little granddaughter upon
her lap; her son Henri sat facing her, and beside her was her
daughter-in-law.

Henri sat back in the carriage and could not speak. His soul was possessed by a pathetic joy that would not admit of speech. He was going back again to the home where he was born, after a banishment of ten long years.

He would hear again the water beat against the green levee-bank with a sound that was not quite like any other that he could remember. He would sit within the sweet and solemn shadow of the deep and overhanging roof; and roam through the wild, rich solitude of the old garden, where he had played his pranks of boyhood and dreamed his dreams of youth. He would listen to his mother's voice calling him, 'mon fils,' as it had always done before that day he had had to choose between mother and wife. No; he could not speak.

But his wife chatted much and pleasantly – in a French, however, that must have been trying to old madame to listen to.

'I am so sorry, ma mère,' she said, 'that our little one does not speak French. It is not my fault, I assure you,' and she flushed and hesitated a little. 'It – it was Henri who would not permit it.'

'That is nothing,' replied madame, amiably, drawing the child close to her. 'Her grandmother will teach her French; and she will teach her grandmother English. You see, I have no prejudices. I am not like my son. Henri was always a stubborn boy. Heaven only knows how he came by such a character!'

La Belle Zoraïde

The summer night was hot and still; not a ripple of air swept over the *marais*. Yonder, across Bayou St. John, lights twinkled here and there in the darkness, and in the dark sky above a few stars were blinking. A lugger that had come out of the lake was moving with slow, lazy motion down the bayou. A man in the boat was singing a song.

The notes of the song came faintly to the ears of old Manna-Loulou, herself as black as the night, who had gone out upon the gallery to open the shutters wide.

Something in the refrain reminded the woman of an old, half-forgotten Creole romance, and she began to sing it low to herself while she threw the shutters open:—

> 'Lisett' to kité la plaine,
> Mo perdi bonhair à moué;
> Ziés à moué semblé fontaine,
> Dépi mo pa miré toué.'

And then this old song, a lover's lament for the loss of his mistress, floating into her memory, brought with it the story she would tell to Madame, who lay in her sumptuous mahogany bed, waiting to be fanned and put to sleep to the sound of one of Manna-Loulou's stories. The old negress had already bathed her mistress's pretty white feet and kissed them lovingly, one, then the other. She had brushed her mistress's beautiful hair, that was as soft and shining as satin, and was the color of Madame's wedding-ring. Now, when she reëntered the room, she moved softly toward the bed, and seating herself there began gently to fan Madame Delisle.

Manna-Loulou was not always ready with her story, for Madame would hear none but those which were true. But tonight the story was all there in Manna-Loulou's head – the story of la belle Zoraïde – and she told it to her mistress in the soft creole patois, whose music and charm no English words can convey.

'La belle Zoraïde had eyes that were so dusky, so beautiful, that any man who gazed too long into their depths was sure to lose his head, and even his heart sometimes. Her soft, smooth skin was the color of *café-au-lait*. As for her elegant manners, her *svelte* and graceful figure, they were the envy of half the ladies who visited her mistress, Madame Delarivière.

'No wonder Zoraïde was as charming and as dainty as the finest lady of la rue Royale: from a toddling thing she had been brought up at her mistress's side; her fingers had never done rougher work than sewing a fine muslin seam; and she even had her own little black servant to wait upon her. Madame, who was her godmother as well as her mistress, would often say to her:

'"Remember, Zoraïde, when you are ready to marry, it must be in a way to do honor to your bringing up. It will be at the Cathedral. Your wedding gown, your *corbeille*, all will be of the best; I shall see to that myself. You know, M'sieur Ambroise is ready whenever you say the word; and his master is willing to do as much for him as I shall do for you. It is a union that will please me in every way."

'M'sieur Ambroise was then the body servant of Dr Langlé. La belle Zoraïde detested the little mulatto, with his shining whiskers like a white man's, and his small eyes, that were cruel and false as a snake's. She would cast down her own mischievous eyes, and say:

'"Ah, nénaine, I am so happy, so contented here at your side just as I am. I don't want to marry now; next year, perhaps, or the next." And Madame would smile indulgently and remind Zoraïde that a woman's charms are not everlasting.

'But the truth of the matter was, Zoraïde had seen le beau Mézor dance the Bamboula in Congo Square. That was a sight to hold one rooted to the ground. Mézor was as straight as a cypress-tree and as proud looking as a king. His body, bare to the waist, was like a column of ebony and it glistened like oil.

'Poor Zoraïde's heart grew sick in her bosom with love for le beau Mézor from the moment she saw the fierce gleam of his eye, lighted by the inspiring strains of the Bamboula, and beheld the stately movements of his splendid body swaying and quivering through the figures of the dance.

'But when she knew him later, and he came near her to speak with her, all the fierceness was gone out of his eyes, and she saw only kindness in them and heard only gentleness in his voice; for love had taken possession of him also, and Zoraïde was more distracted than ever. When Mézor was not dancing Bamboula in Congo Square, he was hoeing sugar cane, barefooted and half naked, in his master's field outside of the city. Dr Langlé was his master as well as M'sieur Ambroise's.

'One day, when Zoraïde kneeled before her mistress, drawing on Madame's silken stockings, that were of the finest, she said:

'"Nénaine, you have spoken to me often of marrying. Now, at last, I have chosen a husband, but it is not M'sieur Ambroise; it is le beau Mézor that I want and no other." And Zoraïde hid her face in her hands when she had said that, for she guessed, rightly enough, that her mistress would be very angry. And, indeed, Madame Delarivière was at first speechless with rage. When she finally spoke it was only to gasp out, exasperated:

'"That Negro! That Negro! Bon Dieu Seigneur, but this is too much!"

'"Am I white, nénaine?" pleaded Zoraïde.

'"You white! *Malheureuse!* You deserve to have the lash laid upon you like any other slave; you have proven yourself no better than the worst."

'"I am not white," persisted Zoraïde, respectfully and gently. "Dr Langlé gives me his slave to marry, but he would not give me his son. Then, since I am not white, let me have from out of my own race the one whom my heart has chosen."

'However, you may well believe that Madame would not hear to that. Zoraïde was forbidden to speak to Mézor, and Mézor was cautioned against seeing Zoraïde again. But you know how the Negroes are, Ma'zélle Titite,' added Manna-Loulou, smiling a little sadly. 'There is no mistress, no master, no king nor priest who can hinder them from loving when they will. And these two found ways and means.

'When months had passed by, Zoraïde, who had grown unlike herself – sober and preoccupied – said again to her mistress:

'"Nénaine, you would not let me have Mézor for my husband; but I have disobeyed you, I have sinned. Kill me if you wish, nénaine: forgive me if you will; but when I heard le beau Mézor say to me, 'Zoraïde, mo l'aime toi,' I could have died, but I could not have helped loving him."

'This time Madame Delarivière was so actually pained, so

wounded at hearing Zoraïde's confession, that there was no place
left in her heart for anger. She could utter only confused
reproaches. But she was a woman of action rather than of words,
and she acted promptly. Her first step was to induce Dr Langlé to
sell Mézor. Dr Langlé, who was a widower, had long wanted to
marry Madame Delarivière, and he would willingly have walked
on all fours at noon through the Place d'Armes if she wanted him
to. Naturally he lost no time in disposing of le beau Mézor, who
was sold away into Georgia, or the Carolinas, or one of those
distant countries far away, where he would no longer hear his
Creole tongue spoken, nor dance Calinda, nor hold la belle
Zoraïde in his arms.

'The poor thing was heartbroken when Mézor was sent away
from her, but she took comfort and hope in the thought of her
baby that she would soon be able to clasp to her breast.

'La belle Zoraïde's sorrows had now begun in earnest. Not only
sorrows but sufferings, and with the anguish of maternity came
the shadow of death. But there is no agony that a mother will not
forget when she holds her first-born to her heart, and presses her
lips upon the baby flesh that is her own, yet far more precious
than her own.

'So, instinctively, when Zoraïde came out of the awful shadow
she gazed questioningly about her and felt with her trembling
hands upon either side of her. "Où li, mo piti a moin? (Where is
my little one?)" she asked imploringly. Madame who was there
and the nurse who was there both told her in turn, "To piti à toi,
li mouri" ("Your little one is dead"), which was a wicked
falsehood that must have caused the angels in heaven to weep.
For the baby was living and well and strong. It had at once been
removed from its mother's side, to be sent away to Madame's
plantation, far up the coast. Zoraïde could only moan in reply, "Li
mouri, li mouri," and she turned her face to the wall.

'Madame had hoped, in thus depriving Zoraïde of her child, to
have her young waiting-maid again at her side free, happy, and
beautiful as of old. But there was a more powerful will than
Madame's at work – the will of the good God, who had already
designed that Zoraïde should grieve with a sorrow that was never
more to be lifted in this world. La belle Zoraïde was no more. In
her stead was a sad-eyed woman who mourned night and day for
her baby. "Li mouri, li mouri," she would sigh over and over

again to those about her, and to herself when others grew weary of her complaint.

'Yet, in spite of all, M'sieur Ambroise was still in the notion to marry her. A sad wife or a merry one was all the same to him so long as that wife was Zoraïde. And she seemed to consent, or rather submit, to the approaching marriage as though nothing mattered any longer in this world.

'One day, a black servant entered a little noisily the room in which Zoraïde sat sewing. With a look of strange and vacuous happiness upon her face, Zoraïde arose hastily. "Hush, hush," she whispered, lifting a warning finger, "my little one is asleep; you must not awaken her."

'Upon the bed was a senseless bundle of rags shaped like an infant in swaddling clothes. Over this dummy the woman had drawn the mosquito bar, and she was sitting contentedly beside it. In short, from that day Zoraïde was demented. Night nor day did she lose sight of the doll that lay in her bed or in her arms.

'And now was Madame stung with sorrow and remorse at seeing this terrible affliction that had befallen her dear Zoraïde. Consulting with Dr Langlé, they decided to bring back to the mother the real baby of flesh and blood that was now toddling about, and kicking its heels in the dust yonder upon the plantation.

'It was Madame herself who led the pretty, tiny little "griffe" girl to her mother. Zoraïde was sitting upon a stone bench in the courtyard, listening to the soft splashing of the fountain, and watching the fitful shadows of the palm leaves upon the broad, white flagging.

'"Here," said Madame, approaching, "here, my poor dear Zoraïde, is your own little child. Keep her; she is yours. No one will ever take her from you again."

'Zoraïde looked with sullen suspicion upon her mistress and the child before her. Reaching out a hand she thrust the little one mistrustfully away from her. With the other hand she clasped the rag bundle fiercely to her breast; for she suspected a plot to deprive her of it.

'Nor could she ever be induced to let her own child approach her; and finally the little one was sent back to the plantation, where she was never to know the love of mother or father.

'And now this is the end of Zoraïde's story. She was never

known again as la belle Zoraïde, but ever after as Zoraïde la folle, whom no one ever wanted to marry – not even M'sieur Ambroise. She lived to be an old woman, whom some people pitied and others laughed at – always clasping her bundle of rags – her "piti."

'Are you asleep, Ma'zélle Titite?'

'No, I am not asleep; I was thinking. Ah, the poor little one, Man Loulou, the poor little one! better had she died!'

But this is the way Madame Delisle and Manna-Loulou really talked to each other:—

'Vou pré droumi, Ma'zélle Titite?'

'Non, pa pré droumi; mo yapré zongler. Ah, la pauv' piti, Man Loulou. La pauv' piti! Mieux li mouri!'

At Chênière Caminada

I

There was no clumsier looking fellow in church that Sunday morning than Antoine Bocaze – the one they called Tonie. But Tonie did not really care if he were clumsy or not. He felt that he could speak intelligibly to no woman save his mother; but since he had no desire to inflame the hearts of any of the island maidens, what difference did it make?

He knew there was no better fisherman on the Chênière Caminada than himself, if his face was too long and bronzed, his limbs too unmanageable and his eyes too earnest – almost too honest.

It was a midsummer day, with a lazy, scorching breeze blowing from the Gulf straight into the church windows. The ribbons on the young girls' hats fluttered like the wings of birds, and the old women clutched the flapping ends of the veils that covered their heads.

A few mosquitoes, floating through the blistering air, with their nipping and humming fretted the people to a certain degree of attention and consequent devotion. The measured tones of the priest at the altar rose and fell like a song: 'Credo in unum Deum patrem omnipotentem' he chanted. And then the people all looked at one another, suddenly electrified.

Some one was playing upon the organ whose notes no one on the whole island was able to awaken; whose tones had not been heard during the many months since a passing stranger had one day listlessly dragged his fingers across its idle keys. A long, sweet strain of music floated down from the loft and filled the church.

It seemed to most of them – it seemed to Tonie standing there beside his old mother – that some heavenly being must have descended upon the Church of Our Lady of Lourdes and chosen this celestial way of communicating with its people.

But it was no creature from a different sphere; it was only a young lady from Grand Isle. A rather pretty young person with blue eyes and nut-brown hair, who wore a dotted lawn of fine texture and fashionable make, and a white Leghorn sailor-hat.

Tonie saw her standing outside of the church after mass, receiving the priest's voluble praises and thanks for her graceful service.

She had come over to mass from Grand Isle in Baptiste Beaudelet's lugger, with a couple of young men, and two ladies who kept a pension over there. Tonie knew these two ladies – the widow Lebrun and her old mother – but he did not attempt to speak with them; he would not have known what to say. He stood aside gazing at the group, as others were doing, his serious eyes fixed earnestly upon the fair organist.

Tonie was late at dinner that day. His mother must have waited an hour for him, sitting patiently with her coarse hands folded in her lap, in that little still room with its 'brick-painted' floor, its gaping chimney and homely furnishings.

He told her that he had been walking – walking he hardly knew where, and he did not know why. He must have tramped from one end of the island to the other; but he brought her no bit of news or gossip. He did not know if the Cotures had stopped for dinner with the Avendettes; whether old Pierre François was worse, or better, or dead, or if lame Philibert was drinking again this morning. He knew nothing; yet he had crossed the village, and passed every one of its small houses that stood close together in a long jagged line facing the sea; they were gray and battered by time and the rude buffets of the salt sea winds.

He knew nothing though the Cotures had all bade him 'good day' as they filed into Avendette's, where a steaming plate of crab gumbo was waiting for each. He had heard some woman screaming, and others saying it was because old Pierre François had just passed away. But he did not remember this, nor did he recall the fact that lame Philibert had staggered against him when he stood absently watching a 'fiddler' sidling across the sun-baked sand. He could tell his mother nothing of all this; but he said he had noticed that the wind was fair and must have driven Baptiste's boat, like a flying bird, across the water.

Well, that was something to talk about, and old Ma'me Antoine, who was fat, leaned comfortably upon the table after she had helped Tonie to his courtbouillon, and remarked that she found Madame was getting old. Tonie thought that perhaps she was aging and her hair was getting whiter. He seemed glad to talk about her, and reminded his mother of old Madame's kindness and sympathy at the time his father and brothers had perished. It was when he was a little fellow, ten years before, during a squall in Barataria Bay.

Ma'me Antoine declared that she could never forget that sympathy, if she lived till Judgment Day; but all the same she was sorry to see that Madame Lebrun was also not so young or fresh as she used to be. Her chances of getting a husband were surely lessening every year; especially with the young girls around her, budding each spring like flowers to be plucked. The one who had played upon the organ was Mademoiselle Duvigné, Claire Duvigné, a great belle, the daughter of the famous lawyer who lived in New Orleans, on Rampart street. Ma'me Antoine had found that out during the ten minutes she and others had stopped after mass to gossip with the priest.

'Claire Duvigné,' muttered Tonie, not even making a pretense to taste his courtbouillon, but picking little bits from the half loaf of crusty brown bread that lay beside his plate. 'Claire Duvigné; that is a pretty name. Don't you think so, mother? I can't think of anyone on the Chênière who has so pretty a one, nor at Grand Isle, either, for that matter. And you say she lives on Rampart street?'

It appeared to him a matter of great importance that he should have his mother repeat all that the priest had told her.

II

Early the following morning Tonie went out in search of lame Philibert, than whom there was no cleverer workman on the island when he could be caught sober.

Tonie had tried to work on his big lugger that lay bottom upward under the shed, but it had seemed impossible. His mind, his hands, his tools refused to do their office, and in sudden desperation he desisted. He found Philibert and set him to work in his own place under the shed. Then he got into his small boat with the red lateen-sail and went over to Grand Isle.

There was no one at hand to warn Tonie that he was acting

the part of a fool. He had, singularly, never felt those premonitory symptoms of love which afflict the greater portion of mankind before they reach the age which he had attained. He did not at first recognize this powerful impulse that had, without warning, possessed itself of his entire being. He obeyed it without a struggle, as naturally as he would have obeyed the dictates of hunger and thirst.

Tonie left his boat at the wharf and proceeded at once to Mme. Lebrun's pension, which consisted of a group of plain, stoutly built cottages that stood in mid island, about half a mile from the sea.

The day was bright and beautiful with soft, velvety gusts of wind blowing from the water. From a cluster of orange trees a flock of doves ascended, and Tonic stopped to listen to the beating of their wings and follow their flight toward the water oaks whither he himself was moving.

He walked with a dragging, uncertain step through the yellow, fragrant camomile, his thoughts traveling before him. In his mind was always the vivid picture of the girl as it had stamped itself there yesterday, connected in some mystical way with that celestial music which had thrilled him and was vibrating yet in his soul.

But she did not look the same to-day. She was returning from the beach when Tonie first saw her, leaning upon the arm of one of the men who had accompanied her yesterday. She was dressed differently – in a dainty blue cotton gown. Her companion held a big white sunshade over them both. They had exchanged hats and were laughing with great abandonment.

Two young men walked behind them and were trying to engage her attention. She glanced at Tonie, who was leaning against a tree when the group passed by; but of course she did not know him. She was speaking English, a language which he hardly understood.

There were other young people gathered under the water oaks – girls who were, many of them, more beautiful than Mlle. Duvigné; but for Tonie they simply did not exist. His whole universe had suddenly become converted into a glamorous background for the person of Mlle. Duvigné, and the shadowy figures of men who were about her.

Tonie went to Mme. Lebrun and told her he would bring her oranges next day from the Chênière. She was well pleased, and commissioned him to bring her other things from the stores there, which she could not procure at Grand Isle. She did not question his presence, knowing that these summer days were idle ones for the Chênière fishermen. Nor did she seem surprised when he told her that his boat was at the wharf, and would be there every day at her service. She knew his frugal habits, and supposed he wished to hire it, as others did. He intuitively felt that this could be the only way.

And that is how it happened that Tonie spent so little of his time at the Chênière Caminada that summer. Old Ma'me Antoine grumbled enough about it. She herself had been twice in her life to Grand Isle and once to Grand Terre, and each time had been more than glad to get back to the Chênière. And why Tonie should want to spend his days, and even his nights, away from home, was a thing she could not comprehend, especially as he would have to be away the whole winter; and meantime there was much work to be done at his own hearthside and in the company of his own mother. She did not know that Tonie had much, much more to do at Grand Isle than at the Chênière Caminada.

He had to see how Claire Duvigné sat upon the gallery in the big rocking chair that she kept in motion by the impetus of her slender, slippered foot; turning her head this way and that way to speak to the men who were always near her. He had to follow her little motions at tennis or croquet, that she often played with the children under the trees. Some days he wanted to see how she spread her bare, white arms, and walked out to meet the foam-crested waves. Even here there were men with her. And then at night, standing alone like a still shadow under the stars, did he not have to listen to her voice when she talked and laughed and sang? Did he not have to follow her slim figure whirling through the dance, in the arms of men who must have loved her and wanted her as he did. He did not dream that they could help it more than he could help it. But the days when she stepped into his boat, the one with the red lateen sail, and sat for hours within a few feet of him, were days that he would have given up for nothing else that he could think of.

III

There were always others in her company at such times, young people with jests and laughter on their lips. Only once she was alone.

She had foolishly brought a book with her, thinking she would want to read. But with the breath of the sea stinging her she could not read a line. She looked precisely as she had looked the day he first saw her, standing outside of the church at Chênière Caminada.

She laid the book down in her lap, and let her soft eyes sweep dreamily along the line of the horizon where the sky and water met. Then she looked straight at Tonie, and for the first time spoke directly to him.

She called him Tonie, as she had heard others do, and questioned him about his boat and his work. He trembled, and answered her vaguely and stupidly. She did not mind, but spoke to him anyhow, satisfied to talk herself when she found that he could not or would not. She spoke French, and talked about the Chênière Caminada, its people and its church. She talked of the day she had played upon the organ there, and complained of the instrument being woefully out of tune.

Tonie was perfectly at home in the familiar task of guiding his boat before the wind that bellied its taut, red sail. He did not seem clumsy and awkward as when he sat in church. The girl noticed that he appeared as strong as an ox.

As she looked at him and surprised one of his shifting glances, a glimmer of the truth began to dawn faintly upon her. She remembered how she had encountered him daily in her path, with his earnest, devouring eyes always seeking her out. She recalled – but there was no need to recall anything. There are women whose perception of passion is very keen; they are the women who most inspire it.

A feeling of complacency took possession of her with this conviction. There was some softness and sympathy mingled with it. She would have liked to lean over and pat his big, brown hand, and tell him she felt sorry and would have helped it if she could. With this belief he ceased to be an object of complete indifference in her eyes. She had thought, awhile before, of having him turn about and take her back home. But now it was really piquant to pose for an hour longer before a man – even a rough fisherman – to whom she felt herself to be an object of silent and consuming devotion. She could think of nothing more interesting to do on shore.

She was incapable of conceiving the full force and extent of his infatuation. She did not dream that under the rude, calm exterior before her a man's heart was beating clamorously, and his reason yielding to the savage instinct of his blood.

'I hear the Angelus ringing at Chênière, Tonie,' she said. 'I didn't know it was so late; let us go back to the island.' There had been a long silence which her musical voice interrupted.

Tonie could now faintly hear the Angelus bell himself. A vision of the church came with it, the odor of incense and the sound of the organ. The girl before him was again that celestial being whom our Lady of Lourdes had once offered to his immortal vision.

It was growing dusk when they landed at the pier, and frogs had begun to croak among the reeds in the pools. There were two of Mlle. Duvigné's usual attendants anxiously awaiting her return. But she chose to let Tonie assist her out of the boat. The touch of her hand fired his blood again.

She said to him very low and half-laughing, 'I have no money tonight, Tonie; take this instead,' pressing into his palm a delicate silver chain, which she had worn twined about her bare wrist. It was purely a spirit of coquetry that prompted the action, and a touch of the sentimentality which most women possess. She had read in some romance of a young girl doing something like that.

As she walked away between her two attendants she fancied Tonie pressing the chain to his lips. But he was standing quite still, and held it buried in his tightly-closed hand; wanting to hold as long as he might the warmth of the body that still penetrated the bauble when she thrust it into his hand.

He watched her retreating figure like a blotch against the fading sky. He was stirred by a terrible, an overmastering regret, that he had not clasped her in his arms when they were out there alone, and sprung with her into the sea. It was what he had vaguely meant to do when the sound of the Angelus had weakened and palsied his resolution. Now she was going from him, fading away into the mist with those figures on either side of her, leaving him alone. He resolved within himself that if ever again she were out there on the sea at his mercy, she would have to perish in his arms. He would go far, far out where the sound of no bell could reach him. There was some comfort for him in the thought.

But as it happened, Mlle. Duvigné never went out alone in the boat with Tonie again.

IV

It was one morning in January. Tonie had been collecting a bill from one of the fishmongers at the French Market, in New Orleans, and had turned his steps toward St. Philip street. The day was chilly; a keen wind was blowing. Tonie mechanically buttoned his rough, warm coat and crossed over into the sun.

There was perhaps not a more wretched-hearted being in the whole district, that morning, than he. For months the woman he so hopelessly loved had been lost to his sight. But all the more she dwelt in his thoughts, preying upon his mental and bodily forces until his unhappy condition became apparent to all who knew him. Before leaving his home for the winter fishing grounds he had opened his whole heart to his mother, and told her of the trouble that was killing him. She hardly expected that he would ever come back to her when he went away. She feared that he would not, for he had spoken wildly of the rest and peace that could only come to him with death.

That morning when Tonie had crossed St. Philip street he found himself accosted by Madame Lebrun and her mother. He had not noticed them approaching, and, moreover, their figures in winter garb appeared unfamiliar to him. He had never seen them elsewhere than at Grand Isle and the Chênière during the summer. They were glad to meet him, and shook his hand cordially. He stood as usual a little helplessly before them. A pulse in his throat was beating and almost choking him, so poignant were the recollections which their presence stirred up.

They were staying in the city this winter, they told him. They wanted to hear the opera as often as possible, and the island was really too dreary with everyone gone. Madame Lebrun had left her son there to keep order and superintend repairs, and so on.

'You are both well?' stammered Tonie.

'In perfect health, my dear Tonie,' Madame Lebrun replied. She was wondering at his haggard eyes and thin, gaunt cheeks; but possessed too much tact to mention them.

'And – the young lady who used to go sailing – is she well?' he inquired lamely.

'You mean Mlle. Favette? She was married just after leaving Grand Isle.'

'No; I mean the one you called Claire – Mamzelle Duvigné – is she well?'

Mother and daughter exclaimed together: 'Impossible! You haven't heard? Why, Tonie,' madame continued, 'Mlle. Duvigné died three weeks ago! But that was something sad, I tell you ... Her family heartbroken ... Simply from a cold caught by standing in thin slippers, waiting for her carriage after the opera.... What a warning!'

The two were talking at once. Tonie kept looking from one to the other. He did not know what they were saying, after madame had told him, 'Elle est morte.'

As in a dream he finally heard that they said good-by to him, and sent their love to his mother.

He stood still in the middle of the banquette when they had left him, watching them go toward the market. He could not stir. Something had happened to him – he did not know what. He wondered if the news was killing him.

Some women passed by, laughing coarsely. He noticed how they laughed and tossed their heads. A mockingbird was singing in a cage which hung from a window above his head. He had not heard it before.

Just beneath the window was the entrance to a barroom. Tonie turned and plunged through its swinging doors. He asked the bartender for whiskey. The man thought he was already drunk, but pushed the bottle toward him nevertheless. Tonie poured a great quantity of the fiery liquor into a glass and swallowed it at a draught. The rest of the day he spent among the fishermen and Barataria oystermen; and that night he slept soundly and peacefully until morning.

He did not know why it was so; he could not understand. But from that day he felt that he began to live again, to be once more a part of the moving world about him. He would ask himself over and over again why it was so, and stay bewildered before this truth that he could not answer or explain, and which he began to accept as a holy mystery.

One day in early spring Tonie sat with his mother upon a piece of drift-wood close to the sea.

He had returned that day to the Chênière Caminada. At first she thought he was like his former self again, for all his old strength and courage had returned. But she found that there was a new brightness in his face which had not been there before. It made her think of the Holy Ghost descending and bringing some kind of light to a man.

She knew that Mademoiselle Duvigné was dead, and all along had feared that this knowledge would be the death of Tonie. When she saw him come back to her like a new being, at once she dreaded that he did not know. All day the doubt had been fretting her, and she could bear the uncertainty no longer.

'You know, Tonie – that young lady whom you cared for – well, some one read it to me in the papers – she died last winter.' She had tried to speak as cautiously as she could.

'Yes, I know she is dead. I am glad.'

It was the first time he had said this in words, and it made his heart beat quicker.

Ma'me Antoine shuddered and drew aside from him. To her it was somehow like murder to say such a thing.

'What do you mean? Why are you glad?' she demanded, indignantly.

Tonie was sitting with his elbows on his knees. He wanted to answer his mother, but it would take time; he would have to think. He looked out across the water that glistened gem-like with the sun upon it, but there was nothing there to open his thought. He looked down into his open palm and began to pick at the callous flesh that was hard as a horse's hoof. Whilst he did this his ideas began to gather and take form.

'You see, while she lived I could never hope for anything,' he began, slowly feeling his way. 'Despair was the only thing for me. There were always men about her. She walked and sang and danced with them. I knew it all the time, even when I didn't see her. But I saw her often enough. I knew that some day one of them would please her and she would give herself to him – she would marry him. That thought haunted me like an evil spirit.'

Tonie passed his hand across his forehead as if to sweep away anything of the horror that might have remained there.

'It kept me awake at night,' he went on. 'But that was not so bad; the worst torture was to sleep, for then I would dream that it was all true.

'Oh, I could see her married to one of them – his wife – coming year after year to Grand Isle and bringing her little children with her! I can't tell you all that I saw – all that was driving me mad! But now' – and Tonie clasped his hands together and smiled as he looked again across the water – 'she is where she belongs; there is no difference up there; the curé has often told us there is no difference between men. It is with the soul that we approach each other there. Then she will know who has loved her best. That is why I am so contented. Who knows what may happen up there?'

Ma'me Antoine could not answer. She only took her son's big, rough hand and pressed it against her.

'And now, ma mère,' he exclaimed, cheerfully, rising, 'I shall go light the fire for your bread; it is a long time since I have done anything for you,' and he stooped and pressed a warm kiss on her withered old cheek.

With misty eyes she watched him walk away in the direction of the big brick oven that stood open-mouthed under the lemon trees.

In Sabine

The sight of a human habitation, even if it was a rude log cabin with a mud chimney at one end, was a very gratifying one to Grégoire.

He had come out of Natchitoches parish, and had been riding a great part of the day through the big lonesome parish of Sabine. He was not following the regular Texas road, but, led by his erratic fancy, was pushing toward the Sabine River by circuitous paths through the rolling pine forests.

As he approached the cabin in the clearing, he discerned behind a palisade of pine saplings an old negro man chopping wood.

'Howdy, Uncle,' called out the young fellow, reining his horse. The negro looked up in blank amazement at so unexpected an apparition, but he only answered: 'How you do, suh,' accompanying his speech by a series of polite nods.

'Who lives yere?'

'Hit 's Mas' Bud Aiken w'at live' heah, suh.'

'Well, if Mr. Bud Aiken c'n affo'd to hire a man to chop his wood, I reckon he won't grudge me a bite o' suppa an' a couple hours' res' on his gall'ry. W'at you say, ole man?'

'I say dit Mas' Bud Aiken don't hires me to chop 'ood. Ef I don't chop dis heah, his wife got it to do. Dat w'y I chops 'ood, suh. Go right 'long in, suh; you g'ine fine Mas' Bud some'eres roun', ef he ain't drunk an' gone to bed.'

Grégoire, glad to stretch his legs, dismounted, and led his horse into the small inclosure which surrounded the cabin. An unkempt, vicious looking little Texas pony stopped nibbling the stubble there to look maliciously at him and his fine sleek horse, as they passed by. Back of the hut, and running plumb up against the pine wood, was a small, ragged specimen of a cotton-field.

Grégoire was rather undersized, with a square, well-knit figure, upon which his clothes sat well and easily. His corduroy trousers were thrust into the legs of his boots; he wore a blue flannel shirt; his coat was thrown across the saddle. In his keen black eyes had

come a puzzled expression, and he tugged thoughtfully at the
brown moustache that lightly shaded his upper lip.

He was trying to recall when and under what circumstances
he had before heard the name of Bud Aiken. But Bud Aiken
himself saved Grégoire the trouble of further speculation on the
subject. He appeared suddenly in the small doorway, which his
big body quite filled; and then Grégoire remembered. This was the
disreputable so-called 'Texan' who a year ago had run away with
and married Baptiste Choupic's pretty daughter, 'Tite Reine,
yonder on Bayou Pierre, in Natchitoches parish. A vivid picture
of the girl as he remembered her appeared to him: her trim
rounded figure; her piquant face with its saucy black coquettish
eyes; her little exacting, imperious ways that had obtained for her
the nickname of 'Tite Reine, little queen. Grégoire had known her
at the 'Cadian balls that he sometimes had the hardihood to
attend.

These pleasing recollections of 'Tite Reine lent a warmth that
might otherwise have been lacking to Grégoire's manner, when
he greeted her husband.

'I hope I fine you well, Mr. Aiken,' he exclaimed cordially, as
he approached and extended his hand.

'You find me damn' porely, suh; but you 've got the better o'
me, ef I may so say.' He was a big good-looking brute, with a
straw-colored 'horse-shoe' moustache quite concealing his
mouth, and a several days' growth of stubble on his rugged face.
He was fond of reiterating that women's admiration had wrecked
his life, quite forgetting to mention the early and sustained
influence of 'Pike's Magnolia' and other brands, and wholly
ignoring certain inborn propensities capable of wrecking unaided
any ordinary existence. He had been lying down, and looked
frouzy and half asleep.

'Ef I may so say, you 've got the better o' me, Mr. – er'—

'Santien, Grégoire Santien. I have the pleasure o' knowin' the
lady you married, suh; an' I think I met you befo', – somew'ere o'
'nother,' Grégoire added vaguely.

'Oh,' drawled Aiken, waking up, 'one o' them Red River
Sanchuns!' and his face brightened at the prospect before him of
enjoying the society of one of the Santien boys. 'Mortimer!' he
called in ringing chest tones worthy a commander at the head of
his troop. The negro had rested his axe and appeared to be

listening to their talk, though he was too far to hear what they said.

'Mortimer, come along here an' take my frien' Mr. Sanchun's hoss. Git a move thar, git a move!' Then turning toward the entrance of the cabin he called back through the open door: 'Rain!' it was his way of pronouncing 'Tite Reine's name. 'Rain!' he cried again peremptorily; and turning to Grégoire: 'she 's 'tendin' to some or other housekeepin' truck.' 'Tite Reine was back in the yard feeding the solitary pig which they owned, and which Aiken had mysteriously driven up a few days before, saying he had bought it at Many.

Grégoire could hear her calling out as she approached: 'I 'm comin', Bud. Yere I come. W'at you want, Bud?' breathlessly, as she appeared in the door frame and looked out upon the narrow sloping gallery where stood the two men. She seemed to Grégoire to have changed a good deal. She was thinner, and her eyes were larger, with an alert, uneasy look in them; he fancied the startled expression came from seeing him there unexpectedly. She wore cleanly homespun garments, the same she had brought with her from Bayou Pierre; but her shoes were in shreds. She uttered only a low, smothered exclamation when she saw Grégoire.

'Well, is that all you got to say to my frien' Mr. Sanchun? That 's the way with them Cajuns,' Aiken offered apologetically to his guest; 'ain't got sense enough to know a white man when they see one.' Grégoire took her hand.

'I 'm mighty glad to see you, 'Tite Reine,' he said from his heart. She had for some reason been unable to speak; now she panted somewhat hysterically:—

'You mus' escuse me, Mista Grégoire. It 's the truth I did n' know you firs', stan'in' up there.' A deep flush had supplanted the former pallor of her face, and her eyes shone with tears and ill-concealed excitement.

'I thought you all lived yonda in Grant,' remarked Grégoire carelessly, making talk for the purpose of diverting Aiken's attention away from his wife's evident embarrassment, which he himself was at a loss to understand.

'Why, we did live a right smart while in Grant; but Grant ain't no parish to make a livin' in. Then I tried Winn and Caddo a spell; they was n't no better. But I tell you, suh, Sabine 's a damn' sight worse than any of 'em. Why, a man can't git a drink o' whiskey here without going out of the parish fer it, or across into Texas. I'm fixin' to sell out an' try Vernon.'

Bud Aiken's household belongings surely would not count for much in the contemplated 'selling out.' The one room that constituted his home was extremely bare of furnishing, – a cheap bed, a pine table, and a few chairs, that was all. On a rough shelf were some paper parcels representing the larder. The mud daubing had fallen out here and there from between the logs of the cabin; and into the largest of these apertures had been thrust pieces of ragged bagging and wisps of cotton. A tin basin outside on the gallery offered the only bathing facilities to be seen. Notwithstanding these drawbacks, Grégoire announced his intention of passing the night with Aiken.

'I'm jus' goin' to ask the privilege o' layin' down yere on yo' gall'ry to-night, Mr Aiken. My hoss ain't in firs'-class trim; an' a night's res' ain't goin' to hurt him o' me either.' He had begun by declaring his intention of pushing on across the Sabine, but an imploring look from 'Tite Reine's eyes had stayed the words upon his lips. Never had he seen in a woman's eyes a look of such heartbroken entreaty. He resolved on the instant to know the meaning of it before setting foot on Texas soil. Grégoire had never learned to steel his heart against a woman's eyes, no matter what language they spoke.

An old patchwork quilt folded double and a moss pillow which 'Tite Reine gave him out on the gallery made a bed that was, after all, not too uncomfortable for a young fellow of rugged habits.

Grégoire slept quite soundly after he laid down upon his improvised bed at nine o'clock. He was awakened toward the middle of the night by some one gently shaking him. It was 'Tite Reine stooping over him; he could see her plainly, for the moon was shining. She had not removed the clothing she had worn during the day; but her feet were bare and looked wonderfully small and white. He arose on his elbow, wide awake at once. 'W'y, 'Tite Reine! w'at the devil you mean? w'ere 's yo' husban'?'

'The house kin fall on 'im, 't en goin' wake up Bud w'en he 's sleepin'; he drink' too much.' Now that she had aroused Grégoire, she stood up, and sinking her face in her bended arm like a child, began to cry softly. In an instant he was on his feet. 'My God, 'Tite Reine! w'at 's the matta? you got to tell me w'at 's the matta.' He could no longer recognize the imperious 'Tite Reine, whose will had been the law in her father's household. He led her to the edge of the low gallery and there they sat down.

Grégoire loved women. He liked their nearness, their atmosphere; the tones of their voices and the things they said; their ways of moving and turning about; the brushing of their garments when they passed him by pleased him. He was fleeing now from the pain that a woman had inflicted upon him. When any overpowering sorrow came to Grégoire he felt a singular longing to cross the Sabine River and lose himself in Texas. He had done this once before when his home, the old Santien place, had gone into the hands of creditors. The sight of 'Tite Reine's distress now moved him painfully.

'W'at is it, 'Tite Reine? tell me w'at it is,' he kept asking her. She was attempting to dry her eyes on her coarse sleeve. He drew a handkerchief from his back pocket and dried them for her.

'They all well, yonda?' she asked, haltingly, 'my popa? my moma? the chil'en?' Grégoire knew no more of the Baptiste Choupic family than the post beside him. Nevertheless he answered: 'They all right well, 'Tite Reine, but they mighty lonesome of you.'

'My popa, he got a putty good crop this yea'?'

'He made right smart o' cotton fo' Bayou Pierre.'

'He done haul it to the relroad?'

'No, he ain't quite finish pickin'.'

'I hope they all ent sole "Putty Girl"?' she inquired solicitously.

'Well, I should say not! Yo' pa says they ain't anotha piece o' hossflesh in the pa'ish he 'd want to swap fo' "Putty Girl."' She turned to him with vague but fleeting amazement, – 'Putty Girl' was a cow!

The autumn night was heavy about them. The black forest seemed to have drawn nearer; its shadowy depths were filled with the gruesome noises that inhabit a southern forest at night time.

'Ain't you 'fraid sometimes yere, 'Tite Reine?' Grégoire asked, as he felt a light shiver run through him at the weirdness of the scene.

'No,' she answered promptly, 'I ent 'fred o' nothin' 'cep' Bud.'

'Then he treats you mean? I thought so!'

'Mista Grégoire,' drawing close to him and whispering in his

face, 'Bud 's killin' me.' He clasped her arm, holding her near
him, while an expression of profound pity escaped him. 'Nobody
don' know, 'cep' Unc' Mort'mer,' she went on. 'I tell you, he
beats me; my back an' arms – you ought to see – it 's all blue. He
would 'a' choke' me to death one day w'en he was drunk, if Unc'
Mort'mer had n' make 'im lef go – with his axe ov' his head.'
Grégoire glanced back over his shoulder toward the room where
the man lay sleeping. He was wondering if it would really be a
criminal act to go then and there and shoot the top of Bud
Aiken's head off. He himself would hardly have considered it a
crime, but he was not sure of how others might regard the act.

'That 's w'y I wake you up, to tell you,' she continued. 'Then
sometime' he plague me mos' crazy; he tell me 't ent no preacher,
it 's a Texas drummer w'at marry him an' me; an' w'en I don'
know w'at way to turn no mo', he say no, it 's a Meth'dis'
archbishop, an' keep on laughin' 'bout me, an' I don' know w'at
the truth!'

Then again, she told how Bud had induced her to mount the
vicious little mustang 'Buckeye,' knowing that the little brute
would n't carry a woman; and how it had amused him to witness
her distress and terror when she was thrown to the ground.

'If I would know how to read an' write, an' had some pencil
an' paper, it 's long 'go I would wrote to my popa. But it 's no
pos'office, it 's no relroad, – nothin' in Sabine. An' you know,
Mista Grégoire, Bud say he 's goin' carry me yonda to Vernon,
an' fu'ther off yet, – 'way yonda, an' he 's goin' turn me loose.
Oh, don' leave me yere, Mista Grégoire! don' leave me behine
you!' she entreated, breaking once more into sobs.

''Tite Reine,' he answered, 'do you think I 'm such a low-down
scound'el as to leave you yere with that' – He finished the
sentence mentally, not wishing to offend the ears of 'Tite Reine.

They talked on a good while after that. She would not return
to the room where her husband lay; the nearness of a friend had
already emboldened her to inward revolt. Grégoire induced her to
lie down and rest upon the quilt that she had given to him for a
bed. She did so, and broken down by fatigue was soon fast asleep.

He stayed seated on the edge of the gallery and began to smoke
cigarettes which he rolled himself of périque tobacco. He might
have gone in and shared Bud Aiken's bed, but preferred to stay

there near 'Tite Reine. He watched the two horses, tramping
slowly about the lot, cropping the dewy wet tufts of grass.

Grégoire smoked on. He only stopped when the moon sank
down behind the pine-trees, and the long deep shadow reached
out and enveloped him. Then he could no longer see and follow
the filmy smoke from his cigarette, and he threw it away. Sleep
was pressing heavily upon him. He stretched himself full length
upon the rough bare boards of the gallery and slept until day-
break.

Bud Aiken's satisfaction was very genuine when he learned
that Grégoire proposed spending the day and another night with
him. He had already recognized in the young creole a spirit not
altogether uncongenial to his own.

'Tite Reine cooked breakfast for them. She made coffee; of
course there was no milk to add to it, but there was sugar. From
a meal bag that stood in the corner of the room she took a
measure of meal, and with it made a pone of corn bread. She fried
slices of salt pork. Then Bud sent her into the field to pick cotton
with old Uncle Mortimer. The negro's cabin was the counterpart
of their own, but stood quite a distance away hidden in the
woods. He and Aiken worked the crop on shares.

Early in the day Bud produced a grimy pack of cards from
behind a parcel of sugar on the shelf. Grégoire threw the cards
into the fire and replaced them with a spic and span new 'deck'
that he took from his saddlebags. He also brought forth from the
same receptacle a bottle of whiskey, which he presented to his
host, saying that he himself had no further use for it, as he had
'sworn off' since day before yesterday, when he had made a fool
of himself in Cloutierville.

They sat at the pine table smoking and playing cards all the
morning, only desisting when 'Tite Reine came to serve them
with the gumbo-filé that she had come out of the field to cook at
noon. She could afford to treat a guest to chicken gumbo, for she
owned a half dozen chickens that Uncle Mortimer had presented
to her at various times. There were only two spoons, and 'Tite
Reine had to wait till the men had finished before eating her
soup. She waited for Grégoire's spoon, though her husband was
the first to get through. It was a very childish whim.

In the afternoon she picked cotton again; and the men played
cards, smoked, and Bud drank.

It was a very long time since Bud Aiken had enjoyed himself so well, and since he had encountered so sympathetic and appreciative a listener to the story of his eventful career. The story of 'Tite Reine's fall from the horse he told with much spirit, mimicking quite skillfully the way in which she had complained of never being permitted 'to teck a li'le pleasure,' whereupon he had kindly suggested horseback riding. Grégoire enjoyed the story amazingly, which encouraged Aiken to relate many more of a similar character. As the afternoon wore on, all formality of address between the two had disappeared: they were 'Bud' and 'Grégoire' to each other, and Grégoire had delighted Aiken's soul by promising to spend a week with him. 'Tite Reine was also touched by the spirit of recklessness in the air; it moved her to fry two chickens for supper. She fried them deliciously in bacon fat. After supper she again arranged Grégoire's bed out on the gallery.

The night fell calm and beautiful, with the delicious odor of the pines floating upon the air. But the three did not sit up to enjoy it. Before the stroke of nine, Aiken had already fallen upon his bed unconscious of everything about him in the heavy drunken sleep that would hold him fast through the night. It even clutched him more relentlessly than usual, thanks to Grégoire's free gift of whiskey.

The sun was high when he awoke. He lifted his voice and called imperiously for 'Tite Reine, wondering that the coffee-pot was not on the hearth, and marveling still more that he did not hear her voice in quick response with its, 'I'm comin', Bud. Yere I come.' He called again and again. Then he arose and looked out through the back door to see if she were picking cotton in the field, but she was not there. He dragged himself to the front entrance. Grégoire's bed was still on the gallery, but the young fellow was nowhere to be seen.

Uncle Mortimer had come into the yard, not to cut wood this time, but to pick up the axe which was his own property, and lift it to his shoulder.

'Mortimer,' called out Aiken, 'whur 's my wife?' at the same time advancing toward the negro. Mortimer stood still, waiting for him. 'Whur 's my wife an' that Frenchman? Speak out, I say, before I send you to h—l.'

Uncle Mortimer never had feared Bud Aiken; and with the

trusty axe upon his shoulder, he felt a double hardihood in the man's presence. The old fellow passed the back of his black, knotty hand unctuously over his lips, as though he relished in advance the words that were about to pass them. He spoke carefully and deliberately:

'Miss Reine,' he said, 'I reckon she mus' of done struck Natchitoches pa'ish sometime to'ard de middle o' de night, on dat 'ar swif' hoss o' Mr. Sanchun's.'

Aiken uttered a terrific oath. 'Saddle up Buckeye,' he yelled, 'before I count twenty, or I'll rip the black hide off yer. Quick, thar! Thur ain't nothin' fourfooted top o' this earth that Buckeye can't run down.' Uncle Mortimer scratched his head dubiously, as he answered:—

'Yas, Mas' Bud, but you see, Mr. Sanchun, he done cross de Sabine befo' sun-up on Buckeye.'

A Respectable Woman

Mrs. Baroda was a little provoked to learn that her husband expected his friend, Gouvernail, up to spend a week or two on the plantation.

They had entertained a good deal during the winter; much of the time had also been passed in New Orleans in various forms of mild dissipation. She was looking forward to a period of unbroken rest, now, and undisturbed tête-à-tête with her husband, when he informed her that Gouvernail was coming up to stay a week or two.

This was a man she had heard much of but never seen. He had been her husband's college friend; was now a journalist, and in no sense a society man or 'a man about town,' which were, perhaps, some of the reasons she had never met him. But she had unconsciously formed an image of him in her mind. She pictured him tall, slim, cynical; with eye-glasses, and his hands in his pockets; and she did not like him. Gouvernail was slim enough, but he wasn't very tall nor very cynical; neither did he wear eye-glasses nor carry his hands in his pockets. And she rather liked him when he first presented himself.

But why she liked him she could not explain satisfactorily to herself when she partly attempted to do so. She could discover in him none of those brilliant and promising traits which Gaston, her husband, had often assured her that he possessed. On the contrary, he sat rather mute and receptive before her chatty eagerness to make him feel at home and in face of Gaston's frank and wordy hospitality. His manner was as courteous toward her as the most exacting woman could require; but he made no direct appeal to her approval or even esteem.

Once settled at the plantation he seemed to like to sit upon the wide portico in the shade of one of the big Corinthian pillars, smoking his cigar lazily and listening attentively to Gaston's experience as a sugar planter.

'This is what I call living,' he would utter with deep satisfaction, as the air that swept across the sugar field caressed him with its warm and scented velvety touch. It pleased him also to get on familiar terms with the big dogs that came about him, rubbing themselves sociably against his legs. He did not care to fish, and displayed no eagerness to go out and kill grosbecs when Gaston proposed doing so.

Gouvernail's personality puzzled Mrs. Baroda, but she liked him. Indeed, he was a lovable, inoffensive fellow. After a few days, when she could understand him no better than at first, she gave over being puzzled and remained piqued. In this mood she left her husband and her guest, for the most part, alone together. Then finding that Gouvernail took no manner of exception to her action, she imposed her society upon him, accompanying him in his idle strolls to the mill and walks along the batture. She persistently sought to penetrate the reserve in which he had unconsciously enveloped himself.

'When is he going – your friend?' she one day asked her husband. 'For my part, he tires me frightfully.'

'Not for a week yet, dear. I can't understand; he gives you no trouble.'

'No. I should like him better if he did; if he were more like others, and I had to plan somewhat for his comfort and enjoyment.'

Gaston took his wife's pretty face between his hands and looked tenderly and laughingly into her troubled eyes. They were making a bit of toilet sociably together in Mrs. Baroda's dressing-room.

'You are full of surprises, ma belle,' he said to her. 'Even I can never count upon how you are going to act under given conditions.' He kissed her and turned to fasten his cravat before the mirror.

'Here you are,' he went on, 'taking poor Gouvernail seriously and making a commotion over him, the last thing he would desire or expect.'

'Commotion!' she hotly resented. 'Nonsense! How can you say such a thing? Commotion, indeed! But, you know, you said he was clever.'

'So he is. But the poor fellow is run down by overwork now. That's why I asked him here to take a rest.'

'You used to say he was a man of ideas,' she retorted, unconciliated. 'I expected him to be interesting, at least. I'm going to the city in the morning to have my spring gowns fitted. Let me know when Mr. Gouvernail is gone; I shall be at my Aunt Octavie's.'

That night she went and sat alone upon a bench that stood beneath a live oak tree at the edge of the gravel walk.

She had never known her thoughts or her intentions to be so confused. She could gather nothing from them but the feeling of a distinct necessity to quit her home in the morning.

Mrs. Baroda heard footsteps crunching the gravel; but could discern in the darkness only the approaching red point of a lighted cigar. She knew it was Gouvernail, for her husband did not smoke. She hoped to remain unnoticed, but her white gown revealed her to him. He threw away his cigar and seated himself upon the bench beside her; without a suspicion that she might object to his presence.

'Your husband told me to bring this to you, Mrs. Baroda,' he said, handing her a filmy, white scarf with which she sometimes enveloped her head and shoulders. She accepted the scarf from him with a murmur of thanks, and let it lie in her lap.

He made some commonplace observation upon the baneful effect of the night air at that season. Then as his gaze reached out into the darkness, he murmured, half to himself:

'"Night of south winds – night of the large few stars! Still nodding night—"'

She made no reply to this apostrophe to the night, which indeed, was not addressed to her.

Gouvernail was in no sense a diffident man, for he was not a self-conscious one. His periods of reserve were not constitutional, but the result of moods. Sitting there beside Mrs. Baroda, his silence melted for the time.

He talked freely and intimately in a low, hesitating drawl that was not unpleasant to hear. He talked of the old college days when he and Gaston had been a good deal to each other; of the days of keen and blind ambitions and large intentions. Now there was left with him, at least, a philosophic acquiescence to the existing order – only a desire to be permitted to exist, with now and then a little whiff of genuine life, such as he was breathing now.

Her mind only vaguely grasped what he was saying. Her

physical being was for the moment predominant. She was not thinking of his words, only drinking in the tones of his voice. She wanted to reach out her hand in the darkness and touch him with the sensitive tips of her fingers upon the face or the lips. She wanted to draw close to him and whisper against his cheek – she did not care what – as she might have done if she had not been a respectable woman.

The stronger the impulse grew to bring herself near him, the further, in fact, did she draw away from him. As soon as she could do so without an appearance of too great rudeness, she rose and left him there alone.

Before she reached the house, Gouvernail had lighted a fresh cigar and ended his apostrophe to the night.

Mrs. Baroda was greatly tempted that night to tell her husband – who was also her friend – of this folly that had seized her. But she did not yield to the temptation. Beside being a respectable woman she was a very sensible one; and she knew there are some battles in life which a human being must fight alone.

When Gaston arose in the morning, his wife had already departed. She had taken an early morning train to the city. She did not return till Gouvernail was gone from under her roof.

There was some talk of having him back during the summer that followed. That is, Gaston greatly desired it; but this desire yielded to his wife's strenuous opposition.

However, before the year ended, she proposed, wholly from herself, to have Gouvernail visit them again. Her husband was surprised and delighted with the suggestion coming from her.

'I am glad, chère amie, to know that you have finally overcome your dislike for him; truly he did not deserve it.'

'Oh,' she told him, laughingly, after pressing a long, tender kiss upon his lips, 'I have overcome everything! you will see. This time I shall be very nice to him.'

A Dresden Lady in Dixie

Madame Valtour had been in the sitting-room some time before she noticed the absence of the Dresden china figure from the corner of the mantel-piece, where it had stood for years. Aside from the intrinsic value of the piece, there were some very sad and tender memories associated with it. A baby's lips that were now forever still had loved once to kiss the painted 'pitty 'ady'; and the baby arms had often held it in a close and smothered embrace.

Madame Valtour gave a rapid, startled glance around the room, to see perchance if it had been misplaced; but she failed to discover it.

Viny, the house-maid, when summoned, remembered having carefully dusted it that morning, and was rather indignantly positive that she had not broken the thing to bits and secreted the pieces.

'Who has been in the room during my absence?' questioned Madame Valtour, with asperity. Viny abandoned herself to a moment's reflection.

'Pa-Jeff comed in yere wid de mail—' If she had said St. Peter came in with the mail, the fact would have had as little bearing on the case from Madame Valtour's point of view.

Pa-Jeff's uprightness and honesty were so long and firmly established as to have become proverbial on the plantation. He had not served the family faithfully since boyhood and been all through the war with 'old Marse Valtour' to descend at his time of life to tampering with household bric-a-brac.

'Has any one else been here?' Madame Valtour naturally inquired.

'On'y Agapie w'at brung you some Creole aiggs. I tole 'er to sot 'em down in de hall. I don' know she comed in de settin'-room o' not.'

Yes, there they were; eight, fresh 'Creole eggs' reposing on the muslin in the sewing basket. Viny herself had been seated on the gallery brushing her mistress' gowns during the hours of that lady's absence, and could think of no one else having penetrated to the sitting-room.

Madame Valtour did not entertain the thought that Agapie had stolen the relic. Her worst fear was, that the girl, finding herself alone in the room, had handled the frail bit of porcelain and inadvertently broken it.

Agapie came often to the house to play with the children and amuse them – she loved nothing better. Indeed, no other spot known to her on earth so closely embodied her confused idea of paradise, as this home with its atmosphere of love, comfort and good cheer. She was, herself, a cheery bit of humanity, overflowing with kind impulses and animal spirits.

Madame Valtour recalled the fact that Agapie had often admired this Dresden figure (but what had she not admired!); and she remembered having heard the girl's assurance that if ever she became possessed of 'fo' bits' to spend as she liked, she would have some one buy her just such a china doll in town or in the city.

Before night, the fact that the Dresden lady had strayed from her proud eminence on the sitting-room mantel, became, through Viny's indiscreet babbling, pretty well known on the place.

The following morning Madame Valtour crossed the field and went over to the Bedauts' cabin. The cabins on the plantation were not grouped; but each stood isolated upon the section of land which its occupants cultivated. Pa-Jeff's cabin was the only one near enough to the Bedauts to admit of neighborly intercourse.

Seraphine Bedaut was sitting on her small gallery, stringing red peppers, when Madame Valtour approached.

'I'm so distressed, Madame Bedaut,' began the planter's wife, abruptly. But the 'Cadian woman arose politely and interrupted, offering her visitor a chair.

'Come in, set down, Ma'me Valtour.'

'No, no; it's only for a moment. You know, Madame Bedaut, yesterday when I returned from making a visit, I found that an ornament was missing from my sitting-room mantel-piece. It's a thing I prize very, very much –' with sudden tears filling her eyes – 'and I would not willingly part with it for many times its value.'

Seraphine Bedaut was listening, with her mouth partly open, looking, in truth, stupidly puzzled.

'No one entered the room during my absence,' continued Madame Valtour, 'but Agapie.' Seraphine's mouth snapped like a steel trap and her black eyes gleamed with a flash of anger.

'You wan' say Agapie stole some'in' in yo' house!' she cried out in a shrill voice, tremulous from passion.

'No; oh no! I'm sure Agapie is an honest girl and we all love her; but you know how children are. It was a small Dresden figure. She may have handled and broken the thing and perhaps is afraid to say so. She may have thoughtlessly misplaced it; oh, I don't know what! I want to ask if she saw it.'

'Come in; you got to come in, Ma'me Valtour,' stubbornly insisted Seraphine, leading the way into the cabin. 'I sen' 'er to de house yistiddy wid some Creole aiggs,' she went on in her rasping voice, 'like I all time do, because you all say you can't eat dem sto' aiggs no mo'. Yere de basket w'at I sen' 'em in,' reaching for an Indian basket which hung against the wall – and which was partly filled with cotton seed.

'Oh, never mind,' interrupted Madame Valtour, now thoroughly distressed at witnessing the woman's agitation.

'Ah, bien non. I got to show you, Agapie en't no mo' thief 'an yo' own child'en is.' She led the way into the adjoining room of the hut.

'Yere all her things w'at she 'muse herse'f wid,' continued Seraphine, pointing to a soapbox which stood on the floor just beneath the open window. The box was filled with an indescribable assortment of odds and ends, mostly doll-rags. A catechism and a blue-backed speller poked dog-eared corners from out of the confusion; for the Valtour children were making heroic and patient efforts toward Agapie's training.

Seraphine cast herself upon her knees before the box and dived her thin brown hands among its contents. 'I wan' show you; I goin' show you,' she kept repeating excitedly. Madame Valtour was standing beside her.

Suddenly the woman drew forth from among the rags, the Dresden lady, as dapper, sound, and smiling as ever. Seraphine's hand shook so violently that she was in danger of letting the image fall to the floor. Madame Valtour reached out and took it very quietly from her. Then Seraphine rose tremblingly to her feet and broke into a sob that was pitiful to hear.

Agapie was approaching the cabin. She was a chubby girl of twelve. She walked with bare, callous feet over the rough ground and bare-headed under the hot sun. Her thick, short, black hair covered her head like a mane. She had been dancing along the path, but slackened her pace upon catching sight of the two women who had returned to the gallery. But when she perceived that her mother was crying she darted impetuously forward. In an instant she had her arms around her mother's neck, clinging so tenaciously in her youthful strength as to make the frail woman totter.

Agapie had seen the Dresden figure in Madame Valtour's possession and at once guessed the whole accusation.

'It en't so! I tell you, maman, it en't so! I neva touch' it. Stop cryin'; stop cryin'!' and she began to cry most piteously herself.

'But Agapie, we fine it in yo' box,' moaned Seraphine through her sobs.

'Then somebody put it there. Can't you see somebody put it there? 'Ten't so, I tell you.'

The scene was extremely painful to Madame Valtour. Whatever she might tell these two later, for the time she felt herself powerless to say anything befitting, and she walked away. But she turned to remark, with a hardness of expression and intention which she seldom displayed: 'No one will know of this through me. But, Agapie, you must not come into my house again; on account of the children; I could not allow it.'

As she walked away she could hear Agapie comforting her mother with renewed protestations of innocence.

Pa-Jeff began to fail visibly that year. No wonder, considering his great age, which he computed to be about one hundred. It was, in fact, some ten years less than that, but a good old age all the same. It was seldom that he got out into the field; and then, never to do any heavy work – only a little light hoeing. There were days when the 'misery' doubled him up and nailed him down to his chair so that he could not set foot beyond the door of his cabin. He would sit there courting the sunshine and blinking, as he gazed across the fields with the patience of the savage.

The Bedauts seemed to know almost instinctively when Pa-Jeff was sick. Agapie would shade her eyes and look searchingly towards the old man's cabin.

'I don' see Pa-Jeff this mo'nin',' or 'Pa-Jeff en't open his winda,' or 'I didn' see no smoke yet yonda to Pa-Jeff's.' And in a little while the girl would be over there with a pail of soup or coffee, or whatever there was at hand which she thought the old negro might fancy. She had lost all the color out of her cheeks and was pining like a sick bird.

She often sat on the steps of the gallery and talked with the old man while she waited for him to finish his soup from her tin pail.

'I tell you, Pa-Jeff, its neva been no thief in the Bedaut family. My pa say he couldn' hole up his head if he think I been a thief, me. An' maman say it would make her sick in bed, she don' know she could ever git up. Sosthène tell me the chil'en been cryin' fo' me up yonda. Li'le Lulu cry so hard M'sieur Valtour want sen' afta me, an' Ma'me Valtour say no.'

And with this, Agapie flung herself at length upon the gallery with her face buried in her arms, and began to cry so hysterically as seriously to alarm Pa-Jeff. It was well he had finished his soup, for he could not have eaten another mouthful.

'Hole up yo' head, chile. God save us! W'at you kiarrin' on dat away?' he exclaimed in great distress. 'You gwine to take a fit? Hole up yo' head.'

Agapie rose slowly to her feet, and drying her eyes upon the sleeve of her 'josie,' reached out for the tin bucket. Pa-Jeff handed it to her, but without relinquishing his hold upon it.

'War hit you w'at tuck it?' he questioned in a whisper. 'I isn' gwine tell; you knows I isn' gwine tell.' She only shook her head, attempting to draw the pail forcibly away from the old man.

'Le' me go, Pa-Jeff. W'at you doin'! Gi' me my bucket!'

He kept his old blinking eyes fastened for a while questioningly upon her disturbed and tear-stained face. Then he let her go and she turned and ran swiftly away towards her home.

He sat very still watching her disappear; only his furrowed old face twitched convulsively, moved by an unaccustomed train of reasoning that was at work in him.

'She w'ite, I is black,' he muttered calculatingly. 'She young, I is ole; sho I is ole. She good to Pa-Jeff like I her own kin an' color.' This line of thought seemed to possess him to the exclusion of every other. Late in the night he was still muttering.

'Sho I is ole. She good to Pa-Jeff, yas.'

A few days later, when Pa-Jeff happened to be feeling comparatively well, he presented himself at the house just as the family had assembled at their early dinner. Looking up suddenly, Monsieur Valtour was astonished to see him standing there in the room near the open door. He leaned upon his cane and his grizzled head was bowed upon his breast. There was general satisfaction expressed at seeing Pa-Jeff on his legs once more.

'Why, old man, I'm glad to see you out again,' exclaimed the planter, cordially, pouring a glass of wine, which he instructed Viny to hand to the old fellow. Pa-Jeff accepted the glass and set it solemnly down upon a small table near by.

'Marse Albert,' he said, 'I is come heah to-day fo' to make a statement of de rights an' de wrongs w'at is done hang heavy on my soul dis heah long time. Arter you heahs me an' de missus heahs me an' de chillun an' ev'body, den ef you says: "Pa-Jeff you kin tech yo' lips to dat glass o' wine," all well an' right.'

His manner was impressive and caused the family to exchange surprised and troubled glances. Foreseeing that his recital might be long, a chair was offered to him, but he declined it.

'One day,' he began, 'w'en I ben hoein' de madam's flower bed close to de fence, Sosthène he ride up, he say: "Heah, Pa-Jeff, heah de mail." I takes de mail f'om 'im an' I calls out to Viny w'at settin' on de gallery: "Heah Marse Albert's mail, gal; come git it."

'But Viny she answer, pert-like – des like Viny: "You is got two laigs, Pa-Jeff, des well as me." I ain't no han' fo' disputin' wid gals, so I brace up an' I come 'long to de house an' goes on in dat settin'-room dah, naix' to de dinin'-room. I lays dat mail down on Marse Albert's table; den I looks roun'.

'Ev'thing do look putty, sho! De lace cu'tains was a-flappin' an' de flowers was a-smellin' sweet, an' de pictures a-settin' back on de wall. I keep on lookin' roun'. To reckly my eye hit fall on de li'le gal w'at al'ays sets on de een' o' de mantel-shelf. She do look mighty sassy dat day, wid 'er toe a-stickin' out, des so; an' holdin' her skirt des dat away; an' lookin' at me wid her head twis'.

'I laff out. Viny mus' heahed me. I say, "g'long 'way f'om dah, gal." She keep on smilin'. I reaches out my han'. Den Satan an' de good Sperrit, dey begins to wrastle in me. De Sperrit say: "You ole fool-nigga, you; mine w'at you about." Satan keep on shovin' my han' – des so – keep on shovin'. Satan he mighty powerful dat day, an' he win de fight. I kiar dat li'le trick home in my pocket.'

Pa-Jeff lowered his head for a moment in bitter confusion. His hearers were moved with distressful astonishment. They would have had him stop the recital right there, but Pa-Jeff resumed, with an effort:

'Come dat night I heah tell how dat li'le trick, wo'th heap money; how madam, she cryin' 'cause her li'le blessed lamb was use' to play wid dat, an' kiar-on ov' it. Den I git scared. I say, "w'at I gwine do?" An' up jump Satan an' de Sperrit a-wrastlin' again.

'De Sperrit say: "Kiar hit back whar it come f'om, Pa-Jeff." Satan 'low: "Fling it in de bayeh, you ole fool." De Sperrit say: "You won't fling dat in de bayeh, whar de madam kain't neva sot eyes on hit no mo'?" Den Satan he kine give in; he 'low he plumb sick o' disputin' so long; tell me go hide it some 'eres whar dey nachelly gwine fine it. Satan he win dat fight.

'Des w'en de day g'ine break, I creeps out an' goes 'long de fiel' road. I pass by Ma'me Bedaut's house. I riclic how dey says li'le Bedaut gal ben in de sittin'-room, too, day befo'. De winda war open. Ev'body sleepin'. I tres' in my head, des like a dog w'at shame hisse'f. I sees dat box o' rags befo' my eyes; an' I drops dat li'le imp'dence 'mongst dem rags.

'Mebby yo' all t'ink Satan an' de Sperrit lef' me 'lone, arter dat?' continued Pa-Jeff, straightening himself from the relaxed position in which his members seemed to have settled.

'No, suh; dey ben desputin' straight 'long. Las' night dey come nigh onto en'in' me up. De Sperrit say: "Come 'long, I gittin' tired dis heah, you g'long up yonda an' tell de truf an' shame de devil." Satan 'low: "Stay whar you is; you heah me!" Dey clutches me. Dey twis'es an' twines me. Dey dashes me down an' jerks me up. But de Sperrit he win dat fight in de en', an' heah I is, mist'ess, master, chillun'; heah I is.'

Years later Pa-Jeff was still telling the story of his temptation and fall. The negroes especially seemed never to tire of hearing him relate it. He enlarged greatly upon the theme as he went, adding new and dramatic features which gave fresh interest to its every telling.

Agapie grew up to deserve the confidence and favors of the family. She redoubled her acts of kindness toward Pa-Jeff; but somehow she could not look into his face again.

Yet she need not have feared. Long before the end came, poor old Pa-Jeff, confused, bewildered, believed the story himself as firmly as those who had heard him tell it over and over for so many years.

The Story of an Hour

Knowing that Mrs. Mallard was afflicted with a heart trouble, great care was taken to break to her as gently as possible the news of her husband's death.

It was her sister Josephine who told her, in broken sentences; veiled hints that revealed in half concealing. Her husband's friend Richards was there, too, near her. It was he who had been in the newspaper office when intelligence of the railroad disaster was received, with Brently Mallard's name leading the list of 'killed.' He had only taken the time to assure himself of its truth by a second telegram, and had hastened to forestall any less careful, less tender friend in bearing the sad message.

She did not hear the story as many women have heard the same, with a paralyzed inability to accept its significance. She wept at once, with sudden, wild abandonment, in her sister's arms. When the storm of grief had spent itself she went away to her room alone. She would have no one follow her.

There stood, facing the open window, a comfortable, roomy armchair. Into this she sank, pressed down by a physical exhaustion that haunted her body and seemed to reach into her soul.

She could see in the open square before her house the tops of trees that were all aquiver with the new spring life. The delicious breath of rain was in the air. In the street below a peddler was crying his wares. The notes of a distant song which some one was singing reached her faintly, and countless sparrows were twittering in the eaves.

There were patches of blue sky showing here and there through the clouds that had met and piled one above the other in the west facing her window.

She sat with her head thrown back upon the cushion of the chair, quite motionless, except when a sob came up into her throat and shook her, as a child who has cried itself to sleep continues to sob in its dreams.

She was young, with a fair, calm face, whose lines bespoke

repression and even a certain strength. But now there was a dull stare in her eyes, whose gaze was fixed away off yonder on one of those patches of blue sky. It was not a glance of reflection, but rather indicated a suspension of intelligent thought.

There was something coming to her and she was waiting for it, fearfully. What was it? She did not know; it was too subtle and elusive to name. But she felt it, creeping out of the sky, reaching toward her through the sounds, the scents, the color that filled the air.

Now her bosom rose and fell tumultuously. She was beginning to recognize this thing that was approaching to possess her, and she was striving to beat it back with her will – as powerless as her two white slender hands would have been.

When she abandoned herself a little whispered word escaped her slightly parted lips. She said it over and over under her breath: 'free, free, free!' The vacant stare and the look of terror that had followed it went from her eyes. They stayed keen and bright. Her pulses beat fast, and the coursing blood warmed and relaxed every inch of her body.

She did not stop to ask if it were or were not a monstrous joy that held her. A clear and exalted perception enabled her to dismiss the suggestion as trivial.

She knew that she would weep again when she saw the kind, tender hands folded in death; the face that had never looked save with love upon her, fixed and gray and dead. But she saw beyond that bitter moment a long procession of years to come that would belong to her absolutely. And she opened and spread her arms out to them in welcome.

There would be no one to live for her during those coming years; she would live for herself. There would be no powerful will bending hers in that blind persistence with which men and women believe they have a right to impose a private will upon a fellow-creature. A kind intention or a cruel intention made the act seem no less a crime as she looked upon it in that brief moment of illumination.

And yet she had loved him – sometimes. Often she had not. What did it matter! What could love, the unsolved mystery, count for in face of this possession of self-assertion which she suddenly recognized as the strongest impulse of her being!

'Free! Body and soul free!' she kept whispering.

Josephine was kneeling before the closed door with her lips to the key-hole, imploring for admission. 'Louise, open the door! I beg; open the door – you will make yourself ill. What are you doing, Louise? For heaven's sake open the door.'

'Go away. I am not making myself ill.' No; she was drinking in a very elixir of life through that open window.

Her fancy was running riot along those days ahead of her. Spring days, and summer days, and all sorts of days that would be her own. She breathed a quick prayer that life might be long. It was only yesterday she had thought with a shudder that life might be long.

She arose at length and opened the door to her sister's importunities. There was a feverish triumph in her eyes, and she carried herself unwittingly like a goddess of Victory. She clasped her sister's waist, and together they descended the stairs. Richards stood waiting for them at the bottom.

Some one was opening the front door with a latchkey. It was Brently Mallard who entered, a little travel-stained, composedly carrying his grip-sack and umbrella. He had been far from the scene of accident, and did not even know there had been one. He stood amazed at Josephine's piercing cry; at Richards' quick motion to screen him from the view of his wife.

But Richards was too late.

When the doctors came they said she had died of heart disease – of joy that kills.

Lilacs

Mme. Adrienne Farival never announced her coming; but the good nuns knew very well when to look for her. When the scent of the lilac blossoms began to permeate the air, Sister Agathe would turn many times during the day to the window; upon her face the happy, beatific expression with which pure and simple souls watch for the coming of those they love.

But it was not Sister Agathe; it was Sister Marceline who first espied her crossing the beautiful lawn that sloped up to the convent. Her arms were filled with great bunches of lilacs which she had gathered along her path. She was clad all in brown; like one of the birds that come with the spring, the nuns used to say. Her figure was rounded and graceful, and she walked with a happy, buoyant step. The cabriolet which had conveyed her to the convent moved slowly up the gravel drive that led to the imposing entrance. Beside the driver was her modest little black trunk, with her name and address printed in white letters upon it: 'Mme. A. Farival, Paris.' It was the crunching of the gravel which had attracted Sister Marceline's attention. And then the commotion began.

White-capped heads appeared suddenly at the windows; she waved her parasol and her bunch of lilacs at them. Sister Marceline and Sister Marie Anne appeared, fluttered and expectant at the doorway. But Sister Agathe, more daring and impulsive than all, descended the steps and flew across the grass to meet her. What embraces, in which the lilacs were crushed between them! What ardent kisses! What pink flushes of happiness mounting the cheeks of the two women!

Once within the convent Adrienne's soft brown eyes moistened with tenderness as they dwelt caressingly upon the familiar objects about her, and noted the most trifling details. The white, bare boards of the floor had lost nothing of their luster. The stiff, wooden chairs, standing in rows against the walls of hall and parlor, seemed to have taken on an extra polish since she had seen them, last lilac time. And there was a new picture of the

Sacré-Coeur hanging over the hall table. What had they done with Ste. Catherine de Sienne, who had occupied that position of honor for so many years? In the chapel – it was no use trying to deceive her – she saw at a glance that St. Joseph's mantle had been embellished with a new coat of blue, and the aureole about his head freshly gilded. And the Blessed Virgin there neglected! Still wearing her garb of last spring, which looked almost dingy by contrast. It was not just – such partiality! The Holy Mother had reason to be jealous and to complain.

But Adrienne did not delay to pay her respects to the Mother Superior, whose dignity would not permit her to so much as step outside the door of her private apartments to welcome this old pupil. Indeed, she was dignity in person; large, uncompromising, unbending. She kissed Adrienne without warmth, and discussed conventional themes learnedly and prosaically during the quarter of an hour which the young woman remained in her company.

It was then that Adrienne's latest gift was brought in for inspection. For Adrienne always brought a handsome present for the chapel in her little black trunk. Last year it was a necklace of gems for the Blessed Virgin, which the Good Mother was only permitted to wear on extra occasions, such as great feast days of obligation. The year before it had been a precious crucifix – an ivory figure of Christ suspended from an ebony cross, whose extremities were tipped with wrought silver. This time it was a linen embroidered altar cloth of such rare and delicate workmanship that the Mother Superior, who knew the value of such things, chided Adrienne for the extravagance.

'But, dear Mother, you know it is the greatest pleasure I have in life – to be with you all once a year, and to bring some such trifling token of my regard.'

The Mother Superior dismissed her with the rejoinder: 'Make yourself at home, my child. Sister Thérèse will see to your wants. You will occupy Sister Marceline's bed in the end room, over the chapel. You will share the room with Sister Agathe.'

There was always one of the nuns detailed to keep Adrienne company during her fortnight's stay at the convent. This had become almost a fixed regulation. It was only during the hours of recreation that she found herself with them all together. Those were hours of much harmless merry-making under the trees or in the nuns' refectory.

This time it was Sister Agathe who waited for her outside of the Mother Superior's door. She was taller and slenderer than Adrienne, and perhaps ten years older. Her fair blonde face flushed and paled with every passing emotion that visited her soul. The two women linked arms and went together out into the open air.

There was so much which Sister Agathe felt that Adrienne must see. To begin with, the enlarged poultry yard, with its dozens upon dozens of new inmates. It took now all the time of one of the lay sisters to attend to them. There had been no change made in the vegetable garden, but – yes there had; Adrienne's quick eye at once detected it. Last year old Philippe had planted his cabbages in a large square to the right. This year they were set out in an oblong bed to the left. How it made Sister Agathe laugh to think Adrienne should have noticed such a trifle! And old Philippe, who was nailing a broken trellis not far off, was called forward to be told about it.

He never failed to tell Adrienne how well she looked, and how she was growing younger each year. And it was his delight to recall certain of her youthful and mischievous escapades. Never would he forget that day she disappeared; and the whole convent in a hubbub about it! And how at last it was he who discovered her perched among the tallest branches of the highest tree on the grounds, where she had climbed to see if she could get a glimpse of Paris! And her punishment afterwards! – half of the Gospel of Palm Sunday to learn by heart!

'We may laugh over it, my good Philippe, but we must remember that Madame is older and wiser now.'

'I know well, Sister Agathe, that one ceases to commit follies after the first days of youth.' And Adrienne seemed greatly impressed by the wisdom of Sister Agathe and old Philippe, the convent gardener.

A little later when they sat upon a rustic bench which overlooked the smiling landscape about them, Adrienne was saying to Sister Agathe, who held her hand and stroked it fondly:

'Do you remember my first visit, four years ago, Sister Agathe? and what a surprise it was to you all!'

'As if I could forget it, dear child!'

'And I! Always shall I remember that morning as I walked along the boulevard with a heaviness of heart – oh, a heaviness which I hate to recall. Suddenly there was wafted to me the sweet odor of lilac blossoms. A young girl had passed me by, carrying a great bunch of them. Did you ever know, Sister Agathe, that there is nothing which so keenly revives a memory as a perfume – an odor?'

'I believe you are right, Adrienne. For now that you speak of it, I can feel how the odor of fresh bread – when Sister Jeanne bakes – always makes me think of the great kitchen of ma tante de Sierge, and crippled Julie, who sat always knitting at the sunny window. And I never smell the sweet scented honeysuckle without living again through the blessed day of my first communion.'

'Well, that is how it was with me, Sister Agathe, when the scent of the lilacs at once changed the whole current of my thoughts and my despondency. The boulevard, its noises, its passing throng, vanished from before my senses as completely as if they had been spirited away. I was standing here with my feet sunk in the green sward as they are now. I could see the sunlight glancing from that old white stone wall, could hear the notes of birds, just as we hear them now, and the humming of insects in the air. And through all I could see and could smell the lilac blossoms, nodding invitingly to me from their thick-leaved branches. It seems to me they are richer than ever this year, Sister Agathe. And do you know, I became like an *enragée*; nothing could have kept me back. I do not remember now where I was going; but I turned and retraced my steps homeward in a perfect fever of agitation: "Sophie! my little trunk – quick – the black one! A mere handful of clothes! I am going away. Don't ask me any questions. I shall be back in a fortnight." And every year since then it is the same. At the very first whiff of a lilac blossom, I am gone! There is no holding me back.'

'And how I wait for you, and watch those lilac bushes, Adrienne! If you should once fail to come, it would be like the spring coming without the sunshine or the song of birds.

'But do you know, dear child, I have sometimes feared that in moments of despondency such as you have just described, I fear that you do not turn as you might to our Blessed Mother in heaven, who is ever ready to comfort and solace an afflicted heart with the precious balm of her sympathy and love.'

'Perhaps I do not, dear Sister Agathe. But you cannot picture the annoyances which I am constantly submitted to. That Sophie alone, with her detestable ways! I assure you she of herself is enough to drive me to St. Lazare.'

'Indeed, I do understand that the trials of one living in the world must be very great, Adrienne; particularly for you, my poor child, who have to bear them alone, since Almighty God was pleased to call to himself your dear husband. But on the other hand, to live one's life along the lines which our dear Lord traces for each one of us, must bring with it resignation and even a certain comfort. You have your household duties, Adrienne, and your music, to which, you say, you continue to devote yourself. And then, there are always good works – the poor – who are always with us – to be relieved; the afflicted to be comforted.'

'But, Sister Agathe! Will you listen! Is it not La Rose that I hear moving down there at the edge of the pasture? I fancy she is reproaching me with being an ingrate, not to have pressed a kiss yet on that white forehead of hers. Come, let us go.'

The two women arose and walked again, hand in hand this time, over the tufted grass down the gentle decline where it sloped toward the broad, flat meadow, and the limpid stream that flowed cool and fresh from the woods. Sister Agathe walked with her composed, nunlike tread; Adrienne with a balancing motion, a bounding step, as though the earth responded to her light footfall with some subtle impulse all its own.

They lingered long upon the foot-bridge that spanned the narrow stream which divided the convent grounds from the meadow beyond. It was to Adrienne indescribably sweet to rest there in soft, low converse with this gentle-faced nun, watching the approach of evening. The gurgle of the running water beneath them; the lowing of cattle approaching in the distance, were the only sounds that broke upon the stillness, until the clear tones of the angelus bell pealed out from the convent tower. At the sound both women instinctively sank to their knees, signing themselves with the sign of the cross. And Sister Agathe repeated the customary invocation, Adrienne responding in musical tones:

'The Angel of the Lord declared unto Mary,

And she conceived by the Holy Ghost—'
and so forth, to the end of the brief prayer, after which they arose
and retraced their steps toward the convent.

It was with subtle and naïve pleasure that Adrienne prepared
herself that night for bed. The room which she shared with Sister
Agathe was immaculately white. The walls were a dead white,
relieved only by one florid print depicting Jacob's dream at the
foot of the ladder, upon which angels mounted and descended.
The bare floors, a soft yellow-white, with two little patches of
gray carpet beside each spotless bed. At the head of the white-
draped beds were two *bénitiers* containing holy water absorbed in
sponges.

Sister Agathe disrobed noiselessly behind her curtains and
glided into bed without having revealed, in the faint candlelight,
as much as a shadow of herself. Adrienne pattered about the
room, shook and folded her garments with great care, placing
them on the back of a chair as she had been taught to do when a
child at the convent. It secretly pleased Sister Agathe to feel that
her dear Adrienne clung to the habits acquired in her youth.

But Adrienne could not sleep. She did not greatly desire to do
so. These hours seemed too precious to be cast into the oblivion of
slumber.

'Are you not asleep, Adrienne?'

'No, Sister Agathe. You know it is always so the first night. The
excitement of my arrival – I don't know what – keeps me awake.'

'Say your "Hail, Mary," dear child, over and over.'

'I have done so, Sister Agathe; it does not help.'

'Then lie quite still on your side and think of nothing but your
own respiration. I have heard that such inducement to sleep
seldom fails.'

'I will try. Good night, Sister Agathe.'

'Good night, dear child. May the Holy Virgin guard you.'

An hour later Adrienne was still lying with wide, wakeful eyes,
listening to the regular breathing of Sister Agathe. The trailing of
the passing wind through the treetops, the ceaseless babble of the
rivulet were some of the sounds that came to her faintly through
the night.

The days of the fortnight which followed were in character
much like the first peaceful, uneventful day of her arrival, with
the exception only that she devoutly heard mass every morning

at an early hour in the convent chapel, and on Sundays sang in the choir in her agreeable, cultivated voice, which was heard with delight and the warmest appreciation.

When the day of her departure came, Sister Agathe was not satisfied to say good-by at the portal as the others did. She walked down the drive beside the creeping old cabriolet, chattering her pleasant last words. And then she stood – it was as far as she might go – at the edge of the road, waving good-by in response to the fluttering of Adrienne's handkerchief. Four hours later Sister Agathe, who was instructing a class of little girls for their first communion, looked up at the classroom clock and murmured: 'Adrienne is at home now.'

Yes, Adrienne was at home. Paris had engulfed her.

At the very hour when Sister Agathe looked up at the clock, Adrienne, clad in a charming negligé, was reclining indolently in the depths of a luxurious armchair. The bright room was in its accustomed state of picturesque disorder. Musical scores were scattered upon the open piano. Thrown carelessly over the backs of chairs were puzzling and astonishing-looking garments.

In a large gilded cage near the window perched a clumsy green parrot. He blinked stupidly at a young girl in street dress who was exerting herself to make him talk.

In the centre of the room stood Sophie, that thorn in her mistress's side. With hands plunged in the deep pockets of her apron, her white starched cap quivering with each emphatic motion of her grizzled head, she was holding forth, to the evident ennui of the two young women. She was saying:

'Heaven knows I have stood enough in the six years I have been with Mademoiselle; but never such indignities as I have had to endure in the past two weeks at the hands of that man who calls himself a manager! The very first day – and I, good enough to notify him at once of Mademoiselle's flight – he arrives like a lion; I tell you, like a lion. He insists upon knowing Mademoiselle's whereabouts. How can I tell him any more than the statue out there in the square? He calls me a liar! Me, me – a liar! He declares he is ruined. The public will not stand La Petite Gilberta in the role which Mademoiselle has made so famous – La Petite Gilberta, who dances like a jointed wooden figure and sings like a *traînée* of a *café chantant*. If I were to tell La Gilberta that, as I

easily might, I guarantee it would not be well for the few
straggling hairs which he has left on that miserable head of his!

'What could he do? He was obliged to inform the public that
Mademoiselle was ill; and then began my real torment! Answer-
ing this one and that one with their cards, their flowers, their
dainties in covered dishes! which, I must admit, saved Florine
and me much cooking. And all the while having to tell them that
the physician had advised for Mademoiselle a rest of two weeks at
some watering-place, the name of which I had forgotten!'

Adrienne had been contemplating old Sophie with quizzical,
half-closed eyes, and pelting her with hot-house roses which lay
in her lap, and which she nipped off short from their graceful
stems for that purpose. Each rose struck Sophie full in the face;
but they did not disconcert her or once stem the torrent of her
talk.

'Oh, Adrienne!' entreated the young girl at the parrot's cage.
'Make her hush; please do something. How can you ever expect
Zozo to talk? A dozen times he has been on the point of saying
something! I tell you, she stupefies him with her chatter.'

'My good Sophie,' remarked Adrienne, not changing her
attitude, 'you see the roses are all used up. But I assure you,
anything at hand goes,' carelessly picking up a book from the
table beside her. 'What is this? Mons. Zola! Now I warn you,
Sophie, the weightiness, the heaviness of Mons. Zola are such
that they cannot fail to prostrate you; thankful you may be if
they leave you with energy to regain your feet.'

'Mademoiselle's pleasantries are all very well; but if I am to be
shown the door for it – if I am to be crippled for it – I shall say
that I think Mademoiselle is a woman without conscience and
without heart. To torture a man as she does! A man? No, an
angel!

'Each day he has come with sad visage and drooping mien.
"No news, Sophie?"

'"None, Monsieur Henri." "Have you no idea where she has
gone?" "Not any more than the statue in the square, Monsieur."
"Is it perhaps possible that she may not return at all?" with his
face blanching like that curtain.

'I assure him you will be back at the end of the fortnight. I
entreat him to have patience. He drags himself, *désolé*, about the
room, picking up Mademoiselle's fan, her gloves, her music, and

turning them over and over in his hands. Mademoiselle's slipper, which she took off to throw at me in the impatience of her departure, and which I purposely left lying where it fell on the chiffonier – he kissed it – I saw him do it – and thrust it into his pocket, thinking himself unobserved.

'The same song each day. I beg him to eat a little good soup which I have prepared. "I cannot eat, my dear Sophie." The other night he came and stood long gazing out of the window at the stars. When he turned he was wiping his eyes; they were red. He said he had been riding in the dust, which had inflamed them. But I knew better; he had been crying.

'*Ma foi!* in his place I would snap my finger at such cruelty. I would go out and amuse myself. What is the use of being young!'

Adrienne arose with a laugh. She went and seizing old Sophie by the shoulders shook her till the white cap wobbled on her head.

'What is the use of all this litany, my good Sophie? Year after year the same! Have you forgotten that I have come a long, dusty journey by rail, and that I am perishing of hunger and thirst? Bring us a bottle of Château Yquem and a biscuit and my box of cigarettes.' Sophie had freed herself, and was retreating toward the door. 'And, Sophie! If Monsieur Henri is still waiting, tell him to come up.'

It was precisely a year later. The spring had come again, and Paris was intoxicated.

Old Sophie sat in her kitchen discoursing to a neighbor who had come in to borrow some trifling kitchen utensil from the old *bonne*.

'You know, Rosalie, I begin to believe it is an attack of lunacy which seizes her once a year. I wouldn't say it to everyone, but with you I know it will go no further. She ought to be treated for it; a physician should be consulted; it is not well to neglect such things and let them run on.

'It came this morning like a thunder clap. As I am sitting here, there had been no thought or mention of a journey. The baker had come into the kitchen – you know what a gallant he is – with always a girl in his eye. He laid the bread down upon the table and beside it a bunch of lilacs. I didn't know they had

bloomed yet. "For Mam'selle Florine, with my regards," he said
with his foolish simper.

'Now, you know I was not going to call Florine from her work
in order to present her the baker's flowers. All the same, it would
not do to let them wither. I went with them in my hand into the
dining room to get a majolica pitcher which I had put away in
the closet there, on an upper shelf, because the handle was
broken. Mademoiselle, who rises early, had just come from her
bath, and was crossing the hall that opens into the dining room.
Just as she was, in her white *peignoir*, she thrust her head into the
dining room, snuffling the air and exclaiming, "What do I smell?"

'She espied the flowers in my hand and pounced upon them
like a cat upon a mouse. She held them up to her, burying her
face in them for the longest time, only uttering a long "Ah!"

'Sophie, I am going away. Get out the little black trunk; a few
of the plainest garments I have; my brown dress that I have not
yet worn.'

'"But, Mademoiselle," I protested, "you forget that you have
ordered a breakfast of a hundred francs for tomorrow."

'"Shut up!" she cried, stamping her foot.

'"You forget how the manager will rave," I persisted, "and
vilify me. And you will go like that without a word of adieu to
Monsieur Paul, who is an angel if ever one trod the earth."

'I tell you, Rosalie, her eyes flamed.

'"Do as I tell you this instant," she exclaimed, "or I will
strangle you – with your Monsieur Paul and your manager and
your hundred francs!"'

'Yes,' affirmed Rosalie, 'it is insanity. I had a cousin seized in
the same way one morning, when she smelled calf's liver frying
with onions. Before night it took two men to hold her.'

'I could well see it was insanity, my dear Rosalie, and I uttered
not another word as I feared for my life. I simply obeyed her
every command in silence. And now – whiff, she is gone! God
knows where. But between us, Rosalie – I wouldn't say it to
Florine – but I believe it is for no good. I, in Monsieur Paul's
place, should have her watched. I would put a detective upon her
track.

'Now I am going to close up; barricade the entire establish-
ment. Monsieur Paul, the manager, visitors, all – all may ring

and knock and shout themselves hoarse. I am tired of it all. To be vilified and called a liar – at my age, Rosalie!'

Adrienne left her trunk at the small railway station, as the old cabriolet was not at the moment available; and she gladly walked the mile or two of pleasant roadway which led to the convent. How infinitely calm, peaceful, penetrating was the charm of the verdant, undulating country spreading out on all sides of her! She walked along the clear smooth road, twirling her parasol; humming a gay tune; nipping here and there a bud or a waxlike leaf from the hedges along the way; and all the while drinking deep draughts of complacency and content.

She stopped, as she had always done, to pluck lilacs in her path.

As she approached the convent she fancied that a whitecapped face had glanced fleetingly from a window; but she must have been mistaken. Evidently she had not been seen, and this time would take them by surprise. She smiled to think how Sister Agathe would utter a little joyous cry of amazement, and in fancy she already felt the warmth and tenderness of the nun's embrace. And how Sister Marceline and the others would laugh, and make game of her puffed sleeves! For puffed sleeves had come into fashion since last year; and the vagaries of fashion always afforded infinite merriment to the nuns. No, they surely had not seen her.

She ascended lightly the stone steps and rang the bell. She could hear the sharp metallic sound reverberate through the halls. Before its last note had died away the door was opened very slightly, very cautiously by a lay sister who stood there with downcast eyes and flaming cheeks. Through the narrow opening she thrust forward toward Adrienne a package and a letter, saying, in confused tones: 'By order of our Mother Superior.' After which she closed the door hastily and turned the heavy key in the great lock.

Adrienne remained stunned. She could not gather her faculties to grasp the meaning of this singular reception. The lilacs fell from her arms to the stone portico on which she was standing. She turned the note and the parcel stupidly over in her hands, instinctively dreading what their contents might disclose.

The outlines of the crucifix were plainly to be felt through the wrapper of the bundle, and she guessed, without having courage to assure herself, that the jeweled necklace and the altar cloth accompanied it.

Leaning against the heavy oaken door for support, Adrienne opened the letter. She did not seem to read the few bitter reproachful lines word by word – the lines that banished her forever from this haven of peace, where her soul was wont to come and refresh itself. They imprinted themselves as a whole upon her brain, in all their seeming cruelty – she did not dare to say injustice.

There was no anger in her heart; that would doubtless possess her later, when her nimble intelligence would begin to seek out the origin of this treacherous turn. Now, there was only room for tears. She leaned her forehead against the heavy oaken panel of the door and wept with the abandonment of a little child.

She descended the steps with a nerveless and dragging tread. Once as she was walking away, she turned to look back at the imposing façade of the convent, hoping to see a familiar face, or a hand, even, giving a faint token that she was still cherished by some one faithful heart. But she saw only the polished windows looking down at her like so many cold and glittering and reproachful eyes.

In the little white room above the chapel, a woman knelt beside the bed on which Adrienne had slept. Her face was pressed deep in the pillow in her efforts to smother the sobs that convulsed her frame. It was Sister Agathe.

After a short while, a lay sister came out of the door with a broom, and swept away the lilac blossoms which Adrienne had let fall upon the portico.

The Night Came Slowly

I am losing my interest in human beings; in the significance of their lives and their actions. Some one has said it is better to study one man than ten books. I want neither books nor men; they make me suffer. Can one of them talk to me like the night – the Summer night? Like the stars or the caressing wind?

The night came slowly, softly, as I lay out there under the maple tree. It came creeping, creeping stealthily out of the valley, thinking I did not notice. And the outlines of trees and foliage nearby blended in one black mass and the night came stealing out from them, too, and from the east and west, until the only light was in the sky, filtering through the maple leaves and a star looking down through every cranny.

The night is solemn and it means mystery.

Human shapes flitted by like intangible things. Some stole up like little mice to peep at me. I did not mind. My whole being was abandoned to the soothing and penetrating charm of the night.

The katydids began their slumber song: they are at it yet. How wise they are. They do not chatter like people. They tell me only: 'sleep, sleep, sleep.' The wind rippled the maple leaves like little warm love thrills.

Why do fools cumber the Earth! It was a man's voice that broke the necromancer's spell. A man came to-day with his 'Bible Class.' He is detestable with his red cheeks and bold eyes and coarse manner and speech. What does he know of Christ? Shall I ask a young fool who was born yesterday and will die tomorrow to tell me things of Christ? I would rather ask the stars: they have seen him.

Juanita

To all appearances and according to all accounts, Juanita is a character who does not reflect credit upon her family or her native town of Rock Springs. I first met her there three years ago in the little back room behind her father's store. She seemed very shy, and inclined to efface herself; a heroic feat to attempt, considering the narrow confines of the room; and a hopeless one, in view of her five-feet-ten, and more than two-hundred pounds of substantial flesh, which, on that occasion, and every subsequent one when I saw her, was clad in a soiled calico 'Mother Hubbard.'

Her face, and particularly her mouth had a certain fresh and sensuous beauty, though I would rather not say 'beauty' if I might say anything else.

I often saw Juanita that summer, simply because it was so difficult for the poor thing not to be seen. She usually sat in some obscure corner of their small garden, or behind an angle of the house, preparing vegetables for dinner or sorting her mother's flower-seed.

It was even at that day said, with some amusement, that Juanita was not so unattractive to men as her appearance might indicate; that she had more than one admirer, and great hopes of marrying well if not brilliantly.

Upon my return to the 'Springs' this summer, in asking news of the various persons who had interested me three years ago, Juanita came naturally to my mind, and her name to my lips. There were many ready to tell me of Juanita's career since I had seen her.

The father had died and she and the mother had had ups and downs, but still continued to keep the store. Whatever else happened, however, Juanita had never ceased to attract admirers, young and old. They hung on her fence at all hours; they met her in the lanes; they penetrated to the store and back to the living-room. It was even talked about that a gentleman in a plaid suit had come all the way from the city by train for no other purpose than to call upon her. It is not astonishing, in face of these persistent attentions, that speculation grew rife in Rock Springs as to whom and what Juanita would marry in the end.

For a while she was said to be engaged to a wealthy South Missouri farmer, though no one could guess when or where she had met him. Then it was learned that the man of her choice was a Texas millionaire who possessed a hundred white horses, one of which spirited animals Juanita began to drive about that time.

But in the midst of speculation and counter speculation on the subject of Juanita and her lovers, there suddenly appeared upon the scene a one-legged man; a very poor and shabby, and decidedly one-legged man. He first became known to the public through Juanita's soliciting subscriptions towards buying the unhappy individual a cork-leg.

Her interest in the one-legged man continued to show itself in various ways, not always apparent to a curious public; as was proven one morning when Juanita became the mother of a baby, whose father, she announced, was her husband, the one-legged man. The story of a wandering preacher was told; a secret marriage in the State of Illinois; and a lost certificate.

However that may be, Juanita has turned her broad back upon the whole race of masculine bipeds, and lavishes the wealth of her undivided affections upon the one-legged man.

I caught a glimpse of the curious couple when I was in the village. Juanita had mounted her husband upon a dejected looking pony which she herself was apparently leading by the bridle, and they were moving up the lane towards the woods, whither, I am told, they often wander in this manner. The picture which they presented was a singular one; she with a man's big straw hat shading her inflamed moon-face, and the breeze bellying her soiled 'Mother Hubbard' into monstrous proportions. He puny, helpless, but apparently content with his fate which had not even vouchsafed him the coveted cork-leg.

They go off thus to the woods together where they may love each other away from all prying eyes save those of the birds and the squirrels. But what do the squirrels care!

For my part I never expected Juanita to be more respectable than a squirrel; and I don't see how any one else could have expected it.

Her Letters

I

She had given orders that she wished to remain undisturbed and moreover had locked the doors of her room.

The house was very still. The rain was falling steadily from a leaden sky in which there was no gleam, no rift, no promise. A generous wood fire had been lighted in the ample fireplace and it brightened and illumined the luxurious apartment to its furthermost corner.

From some remote nook of her writing desk the woman took a thick bundle of letters, bound tightly together with strong, coarse twine, and placed it upon the table in the centre of the room.

For weeks she had been schooling herself for what she was about to do. There was a strong deliberation in the lines of her long, thin, sensitive face; her hands, too, were long and delicate and blue-veined.

With a pair of scissors she snapped the cord binding the letters together. Thus released the ones which were top-most slid down to the table and she, with a quick movement thrust her fingers among them, scattering and turning them over till they quite covered the broad surface of the table.

Before her were envelopes of various sizes and shapes, all of them addressed in the handwriting of one man and one woman. He had sent her letters all back to her one day when, sick with dread of possibilities, she had asked to have them returned. She had meant, then, to destroy them all, his and her own. That was four years ago, and she had been feeding upon them ever since; they had sustained her, she believed, and kept her spirit from perishing utterly.

But now the days had come when the premonition of danger could no longer remain unheeded. She knew that before many months were past she would have to part from her treasure, leaving it unguarded. She shrank from inflicting the pain, the anguish which the discovery of those letters would bring to others; to one, above all, who was near to her, and whose tenderness and years of devotion had made him, in a manner, dear to her.

She calmly selected a letter at random from the pile and cast it into the roaring fire. A second one followed almost as calmly, with the third her hand began to tremble; when, in a sudden paroxysm she cast a fourth, a fifth, and a sixth into the flames in breathless succession.

Then she stopped and began to pant – for she was far from strong, and she stayed staring into the fire with pained and savage eyes. Oh, what had she done! What had she not done! With feverish apprehension she began to search among the letters before her. Which of them had she so ruthlessly, so cruelly put out of her existence? Heaven grant, not the first, that very first one, written before they had learned, or dared to say to each other 'I love you.' No, no; there it was, safe enough. She laughed with pleasure, and held it to her lips. But what if that other most precious and most imprudent one were missing! in which every word of untempered passion had long ago eaten its way into her brain; and which stirred her still to-day, as it had done a hundred times before when she thought of it. She crushed it between her palms when she found it. She kissed it again and again. With her sharp white teeth she tore the far corner from the letter, where the name was written; she bit the torn scrap and tasted it between her lips and upon her tongue like some god-given morsel.

What unbounded thankfulness she felt at not having destroyed them all! How desolate and empty would have been her remaining days without them; with only her thoughts, illusive thoughts that she could not hold in her hands and press, as she did these, to her cheeks and her heart.

This man had changed the water in her veins to wine, whose taste had brought delirium to both of them. It was all one and past now, save for these letters that she held encircled in her arms. She stayed breathing softly and contentedly, with the hectic cheek resting upon them.

She was thinking, thinking of a way to keep them without possible ultimate injury to that other one whom they would stab more cruelly than keen knife blades.

At last she found the way. It was a way that frightened and

bewildered her to think of at first, but she had reached it by deduction too sure to admit of doubt. She meant, of course, to destroy them herself before the end came. But how does the end come and when? Who may tell? She would guard against the possibility of accident by leaving them in charge of the very one who, above all, should be spared a knowledge of their contents.

She roused herself from the stupor of thought and gathered the scattered letters once more together, binding them again with the rough twine. She wrapped the compact bundle in a thick sheet of white polished paper. Then she wrote in ink upon the back of it, in large, firm characters:

'I leave this package to the care of my husband. With perfect faith in his loyalty and his love, I ask him to destroy it unopened.'

It was not sealed; only a bit of string held the wrapper, which she could remove and replace at will whenever the humor came to her to pass an hour in some intoxicating dream of the days when she felt she had lived.

II

If he had come upon that bundle of letters in the first flush of his poignant sorrow there would not have been an instant's hesitancy. To destroy it promptly and without question would have seemed a welcome expression of devotion – a way of reaching her, of crying out his love to her while the world was still filled with the illusion of her presence. But months had passed since that spring day when they had found her stretched upon the floor, clutching the key of her writing desk, which she appeared to have been attempting to reach when death overtook her.

The day was much like that day a year ago when the leaves were falling and rain pouring steadily from a leaden sky which held no gleam, no promise. He had happened accidentally upon the package in that remote nook of her desk. And just as she herself had done a year ago, he carried it to the table and laid it down there, standing, staring with puzzled eyes at the message which confronted him:

'I leave this package to the care of my husband. With perfect faith in his loyalty and his love, I ask him to destroy it unopened.'

She had made no mistake; every line of his face – no longer

young – spoke loyalty and honesty, and his eyes were as faithful as a dog's and as loving. He was a tall, powerful man, standing there in the firelight, with shoulders that stooped a little, and hair that was growing somewhat thin and gray, and a face that was distinguished, and must have been handsome when he smiled. But he was slow. 'Destroy it unopened,' he re-read, half-aloud, 'but why unopened?'

He took the package again in his hands, and turning it about and feeling it, discovered that it was composed of many letters tightly packed together.

So here were letters which she was asking him to destroy unopened. She had never seemed in her lifetime to have had a secret from him. He knew her to have been cold and passionless, but true, and watchful of his comfort and his happiness. Might he not be holding in his hands the secret of some other one, which had been confided to her and which she had promised to guard? But, no, she would have indicated the fact by some additional word or line. The secret was her own, something contained in these letters, and she wanted it to die with her.

If he could have thought of her as on some distant shadowy shore waiting for him throughout the years with outstretched hands to come and join her again, he would not have hesitated. With hopeful confidence he would have thought 'in that blessed meeting-time, soul to soul, she will tell me all; till then I can wait and trust.' But he could not think of her in any far-off paradise awaiting him. He felt that there was no smallest part of her anywhere in the universe, more than there had been before she was born into the world. But she had embodied herself with terrible significance in an intangible wish, uttered when life still coursed through her veins; knowing that it would reach him when the annihilation of death was between them, but uttered with all confidence in its power and potency. He was moved by the splendid daring of the act, which at the same time exalted him and lifted him above the head of common mortals.

What secret save one could a woman choose to have die with her? As quickly as the suggestion came to his mind, so swiftly did the man-instinct of possession stir in his blood. His fingers cramped about the package in his hands, and he sank into a chair beside the table. The agonizing suspicion that perhaps another had shared with him her thoughts, her affections, her life, deprived him for a swift instant of honor and reason. He thrust the end of his strong thumb beneath the string which, with a single turn would have yielded – 'with perfect faith in your loyalty and your love.' It was not the written characters addressing themselves to the eye; it was like a voice speaking to his soul. With a tremor of anguish he bowed his head down upon the letters.

A half-hour passed before he lifted his head. An unspeakable conflict had raged within him, but his loyalty and his love had conquered. His face was pale and deep-lined with suffering, but there was no more hesitancy to be seen there.

He did not for a moment think of casting the thick package into the flames to be licked by the fiery tongues, and charred and half-revealed to his eyes. That was not what she meant. He arose, and taking a heavy bronze paper-weight from the table, bound it securely to the package. He walked to the window and looked out into the street below. Darkness had come, and it was still raining. He could hear the rain dashing against the window-panes, and could see it falling through the dull yellow rim of light cast by the lighted street lamp.

He prepared himself to go out, and when quite ready to leave the house thrust the weighted package into the deep pocket of his top-coat.

He did not hurry along the street as most people were doing at that hour, but walked with a long, slow, deliberate step, not seeming to mind the penetrating chill and rain driving into his face despite the shelter of his umbrella.

His dwelling was not far removed from the business section of the city; and it was not a great while before he found himself at the entrance of the bridge that spanned the river – the deep, broad, swift, black river dividing two States. He walked on and out to the very centre of the structure. The wind was blowing fiercely and keenly. The darkness where he stood was impenetrable. The thousands of lights in the city he had left seemed like all the stars of heaven massed together, sinking into some distant mysterious horizon, leaving him alone in a black, boundless universe.

He drew the package from his pocket and leaning as far as he could over the broad stone rail of the bridge, cast it from him into the river. It fell straight and swiftly from his hand. He could not follow its descent through the darkness, nor hear its dip into the water far below. It vanished silently; seemingly into some inky unfathomable space. He felt as if he were flinging it back to her in that unknown world whither she had gone.

III

An hour or two later he sat at his table in the company of several men whom he had invited that day to dine with him. A weight had settled upon his spirit, a conviction, a certitude that there could be but one secret which a woman would choose to have die with her. This one thought was possessing him. It occupied his brain, keeping it nimble and alert with suspicion. It clutched his heart, making every breath of existence a fresh moment of pain.

The men about him were no longer the friends of yesterday; in each one he discerned a possible enemy. He attended absently to their talk. He was remembering how she had conducted herself toward this one and that one; striving to recall conversations, subtleties of facial expression that might have meant what he did not suspect at the moment, shades of meaning in words that had seemed the ordinary interchange of social amenities.

He led the conversation to the subject of women, probing these men for their opinions and experiences. There was not one but claimed some infallible power to command the affections of any woman whom his fancy might select. He had heard the empty boast before from the same group and had always met it with good-humored contempt. But to-night every flagrant, inane utterance was charged with a new meaning, revealing possibilities that he had hitherto never taken into account.

He was glad when they were gone. He was eager to be alone, not from any desire or intention to sleep. He was impatient to regain her room, that room in which she had lived a large portion of her life, and where he had found those letters. There must surely be more of them somewhere, he thought; some forgotten scrap, some written thought or expression lying unguarded by an inviolable command.

At the hour when he usually retired for the night he sat himself down before her writing desk and began the search of drawers, slides, pigeon-holes, nooks and corners. He did not leave a scrap of anything unread. Many of the letters which he found were old; some he had read before; others were new to him. But in none did he find a faintest evidence that his wife had not been the true and loyal woman he had always believed her to be. The night was nearly spent before the fruitless search ended. The brief, troubled sleep which he snatched before his hour for rising was freighted with feverish, grotesque dreams, through all of which he could hear and could see dimly the dark river rushing by, carrying away his heart, his ambitions, his life.

But it was not alone in letters that women betrayed their emotions, he thought. Often he had known them, especially when in love, to mark fugitive, sentimental passages in books of verse or prose, thus expressing and revealing their own hidden thought. Might she not have done the same?

Then began a second and far more exhausting and arduous quest than the first, turning, page by page, the volumes that crowded her room – books of fiction, poetry, philosophy. She had read them all; but nowhere, by the shadow of a sign, could he find that the author had echoed the secret of her existence – the secret which he had held in his hands and had cast into the river.

He began cautiously and gradually to question this one and that one, striving to learn by indirect ways what each had thought of her. Foremost he learned she had been unsympathetic because of her coldness of manner. One had admired her intellect; another her accomplishments; a third had thought her beautiful before disease claimed her, regretting, however, that her beauty had lacked warmth of color and expression. She was praised by some for gentleness and kindness, and by others for cleverness and tact. Oh, it was useless to try to discover anything from men! He might have known. It was women who would talk of what they knew.

They did talk, unreservedly. Most of them had loved her; those who had not had held her in respect and esteem.

IV

And yet, and yet, 'there is but one secret which a woman would choose to have die with her,' was the thought which continued to haunt him and deprive him of rest. Days and nights of uncertainty began slowly to unnerve him and to torture him. An assurance of the worst that he dreaded would have offered him peace most welcome, even at the price of happiness.

It seemed no longer of any moment to him that men should come and go; and fall or rise in the world; and wed and die. It did not signify if money came to him by a turn of chance or eluded him. Empty and meaningless seemed to him all devices which the world offers for man's entertainment. The food and the drink set before him had lost their flavor. He did not longer know or care if the sun shone or the clouds lowered about him. A cruel hazard had struck him there where he was weakest, shattering his whole being, leaving him with but one wish in his soul, one gnawing desire, to know the mystery which he had held in his hands and had cast into the river.

One night when there were no stairs shining he wandered, restless, upon the streets. He no longer sought to know from men and women what they dared not or could not tell him. Only the river knew. He went and stood again upon the bridge where he had stood many an hour since that night when the darkness then had closed around him and engulfed his manhood.

Only the river knew. It babbled, and he listened to it, and it told him nothing, but it promised all. He could hear it promising him with caressing voice, peace and sweet repose. He could hear the sweep, the song of the water inviting him.

A moment more and he had gone to seek her, and to join her and her secret thought in the immeasurable rest.

Odalie Misses Mass

Odalie sprang down from the mulecart, shook out her white skirts, and firmly grasping her parasol, which was blue to correspond with her sash, entered Aunt Pinky's gate and proceeded towards the old woman's cabin. She was a thick-waisted young thing who walked with a firm tread and carried her head with a determined poise. Her straight brown hair had been rolled up over night in papillotes, and the artificial curls stood out in clusters, stiff and uncompromising beneath the rim of her white chip hat. Her mother, sister and brother remained seated in the cart before the gate.

It was the fifteenth of August, the great feast of the Assumption, so generally observed in the Catholic parishes of Louisiana. The Chotard family were on their way to mass, and Odalie had insisted upon stopping to 'show herself' to her old friend and protégée, Aunt Pinky.

The helpless, shrivelled old negress sat in the depths of a large, rudely-fashioned chair. A loosely hanging unbleached cotton gown enveloped her mite of a figure. What was visible of her hair beneath the bandana turban, looked like white sheep's wool. She wore round, silver-rimmed spectacles, which gave her an air of wisdom and respectability, and she held in her hand the branch of a hickory sapling, with which she kept mosquitoes and flies at bay, and even chickens and pigs that sometimes penetrated the heart of her domain.

Odalie walked straight up to the old woman and kissed her on the cheek.

'Well, Aunt Pinky, yere I am,' she announced with evident self-complacency, turning herself slowly and stiffly around like a mechanical dummy. In one hand she held her prayer-book, fan and handkerchief, in the other the blue parasol, still open; and on her plump hands were blue cotton mitts. Aunt Pinky beamed and chuckled; Odalie hardly expected her to be able to do more.

'Now you saw me,' the child continued. 'I reckon you satisfied.

I mus' go; I ain't got a minute to was'e.' But at the threshold she
turned to inquire, bluntly:

'W'ere's Pug?'

'Pug,' replied Aunt Pinky, in her tremulous old-woman's voice.
'She's gone to chu'ch; done gone; she done gone,' nodding her
head in seeming approval of Pug's action.

'To church!' echoed Odalie with a look of consternation
settling in her round eyes.

'She gone to chu'ch,' reiterated Aunt Pinky. 'Say she kain't
miss chu'ch on de fifteent'; de debble gwine pester her twell
jedgment, she miss chu'ch on de fifteent'.'

Odalie's plump cheeks fairly quivered with indignation and she
stamped her foot. She looked up and down the long, dusty road
that skirted the river. Nothing was to be seen save the blue cart
with its dejected looking mule and patient occupants. She walked
to the end of the gallery and called out to a negro boy whose
black bullet-head showed up in bold relief against the white of
the cotton patch:

'He, Baptiste! w'ere's yo' ma? Ask yo' ma if she can't come set
with Aunt Pinky.'

'Mammy, she gone to chu'ch,' screamed Baptiste in answer.

'Bonté! w'at's taken you all darkies with yo' "church" to-day?
You come along yere Baptiste an' set with Aunt Pinky. That Pug!
I'm goin' to make yo' ma wear her out fo' that trick of hers –
leavin' Aunt Pinky like that.'

But at the first intimation of what was wanted of him, Baptiste
dipped below the cotton like a fish beneath water, leaving no
sight nor sound of himself to answer Odalie's repeated calls. Her
mother and sister were beginning to show signs of impatience.

'But, I can't go,' she cried out to them. 'It's nobody to stay with
Aunt Pinky. I can't leave Aunt Pinky like that, to fall out of her
chair, maybe, like she already fell out once.'

'You goin' to miss mass on the fifteenth, you, Odalie! W'at you
thinkin' about?' came in shrill rebuke from her sister. But her
mother offering no objection, the boy lost not a moment in
starting the mule forward at a brisk trot. She watched them
disappear in a cloud of dust; and turning with a dejected, almost
tearful countenance, re-entered the room.

Aunt Pinky seemed to accept her reappearance as a matter of
course; and even evinced no surprise at seeing her remove her

hat and mitts, which she laid carefully, almost religiously, on the bed, together with her book, fan and handkerchief.

Then Odalie went and seated herself some distance from the old woman in her own small, low rocking-chair. She rocked herself furiously, making a great clatter with the rockers over the wide, uneven boards of the cabin floor; and she looked out through the open door.

'Puggy, she done gone to chu'ch; done gone. Say de debble gwine pester her twell jedgment—'

'You done tole me that, Aunt Pinky; neva mine; don't le's talk about it.'

Aunt Pinky thus rebuked, settled back into silence and Odalie continued to rock and stare out of the door.

Once she arose, and taking the hickory branch from Aunt Pinky's nerveless hand, made a bold and sudden charge upon a little pig that seemed bent upon keeping her company. She pursued him with flying heels and loud cries as far as the road. She came back flushed and breathless and her curls hanging rather limp around her face; she began again to rock herself and gaze silently out of the door.

'You gwine make yo' fus' c'mmunion?'

This seemingly sober inquiry on the part of Aunt Pinky at once shattered Odalie's ill-humor and dispelled every shadow of it. She leaned back and laughed with wild abandonment.

'Mais w'at you thinkin' about, Aunt Pinky? How you don't remember I made my firs' communion las' year, with this same dress w'at maman let out the tuck,' holding up the altered skirt for Aunt Pinky's inspection. 'An' with this same petticoat w'at maman added this ruffle an' crochet' edge; excep' I had a w'ite sash.'

These evidences proved beyond question convincing and seemed to satisfy Aunt Pinky. Odalie rocked as furiously as ever, but she sang now, and the swaying chair had worked its way nearer to the old woman.

'You gwine git mar'ied?'

'I declare, Aunt Pinky,' said Odalie, when she had ceased laughing and was wiping her eyes, 'I declare, sometime' I think you gittin' plumb foolish. How you expec' me to git married w'en I'm on'y thirteen?'

Evidently Aunt Pinky did not know why or how she expected

anything so preposterous; Odalie's holiday attire that filled her with contemplative rapture, had doubtless incited her to these vagaries.

The child now drew her chair quite close to the old woman's knee after she had gone out to the rear of the cabin to get herself some water and had brought a drink to Aunt Pinky in the gourd dipper.

There was a strong, hot breeze blowing from the river, and it swept fitfully and in gusts through the cabin, bringing with it the weedy smell of cacti that grew thick on the bank, and occasionally a shower of reddish dust from the road. Odalie for a while was greatly occupied in keeping in place her filmy skirt, which every gust of wind swelled balloon-like about her knees. Aunt Pinky's little black, scrawny hand had found its way among the droopy curls, and strayed often caressingly to the child's plump neck and shoulders.

'You riclics, honey, dat day yo' granpappy say it wur pinchin' times an' he reckin he bleege to sell Yallah Tom an' Susan an' Pinky? Don' know how come he think 'bout Pinky, 'less caze he sees me playin' an' trapsin' roun' wid you alls, day in an' out. I riclics yit how you tu'n w'ite like milk an' fling yo' arms roun' li'le black Pinky; an' you cries out you don' wan' no saddle-mar'; you don' wan' no silk dresses and fing' rings an' sich; an' don' wan' no idication; des wants Pinky. An' you cries an' screams an' kicks, an' 'low you gwine kill fus' pusson w'at dar come an' buy Pinky an' kiars her off. You riclics dat, honey?'

Odalie had grown accustomed to these flights of fancy on the part of her old friend; she liked to humor her as she chose to sometimes humor very small children; so she was quite used to impersonating one dearly beloved but impetuous, 'Paulette,' who seemed to have held her place in old Pinky's heart and imagination through all the years of her suffering life.

'I rec'lec' like it was yesterday, Aunt Pinky. How I scream an' kick an' maman gave me some med'cine; an' how you scream an' kick an' Susan took you down to the quarters an' give you "twenty".'

'Das so, honey; des like you says,' chuckled Aunt Pinky. 'But you don' riclic dat time you cotch Pinky cryin' down in de holler behine de gin; an' you say you gwine give me "twenty" ef I don' tell you w'at I cryin' 'bout?'

'I rec'lec' like it happen'd to-day, Aunt Pinky. You been cryin' because you want to marry Hiram, ole Mr. Benitou's servant.'

'Das true like you says, Miss Paulette; an' you goes home an' cries and kiars on an' won' eat, an' breaks dishes, an' pesters yo' gran'pap 'tell he bleedge to buy Hi'um fom de Benitous.'

'Don't talk, Aunt Pink! I can see all that jus' as plain!' responded Odalie sympathetically, yet in truth she took but a languid interest in these reminiscences which she had listened to so often before.

She leaned her flushed cheek against Aunt Pinky's knee.

The air was rippling now, and hot and caressing. There was the hum of bumble bees outside; and busy mud-daubers kept flying in and out through the door. Some chickens had penetrated to the very threshold in their aimless roamings, and the little pig was approaching more cautiously. Sleep was fast overtaking the child, but she could still hear through her drowsiness the familiar tones of Aunt Pinky's voice.

'But Hi'um, he done gone; he nuva come back; an' Yallah Tom nuva come back; an' ole Marster an' de chillun – all gone – nuva come back. Nobody nuva come back to Pinky 'cep you, my honey. You ain' gwine 'way fom Pinky no mo', is you, Miss Paulette?'

'Don' fret, Aunt Pinky – I'm goin' – to stay with – you.'

'No pussun nuva come back 'cep' you.'

Odalie was fast asleep. Aunt Pinky was asleep with her head leaning back on her chair and her fingers thrust into the mass of tangled brown hair that swept across her lap. The chickens and little pig walked fearlessly in and out. The sunlight crept close up to the cabin door and stole away again.

Odalie awoke with a start. Her mother was standing over her arousing her from sleep. She sprang up and rubbed her eyes. 'Oh, I been asleep!' she exclaimed. The cart was standing in the road waiting. 'An' Aunt Pinky, she's asleep, too.'

'Yes, chérie, Aunt Pinky is asleep,' replied her mother, leading Odalie away. But she spoke low and trod softly as gentle-souled women do, in the presence of the dead.

Athénaïse

I

Athénaïse went away in the morning to make a visit to her parents, ten miles back on rigolet de Bon Dieu. She did not return in the evening, and Cazeau, her husband, fretted not a little. He did not worry much about Athénaïse, who, he suspected, was resting only too content in the bosom of her family; his chief solicitude was manifestly for the pony she had ridden. He felt sure those 'lazy pigs,' her brothers, were capable of neglecting it seriously. This misgiving Cazeau communicated to his servant, old Félicité, who waited upon him at supper.

His voice was low pitched, and even softer than Félicité's. He was tall, sinewy, swarthy, and altogether severe looking. His thick black hair waved, and it gleamed like the breast of a crow. The sweep of his mustache, which was not so black, outlined the broad contour of the mouth. Beneath the under lip grew a small tuft which he was much given to twisting, and which he permitted to grow, apparently for no other purpose. Cazeau's eyes were dark blue, narrow and overshadowed. His hands were coarse and stiff from close acquaintance with farming tools and implements, and he handled his fork and knife clumsily. But he was distinguished looking, and succeeded in commanding a good deal of respect, and even fear sometimes.

He ate his supper alone, by the light of a single coal-oil lamp that but faintly illuminated the big room, with its bare floor and huge rafters, and its heavy pieces of furniture that loomed dimly in the gloom of the apartment. Félicité, ministering to his wants, hovered about the table like a little, bent, restless shadow.

She served him with a dish of sunfish fried crisp and brown. There was nothing else set before him beside the bread and butter and the bottle of red wine which she locked carefully in the buffet after he had poured his second glass. She was occupied with her mistress's absence, and kept reverting to it after he had expressed his solicitude about the pony.

'Dat beat me! on'y marry two mont', an' got de head turn' a'ready to go 'broad. C'est pas Chrétien, tenez!'

Cazeau shrugged his shoulders for answer, after he had drained his glass and pushed aside his plate. Félicité's opinion of the unchristianlike behavior of his wife in leaving him thus alone after two months of marriage weighed little with him. He was used to solitude, and did not mind a day or a night or two of it. He had lived alone ten years, since his first wife died, and Félicité might have known better than to suppose that he cared. He told her she was a fool. It sounded like a compliment in his modulated, caressing voice. She grumbled to herself as she set about clearing the table, and Cazeau arose and walked outside on the gallery; his spur, which he had not removed upon entering the house, jangled at every step.

The night was beginning to deepen, and to gather black about the clusters of trees and shrubs that were grouped in the yard. In the beam of light from the open kitchen door a black boy stood feeding a brace of snarling, hungry dogs; further away, on the steps of a cabin, some one was playing the accordion; and in still another direction a little negro baby was crying lustily. Cazeau walked around to the front of the house, which was square, squat and one-story.

A belated wagon was driving in at the gate, and the impatient driver was swearing hoarsely at his jaded oxen. Félicité stepped out on the gallery, glass and polishing towel in hand, to investigate, and to wonder, too, who could be singing out on the river. It was a party of young people paddling around, waiting for the moon to rise, and they were singing Juanita, their voices coming tempered and melodious through the distance and the night.

Cazeau's horse was waiting, saddled, ready to be mounted, for Cazeau had many things to attend to before bed-time; so many things that there was not left to him a moment in which to think of Athénaïse. He felt her absence, though, like a dull, insistent pain.

However, before he slept that night he was visited by the thought of her, and by a vision of her fair young face with its drooping lips and sullen and averted eyes. The marriage had been a blunder; he had only to look into her eyes to feel that, to discover her growing aversion. But it was a thing not by any possibility to be undone. He was quite prepared to make the best of it, and expected no less than a like effort on her part. The less she revisited the rigolet, the better. He would find means to keep her at home hereafter.

These unpleasant reflections kept Cazeau awake far into the night, notwithstanding the craving of his whole body for rest and sleep. The moon was shining, and its pale effulgence reached dimly into the room, and with it a touch of the cool breath of the spring night. There was an unusual stillness abroad; no sound to be heard save the distant, tireless, plaintive notes of the accordion.

II

Athénaïse did not return the following day, even though her husband sent her word to do so by her brother, Montéclin, who passed on his way to the village early in the morning.

On the third day Cazeau saddled his horse and went himself in search of her. She had sent no word, no message, explaining her absence, and he felt that he had good cause to be offended. It was rather awkward to have to leave his work, even though late in the afternoon, – Cazeau had always so much to do; but among the many urgent calls upon him, the task of bringing his wife back to a sense of her duty seemed to him for the moment paramount.

The Michés, Athénaïse's parents, lived on the old Gotrain place. It did not belong to them; they were 'running' it for a merchant in Alexandria. The house was far too big for their use. One of the lower rooms served for the storing of wood and tools; the person 'occupying' the place before Miché having pulled up the flooring in despair of being able to patch it. Upstairs, the rooms were so large, so bare, that they offered a constant temptation to lovers of the dance, whose importunities Madame Miché was accustomed to meet with amiable indulgence. A dance at Miché's and a plate of Madame Miché's gumbo filé at midnight were pleasures not to be neglected or despised, unless by such serious souls as Cazeau.

Long before Cazeau reached the house his approach had been observed, for there was nothing to obstruct the view of the outer road; vegetation was not yet abundantly advanced, and there was but a patchy, straggling stand of cotton and corn in Miché's field.

Madame Miché, who had been seated on the gallery in a rocking-chair, stood up to greet him as he drew near. She was short and fat, and wore a black skirt and loose muslin sack fastened at the throat with a hair brooch. Her own hair, brown and glossy, showed but a few threads of silver. Her round pink face was cheery, and her eyes were bright and good humored. But she was plainly perturbed and ill at ease as Cazeau advanced.

Montéclin, who was there too, was not ill at ease, and made no attempt to disguise the dislike with which his brother-in-law inspired him. He was a slim, wiry fellow of twenty-five, short of stature like his mother, and resembling her in feature. He was in shirt-sleeves, half leaning, half sitting, on the insecure railing of the gallery, and fanning himself with his broad-rimmed felt hat.

'Cochon!' he muttered under his breath as Cazeau mounted the stairs, – 'sacré cochon!'

'Cochon' had sufficiently characterized the man who had once on a time declined to lend Montéclin money. But when this same man had had the presumption to propose marriage to his well-beloved sister, Athénaïse, and the honor to be accepted by her, Montéclin felt that a qualifying epithet was needed fully to express his estimate of Cazeau.

Miché and his oldest son were absent. They both esteemed Cazeau highly, and talked much of his qualities of head and heart, and thought much of his excellent standing with city merchants.

Athénaïse had shut herself up in her room. Cazeau had seen her rise and enter the house at perceiving him. He was a good deal mystified, but no one could have guessed it when he shook hands with Madame Miché. He had only nodded to Montéclin, with a muttered 'Comment ça va?'

'Tiens! something tole me you were coming to-day!' exclaimed Madame Miché, with a little blustering appearance of being cordial and at ease, as she offered Cazeau a chair.

He ventured a short laugh as he seated himself.

'You know, nothing would do,' she went on, with much gesture of her small, plump hands, 'nothing would do but

Athénaïse mus' stay las' night fo' a li'le dance. The boys wouldn' year to their sister leaving.'

Cazeau shrugged his shoulders significantly, telling as plainly as words that he knew nothing about it.

'Comment! Montéclin didn' tell you we were going to keep Athénaïse?' Montéclin had evidently told nothing.

'An' how about the night befo',' questioned Cazeau, 'an' las' night? It isn't possible you dance every night out yere on the Bon Dieu!'

Madame Miché laughed, with amiable appreciation of the sarcasm; and turning to her son, 'Montéclin, my boy, go tell yo' sister that Monsieur Cazeau is yere.'

Montéclin did not stir except to shift his position and settle himself more securely on the railing.

'Did you year me, Montéclin?'

'Oh yes, I yeard you plain enough,' responded her son, 'but you know as well as me it's no use to tell 'Thénaïse anything. You been talkin' to her yo'se'f since Monday; an' pa's preached himse'f hoa'se on the subject; an' you even had uncle Achille down yere yesterday to reason with her. W'en 'Thénaïse said she wasn' goin' to set her foot back in Cazeau's house, she meant it.'

This speech, which Montéclin delivered with thorough unconcern, threw his mother into a condition of painful but dumb embarrassment. It brought two fiery red spots to Cazeau's cheeks, and for the space of a moment he looked wicked.

What Montéclin had spoken was quite true, though his taste in the manner and choice of time and place in saying it were not of the best. Athénaïse, upon the first day of her arrival, had announced that she came to stay, having no intention of returning under Cazeau's roof. The announcement had scattered consternation, as she knew it would. She had been implored, scolded, entreated, stormed at, until she felt herself like a dragging sail that all the winds of heaven had beaten upon. Why in the name of God had she married Cazeau? Her father had lashed her with the question a dozen times. Why indeed? It was difficult now for her to understand why, unless because she supposed it was customary for girls to marry when the right opportunity came. Cazeau, she knew, would make life more comfortable for her; and again, she had liked him, and had even been rather flustered when he pressed her hands and kissed them, and kissed her lips and cheeks and eyes, when she accepted him.

Montéclin himself had taken her aside to talk the thing over. The turn of affairs was delighting him.

'Come, now, 'Thénaïse, you mus' explain to me all about it, so we can settle on a good cause, an' secu' a separation fo' you. Has he been mistreating an' abusing you, the sacré cochon?' They were alone together in her room, whither she had taken refuge from the angry domestic elements.

'You please to reserve yo' disgusting expressions, Montéclin. No, he has not abused me in any way that I can think.'

'Does he drink? Come 'Thénaïse, think well over it. Does he ever get drunk?'

'Drunk! Oh, mercy, no, – Cazeau never gets drunk.'

'I see; it's jus' simply you feel like me; you hate him.'

'No, I don't hate him,' she returned reflectively; adding with a sudden impulse, 'It's jus' being married that I detes' an' despise. I hate being Mrs. Cazeau, an' would want to be Athénaïse Miché again. I can't stan' to live with a man; to have him always there; his coats an' pantaloons hanging in my room; his ugly bare feet – washing them in my tub, befo' my very eyes, ugh!' She shuddered with recollections, and resumed, with a sigh that was almost a sob: 'Mon Dieu, mon Dieu! Sister Marie Angélique knew w'at she was saying; she knew me better than myse'f w'en she said God had sent me a vocation an' I was turning deaf ears. W'en I think of a blessed life in the convent, at peace! Oh, w'at was I dreaming of!' and then the tears came.

Montéclin felt disconcerted and greatly disappointed at having obtained evidence that would carry no weight with a court of justice. The day had not come when a young woman might ask the court's permission to return to her mamma on the sweeping ground of a constitutional disinclination for marriage. But if there was no way of untying this Gordian knot of marriage, there was surely a way of cutting it.

'Well, 'Thénaïse, I'm mighty durn sorry you got no better groun's 'an w'at you say. But you can count on me to stan' by you w'atever you do. God knows I don' blame you fo' not wantin' to live with Cazeau.'

And now there was Cazeau himself, with the red spots flaming in his swarthy cheeks, looking and feeling as if he wanted to thrash Montéclin into some semblance of decency. He arose abruptly, and approaching the room which he had seen his wife enter, thrust open the door after a hasty preliminary knock. Athénaïse, who was standing erect at a far window, turned at his entrance.

She appeared neither angry nor frightened, but thoroughly unhappy, with an appeal in her soft dark eyes and a tremor on her lips that seemed to him expressions of unjust reproach, that wounded and maddened him at once. But whatever he might feel, Cazeau knew only one way to act toward a woman.

'Athénaïse, you are not ready?' he asked in his quiet tones. 'It's getting late; we havn' any time to lose.'

She knew that Montéclin had spoken out, and she had hoped for a wordy interview, a stormy scene, in which she might have held her own as she had held it for the past three days against her family, with Montéclin's aid. But she had no weapon with which to combat subtlety. Her husband's looks, his tones, his mere presence, brought to her a sudden sense of hopelessness, an instinctive realization of the futility of rebellion against a social and sacred institution.

Cazeau said nothing further, but stood waiting in the doorway. Madame Miché had walked to the far end of the gallery, and pretended to be occupied with having a chicken driven from her parterre. Montéclin stood by, exasperated, fuming, ready to burst out.

Athénaïse went and reached for her riding skirt that hung against the wall. She was rather tall, with a figure which, though not robust, seemed perfect in its fine proportions. 'La fille de son père,' she was often called, which was a great compliment to Miché. Her brown hair was brushed all fluffily back from her temples and low forehead, and about her features and expression lurked a softness, a prettiness, a dewiness, that were perhaps too childlike, that savored of immaturity.

She slipped the riding-skirt, which was of black alpaca, over her head, and with impatient fingers hooked it at the waist over her pink linen-lawn. Then she fastened on her white sunbonnet and reached for her gloves on the mantelpiece.

'If you don' wan' to go, you know w'at you got to do, 'Thénaïse,' fumed Montéclin. 'You don' set yo' feet back on Cane River, by God, unless you want to, – not w'ile I'm alive.'

Cazeau looked at him as if he were a monkey whose antics fell short of being amusing.

Athénaïse still made no reply, said not a word. She walked rapidly past her husband, past her brother; bidding good-bye to no one, not even to her mother. She descended the stairs, and without assistance from any one mounted the pony, which Cazeau had ordered to be saddled upon his arrival. In this way she obtained a fair start of her husband, whose departure was far more leisurely, and for the greater part of the way she managed to keep an appreciable gap between them. She rode almost madly at first, with the wind inflating her skirt balloon-like about her knees, and her sunbonnet falling back between her shoulders.

At no time did Cazeau make an effort to overtake her until traversing an old fallow meadow that was level and hard as a table. The sight of a great solitary oak-tree, with its seemingly immutable outlines, that had been a landmark for ages – or was it the odor of elderberry stealing up from the gully to the south? or what was it that brought vividly back to Cazeau, by some association of ideas, a scene of many years ago? He had passed that old live-oak hundreds of times, but it was only now that the memory of one day came back to him. He was a very small boy that day, seated before his father on horse-back. They were proceeding slowly, and Black Gabe was moving on before them at a little dog-trot. Black Gabe had run away, and had been discovered back in the Gotrain swamp. They had halted beneath this big oak to enable the negro to take breath; for Cazeau's father was a kind and considerate master, and every one had agreed at the time that Black Gabe was a fool, a great idiot indeed, for wanting to run away from him.

The whole impression was for some reason hideous, and to dispel it Cazeau spurred his horse to a swift gallop. Overtaking his wife, he rode the remainder of the way at her side in silence.

It was late when they reached home. Félicité was standing on the grassy edge of the road, in the moonlight, waiting for them.

Cazeau once more ate his supper alone; for Athénaïse went to her room, and there she was crying again.

III

Athénaïse was not one to accept the inevitable with patient resignation, a talent born in the souls of many women; neither was she the one to accept it with philosophical resignation, like her husband. Her sensibilities were alive and keen and responsive. She met the pleasurable things of life with frank, open appreciation, and against distasteful conditions she rebelled. Dissimulation was as foreign to her nature as guile to the breast of a babe, and her rebellious outbreaks, by no means rare, had hitherto been quite open and aboveboard. People often said that Athénaïse would know her own mind some day, which was equivalent to saying that she was at present unacquainted with it. If she ever came to such knowledge, it would be by no intellectual research, by no subtle analyses or tracing the motives of actions to their source. It would come to her as the song to the bird, the perfume and color to the flower.

Her parents had hoped – not without reason and justice – that marriage would bring the poise, the desirable pose, so glaringly lacking in Athénaïse's character. Marriage they knew to be a wonderful and powerful agent in the development and formation of a woman's character; they had seen its effect too often to doubt it.

'And if this marriage does nothing else,' exclaimed Miché in an outburst of sudden exasperaton, 'it will rid us of Athénaïse; for I am at the end of my patience with her! You have never had the firmness to manage her,' – he was speaking to his wife, – 'I have not had the time, the leisure, to devote to her training; and what good we might have accomplished, that maudit Montéclin – Well, Cazeau is the one! It takes just such a steady hand to guide a disposition like Athénaïse's, a master hand, a strong will that compels obedience.'

And now, when they had hoped for so much, here was Athénaïse, with gathered and fierce vehemence, beside which her former outbursts appeared mild, declaring that she would not, and she would not, and she would not continue to enact the role of wife to Cazeau. If she had had a reason! as Madame Miché lamented; but it could not be discovered that she had any sane one. He had never scolded, or called names, or deprived her of comforts, or been guilty of any of the many reprehensible acts commonly attributed to objectionable husbands. He did not slight nor neglect her. Indeed, Cazeau's chief offense seemed to be that he loved her, and Athénaïse was not the woman to be loved against her will. She called marriage a trap set for the feet of unwary and unsuspecting girls, and in round, unmeasured terms reproached her mother with treachery and deceit.

'I told you Cazeau was the man,' chuckled Miché, when his wife had related the scene that had accompanied and influenced Athénaïse's departure.

Athénaïse again hoped, in the morning, that Cazeau would scold or make some sort of a scene, but he apparently did not dream of it. It was exasperating that he should take her acquiescence so for granted. It is true he had been up and over the fields and across the river and back long before she was out of bed, and he may have been thinking of something else, which was no excuse, which was even in some sense an aggravation. But he did say to her at breakfast, 'That brother of yo's, that Montéclin, is unbearable.'

'Montéclin? Par exemple!'

Athénaïse, seated opposite to her husband, was attired in a white morning wrapper. She wore a somewhat abused, long face, it is true, – an expression of countenance familiar to some husbands, – but the expression was not sufficiently pronounced to mar the charm of her youthful freshness. She had little heart to eat, only playing with the food before her, and she felt a pang of resentment at her husband's healthy appetite.

'Yes, Montéclin,' he reasserted. 'He's developed into a firs'-class nuisance; an' you better tell him, Athénaïse, – unless you want me to tell him, – to confine his energies after this to matters that concern him. I have no use fo' him or fo' his interference in w'at regards you an' me alone.'

This was said with unusual asperity. It was the little breach that Athenaïse had been watching for, and she charged rapidly: 'It's strange, if you detes' Montéclin so heartily, that you would desire to marry his sister.' She knew it was a silly thing to say, and was not surprised when he told her so. It gave her a little foothold for further attack, however. 'I don't see, anyhow, w'at reason you had to marry me, w'en there wére so many others,' she complained, as if accusing him of persecution and injury. 'There was Marianne running after you fo' the las' five years till it was disgraceful; an' any one of the Dortrand girls would have been glad to marry you. But no, nothing would do; you mus' come out on the rigolet fo' me.' Her complaint was pathetic, and at the same time so amusing that Cazeau was forced to smile.

'I can't see w'at the Dortrand girls or Marianne have to do with it,' he rejoined; adding, with no trace of amusement, 'I married you because I loved you; because you were the woman I wanted to marry, an' the only one. I reckon I tole you that befo'. I thought – of co'se I was a fool fo' taking things fo' granted – but I did think that I might make you happy in making things easier an' mo' comfortable fo' you. I expected – I was even that big a fool – I believed that yo' coming yere to me would be like the sun shining out of the clouds, an' that our days would be like w'at the story-books promise after the wedding. I was mistaken. But I can't imagine w'at induced you to marry me. W'atever it was, I reckon you foun' out you made a mistake, too. I don' see anything to do but make the best of a bad bargain, an' shake han's over it.' He had arisen from the table, and, approaching, held out his hand to her. What he had said was commonplace enough, but it was significant, coming from Cazeau, who was not often so unreserved in expressing himself.

Athénaïse ignored the hand held out to her. She was resting her chin in her palm, and kept her eyes fixed moodily upon the table. He rested his hand, that she would not touch, upon her head for an instant, and walked away out of the room.

She heard him giving orders to workmen who had been waiting for him out on the gallery, and she heard him mount his horse and ride away. A hundred things would distract him and engage his attention during the day. She felt that he had perhaps put her and her grievance from his thoughts when he crossed the threshold; whilst she—

Old Félicité was standing there holding a shining tin pail, asking for flour and lard and eggs from the storeroom, and meal for the chicks.

Athénaïse seized the bunch of keys which hung from her belt and flung them at Félicité's feet.

'Tiens! tu vas les garder comme tu as jadis fait. Je ne veux plus de ce train là, moi!'

The old woman stooped and picked up the keys from the floor.

It was really all one to her that her mistress returned them to her keeping, and refused to take further account of the ménage.

IV

It seemed now to Athénaïse that Montéclin was the only friend left to her in the world. Her father and mother had turned from her in what appeared to be her hour of need. Her friends laughed at her, and refused to take seriously the hints which she threw out, – feeling her way to discover if marriage were as distasteful to other women as to herself. Montéclin alone understood her. He alone had always been ready to act for her and with her, to comfort and solace her with his sympathy and his support. Her only hope for rescue from her hateful surroundings lay in Montéclin. Of herself she felt powerless to plan, to act, even to conceive a way out of this pitfall into which the whole world seemed to have conspired to thrust her.

She had a great desire to see her brother, and wrote asking him to come to her. But it better suited Montéclin's spirit of adventure to appoint a meeting-place at the turn of the lane, where Athénaïse might appear to be walking leisurely for health and recreation, and where he might seem to be riding along, bent on some errand of business or pleasure.

There had been a shower, a sudden downpour, short as it was sudden, that had laid the dust in the road. It had freshened the pointed leaves of the live-oaks, and brightened up the big fields of cotton on either side of the lane till they seemed carpeted with green, glittering gems.

Athénaïse walked along the grassy edge of the road, lifting her crisp skirts with one hand, and with the other twirling a gay sunshade over her bare head. The scent of the fields after the rain was delicious. She inhaled long breaths of their freshness and perfume, that soothed and quieted her for the moment. There were birds splashing and spluttering in the pools, pluming themselves on the fence-rails, and sending out little sharp cries, twitters, and shrill rhapsodies of delight.

She saw Montéclin approaching from a great distance, – almost as far away as the turn of the woods. But she could not feel sure it was he; it appeared too tall for Montéclin, but that was because he was riding a large horse. She waved her parasol to

him; she was so glad to see him. She had never been so glad to
see Montéclin before; not even the day when he had taken her
out of the convent, against her parents' wishes, because she had
expressed a desire to remain there no longer. He seemed to her,
as he drew near, the embodiment of kindness, of bravery, of
chivalry, even of wisdom; for she had never known Montéclin at
a loss to extricate himself from a disagreeable situation.

He dismounted, and, leading his horse by the bridle, started to
walk beside her, after he had kissed her affectionately and asked
her what she was crying about. She protested that she was not
crying, for she was laughing, though drying her eyes at the same
time on her handkerchief, rolled in a soft mop for the purpose.

She took Montéclin's arm, and they strolled slowly down the
lane; they could not seat themselves for a comfortable chat, as
they would have liked, with the grass all sparkling and bristling
wet.

Yes, she was quite as wretched as ever, she told him. The week
which had gone by since she saw him had in no wise lightened
the burden of her discontent. There had even been some
additional provocations laid upon her, and she told Montéclin all
about them, – about the keys, for instance, which in a fit of
temper she had returned to Félicité's keeping; and she told how
Cazeau had brought them back to her as if they were something
she had accidentally lost, and he had recovered; and how he had
said, in that aggravating tone of his, that it was not the custom
on Cane river for the negro servants to carry the keys, when
there was a mistress at the head of the household.

But Athénaïse could not tell Montéclin anything to increase
the disrespect which he already entertained for his brother-in-
law; and it was then he unfolded to her a plan which he had
conceived and worked out for her deliverance from this galling
matrimonial yoke.

It was not a plan which met with instant favor, which she was
at once ready to accept, for it involved secrecy and dissimulation,
hateful alternatives, both of them. But she was filled with
admiration for Montéclin's resources and wonderful talent for
contrivance. She accepted the plan; not with the immediate
determination to act upon it, rather with the intention to sleep
and to dream upon it.

Three days later she wrote to Montéclin that she had

abandoned herself to his counsel. Displeasing as it might be to her sense of honesty, it would yet be less trying than to live on with a soul full of bitterness and revolt, as she had done for the past two months.

V

When Cazeau awoke, one morning at his usual very early hour, it was to find the place at his side vacant. This did not surprise him until he discovered that Athénaïse was not in the adjoining room, where he had often found her sleeping in the morning on the lounge. She had perhaps gone out for an early stroll, he reflected, for her jacket and hat were not on the rack where she had hung them the night before. But there were other things absent, – a gown or two from the armoire; and there was a great gap in the piles of lingerie on the shelf; and her traveling-bag was missing, and so were her bits of jewelry from the toilet tray – and Athénaïse was gone!

But the absurdity of going during the night, as if she had been a prisoner, and he the keeper of a dungeon! So much secrecy and mystery, to go sojourning out on the Bon Dieu! Well, the Michés might keep their daughter after this. For the companionship of no woman on earth would he again undergo the humiliating sensation of baseness that had overtaken him in passing the old oak-tree in the fallow meadow.

But a terrible sense of loss overwhelmed Cazeau. It was not new or sudden; he had felt it for weeks growing upon him, and it seemed to culminate with Athénaïse's flight from home. He knew that he could again compel her return as he had done once before, – compel her to return to the shelter of his roof, compel her cold and unwilling submission to his love and passionate transports; but the loss of self-respect seemed to him too dear a price to pay for a wife.

He could not comprehend why she had seemed to prefer him above others; why she had attracted him with eyes, with voice, with a hundred womanly ways, and finally distracted him with love which she seemed, in her timid, maidenly fashion, to return. The great sense of loss came from the realization of having missed a chance for happiness, – a chance that would come his way again only through a miracle. He could not think of himself loving any other woman, and could not think of Athénaïse ever – even at some remote date – caring for him.

He wrote her a letter, in which he disclaimed any further intention of forcing his commands upon her. He did not desire her presence ever again in his home unless she came of her free will, uninfluenced by family or friends; unless she could be the companion he had hoped for in marrying her, and in some measure return affection and respect for the love which he continued and would always continue to feel for her. This letter he sent out to the rigolet by a messenger early in the day. But she was not out on the rigolet, and had not been there.

The family turned instinctively to Montéclin, and almost literally fell upon him for an explanation; he had been absent from home all night. There was much mystification in his answers, and a plain desire to mislead in his assurances of ignorance and innocence.

But with Cazeau there was no doubt or speculation when he accosted the young fellow. 'Montéclin, w'at have you done with Athénaïse?' he questioned bluntly. They had met in the open road on horseback, just as Cazeau ascended the river bank before his house.

'W'at have you done to Athénaïse?' returned Montéclin for answer.

'I don't reckon you've considered yo' conduct by any light of decency an' propriety in encouraging yo' sister to such an action, but let me tell you'—

'Voyons! you can let me alone with yo' decency an' morality an' fiddlesticks. I know you mus' 'a' done Athénaïse pretty mean that she can't live with you; an' fo' my part, I'm mighty durn glad she had the spirit to quit you.'

'I ain't in the humor to take any notice of yo' impertinence, Montéclin; but let me remine you that Athénaïse is nothing but a chile in character; besides that, she's my wife, an' I hole you responsible fo' her safety an' welfare. If any harm of any description happens to her, I'll strangle you, by God, like a rat, and fling you in Cane river, if I have to hang fo' it!' He had not lifted his voice. The only sign of anger was a savage gleam in his eyes.

'I reckon you better keep yo' big talk fo' the women, Cazeau,' replied Montéclin, riding away.

But he went doubly armed after that, and intimated that the precaution was not needless, in view of the threats and menaces that were abroad touching his personal safety.

VI

Athénaïse reached her destination sound of skin and limb, but a good deal flustered, a little frightened, and altogether excited and interested by her unusual experiences.

Her destination was the house of Sylvie, on Dauphine Street, in New Orleans, – a three-story gray brick, standing directly on the banquette, with three broad stone steps leading to the deep front entrance. From the second-story balcony swung a small sign, conveying to passers-by the intelligence that within were '*chambres garnies.*'

It was one morning in the last week of April that Athénaïse presented herself at the Dauphine Street house. Sylvie was expecting her, and introduced her at once to her apartment, which was in the second story of the back ell, and accessible by an open, outside gallery. There was a yard below, paved with broad stone flagging; many fragrant flowering shrubs and plants grew in a bed along the side of the opposite wall, and others were distributed about in tubs and green boxes.

It was a plain but large enough room into which Athénaïse was ushered, with matting on the floor, green shades and Nottingham-lace curtains at the windows that looked out on the gallery, and furnished with a cheap walnut suit. But everything looked exquisitely clean, and the whole place smelled of cleanliness.

Athénaïse at once fell into the rocking-chair, with the air of exhaustion and intense relief of one who has come to the end of her troubles. Sylvie, entering behind her, laid the big traveling-bag on the floor and deposited the jacket on the bed.

She was a portly quadroon of fifty or there-about, clad in an ample *volante* of the old-fashioned purple calico so much affected by her class. She wore large golden hoop-earrings, and her hair was combed plainly, with every appearance of effort to smooth out the kinks. She had broad, coarse features, with a nose that turned up, exposing the wide nostrils, and that seemed to emphasize the loftiness and command of her bearing, – a dignity that in the presence of white people assumed a character of respectfulness, but never of obsequiousness. Sylvie believed firmly in maintaining the color line, and would not suffer a white person, even a child, to call her 'Madame Sylvie,' – a title which she exacted religiously, however, from those of her own race.

'I hope you be please' wid yo' room, madame,' she observed amiably. 'Dat's de same room w'at yo' brother, M'sieur Miché, all time like w'en he come to New Orlean'. He well, M'sieur Miché? I receive' his letter las' week, an' dat same day a gent'man want I give 'im dat room. I say, "No, dat room already ingage'." Ev-body like dat room on 'count it so quite (quiet). M'sieur Gouvernail, dere in nax' room, you can't pay 'im! He been stay t'ree year' in dat room; but all fix' up fine wid his own furn'ture an' books, 'tel you can't see! I say to 'im plenty time', "M'sieur Gouvernail, w'y you don't take dat t'ree-story front, now, long it's empty?" He tells me, "Leave me 'lone, Sylvie; I know a good room w'en I fine it, me."'

She had been moving slowly and majestically about the apartment, straightening and smoothing down bed and pillows, peering into ewer and basin, evidently casting an eye around to make sure that everything was as it should be.

'I sen' you some fresh water, madame,' she offered upon retiring from the room. 'An' w'en you want an't'ing, you jus' go out on de gall'ry an' call Pousette: she year you plain, – she right down dere in de kitchen.'

Athénaïse was really not so exhausted as she had every reason to be after that interminable and circuitous way by which Montéclin had seen fit to have her conveyed to the city.

Would she ever forget that dark and truly dangerous midnight ride along the 'coast' to the mouth of Cane river! There Montéclin had parted with her, after seeing her aboard the St. Louis and Shreveport packet which he knew would pass there before dawn. She had received instructions to disembark at the mouth of Red river, and there transfer to the first south-bound steamer for New Orleans; all of which instructions she had followed implicitly, even to making her way at once to Sylvie's upon her arrival in the city. Montéclin had enjoined secrecy and much caution; the clandestine nature of the affair gave it a savor of adventure which was highly pleasing to him. Eloping with his sister was only a little less engaging than eloping with some one else's sister.

But Montéclin did not do the *grand seigneur* by halves. He had paid Sylvie a whole month in advance for Athénaïse's board and lodging. Part of the sum he had been forced to borrow, it is true, but he was not niggardly.

Athénaïse was to take her meals in the house which none of the other lodgers did; the one exception being that Mr. Gouvernail was served with breakfast on Sunday mornings.

Sylvie's clientèle came chiefly from the southern parishes; for the most part, people spending but a few days in the city. She prided herself upon the quality and highly respectable character of her patrons, who came and went unobtrusively.

The large parlor opening upon the front balcony was seldom used. Her guests were permitted to entertain in this sanctuary of elegance, – but they never did. She often rented it for the night to parties of respectable and discreet gentlemen desiring to enjoy a quiet game of cards outside the bosom of their families. The second-story hall also led by a long window out on the balcony. And Sylvie advised Athénaïse, when she grew weary of her back room, to go and sit on the front balcony, which was shady in the afternoon, and where she might find diversion in the sounds and sights of the street below.

Athénaïse refreshed herself with a bath, and was soon unpacking her few belongings, which she ranged neatly away in the bureau drawers and the armoire.

She had revolved certain plans in her mind during the past hour or so. Her present intention was to live on indefinitely in this big, cool, clean back room on Dauphine street. She had thought seriously, for moments, of the convent, with all readiness to embrace the vows of poverty and chastity; but what about obedience? Later, she intended, in some roundabout way, to give her parents and her husband the assurance of her safety and welfare; reserving the right to remain unmolested and lost to them. To live on at the expense of Montéclin's generosity was wholly out of the question, and Athénaïse meant to look about for some suitable and agreeable employment.

The imperative thing to be done at present, however, was to go out in search of material for an inexpensive gown or two; for she found herself in the painful predicament of a young woman

having almost literally nothing to wear. She decided upon pure
white for one, and some sort of a sprigged muslin for the other.

VII

On Sunday morning, two days after Athénaïse's arrival in the
city, she went in to breakfast somewhat later than usual, to find
two covers laid at table instead of the one to which she was
accustomed. She had been to mass, and did not remove her hat,
but put her fan, parasol, and prayer-book aside. The dining-room
was situated just beneath her own apartment, and, like all rooms
of the house, was large and airy; the floor was covered with a
glistening oil-cloth.

The small, round table, immaculately set, was drawn near the
open window. There were some tall plants in boxes on the gallery
outside; and Pousette, a little, old, intensely black woman, was
splashing and dashing buckets of water on the flagging, and
talking loud in her Creole patois to no one in particular.

A dish piled with delicate river-shrimps and crushed ice was on
the table; a caraffe of crystal-clear water, a few *hors d'œuvres*,
beside a small golden-brown crusty loaf of French bread at each
plate. A half-bottle of wine and the morning paper were set at the
place opposite Athénaïse.

She had almost completed her breakfast when Gouvernail
came in and seated himself at table. He felt annoyed at finding his
cherished privacy invaded. Sylvie was removing the remains of a
mutton-chop from before Athénaïse and serving her with a cup
of café au lait.

'M'sieur Gouvernail,' offered Sylvie in her most insinuating
and impressive manner, 'you please leave me make you
acquaint' wid Madame Cazeau. Dat's M'sieur Miché's sister; you
meet 'im two t'ree time', you rec'lec', an' been one day to de race
wid 'im. Madame Cazeau, you please leave me make you
acquaint' wid M'sieur Gouvernail.'

Gouvernail expressed himself greatly pleased to meet the sister
of Monsieur Miché, of whom he had not the slightest recollection.
He inquired after Monsieur Miché's health, and politely offered
Athénaïse a part of his newspaper, – the part which contained
the Woman's Page and the social gossip.

Athénaïse faintly remembered that Sylvie had spoken of a

Monsieur Gouvernail occupying the room adjoining hers; living amid luxurious surroundings and a multitude of books. She had not thought of him further than to picture him a stout, middle-aged gentleman, with a bushy beard turning gray, wearing large gold-rimmed spectacles, and stooping somewhat from much bending over books and writing material. She had confused him in her mind with the likeness of some literary celebrity that she had run across in the advertising pages of a magazine.

Gouvernail's appearance was, in truth, in no sense striking. He looked older than thirty and younger than forty, was of medium height and weight, with a quiet, unobtrusive manner which seemed to ask that he be let alone. His hair was light brown, brushed carefully and parted in the middle. His mustache was brown, and so were his eyes, which had a mild, penetrating quality. He was neatly dressed in the fashion of the day; and his hands seemed to Athénaïse remarkably white and soft for a man's.

He had been buried in the contents of his newspaper, when he suddenly realized that some further little attention might be due to Miché's sister. He started to offer her a glass of wine, when he was surprised and relieved to find that she had quietly slipped away while he was absorbed in his own editorial on Corrupt Legislation.

Gouvernail finished his paper and smoked his cigar out on the gallery. He lounged about, gathered a rose for his buttonhole, and had his regular Sunday-morning confab with Pousette, to whom he paid a weekly stipend for brushing his shoes and clothing. He made a great pretense of haggling over the transaction, only to enjoy her uneasiness and garrulous excitement.

He worked or read in his room for a few hours, and when he quitted the house, at three in the afternoon, it was to return no more 'till late at night. It was his almost invariable custom to spend Sunday evenings out in the American quarter, among a congenial set of men and women, – *des esprits forts*, all of them, whose lives were irreproachable, yet whose opinions would startle even the traditional 'sapeur,' for whom 'nothing is sacred.' But for all his 'advanced' opinions, Gouvernail was a liberal-minded fellow; a man or woman lost nothing of his respect by being married.

When he left the house in the afternoon, Athénaïse had already ensconced herself on the front balcony. He could see her through the jalousies when he passed on his way to the front entrance. She had not yet grown lonesome or homesick; the newness of her surroundings made them sufficiently entertaining. She found it diverting to sit there on the front balcony watching people pass by, even though there was no one to talk to. And then the comforting, comfortable sense of not being married!

She watched Gouvernail walk down the street, and could find no fault with his bearing. He could hear the sound of her rockers for some little distance. He wondered what the 'poor little thing' was doing in the city, and meant to ask Sylvie about her when he should happen to think of it.

VIII

The following morning, towards noon, when Gouvernail quitted his room, he was confronted by Athénaïse, exhibiting some confusion and trepidation at being forced to request a favor of him at so early a stage of their acquaintance. She stood in her doorway, and had evidently been sewing, as the thimble on her finger testified, as well as a long-threaded needle thrust in the bosom of her gown. She held a stamped but unaddressed letter in her hand.

And would Mr. Gouvernail be so kind as to address the letter to her brother, Mr. Montéclin Miché? She would hate to detain him with explanations this morning, – another time, perhaps, – but now she begged that he would give himself the trouble.

He assured her that it made no difference, that it was no trouble whatever; and he drew a fountain pen from his pocket and addressed the letter at her dictation, resting it on the inverted rim of his straw hat. She wondered a little at a man of his supposed erudition stumbling over the spelling of 'Montéclin' and 'Miché.'

She demurred at overwhelming him with the additional trouble of posting it, but he succeeded in convincing her that so simple a task as the posting of a letter would not add an iota to the burden of the day. Moreover, he promised to carry it in his hand, and thus avoid any possible risk of forgetting it in his pocket.

After that, and after a second repetition of the favor, when she had told him that she had had a letter from Montéclin, and looked as if she wanted to tell him more, he felt that he knew her better. He felt that he knew her well enough to join her out on the balcony, one night, when he found her sitting there alone. He was not one who deliberately sought the society of women, but he was not wholly a bear. A little commiseration for Athénaïse's aloneness, perhaps some curiosity to know further what manner of woman she was, and the natural influence of her feminine charm were equal unconfessed factors in turning his steps towards the balcony when he discovered the shimmer of her white gown through the open hall window.

It was already quite late, but the day had been intensely hot, and neighboring balconies and doorways were occupied by chattering groups of humanity, loath to abandon the grateful freshness of the outer air. The voices about her served to reveal to Athénaïse the feeling of loneliness that was gradually coming over her. Notwithstanding certain dormant impulses, she craved human sympathy and companionship.

She shook hands impulsively with Gouvernail, and told him how glad she was to see him. He was not prepared for such an admission, but it pleased him immensely, detecting as he did that the expression was as sincere as it was outspoken. He drew a chair up within comfortable conversational distance of Athénaïse, though he had no intention of talking more than was barely necessary to encourage Madame – He had actually forgotten her name!

He leaned an elbow on the balcony rail, and would have offered an opening remark about the oppressive heat of the day, but Athénaïse did not give him the opportunity. How glad she was to talk to some one, and how she talked!

An hour later she had gone to her room, and Gouvernail stayed smoking on the balcony. He knew her quite well after that hour's talk. It was not so much what she had said as what her half saying had revealed to his quick intelligence. He knew that she adored Montéclin, and he suspected that she adored Cazeau without being herself aware of it. He had gathered that she was self-willed, impulsive, innocent, ignorant, unsatisfied, dissatisfied;

for had she not complained that things seemed all wrongly arranged in this world, and no one was permitted to be happy in his own way? And he told her he was sorry she had discovered that primordial fact of existence so early in life.

He commiserated her loneliness, and scanned his bookshelves next morning for something to lend her to read, rejecting everything that offered itself to his view. Philosophy was out of the question, and so was poetry; that is, such poetry as he possessed. He had not sounded her literary tastes, and strongly suspected she had none; that she would have rejected The Duchess as readily as Mrs. Humphry Ward. He compromised on a magazine.

It had entertained her passably, she admitted, upon returning it. A New England story had puzzled her, it was true, and a Creole tale had offended her, but the pictures had pleased her greatly, especially one which had reminded her so strongly of Montéclin after a hard day's ride that she was loath to give it up. It was one of Remington's Cowboys, and Gouvernail insisted upon her keeping it, – keeping the magazine.

He spoke to her daily after that, and was always eager to render her some service or to do something towards her entertainment.

One afternoon he took her out to the lake end. She had been there once, some years before, but in winter; so the trip was comparatively new and strange to her. The large expanse of water studded with pleasure-boats, the sight of children playing merrily along the grassy palisades, the music, all enchanted her. Gouvernail thought her the most beautiful woman he had ever seen. Even her gown – the sprigged muslin – appeared to him the most charming one imaginable. Nor could anything be more becoming than the arrangement of her brown hair under the white sailor hat, all rolled back in a soft puff from her radiant face. And she carried her parasol and lifted her skirts and used her fan in ways that seemed quite unique and peculiar to herself, and which he considered almost worthy of study and imitation.

They did not dine out there at the water's edge, as they might have done, but returned early to the city to avoid the crowd. Athénaïse wanted to go home, for she said Sylvie would have dinner prepared and would be expecting her. But it was not difficult to persuade her to dine instead in the quiet little restaurant that he knew and liked, with its sanded floor, its secluded atmosphere, its delicious menu, and its obsequious waiter wanting to know what he might have the honor of serving to 'monsieur et madame.' No wonder he made the mistake, with Gouvernail assuming such an air of proprietorship! But Athénaïse was very tired after it all; the sparkle went out of her face, and she hung draggingly on his arm in walking home.

He was reluctant to part from her when she bade him good-night at her door and thanked him for the agreeable evening. He had hoped she would sit outside until it was time for him to regain the newspaper office. He knew that she would undress and get into her peignoir and lie upon her bed; and what he wanted to do, what he would have given much to do, was to go and sit beside her, read to her something restful, soothe her, do her bidding, whatever it might be. Of course there was no use in thinking of that. But he was surprised at his growing desire to be serving her. She gave him an opportunity sooner than he looked for.

'Mr. Gouvernail,' she called from her room, 'will you be so kine as to call Pousette an' tell her she fo'got to bring my ice-water?'

He was indignant at Pousette's negligence, and called severely to her over the banisters. He was sitting before his own door, smoking. He knew that Athénaïse had gone to bed, for her room was dark, and she had opened the slats of the door and windows. Her bed was near a window.

Pousette came flopping up with the ice-water, and with a hundred excuses: 'Mo pa oua vou à tab c'te lanuite, mo cri vou pé gagni déja là-bas; parole! Vou pas cri conté ça Madame Sylvie?' She had not seen Athénaïse at table, and thought she was gone. She swore to this, and hoped Madame Sylvie would not be informed of her remissness.

A little later Athénaïse lifted her voice again: 'Mr. Gouvernail, did you remark that young man sitting on the opposite side from us, coming in, with a gray coat an' a blue ban' aroun' his hat?'

Of course Gouvernail had not noticed any such individual, but he assured Athénaïse that he had observed the young fellow particularly.

'Don't you think he looked something, – not very much, of co'se, – but don't you think he had a little faux-air of Montéclin?'

'I think he looked strikingly like Montéclin,' asserted Gouvernail, with the one idea of prolonging the conversation. 'I meant to call your attention to the resemblance, and something drove it out of my head.'

'The same with me,' returned Athénaïse. 'Ah, my dear Montéclin! I wonder w'at he is doing now?'

'Did you receive any news, any letter from him to-day?' asked Gouvernail, determined that if the conversation ceased it should not be through lack of effort on his part to sustain it.

'Not to-day, but yesterday. He tells me that maman was so distracted with uneasiness that finally, to pacify her, he was fo'ced to confess that he knew w'ere I was, but that he was boun' by a vow of secrecy not to reveal it. But Cazeau has not noticed him or spoken to him since he threaten' to throw po' Montéclin in Cane river. You know Cazeau wrote me a letter the morning I lef', thinking I had gone to the rigolet. An' maman opened it, an' said it was full of the mos' noble sentiments, an' she wanted Montéclin to sen' it to me; but Montéclin refuse' poin' blank, so he wrote to me.'

Gouvernail preferred to talk of Montéclin. He pictured Cazeau as unbearable, and did not like to think of him.

A little later Athénaïse called out, 'Good-night, Mr. Gouvernail.'

'Good-night,' he returned reluctantly. And when he thought that she was sleeping, he got up and went away to the midnight pandemonium of his newspaper office.

IX

Athénaïse could not have held out through the month had it not been for Gouvernail. With the need of caution and secrecy always uppermost in her mind, she made no new acquaintances, and she did not seek out persons already known to her; however, she knew so few, it required little effort to keep out of their way. As for Sylvie, almost every moment of her time was occupied in looking after her house; and, moreover, her deferential attitude towards her lodgers forbade anything like the gossipy chats in which Athénaïse might have condescended sometimes to indulge with her land-lady. The transient lodgers, who came and went,

she never had occasion to meet. Hence she was entirely
dependent upon Gouvernail for company.

He appreciated the situation fully; and every moment that he
could spare from his work he devoted to her entertainment. She
liked to be out of doors, and they strolled together in the summer
twilight through the mazes of the old French quarter. They went
again to the lake end, and stayed for hours on the water;
returning so late that the streets through which they passed were
silent and deserted. On Sunday morning he arose at an
unconscionable hour to take her to the French market, knowing
that the sights and sounds there would interest her. And he did
not join the intellectual coterie in the afternoon, as he usually
did, but placed himself all day at the disposition and service of
Athénaïse.

Notwithstanding all, his manner toward her was tactful, and
evinced intelligence and a deep knowledge of her character,
surprising upon so brief an acquaintance. For the time he was
everything to her that she would have him; he replaced home
and friends. Sometimes she wondered if he had ever loved a
woman. She could not fancy him loving any one passionately,
rudely, offensively, as Cazeau loved her. Once she was so naïve as
to ask him outright if he had ever been in love, and he assured
her promptly that he had not. She thought it an admirable trait
in his character, and esteemed him greatly therefor.

He found her crying one night, not openly or violently. She
was leaning over the gallery rail, watching the toads that hopped
about in the moonlight, down on the damp flagstones of the
courtyard. There was an oppressively sweet odor rising from the
cape jessamine. Pousette was down there, mumbling and
quarreling with some one, and seeming to be having it all her
own way, – as well she might, when her companion was only a
black cat that had come in from a neighboring yard to keep her
company.

Athénaïse did admit feeling heart-sick, body-sick, when he
questioned her; she supposed it was nothing but homesick. A
letter from Montéclin had stirred her all up. She longed for her
mother, for Montéclin; she was sick for a sight of the cotton-fields,
the scent of the ploughed earth, for the dim, mysterious charm of
the woods, and the old tumble-down home on the Bon Dieu.

As Gouvernail listened to her, a wave of pity and tenderness swept through him. He took her hands and pressed them against him. He wondered what would happen if he were to put his arms around her.

He was hardly prepared for what happened, but he stood it courageously. She twined her arms around his neck and wept outright on his shoulder; the hot tears scalding his cheek and neck, and her whole body shaken in his arms. The impulse was powerful to strain her to him; the temptation was fierce to seek her lips; but he did neither.

He understood a thousand times better than she herself understood it that he was acting as substitute for Montéclin. Bitter as the conviction was, he accepted it. He was patient; he could wait. He hoped some day to hold her with a lover's arms. That she was married made no particle of difference to Gouvernail. He could not conceive or dream of it making a difference. When the time came that she wanted him, – as he hoped and believed it would come, – he felt he would have a right to her. So long as she did not want him, he had no right to her, – no more than her husband had. It was very hard to feel her warm breath and tears upon his cheek, and her struggling bosom pressed against him and her soft arms clinging to him and his whole body and soul aching for her, and yet to make no sign.

He tried to think what Montéclin would have said and done, and to act accordingly. He stroked her hair, and held her in a gentle embrace, until the tears dried and the sobs ended. Before releasing herself she kissed him against the neck; she had to love somebody in her own way! Even that he endured like a stoic. But it was well he left her, to plunge into the thick of rapid, breathless, exacting work till nearly dawn.

Athénaïse was greatly soothed, and slept well. The touch of friendly hands and caressing arms had been very grateful. Henceforward she would not be lonely and unhappy, with Gouvernail there to comfort her.

X

The fourth week of Athénaïse's stay in the city was drawing to a close. Keeping in view the intention which she had of finding some suitable and agreeable employment, she had made a few tentatives in that direction. But with the exception of two little girls who had promised to take piano lessons at a price that would be embarrassing to mention, these attempts had been fruitless. Moreover, the homesickness kept coming back, and Gouvernail was not always there to drive it away.

She spent much of her time weeding and pottering among the flowers down in the courtyard. She tried to take an interest in the black cat, and a mockingbird that hung in a cage outside the kitchen door, and a disreputable parrot that belonged to the cook next door, and swore hoarsely all day long in bad French.

Beside, she was not well; she was not herself, as she told Sylvie. The climate of New Orleans did not agree with her. Sylvie was distressed to learn this, as she felt in some measure responsible for the health and well-being of Monsieur Miché's sister; and she made it her duty to inquire closely into the nature and character of Athénaïse's malaise.

Sylvie was very wise, and Athénaïse was very ignorant. The extent of her ignorance and the depth of her subsequent enlightenment were bewildering. She stayed a long, long time quite still, quite stunned, after her interview with Sylvie, except for the short, uneven breathing that ruffled her bosom. Her whole being was steeped in a wave of ecstasy. When she finally arose from the chair in which she had been seated, and looked at herself in the mirror, a face met hers which she seemed to see for the first time, so transfigured was it with wonder and rapture.

One mood quickly followed another, in this new turmoil of her senses, and the need of action became uppermost. Her mother must know at once, and her mother must tell Montéclin. And Cazeau must know. As she thought of him, the first purely sensuous tremor of her life swept over her. She half whispered his name, and the sound of it brought red blotches into her cheeks. She spoke it over and over, as if it were some new, sweet sound born out of darkness and confusion, and reaching her for the first time. She was impatient to be with him. Her whole passionate nature was aroused as if by a miracle.

She seated herself to write to her husband. The letter he would get in the morning, and she would be with him at night. What would he say? How would he act? She knew that he would forgive her, for had he not written a letter? – and a pang of resentment toward Montéclin shot through her. What did he mean by withholding that letter? How dared he not have sent it?

Athénaïse attired herself for the street, and went out to post the letter which she had penned with a single thought, a spontaneous impulse. It would have seemed incoherent to most people, but Cazeau would understand.

She walked along the street as if she had fallen heir to some magnificent inheritance. On her face was a look of pride and satisfaction that passers-by noticed and admired. She wanted to talk to some one, to tell some person; and she stopped at the corner and told the oyster-woman, who was Irish, and who God-blessed her, and wished prosperity to the race of Cazeaus for generations to come. She held the oyster-woman's fat, dirty little baby in her arms and scanned it curiously and observingly, as if a baby were a phenomenon that she encountered for the first time in life. She even kissed it!

Then what a relief it was to Athénaïse to walk the streets without dread of being seen and recognized by some chance acquaintance from Red river! No one could have said now that she did not know her own mind.

She went directly from the oyster-woman's to the office of Harding & Offdean, her husband's merchants; and it was with such an air of partnership, almost proprietorship, that she demanded a sum of money on her husband's account, they gave it to her as unhesitatingly as they would have handed it over to Cazeau himself. When Mr. Harding, who knew her, asked politely after her health, she turned so rosy and looked so conscious, he thought it a great pity for so pretty a woman to be such a little goose.

Athénaïse entered a dry-goods store and bought all manner of things, – little presents for nearly everybody she knew. She bought whole bolts of sheerest, softest, downiest white stuff; and when the clerk, in trying to meet her wishes, asked if she intended it for infant's use, she could have sunk through the floor, and wondered how he might have suspected it.

As it was Montéclin who had taken her away from her husband, she wanted it to be Montéclin who should take her back to him. So she wrote him a very curt note, – in fact it was a postal card, – asking that he meet her at the train on the evening following. She felt convinced that after what had gone before, Cazeau would await her at their own home; and she preferred it so.

Then there was the agreeable excitement of getting ready to leave, of packing up her things. Pousette kept coming and going, coming and going; and each time that she quitted the room it was with something that Athénaïse had given her, – a handkerchief, a petticoat, a pair of stockings with two tiny holes at the toes, some broken prayer-beads, and finally a silver dollar.

Next it was Sylvie who came along bearing a gift of what she called 'a set of pattern',' – things of complicated design which never could have been obtained in any new-fangled bazaar or pattern-store, that Sylvie had acquired of a foreign lady of distinction whom she had nursed years before at the St. Charles hotel. Athénaïse accepted and handled them with reverence, fully sensible of the great compliment and favor, and laid them religiously away in the trunk which she had lately acquired.

She was greatly fatigued after the day of unusual exertion, and went early to bed and to sleep. All day long she had not once thought of Gouvernail, and only did think of him when aroused for a brief instant by the sound of his foot-falls on the gallery, as he passed in going to his room. He had hoped to find her up, waiting for him.

But the next morning he knew. Some one must have told him. There was no subject known to her which Sylvie hesitated to discuss in detail with any man of suitable years and discretion.

Athénaïse found Gouvernail waiting with a carriage to convey her to the railway station. A momentary pang visited her for having forgotten him so completely, when he said to her, 'Sylvie tells me you are going away this morning.'

He was kind, attentive, and amiable, as usual, but respected to the utmost the new dignity and reserve that her manner had developed since yesterday. She kept looking from the carriage window, silent, and embarrassed as Eve after losing her ignorance. He talked of the muddy streets and the murky morning, and of Montéclin. He hoped she would find everything comfortable and pleasant in the country, and trusted she would inform him whenever she came to visit the city again. He talked as if afraid or mistrustful of silence and himself.

At the station she handed him her purse, and he bought her ticket, secured for her a comfortable section, checked her trunk, and got all the bundles and things safely aboard the train. She felt very grateful. He pressed her hand warmly, lifted his hat, and left her. He was a man of intelligence, and took defeat gracefully; that was all. But as he made his way back to the carriage, he was thinking, 'By heaven, it hurts, it hurts!'

XI

Athénaïse spent a day of supreme happiness and expectancy. The fair sight of the country unfolding itself before her was balm to her vision and to her soul. She was charmed with the rather unfamiliar, broad, clean sweep of the sugar plantations, with their monster sugar-houses, their rows of neat cabins like little villages of a single street, and their impressive homes standing apart amid clusters of trees. There were sudden glimpses of a bayou curling between sunny, grassy banks, or creeping sluggishly out from a tangled growth of wood, and brush, and fern, and poison-vines, and palmettos. And passing through the long stretches of monotonous woodlands, she would close her eyes and taste in anticipation the moment of her meeting with Cazeau. She could think of nothing but him.

It was night when she reached her station. There was Montéclin, as she had expected, waiting for her with a two-seated buggy, to which he had hitched his own swift-footed, spirited pony. It was good, he felt, to have her back on any terms; and he had no fault to find since she came of her own choice. He more than suspected the cause of her coming; her eyes and her voice and her foolish little manner went far in revealing the secret that was brimming over in her heart. But after he had deposited her at her own gate, and as he continued his way toward the rigolet, he could not help feeling that the affair had taken a very disappointing, an ordinary, a most commonplace turn, after all. He left her in Cazeau's keeping.

Her husband lifted her out of the buggy, and neither said a word until they stood together within the shelter of the gallery. Even then they did not speak at first. But Athénaïse turned to him with an appealing gesture. As he clasped her in his arms, he felt the yielding of her whole body against him. He felt her lips for the first time respond to the passion of his own.

The country night was dark and warm and still, save for the distant notes of an accordion which some one was playing in a cabin away off. A little negro baby was crying somewhere. As

Athénaïse withdrew from her husband's embrace, the sound arrested her.

'Listen, Cazeau! How Juliette's baby is crying! Pauvre ti chou, I wonder w'at is the matter with it?'

Two Summers and Two Souls

I

He was a fine, honest-looking fellow; young, impetuous, candid; and he was bidding her good-bye.

It was in the country, where she lived, and where her soul and senses were slowly unfolding, like the languid petals of some white and fragrant blossom.

Five weeks – only five weeks he had known her. They seemed to him a flash, an eternity, a rapturous breath, an existence – a re-creation of light and life, and soul and senses. He tried to tell her something of this when the hour of parting came. But he could only say that he loved her; nothing else that he wanted to say seemed to mean so much as this. She was glad, and doubtful, and afraid, and kept reiterating:

'Only five weeks! so short! and love and life are so long.'

'Then you don't love me!'

'I don't know. I want to be with you – near you.'

'Then you do love me!'

'I don't know. I thought love meant something different – powerful, overwhelming. No. I am afraid to say.'

He talked like a mad man then, and troubled and bewildered her with his incoherence. He begged for love as a mendicant might beg for alms, without reserve and without shame, and the passion within him gave an unnatural ring to his voice and a new, strange look to his eyes that chilled her unawakened senses and sent her shivering within herself.

'No, no, no!' was all she could say to him.

He willed not to believe it; he had felt so sure of her. And she was not one to play fast and loose, with those honest eyes whose depths had convinced while they ensnared him.

'Don't send me away like this,' he pleaded, 'without a crumb of hope to feed on and keep me living.'

She dismissed him with a promise that it might not be final.

'Who knows! I will think; but leave me alone. Don't trouble me; and I will see – Good-bye.'

He did not once look back after leaving her, but walked straight on with a step that was quick and firm from habit. But he was almost blind and senseless from pain.

She stayed watching him cross the lawn and the long stretch of meadow beyond. She watched him till the deepening shadows of the coming night crept between them. She stayed troubled, uncertain; tearful because she did not know!

II

'I remember quite well the words I told you a year ago when we parted,' she wrote to him. 'I told you I did not know, I wanted to think, I even wanted to pray, but I believe I did not tell you that. And now, will you believe me when I say that I have not been able to think – hardly to pray. I have only been able to feel. When you went away that day you seemed to leave me in an empty world. I kept saying to myself, "to-morrow or next day it will be different; it will be with me as it was before he came." Then your letters coming – three of them, one upon the other – gave voice to the empty places. You were everywhere after that. And still I doubted, and I was cautious; for it has seemed to me that the love which is to hold two beings together through life must be love indeed.

'But what is the use of saying more than that I love you. I would not care to live without you; I think I could not. Come back to me.'

III

When this letter reached him he was in preparation for a journey with a party of friends. It came with a batch of business letters, and in the midst of the city's rush and din which he had meant in another day to leave behind him.

He was all unprepared for its coming and unable at once to master the shock of it, that bewildered and unnerved him.

Then came back to him the recollection of pain – a remembrance always faint and unreal; but there was complete inability to revive the conditions that had engendered it.

How he had loved her and how he had suffered! especially during those first days, and even months, when he slept and waked dreaming of her; when his letters remained unanswered, and when existence was but a name for bitter endurance.

How long had it lasted? Could he tell? The end began when he could wake in the morning without the oppression, and free from the haunting pain. The end was that day, that hour or second, when he thought of her without emotion and without regret; as he thought of her now, with unstirred pulses. There was even with him now the touch of something keener than indifference – something engendered by revolt.

It was as if one loved, and dead and forgotten had returned to life; with the strange illusion that the rush of existence had halted while she lay in her grave; and with the still more singular delusion that love is eternal.

He did not hesitate as though confronted by a problem. He did not think of leaving the letter unnoticed. He did not think of telling her the truth. If he thought of these expedients, it was only to dismiss them.

He simply went to her. As he would have gone unflinchingly to meet the business obligation that he knew would leave him bankrupt.

Two Portraits

I

The Wanton

Alberta having looked not very long into life, had not looked very far. She put out her hands to touch things that pleased her and her lips to kiss them. Her eyes were deep brown wells that were drinking, drinking impressions and treasuring them in her soul. They were mysterious eyes and love looked out of them.

Alberta was very fond of her mama who was really not her mama; and the beatings which alternated with the most amiable and generous indulgence, were soon forgotten by the little one, always hoping that there would never be another, as she dried her eyes.

She liked the ladies who petted her and praised her beauty, and the artists who painted it naked, and the student who held her upon his knee and fondled and kissed her while he taught her to read and spell.

There was a cruel beating about that one day, when her mama happened to be in the mood to think her too old for fondling. And the student had called her mama some very vile names in his wrath, and had asked the woman what else she expected.

There was nothing very fixed or stable about her expectations – whatever they were – as she had forgotten them the following day, and Alberta, consoled with a fantastic bracelet for her plump little arm and a shower of bonbons, installed herself again upon the student's knee. She liked nothing better, and in time was willing to take the beating if she might hold his attentions and her place in his affections and upon his knee.

Alberta cried very bitterly when he went away. The people about her seemed to be always coming and going. She had hardly the time to fix her affections upon the men and the women who came into her life before they were gone again.

Her mama died one day – very suddenly; a self-inflicted death, she heard the people say. Alberta grieved sorely, for she forgot the beatings and remembered only the outbursts of a torrid affection. But she really did not belong anywhere then, nor to anybody. And when a lady and gentleman took her to live with them, she went willingly as she would have gone anywhere, with any one. With them she met with more kindness and indulgence than she had ever known before in her life.

There were no more beatings; Alberta's body was too beautiful to be beaten – it was made for love. She knew that herself; she had heard it since she had heard anything. But now she heard many things and learned many more. She did not lack for instruction in the wiles – the ways of stirring a man's desire and holding it. Yet she did not need instruction – the secret was in her blood and looked out of her passionate, wanton eyes and showed in every motion of her seductive body.

At seventeen she was woman enough, so she had a lover. But as for that, there did not seem to be much difference. Except that she had gold now – plenty of it with which to make herself appear more beautiful, and enough to fling with both hands into the laps of those who came whining and begging to her.

Alberta is a most beautiful woman, and she takes great care of her body, for she knows that it brings her love to squander and gold to squander.

Some one has whispered in her ear:

'Be cautious, Alberta. Save, save your gold. The years are passing. The days are coming when youth slips away, when you will stretch out your hands for money and for love in vain. And what will be left for you but—'

Alberta shrunk in horror before the pictured depths of hideous degradation that would be left for her. But she consoles herself with the thought that such need never be – with death and oblivion always within her reach.

Alberta is capricious. She gives her love only when and where she chooses. One or two men have died because of her withholding it. There is a smooth-faced boy now who teases her with his resistance; for Alberta does not know shame or reserve.

One day he seems to half-relent and another time he plays indifference, and she frets and she fumes and rages.

But he had best have a care; for since Alberta has added much wine to her wantonness she is apt to be vixenish; and she carries a knife.

II

The Nun

Alberta having looked not very long into life, had not looked very far. She put out her hands to touch things that pleased her, and her lips to kiss them. Her eyes were deep brown wells that were drinking, drinking impressions and treasuring them in her soul. They were mysterious eyes and love looked out of them.

It was a very holy woman who first took Alberta by the hand. The thought of God alone dwelt in her mind, and his name and none other was on her lips.

When she showed Alberta the creeping insects, the blades of grass, the flowers and trees; the rain-drops falling from the clouds; the sky and the stars and the men and women moving on the earth, she taught her that it was God who had created all; that God was great, was good, was the Supreme Love.

And when Alberta would have put out her hands and her lips to touch the great and all-loving God, it was then the holy woman taught her that it is not with the hands and lips and eyes that we reach God, but with the soul; that the soul must be made perfect and the flesh subdued. And what is the soul but the inward thought? And this the child was taught to keep spotless – pure, and fit as far as a human soul can be, to hold intercourse with the all-wise and all-seeing God.

Her existence became a prayer. Evil things approached her not. The inherited sin of the blood must have been washed away at the baptismal font; for all the things of this world that she encountered – the pleasures, the trials and even temptations, but turned her gaze within, through her soul up to the fountain of all love and every beatitude.

When Alberta had reached the age when with other women the languor of love creeps into the veins and dreams begin, at such a period an overpowering impulse toward the purely spiritual possessed itself of her. She could no longer abide the sights, the sounds, the accidental happenings of life surrounding her, that tended but to disturb her contemplation of the heavenly existence.

It was then she went into the convent – the white convent on the hill that overlooks the river; the big convent whose long, dim corridors echo with the soft tread of a multitude of holy women;

whose atmosphere of chastity, poverty and obedience penetrates to the soul through benumbed senses.

But of all the holy women in the white convent, there is none so saintly as Alberta. Any one will tell you that who knows them. Even her pious guide and counsellor does not equal her in sanctity. Because Alberta is endowed with the powerful gift of a great love that lifts her above common mortals, close to the invisible throne. Her ears seem to hear sounds that reach no other ears; and what her eyes see, only God and herself know. When the others are plunged in meditation, Alberta is steeped in an oblivious ecstasy. She kneels before the Blessed Sacrament with stiffened, tireless limbs; with absorbing eyes that drink in the holy mystery till it is a mystery no longer, but a real flood of celestial love deluging her soul. She does not hear the sound of bells nor the soft stir of disbanding numbers. She must be touched upon the shoulder; roused, awakened.

Alberta does not know that she is beautiful. If you were to tell her so she would not blush and utter gentle protest and reproof as might the others. She would only smile, as though beauty were a thing that concerned her not. But she is beautiful, with the glow of a holy passion in her dark eyes. Her face is thin and white, but illumined from within by a light which seems not of this world.

She does not walk upright; she could not, overpowered by the Divine Presence and the realization of her own nothingness. Her hands, slender and blue-veined, and her delicate fingers seem to have been fashioned by God to be clasped and uplifted in prayer.

It is said – not broadcast, it is only whispered – that Alberta sees visions. Oh, the beautiful visions! The first of them came to her when she was rapped in suffering, in quivering contemplation of the bleeding and agonizing Christ. Oh, the dear God! Who loved her beyond the power of man to describe, to conceive. The God-Man, the Man-God, suffering, bleeding, dying for her, Alberta, a worm upon the earth; dying that she might be saved from sin and transplanted among the heavenly delights. Oh, if she might die for him in return! But she could only abandon herself to his mercy and his love. 'Into thy hands, Oh Lord! Into thy hands!'

She pressed her lips upon the bleeding wounds and the Divine Blood transfigured her. The Virgin Mary enfolded her in her

mantle. She could not describe in words the ecstasy; that taste of
the Divine love which only the souls of the transplanted could
endure in its awful and complete intensity. She, Alberta, had
received this sign of Divine favor; this fore-taste of heavenly bliss.
For an hour she had swooned in rapture; she had lived in Christ.
Oh, the beautiful visions!

The visions come often to Alberta now, refreshing and
strengthening her soul; it is being talked about a little in
whispers.

And it is said that certain afflicted persons have been helped by
her prayers. And others having abounding faith, have been cured
of bodily ailments by the touch of her beautiful hands.

Aunt Lympy's Interference

The day was warm, and Melitte, cleaning her room, strayed often to the south window that looked out toward the Annibelles' place. She was a slender young body of eighteen with skirts that escaped the ground and a pink-sprigged shirt-waist. She had the beauty that belongs to youth – the freshness, the dewiness – with healthy brown hair that gleamed and honest brown eyes that could be earnest as well as merry.

Looking toward the Annibelles' place, Melitte could see but a speck of the imposing white house through the trees. Men were at work in the field, head and shoulders above the cotton. She could occasionally hear them laugh or shout. The air came in little broken waves from the south, bringing the hot, sweet scent of flowers and sometimes the good smell of the plowed earth.

Melitte always cleaned her room thoroughly on Saturday, because it was her only free day; of late she had been conducting a small school which stood down the road at the far end of the Annibelle place.

Almost every morning, as she trudged to school, she saw Victor Annibelle mending the fence; always mending it, but why so much nailing and bracing were required, no one but himself knew. The spectacle of the young man so persistently at work was one to distress Melitte in the goodness of her soul.

'My! but you have trouble with yo' fence, Victor,' she called out to him in passing.

His good-looking face changed from a healthy brown to the color of one of his own cotton blooms; and never a phrase could his wits find till she was out of ear-shot; for Melitte never stopped to talk. She would but fling him a pleasant word, turning her face to him framed, buried, in a fluted pink sunbonnet.

He had not always been so diffident – when they were youngsters, for instance, and he lent her his pony, or came over to thrash the pecan-tree for her. Now it was different. Since he had been long away from home and had returned at twenty-two, she gave herself the airs and graces of a young lady.

He did not dare to call her 'Melitte,' he was ashamed to call her 'Miss,' so he called her nothing, and hardly spoke to her.

Sometimes Victor went over to visit in the evenings, when he would be amiably entertained by Melitte, her brother, her brother's wife, her two little nieces and one little nephew. On Saturdays the young man was apparently less concerned about the condition of his fences, and passed frequently up and down the road on his white horse.

Melitte thought it was perhaps he, calling upon some pretext, when the little tot of a nephew wabbled in to say that some one wanted to see her on the front gallery. She gave a flurried glance at the mirror and divested her head of the dust-cloth.

'It's Aunt Lympy!' exclaimed the two small nieces, who had followed in the wake of the toddling infant.

'She won't say w'at she wants, *ti tante*,' pursued one of them. 'She don't look pleased, an' she sittin' down proud as a queen in the big chair.'

There, in fact, Melitte found Aunt Lympy, proud and unbending in all the glory of a flowered 'challie' and a black grenadine shawl edged with a purple satin quilling; she was light-colored. Two heavy bands of jet-black hair showed beneath her bandanna and covered her ears down to the gold hoop earrings.

'W'y, Aunt Lympy!' cried the girl, cordially, extending both hands. 'Didn't I hear you were in Alexandria?'

'Tha's true, ma' Melitte.' Aunt Lympy spoke slowly and with emphasis. 'I ben in Alexandria nussin' Judge Morse's wife. She well now, an' I ben sence Chuseday in town. Look like Severin git 'long well 'idout me, an' I ant hurry to go home.' Her dusky eyes glowed far from cheerfully.

'I yeard some'in' yonda in town,' the woman went on, 'w'at I don' wan' to b'lieve. An' I say to myse'f, "Olympe, you don' listen to no sich tale tell you go axen ma' Melitte."'

'Something you heard about me, Aunt Lympy?' Melitte's eyes were wide.

'I don' wan' to spick about befo' de chillun,' said Aunt Lympy.

'I yeard yonda in town, ma' Melitte,' she went on after the children had gone, 'I yeard you was turn school-titcher! Dat ant true?'

The question in her eyes was almost pathetic.

'Oh!' exclaimed Melitte; an utterance that expressed relief, surprise, amusement, commiseration, affirmation.

'Den it's true,' Aunt Lympy almost whispered; 'a De Broussard turn school-titcher!' The shame of it crushed her into silence.

Melitte felt the inutility of trying to dislodge the old family servant's deep-rooted prejudices. All her effort was directed toward convincing Aunt Lympy of her complete self-satisfaction in this new undertaking.

But Aunt Lympy did not listen. She had money in her reticule, if that would do any good. Melitte gently thrust it away. She changed the subject, and kindly offered the woman a bit of refreshment. But Aunt Lympy would not eat, drink, unbend, nor lend herself to the subterfuge of small talk. She said good-by, with solemnity, as we part from those in sore affliction. When she had mounted into her ramshackle open buggy the old vehicle looked someway like a throne.

Scarcely a week after Aunt Lympy's visit Melitte was amazed by receiving a letter from her uncle, Gervais Leplain, of New Orleans. The tone of the letter was sad, self-condemnatory, reminiscent. A flood of tender recollection of his dead sister seemed to have suddenly overflowed his heart and glided from the point of his pen.

He was asking Melitte to come to them there in New Orleans and be as one of his own daughters, who were quite as eager to call her 'sister' as he was desirous of subscribing himself always henceforward, her father. He sent her a sum of money to supply her immediate wants, and informed her that he and one of his daughters would come for her in person at an early date.

Never a word was said of a certain missive dictated and sent to him by Aunt Lympy, every line of which was either a stinging rebuke or an appeal to the memory of his dead sister, whose child was tasting the bitter dregs of poverty. Melitte would never have recognized the overdrawn picture of herself.

From the very first there seemed to be no question about her accepting the offer of her uncle. She had literally not time to lift her voice in protest, before relatives, friends, acquaintances throughout the country raised a very clamor of congratulation. What luck! What a chance! To form one of the Gervais Leplain household!

Perhaps Melitte did not know that they lived in the most

sumptuous style in la rue Esplanade, with a cottage across the lake; and they traveled – they spent summers at the North! Melitte would see the great, the big, the beautiful world! They already pictured little Melitte gowned *en Parisienne;* they saw her name figuring in the society columns of the Sunday papers! as attending balls, dinners, luncheons and card parties.

The whole proceeding had apparently stunned Melitte. She sat with folded hands; except that she put the money carefully aside to return to her uncle. She would in no way get it confounded with her own small hoard; that was something precious and apart, not to be contaminated by gift-money.

'Have you written to yo' uncle to thank him, Melitte?' asked the sister-in-law.

Melitte shook her head. 'No; not yet.'

'But, Melitte!'

'Yes; I know.'

'Do you want yo' brother to write?'

'No! Oh, no!'

'Then don't put it off a day longer, Melitte. Such rudeness! W'at will yo' Uncle Gervais an' yo' cousins think!'

Even the babies that loved her were bitten with this feverish ambition for Melitte's worldly advancement. "Taint you, *ti tante,* that's goin' to wear a sunbonnet any mo', or calico dresses, or an apron, or feed the chickens!'

'Then you want *ti tante* to go away an' leave you all?'

They were not ready to answer, but hung their heads in meditative silence, which lasted until the full meaning of *ti tante's* question had penetrated the inner consciousness of the little man, whereupon he began to howl, loud and deep and long.

Even the curé, happy to see the end of a family estrangement, took Melitte's acceptance wholly for granted. He visited her and discoursed at length and with vivid imagination upon the perils and fascinations of 'the city's' life, presenting impartially, however, its advantages, which he hoped she would use to the betterment of her moral and intellectual faculties. He recommended to her a confessor at the cathedral who had traveled with him from France so many years ago.

'It's time you were dismissing an' closing up that school of yo's, Melitte,' advised her sister-in-law, puzzled and disturbed, as Melitte was preparing to leave for the schoolhouse.

She did not answer. She seemed to have been growing sullen and ill-humored since her great piece of good luck; but perhaps she did not hear, with the pink sunbonnet covering her pink ears.

Melitte was sensible of a strong attachment for the things about her – the dear, familiar things. She did not fully realize that her surroundings were poor and pinched. The thought of entering upon a different existence troubled her.

Why was every one, with single voice, telling her to 'go'? Was it that no one cared? She did not believe this, but chose to nourish the fancy. It furnished her a pretext for tears.

Why should she not go, and live in ease, free from responsibility and care? Why should she stay where no soul had said, 'I can't bear to have you go, Melitte?'

If they had only said, 'I shall miss you, Melitte,' it would have been something – but no! Even Aunt Lympy, who had nursed her as a baby, and in whose affection she had always trusted – even she had made her appearance and spent a whole day upon the scene, radiant, dispensing compliments, self-satisfied, as one who feels that all things are going well in her royal possessions.

'Oh, I'll go! I will go!' Melitte was saying a little hysterically to herself as she walked. The familiar road was a brown and green blur, for the tears in her eyes.

Victor Annibelle was not mending his fence that morning; but there he was, leaning over it as Melitte came along. He had hardly expected she would come, and at that hour he should have been back in the swamp with the men who were hired to cut timber; but the timber could wait, and the men could wait, and so could the work. It did not matter. There would be days enough to work when Melitte was gone.

She did not look at him; her head was down and she walked steadily on, carrying her bag of books. In a moment he was over the fence; he did not take the time to walk around to the gate; and with a few long strides he had joined her.

'Good morning, Melitte.' She gave a little start, for she had not heard him approaching.

'Oh – good morning. How is it you are not at work this morning?'

'I'm going a little later. An' how is it you are at work, Melitte? I didn't expect to see you passing by again.'

'Then you were going to let me leave without coming to say good-by?' she returned with an attempt at sprightliness.

And he, after a long moment's hesitation, 'Yes, I believe I was. W'en do you go?'

'When do you go! When do you go!' There it was again! Even he was urging her. It was the last straw.

'Who said I was going?' She spoke with quick exasperation. It was warm, and he would have lingered beneath the trees that here and there flung a pleasant shade, but she led him a pace through the sun.

'Who said?' he repeated after her. 'W'y, I don't know – everybody. You are going, of co'se?'

'Yes.'

She walked slowly and then fast in her agitation, wondering why he did not leave her instead of remaining there at her side in silence.

'Oh, I can't bear to have you go, Melitte!'

They were so near the school it seemed perfectly natural that she should hurry forward to join the little group that was there waiting for her under a tree. He made no effort to follow her. He expected no reply; the expression that had escaped him was so much a part of his unspoken thought, he was hardly conscious of having uttered it.

But the few spoken words, trifling as they seemed, possessed a power to warm and brighten greater than that of the sun and the moon. What mattered now to Melitte if the hours were heavy and languid; if the children were slow and dull! Even when they asked, 'W'en are you going, Miss Melitte?' she only laughed and said there was plenty of time to think of it. And were they so anxious to be rid of her? she wanted to know. She some way felt that it would not be so very hard to go now. In the afternoon, when she had dismissed the scholars, she lingered a while in the schoolroom. When she went to close the window, Victor Annibelle came up and stood outside with his elbows on the sill.

'Oh!' she said, with a start, 'why are you not working this hour of the day?' She was conscious of reiteration and a sad lack of imagination or invention to shape her utterances. But the question suited his intention well enough.

'I haven't worked all day,' he told her. 'I haven't gone twenty paces from this schoolhouse since you came into it this morning.'

Every particle of diffidence that had hampered his intercourse with her during the past few months had vanished.

'I'm a selfish brute,' he blurted, 'but I reckon it's instinct fo' a man to fight fo' his happiness just as he would fight fo' his life.'

'I mus' be going, Victor. Please move yo' arms an' let me close the window.'

'No, I won't move my arms till I say w'at I came here to say.' And seeing that she was about to withdraw, he seized her hand and held it. 'If you go away, Melitte – if you go I – oh! I don't want you to go. Since morning – I don't know w'y – something you said – or some way, I have felt that maybe you cared a little; that you might stay if I begged you. Would you, Melitte – would you?'

'I believe I would, Victor. Oh – never mind my hand; don't you see I must shut the window?'

So after all Melitte did not go to the city to become a *grande dame*. Why? Simply because Victor Annibelle asked her not to. The old people when they heard it shrugged their shoulders and tried to remember that they, too, had been young once; which is, sometimes, a very hard thing for old people to remember. Some of the younger ones thought she was right, and many of them believed she was wrong to sacrifice so brilliant an opportunity to shine and become a woman of fashion.

Aunt Lympy was not altogether dissatisfied; she felt that her interference had not been wholly in vain.

The Blind Man

A man carrying a small red box in one hand walked slowly down the street. His old straw hat and faded garments looked as if the rain had often beaten upon them, and the sun had as many times dried them upon his person. He was not old, but he seemed feeble; and he walked in the sun, along the blistering asphalt pavement. On the opposite side of the street there were trees that threw a thick and pleasant shade; people were all walking on that side. But the man did not know, for he was blind, and moreover he was stupid.

In the red box were lead pencils, which he was endeavoring to sell. He carried no stick, but guided himself by trailing his foot along the stone copings or his hand along the iron railings. When he came to the steps of a house he would mount them. Sometimes, after reaching the door with great difficulty, he could not find the electric button, whereupon he would patiently descend and go his way. Some of the iron gates were locked – their owners being away for the summer – and he would consume much time in striving to open them, which made little difference, as he had all the time there was at his disposal.

At times he succeeded in finding the electric button; but the man or maid who answered the bell needed no pencil, nor could they be induced to disturb the mistress of the house about so small a thing.

The man had been out long and had walked very far, but had sold nothing. That morning some one who had finally grown tired of having him hanging around had equipped him with this box of pencils, and sent him out to make his living. Hunger, with sharp fangs, was gnawing at his stomach and a consuming thirst parched his mouth and tortured him. The sun was broiling. He wore too much clothing – a vest and coat over his shirt. He might have removed these and carried them on his arm or thrown them away; but he did not think of it. A kind-hearted woman who saw him from an upper window felt sorry for him, and wished that he would cross over into the shade.

The man drifted into a side street, where there was a group of noisy, excited children at play. The color of the box which he carried attracted them and they wanted to know what was in it. One of them attempted to take it away from him. With the instinct to protect his own and his only means of sustenance, he resisted, shouted at the children and called them names. A policeman coming around the corner and seeing that he was the centre of a disturbance, jerked him violently around by the collar; but upon perceiving that he was blind, considerately refrained from clubbing him and sent him on his way. He walked on in the sun.

During his aimless rambling he turned into a street where there were monster electric cars thundering up and down, clanging wild bells and literally shaking the ground beneath his feet with their terrific impetus. He started to cross the street.

Then something happened – something horrible happened that made the women faint and the strongest men who saw it grow sick and dizzy. The motorman's lips were as gray as his face, and that was ashen gray; and he shook and staggered from the superhuman effort he had put forth to stop his car.

Where could the crowds have come from so suddenly, as if by magic? Boys on the run, men and women tearing up on their wheels to see the sickening sight; doctors dashing up in buggies as if directed by Providence.

And the horror grew when the multitude recognized in the dead and mangled figure one of the wealthiest, most useful and most influential men of the town – a man noted for his prudence and foresight. How could such a terrible fate have overtaken him? He was hastening from his business house – for he was late – to join his family, who were to start in an hour or two for their summer home on the Atlantic coast. In his hurry he did not perceive the other car coming from the opposite direction, and the common, harrowing thing was repeated.

The blind man did not know what the commotion was all about. He had crossed the street, and there he was, stumbling on in the sun, trailing his foot along the coping.

The Storm

A Sequel to 'The 'Cadian Ball'

I

The leaves were so still that even Bibi thought it was going to rain. Bobinôt, who was accustomed to converse on terms of perfect equality with his little son, called the child's attention to certain somber clouds that were rolling with sinister intention from the west, accompanied by a sullen, threatening roar. They were at Friedheimer's store and decided to remain there till the storm had passed. They sat within the door on two empty kegs. Bibi was four years old and looked very wise.

'Mama'll be 'fraid, yes,' he suggested with blinking eyes.

'She'll shut the house. Maybe she got Sylvie helpin' her this evenin',' Bobinôt responded reassuringly.

'No; she ent got Sylvie. Sylvie was helpin' her yistiday,' piped Bibi.

Bobinôt arose and going across to the counter purchased a can of shrimps, of which Calixta was very fond. Then he returned to his perch on the keg and sat stolidly holding the can of shrimps while the storm burst. It shook the wooden store and seemed to be ripping great furrows in the distant field. Bibi laid his little hand on his father's knee and was not afraid.

II

Calixta, at home, felt no uneasiness for their safety. She sat at a side window sewing furiously on a sewing machine. She was greatly occupied and did not notice the approaching storm. But she felt very warm and often stopped to mop her face on which the perspiration gathered in beads. She unfastened her white sacque at the throat. It began to grow dark, and suddenly realizing the situation she got up hurriedly and went about closing windows and doors.

Out on the small front gallery she had hung Bobinôt's Sunday clothes to air and she hastened out to gather them before the rain

fell. As she stepped outside, Alcée Laballière rode in at the gate.
She had not seen him very often since her marriage, and never
alone. She stood there with Bobinôt's coat in her hands, and the
big rain drops began to fall. Alcée rode his horse under the shelter
of a side projection where the chickens had huddled and there
were plows and a harrow piled up in the corner.

'May I come and wait on your gallery till the storm is over,
Calixta?' he asked.

'Come 'long in, M'sieur Alcée.'

His voice and her own startled her as if from a trance, and she
seized Bobinôt's vest. Alcée, mounting to the porch, grabbed the
trousers and snatched Bibi's braided jacket that was about to be
carried away by a sudden gust of wind. He expressed an intention
to remain outside, but it was soon apparent that he might as well
have been out in the open: the water beat in upon the boards in
driving sheets, and he went inside, closing the door after him. It
was even necessary to put something beneath the door to keep
the water out.

'My! what a rain! It's good two years sence it rain' like that,'
exclaimed Calixta as she rolled up a piece of bagging and Alcée
helped her to thrust it beneath the crack.

She was a little fuller of figure than five years before when she
married; but she had lost nothing of her vivacity. Her blue eyes
still retained their melting quality; and her yellow hair, dishevelled by the wind and rain, kinked more stubbornly than ever
about her ears and temples.

The rain beat upon the low, shingled roof with a force and
clatter that threatened to break an entrance and deluge them
there. They were in the dining room – the sitting room – the
general utility room. Adjoining was her bed room, with Bibi's
couch along side her own. The door stood open, and the room
with its white, monumental bed, its closed shutters, looked dim
and mysterious.

Alcée flung himself into a rocker and Calixta nervously began
to gather up from the floor the lengths of a cotton sheet which
she had been sewing.

'If this keeps up, *Dieu sait* if the levees goin' to stan' it!' she
exclaimed.

'What have you got to do with the levees?'

'I got enough to do! An' there's Bobinôt with Bibi out in that storm – if he only didn' left Friedheimer's!'

'Let us hope, Calixta, that Bobinôt's got sense enough to come in out of a cyclone.'

She went and stood at the window with a greatly disturbed look on her face. She wiped the frame that was clouded with moisture. It was stiflingly hot. Alcée got up and joined her at the window, looking over her shoulder. The rain was coming down in sheets obscuring the view of far-off cabins and enveloping the distant wood in a gray mist. The playing of the lightning was incessant. A bolt struck a tall chinaberry tree at the edge of the field. It filled all visible space with a blinding glare and the crash seemed to invade the very boards they stood upon.

Calixta put her hands to her eyes, and with a cry, staggered backward. Alcée's arm encircled her, and for an instant he drew her close and spasmodically to him.

'*Bonté!*' she cried, releasing herself from his encircling arm and retreating from the window, 'the house'll go next! If I only knew w'ere Bibi was!' She would not compose herself; she would not be seated. Alcée clasped her shoulders and looked into her face. The contact of her warm, palpitating body when he had unthinkingly drawn her into his arms, had aroused all the old-time infatuation and desire for her flesh.

'Calixta,' he said, 'don't be frightened. Nothing can happen. The house is too low to be struck, with so many tall trees standing about. There! aren't you going to be quiet? say, aren't you?' He pushed her hair back from her face that was warm and steaming. Her lips were as red and moist as pomegranate seed. Her white neck and a glimpse of her full, firm bosom disturbed him powerfully. As she glanced up at him the fear in her liquid blue eyes had given place to a drowsy gleam that unconsciously betrayed a sensuous desire. He looked down into her eyes and there was nothing for him to do but to gather her lips in a kiss. It reminded him of Assumption.

'Do you remember – in Assumption, Calixta?' he asked in a low voice broken by passion. Oh! she remembered; for in Assumption he had kissed her and kissed and kissed her; until his senses would well nigh fail, and to save her he would resort to a desperate flight. If she was not an immaculate dove in those days, she was still inviolate; a passionate creature whose very defense-lessness had made her defense, against which his honor forbade him to prevail. Now – well, now – her lips seemed in a manner free to be tasted, as well as her round, white throat and her whiter breasts.

They did not heed the crashing torrents, and the roar of the elements made her laugh as she lay in his arms. She was a revelation in that dim, mysterious chamber; as white as the couch she lay upon. Her firm, elastic flesh that was knowing for the first time its birthright, was like a creamy lily that the sun invites to contribute its breath and perfume to the undying life of the world.

The generous abundance of her passion, without guile or trickery, was like a white flame which penetrated and found response in depths of his own sensuous nature that had never yet been reached.

When he touched her breasts they gave themselves up in quivering ecstasy, inviting his lips. Her mouth was a fountain of delight. And when he possessed her, they seemed to swoon together at the very borderland of life's mystery.

He stayed cushioned upon her, breathless, dazed, enervated, with his heart beating like a hammer upon her. With one hand she clasped his head, her lips lightly touching his forehead. The other hand stroked with a soothing rhythm his muscular shoulders.

The growl of the thunder was distant and passing away. The rain beat softly upon the shingles, inviting them to drowsiness and sleep. But they dared not yield.

The rain was over; and the sun was turning the glistening green world into a palace of gems. Calixta, on the gallery, watched Alcée ride away. He turned and smiled at her with a beaming face; and she lifted her pretty chin in the air and laughed aloud.

III

Bobinôt and Bibi, trudging home, stopped without at the cistern to make themselves presentable.

'My! Bibi, w'at will yo' mama say! You ought to be ashame'. You oughtn' put on those good pants. Look at 'em! An' that mud on yo' collar! How you got that mud on yo' collar, Bibi? I never saw such a boy!' Bibi was the picture of pathetic resignation.

Bobinôt was the embodiment of serious solicitude as he strove to remove from his own person and his son's the signs of their tramp over heavy roads and through wet fields. He scraped the mud off Bibi's bare legs and feet with a stick and carefully removed all traces from his heavy brogans. Then, prepared for the worst – the meeting with an over-scrupulous housewife, they entered cautiously at the back door.

Calixta was preparing supper. She had set the table and was dripping coffee at the hearth. She sprang up as they came in.

'Oh, Bobinôt! You back! My! but I was uneasy. W'ere you been during the rain? An' Bibi? he ain't wet? he ain't hurt?' She had clasped Bibi and was kissing him effusively. Bobinôt's explanations and apologies which he had been composing all along the way, died on his lips as Calixta felt him to see if he were dry, and seemed to express nothing but satisfaction at their safe return.

'I brought you some shrimps, Calixta,' offered Bobinôt, hauling the can from his ample side pocket and laying it on the table.

'Shrimps! Oh, Bobinôt! you too good fo' anything!' and she gave him a smacking kiss on the cheek that resounded. *'J'vous réponds*, we'll have a feas' to night! umph-umph!'

Bobinôt and Bibi began to relax and enjoy themselves, and when the three seated themselves at table they laughed much and so loud that anyone might have heard them as far away as Laballière's.

IV

Alcée Laballière wrote to his wife, Clarisse, that night. It was a loving letter, full of tender solicitude. He told her not to hurry back, but if she and the babies liked it at Biloxi, to stay a month longer. He was getting on nicely; and though he missed them, he was willing to bear the separation a while longer – realizing that their health and pleasure were the first things to be considered.

V

As for Clarisse, she was charmed upon receiving her husband's letter. She and the babies were doing well. The society was agreeable; many of her old friends and acquaintances were at the bay. And the first free breath since her marriage seemed to restore the pleasant liberty of her maiden days. Devoted as she was to her husband, their intimate conjugal life was something which she was more than willing to forego for a while.

So the storm passed and every one was happy.

The Godmother

I

Tante Elodie attracted youth in some incomprehensible way. It was seldom there was not a group of young people gathered about her fire in winter or sitting with her in summer, in the pleasant shade of the live-oaks that screened the gallery.

There were several persons forming a half circle around her generous chimney early one evening in February. There were Madame Nicolas' two tiny little girls who sat on the floor and played with a cat the whole time; Madame Nicolas herself, who only came for the little girls and insisted on hurrying away because it was time to put the children to bed, and who, moreover, was expecting a caller. There was a fair, blonde girl, one of the younger teachers at the Normal school. Gabriel Lucaze offered to escort her home when she got up to go, after Madame Nicolas' departure. But she had already accepted the company of a silent, studious looking youth who had come there in the hope of meeting her. So they all went away but young Gabriel Lucaze, Tante Elodie's godson, who stayed and played cribbage with her. They played at a small table on which were a shaded lamp, a few magazines and a dish of *pralines* which the lady took great pleasure in nibbling during the reflective pauses of the game. They had played one game and were nearing the end of the second. He laid a queen upon the table.

'Fifteen-two,' she said, playing a five.

'Twenty, and a pair.'

'Twenty-five. Six points for me.'

'Its a "go."'

'Thirty-one and out. That is the second game I've won. Will you play another rubber, Gabriel?'

'Not much, Tante Elodie, when you are playing in such luck. Besides, I've got to get out, it's half-past-eight.' He had played recklessly, often glancing at the bronze clock which reposed majestically beneath its crystal globe on the mantel-piece. He prepared at once to leave, going before the gilt-framed, oval mirror to fold and arrange a silk muffler beneath his great coat.

He was rather good looking. That is, he was healthy looking; his face a little florid, and hair almost black. It was short and curly and parted on one side. His eyes were fine when they were not bloodshot, as they sometimes were. His mouth might have been better. It was not disagreeable or unpleasant, but it was unsatisfactory and drooped a little at the corners. However, he was good to look at as he crossed the muffler over his chest. His face was unusually alert. Tante Elodie looked at him in the glass.

'Will you be warm enough, my boy? It has turned very cold since six o'clock.'

'Plenty warm. Too warm.'

'Where are you going?'

'Now, Tante Elodie,' he said, turning, and laying a hand on her shoulder; he was holding his soft felt hat in the other. 'It is always "where are you going?" "Where have you been?" I have spoiled you. I have told you too much. You expect me to tell you everything; consequently, I must sometimes tell you fibs. I am going to confession. There! are you satisfied?' and he bent down and gave her a hearty kiss.

'I am satisfied, provided you go to the right priestess to confession; not up the hill, mind you!'

'Up the hill' meant up at the Normal School with Tante Elodie. She was a very conservative person. 'The Normal' seemed to her an unpardonable innovation, with its teachers from Minnesota, from Iowa, from God-knows-where, bringing strange ways and manners to the old town. She was one, also, who considered the emancipation of slaves a great mistake. She had many reasons for thinking so and was often called upon to enumerate this in her wordy arguments with her many opponents.

II

Tante Elodie distinctly heard the Doctor leave the Widow Nicolas' at a quarter past ten. He visited the handsome and attractive young woman two evenings in the week and always left at the same hour. Tante Elodie's double glass doors opened upon the wide upper gallery. Around the angle of the gallery were the apartments of Madame Nicolas. Any one visiting the widow was obliged to pass Tante Elodie's door. Beneath was a store occasionally occupied by some merchant or other, but oftener vacant. A stairway led down from the porch to the yard where two enormous live-oaks grew and cast a dense shade upon the gallery above, making it an agreeable retreat and resting place on hot summer afternoons. The high, wooden yard-gate opened directly upon the street.

A half hour went by after the Doctor passed her door. Tante Elodie played 'solitaire.' Another half hour followed and still Tante Elodie was not sleepy nor did she think of going to bed. It was very near midnight when she began to prepare her night toilet and to cover the fire.

The room was very large with heavy rafters across the ceiling. There was an enormous bed over in the corner; a four-posted mahogany covered with a lace spread which was religiously folded every night and laid on a chair. There were some old ambrotypes and photographs about the room; a few comfortable but simple rocking chairs and a broad fire place in which a big log sizzled. It was an attractive room for anyone, not because of anything that was in it except Tante Elodie herself. She was far past fifty. Her hair was still soft and brown and her eyes bright and vivacious. Her figure was slender and nervous. There were many lines in her face, but it did not look care-worn. Had she her youthful flesh, she would have looked very young.

Tante Elodie had spent the evening in munching *pralines* and reading by lamp-light some old magazines that Gabriel Lucaze had brought her from the club.

There was a romance connected with her early days. Romances serve but to feed the imagination of the young; they add nothing to the sum of truth. No one realized this fact more strongly than Tante Elodie herself. While she tacitly condoned the romance, perhaps for the sake of the sympathy it bred, she never thought of Justin Lucaze but with a feeling of gratitude towards the memory of her parents who had prevented her marrying him thirty-five years before. She could have no connection between her deep and powerful affection for young Gabriel Lucaze and her old-time, brief passion for his father. She loved the boy above everything on earth. There was none so attractive to her as he; none so thoughtful of her pleasures and pains. In his devotion there was no trace of a duty-sense; it was the spontaneous expression of affection and seeming dependence.

After Tante Elodie had turned down her bed and undressed, she drew a grey flannel *peignoir* over her nightgown and knelt down to say her prayers; kneeling before a rocker with her bare feet turned to the fire. Prayers were no trifling matter with her. Besides those which she knew by heart, she read litanies and invocations from a book and also a chapter of 'The Following of Christ.' She had said her *Notre Père*, her *Salve Marie* and *Je crois en Dieu* and was deep in the litany of the Blessed Virgin when she fancied she heard footsteps on the stairs. The night was breathlessly still; it was very late.

'*Vierge des Vierges: Priez pour nous. Mère de Dieu: Priez—*'

Surely there was a stealthy step upon the gallery, and now a hand at her door, striving to lift the latch. Tante Elodie was not afraid. She felt the utmost security in her home and had no dread of mischievous intruders in the peaceful old town. She simply realized that there was some one at her door and that she must find out who it was and what they wanted. She got up from her knees, thrust her feet into her slippers that were near the fire and, lowering the lamp by which she had been reading her litanies, approached the door. There was the very softest rap upon the pane. Tante Elodie unbolted and opened the door the least bit.

'*Qui est là?*' she asked.

'Gabriel.' He forced himself into the room before she had time to fully open the door to him.

III

Gabriel strode past her towards the fire, mechanically taking off his hat, and sat down in the rocker before which she had been kneeling. He sat on the prayer books she had left there. He removed them and laid them upon the table. Seeming to realize in a dazed way that it was not their accustomed place, he threw the two books on a nearby chair.

Tante Elodie raised the lamp and looked at him. His eyes were blood-shot, as they were when he drank or experienced any unusual emotion or excitement. But he was pale and his mouth drooped excessively, and twitched with the effort he made to control it. The top button was wrenched from his coat and his

muffler was disarranged. Tante Elodie was grieved to the soul,
seeing him thus. She thought he had been drinking.

'Gabriel, w'at is the matter?' she asked imploringly. 'Oh, my
poor child, w'at is the matter?' He looked at her in a fixed way
and passed a hand over his head. He tried to speak, but his voice
failed, as with one who experiences stage fright. Then he
articulated, hoarsely, swallowing nervously between the slow
words:

'I – killed a man – about an hour ago – yonder in the old
Nigger-Luke Cabin.' Tante Elodie's two hands went suddenly
down to the table and she leaned heavily upon them for support.

'You did not; you did not,' she panted. 'You are drinking. You
do not know w'at you are saying. Tell me, Gabriel, who 'as been
making you drink? Ah! they will answer to me! You do not know
w'at you are saying. *Boute!* how can you know!' She clutched
him and the torn button that hung in the button-hole fell to the
floor.

'I don't know why it happened,' he went on, gazing into the
fire with unseeing eyes, or rather with eyes that saw what was
pictured in his mind and not what was before them.

'I've been in cutting scrapes and shooting scrapes that never
amounted to anything, when I was just as crazy mad as I was to-
night. But I tell you, Tante Elodie, he's dead. I've got to get away.
But how are you going to get out of a place like this, when every
dog and cat' – His effort had spent itself, and he began to tremble
with a nervous chill; his teeth chattered and his lips could not
form an utterance.

Tante Elodie, stumbling rather than walking, went over to a
small buffet and pouring some brandy into a glass, gave it to him.
She took a little herself. She looked much older in the *peignoir* and
the handkerchief tied around her head. She sat down beside
Gabriel and took his hand. It was cold and clammy.

'Tell me everything,' she said with determination, 'everything;
without delay; and do not speak so loud. We shall see what must
be done. Was it a negro? Tell me everything.'

'No, it was a white man, you don't know, from Conshotta,
named Everson. He was half drunk; a hulking bully as strong as
an ox, or I could have licked him. He tortured me until I was
frantic. Did you ever see a cat torment a mouse? The mouse can't

do anything but lose its head. I lost my head, but I had my knife; that big hornhandled knife.'

'Where is it?' she asked sharply. He felt his back pocket.

'I don't know.' He did not seem to care, or to realize the importance of the loss.

'Go on; make haste; tell me the whole story. You went from here – you went – go on.'

'I went down the river a piece,' he said, throwing himself back in the chair and keeping his eyes fixed upon one burning ember on the hearth, 'down to Symund's store where there was a game of cards. A lot of the fellows were there. I played a little and didn't drink anything, and stopped at ten. I was going' – He leaned forward with his elbows on his knees and his hands hanging between. 'I was going to see a woman at eleven o'clock; it was the only time I could see her. I came along and when I got by the old Nigger-Luke Cabin I lit a match and looked at my watch. It was too early and it wouldn't do to hang around. I went into the cabin and started a blaze in the chimney with some fine wood I found there. My feet were cold and I sat on an empty soap-box before the fire to dry them. I remember I kept looking at my watch. It was twenty-five minutes to eleven when Everson came into the cabin. He was half drunk and his face was red and looked like a beast. He had left the game and had followed me. I hadn't spoken of where I was going. But he said he knew I was off for a lark and he wanted to go along. I said he couldn't go where I was going, and there was no use talking. He kept it up. At a quarter to eleven I wanted to go, and he went and stood in the doorway.

'"If I don't go, you don't go", he said, and he kept it up. When I tried to pass him he pushed me back like I was a feather. He didn't get mad. He laughed all the time and drank whiskey out of a bottle he had in his pocket. If I hadn't got mad and lost my head, I might have fooled him or played some trick on him – if I had used my wits. But I didn't know any more what I was doing than the day I threw the inkstand at old Dainean's head when he switched me and made fun of me before the whole school.

'I stooped by the fire and looked at my watch; he was talking all kinds of foolishness I can't repeat. It was eleven o'clock. I was in a killing rage and made a dash for the door. His big body and his big arm were there like an iron bar, and he laughed. I took

out my knife and stuck it into him. I don't believe he knew at first
that I had touched him, for he kept on laughing; then he fell over
like a pig, and the old cabin shook.'

Gabriel had raised his clinched hand with an intensely
dramatic movement when he said, 'I stuck it into him.' Then he
let his head fall back against the chair and finished the
concluding sentences of his story with closed eyes.

'How do you know he is dead?' asked Tante Elodie, whose
voice sounded hard and monotonous.

'I only walked ten steps away and went back to see. He was
dead. Then I came here. The best thing is to go give myself up, I
reckon, and tell the whole story like I've told you. That's about
the best thing I can do if I want any peace of mind.'

'Are you crazy, Gabriel! You have not yet regained your
senses. Listen to me. Listen to me and try to understand what I
say.'

Her face was full of a hard intelligence he had not seen there
before; all the soft womanliness had for the moment faded out of
it.

'You 'ave not killed the man Everson,' she said deliberately.
'You know nothing about 'im. You do not know that he left
Symund's or that he followed you. You left at ten o'clock. You
came straight in town, not feeling well. You saw a light in my
window, came here; rapped on the door; I let you in and gave
you something for cramps in the stomach and made you warm
yourself and lie down on the sofa. Wait a moment. Stay still
there.'

She got up and went shuffling out the door, around the angle
of the gallery and tapped on Madame Nicolas' door. She could
hear the young woman jump out of bed bewildered, asking,
'Who is there? Wait! What is it?'

'It is Tante Elodie.' The door was unbolted at once.

'Oh! how I hate to trouble you, chérie. Poor Gabriel 'as been at
my room for hours with the most severe cramps. Nothing I can
do seems to relieve 'im. Will you let me 'ave the morphine which
Doctor left with you for old Betsy's rheumatism? Ah! thank you. I
think a quarter of a grain will relieve 'im. Poor boy! Such
suffering! I am so sorry dear, to disturb you. Do not stand by the
door, you will take cold. Good night.'

Tante Elodie persuaded Gabriel, if the club were still open, to look in there on his way home. He had a room in a relative's house. His mother was dead and his father lived on a plantation several miles from town. Gabriel feared that his nerve would fail him. But Tante Elodie had him up again with a glass of brandy. She said that he must get the fact lodged in his mind that he was innocent. She inspected the young man carefully before he went away, brushing and arranging his toilet. She sewed the missing button on his coat. She had noticed some blood upon his right hand. He himself had not seen it. With a wet towel she washed his face and hands as though he were a little child. She brushed his hair and sent him away with a thousand reiterated precautions.

IV

Tante Elodie was not overcome in any way after Gabriel left her. She did not indulge in a hysterical moment, but set about accomplishing some purpose which she had evidently had in her mind. She dressed herself again; quickly, nervously, but with much precision. A shawl over her head and a long, black cape across her shoulders made her look like a nun. She quitted her room. It was very dark and very still out of doors. There was only a whispering wail among the live-oak leaves.

Tante Elodie stole noiselessly down the steps and out the gate. If she had met anyone, she intended to say she was suffering with toothache and was going to the doctor or druggist for relief.

But she met not a soul. She knew every plank, every uneven brick of the side walk; every rut of the way, and might have walked with her eyes closed. Strangely enough she had forgotten to pray. Prayer seemed to belong to her moments of contemplation; while now she was all action; prompt, quick, decisive action.

It must have been near upon two o'clock. She did not meet a cat or a dog on her way to the Nigger-Luke Cabin. The hut was well out of town and isolated from a group of tumbled-down shanties some distance off, in which a lazy set of negroes lived. There was not the slightest feeling of fear or horror in her breast. There might have been, had she not already been dominated and possessed by the determination that Gabriel must be shielded from ignominy – maybe, worse.

She glided into the low cabin like a shadow, hugging the side of the open door. She would have stumbled over the dead man's feet if she had not stepped so cautiously. The embers were burning so low that they gave but a faint glow in the sinister cabin with its obscure corners, its black, hanging cobwebs and the dead man lying twisted as he had fallen with his face on his arm.

Once in the cabin the woman crept towards the body on her hands and knees. She was looking for something in the dusky light; something she could not find. Crawling towards the fire over the uneven, creaking boards, she stirred the embers the least bit with a burnt stick that had fallen to one side. She dared not make a blaze. Then she dragged herself once more towards the lifeless body. She pictured how the knife had been thrust in; how it had fallen from Gabriel's hand; how the man had come down like a felled ox. Yes, the knife could not be far off, but she could not discover a trace of it. She slipped her fingers beneath the body and felt all along. The knife lay up under his arm pit. Her hand scraped his chin as she withdrew it. She did not mind. She was exultant at getting the knife. She felt like some other being, possessed by Satan. Some fiend in human shape, some spirit of murder. A cricket began to sing on the hearth.

Tante Elodie noticed the golden gleam of the murdered man's watch chain, and a sudden thought invaded her. With deft, though unsteady fingers, she unhooked the watch and chain. There was money in his pockets. She emptied them, turning the pockets inside out. It was difficult to reach his left hand pockets, but she did so. The money, a few bank notes and some silver coins, together with the watch and knife she tied in her handkerchief. Then she hurried away, taking a long stride across the man's body in order to reach the door.

The stars were like shining pieces of gold upon dark velvet. So Tante Elodie thought as she looked up at them an instant.

There was the sound of disorderly voices away off in the negro shanties. Clasping the parcel close to her breast she began to run. She ran, ran, as fast as some fleet fourfooted creature, ran, panting. She never stopped till she reached the gate that let her in under the live-oaks. The most intent listener could not have heard her as she mounted the stairs; as she let herself in at the door; as she bolted it. Once in the room she began to totter. She was sick to her stomach and her head swam. Instinctively she reached out towards the bed, and fell fainting upon it, face downward.

The gray light of dawn was coming in at her windows. The lamp on the table had burned out. Tante Elodie groaned as she tried to move. And again she groaned with mental anguish, this time as the events of the past night came back to her, one by one, in all their horrifying details. Her labor of love, begun the night before, was not yet ended. The parcel containing the watch and money were there beneath her, pressing into her bosom. When she managed to regain her feet the first thing which she did was to rekindle the fire with splinters of pine and pieces of hickory that were at hand in her wood box. When the fire was burning briskly, Tante Elodie took the paper money from the little bundle and burned it. She did not notice the denomination of the bills, there were five or six, she thrust them into the blaze with the poker and watched them burn. The few loose pieces of silver she put in her purse, apart from her own money; there was sixty-five cents in small coin. The watch she placed between her mattresses; then, seized with misgiving, took it out. She gazed around the room, seeking a safe hiding place and finally put the watch into a large, strong stocking which she pinned securely around her waist beneath her clothing. The knife she washed carefully, drying it with pieces of newspaper which she burned. The water in which she had washed it she also threw in a corner of the large fire place upon a heap of ashes. Then she put the knife into the pocket of one of Gabriel's coats which she had cleaned and mended for him; it was hanging in her closet.

She did all this slowly and with great effort, for she felt very sick. When the unpleasant work was over it was all she could do to undress and get beneath the covers of her bed.

She knew that when she did not appear at breakfast Madame Nicolas would send to investigate the cause of her absence. She took her meals with the young widow around the corner of the gallery. Tante Elodie was not rich. She received a small income from the remains of what had once been a magnificent plantation adjoining the lands which Justin Lucaze owned and cultivated. But she lived frugally, with a hundred small cares and economies and rarely felt the want of extra money except when the generosity of her nature prompted her to help an afflicted neighbor, or to bestow a gift upon some one of whom she was fond. It often seemed to Tante Elodie that all the affection of her heart was centered upon her young protégé, Gabriel; that what she felt for others was simply an emanation – rays, as it were, from this central sun of love that shone for him alone.

In the midst of twinges, of nervous tremors, her thoughts were with him. It was impossible for her to think of anything else. She was filled with unspeakable dread that he might betray himself. She wondered what he had done after he left her: what he was doing at that moment? She wanted to see him again alone, to insist anew upon the necessity of his self-assertion of innocence.

As she expected, Mrs. Wm. Nicolas came around at the breakfast hour to see what was the matter. She was an active woman, very pretty and fresh looking, with willing, deft hands and the kindest voice and eyes. She was distressed at the spectacle of poor Tante Elodie extended in bed with her head tied up, and looking pale and suffering.

'Ah! I suspected it!' she exclaimed, 'coming out in the cold on the gallery last night to get morphine for Gabriel; *ma foi!* as if he could not go to the drug store for his morphine! Where have you pain? Have you any fever, Tante Elodie?'

'It is nothing, *chérie*. I believe I am only tired and want to rest for a day in bed.'

'Then you must rest as long as you want. I will look after your fire and see that you have what you need. I will bring your coffee at once. It is a beautiful day; like spring. When the sun gets very warm I will open the window.'

V

All day long Gabriel did not appear, and she dared not make inquiries about him. Several persons came in to see her, learning that she was sick. The midnight murder in the Nigger-Luke Cabin seemed to be the favorite subject of conversation among her visitors. They were not greatly excited over it as they might have been were the man other than a comparative stranger. But the

subject seemed full of interest, enhanced by the mystery surrounding it. Madame Nicolas did not risk to speak of it.

'That is not a fit conversation for a sick-room. Any doctor –
anybody with sense will tell you. For Mercy's sake! change the
subject.'

But Fifine Delonce could not be silenced.

'And now it appears,' she went on with renewed animation, 'it
appears he was playing cards down at Symund's store. That
shows how they pass their time – those boys! It's a scandal! But
nobody can remember when he left. Some say at nine, some say
it was past eleven. He sort of went away like he didn't want them
to notice.'

'Well, we didn't know the man. My patience! there are
murders every day. If we had to keep up with them, *ma foi!* Who
is going to Lucie's card party to-morrow? I hear she did not invite
her cousin Claire. They have fallen out again it seems.' And
Madame Nicolas, after speaking, went to give Tante Elodie a
drink of *Tisane*.

'Mr. Ben's got about twenty darkies from Niggerville, holding
them on suspicion,' continued Fifine, dancing on the edge of her
chair. 'Without doubt the man was enticed to the cabin and
murdered and robbed there. Not a picayune left in his pockets!
only his pistol – that they didn't take, all loaded, in his back
pocket, that he might have used, and his watch gone! Mr. Ben
thinks his brother in Conshotta, that's very well off, is going to
offer a big reward.'

'What relation was the man to you, Fifine?' asked Madame
Nicolas, sarcastically.

'He was a human being, Amelia; you have no heart, no
feeling. If it makes a woman that hard to associate with a doctor,
then thank God – well – as I was saying, if they can catch those
two strange section hands that left town last night – but you
better bet they're not such fools to keep that watch. But old Uncle
Marte said he saw little foot prints like a woman's, early this
morning, but no one wanted to listen to him or pay any
attention, and the crowd tramped them out in little or no time.
None of the boys want to let on; they don't want us to know
which ones were playing cards at Symund's. Was Gabriel at
Symund's, Tante Elodie?'

Tante Elodie coughed painfully and looked blankly as though she had only heard her name and had been inattentive to what was said.

'For pity sake leave Tante Elodie out of this! it's bad enough she has to listen, suffering as she is. Gabriel spent the evening here, on Tante Elodie's sofa, very sick with cramps. You will have to pursue your detective work in some other quarter, my dear.'

A little girl came in with a huge bunch of blossoms. There was some bustle attending the arrangement of the flowers in vases, and in the midst of it, two or three ladies took their leave.

'I wonder if they're going to send the body off to-night, or if they're going to keep it for the morning train,' Fifine was heard to speculate, before the door closed upon her.

Tante Elodie could not sleep that night. The following day she had some fever and Madame Nicolas insisted upon her seeing the doctor. He gave her a sleeping draught and some fever drops and said she would be all right in a few days; for he could find nothing alarming in her condition.

By a supreme effort of the will she got up on the third day hoping in the accustomed routine of her daily life to get rid, in part, of the uneasiness and unhappiness that possessed her.

The sun shone warm in the afternoon and she went and stood on the gallery watching for Gabriel to pass. He had not been near her. She was wounded, alarmed, miserable at his silence and absence; but determined to see him. He came down the street, presently, never looking up, with his hat drawn over his eyes.

'Gabriel!' she called. He gave a start and glanced around.

'Come up; I want to see you a moment.'

'I haven't time now, Tante Elodie.'

'Come in!' she said sharply.

'All right, you'll have to fix it up with Morrison,' and he opened the gate and went in. She was back in her room by the time he reached it, and in her chair, trembling a little and feeling sick again.

'Gabriel, if you 'ave no heart, it seems to me you would 'ave some intelligence; a moment's reflection would show you the folly of altering your 'abits so suddenly. Did you not know I was sick? did you not guess my uneasiness?'

'I haven't guessed anything or known anything but a taste of hell,' he said, not looking at her. Her heart bled afresh for him and went out to him in full forgiveness. 'You were right,' he went on, 'it would have been horrible to saying anything. There is no suspicion. I'll never say anything unless some one should be falsely accused.'

'There will be no possible evidence to accuse anyone,' she assured him. 'Forget it, forget it. Keep on as though it was something you had dreamed. Not only for the outside, but within yourself. Do not accuse yourself of that act, but the actions, the conduct, the ungovernable temper that made it possible. Promise me it will be a lesson to you, Gabriel; and God, who reads men's hearts, will not call it a crime, but an accident which your unbridled nature invited. I will forget it. You must forget it. 'Ave you been to the office?'

'To-day; not yesterday. I don't know what I did yesterday, but look for the knife — after they — I couldn't go while he was there — and I thought every minute some one was coming to accuse me. And when I realized they weren't — I don't know — I drank too much, I think. Reading law! I might as well have been reading Hebrew. If Morrison thinks — See here Tante Elodie, are there any spots on this coat? Can you see anything here in the light?'

'There are no spots anywhere. Stop thinking of it, I implore you.' But he pulled off the coat and flung it across a chair. He went to the closet to get his other coat which he knew hung there. Tante Elodie, still feeble and suffering, in the depths of her chair, was not quick enough, could think of no way to prevent it. She had at first put the knife in his pocket with the intention of returning it to him. But now she dreaded to have him find it, and thus discover the part she had played in the sickening dream.

He buttoned up his coat briskly and started away.

'Please burn it,' he said, looking at the garment on the chair, 'I never want to see it again.'

VI

When it became distinctly evident that no slightest suspicion would be attached to him for the killing of Everson; when he plainly realized that there was no one upon whom the guilt could be fastened, Gabriel thought he would regain his lost equilibrium.

If in no other way, he fancied he could reason himself back into it. He was suffering, but he someway had no fear that his present condition of mind would last. He thought it would pass away like a malignant fever. It would have to pass away or it would have to kill him.

From Tante Elodie's he went over to Morrison's office where he was reading law. Morrison and his partner were out of town and he had the office to himself. He had been there all morning. There was nothing for him to do now but to see anyone who called on business, and to go on with his reading. He seated himself and spread his book before him, but he looked into the street through the open door. Then he got up and shut the door. He again fastened his eyes upon the pages before him, but his mind was traveling other ways. For the hundredth time he was going over every detail of the fatal night, and trying to justify himself in his own heart.

If it had been an open and fair fight there would have been no trouble in squaring himself with his conscience; if the man had shown the slightest disposition to do him bodily harm, but he had not. On the other hand, he asked himself, what constituted a murder? Why, there was Morrison himself who had once fired at Judge Filips on that very street. His ball had gone wide of the mark, and subsequently he and Filips had adjusted their difficulties and become friends. Was Morrison any less a murderer because his weapon had missed?

Suppose the knife had swerved, had penetrated the arm, had inflicted a harmless scratch or flesh wound, would he be sitting there now, calling himself names? But he would try to think it all out later. He could not bear to be there alone, he never liked to be alone, and now he could not endure it. He closed the book without the slightest recollection of a line his eyes had followed. He went and gazed up and down the street, then he locked the office and walked away.

The fact of Everson having been robbed was very puzzling to Gabriel. He thought about it as he walked along the street.

The complete change that had taken place in his emotions, his sentiments, did not astonish him in the least: we accept such phenomena without question. A week ago – not so long as that – he was in love with the fair-haired girl up at the Normal. He was undeniably in love with her. He knew the symptoms. He wanted to marry her and meant to ask her whenever his position justified him in doing so.

Now, where had that love gone? He thought of her with indifference. Still, he was seeking her at that moment, through habit, without any special motive. He had no positive desire to see her; to see any one; and yet he could not endure to be alone. He had no desire to see Tante Elodie. She wanted him to forget and her presence made him remember.

The girl was walking under the beautiful trees, and she stood and waited for him, when she saw him mounting the hill. As he looked at her, his fondness for her and his intentions toward her, appeared now, like child's play. Life was something terrible of which she had no conception. She seemed to him as harmless, as innocent, as insignificant as a little bird.

'Oh! Gabriel,' she exclaimed. 'I had just written you a note. Why haven't you been here? It was foolish to get offended. I wanted to explain: I couldn't get out of it the other night, at Tante Elodie's, when he asked me. You know I couldn't, and that I would rather have come with you.' Was it possible he would have taken this seriously a week ago?

'Delonce is a good fellow; he's a decent fellow. I don't blame you. That's all right.' She was hurt at his easy complaisance. She did not wish to offend him, and here she was grieved because he was not offended.

'Will you come indoors to the fire?' she asked.

'No; I just strolled up for a minute.' He leaned against a tree and looked bored, or rather, preoccupied with other things than herself. It was not a week ago that he wanted to see her every day; when he said the hours were like minutes that he passed beside her. 'I just strolled up to tell you that I am going away.'

'Oh! going away?' and the pink deepened in her cheeks, and she tried to look indifferent and to clasp her glove tighter. He had not the slightest intention of going away when he mounted the hill. It came to him like an inspiration.

'Where are you going?'

'Going to look for work in the city.'

'And what about your law studies?'

'I have no talent for the law; it's about time I acknowledged it. I want to get into something that will make me hustle. I wouldn't mind – I'd like to get something to do on a railroad that would go tearing through the country night and day. What's the matter?' he asked, perceiving the tears that she could not conceal.

'Nothing's the matter,' she answered with dignity, and a sense of seeming proud.

He took her word for it and, instead of seeking to console her, went rambling on about the various occupations in which he should like to engage for a while.

'When are you going?'

'Just as soon as I can.'

'Shall I see you again?'

'Of course. Good-bye. Don't stay out here too long; you might take cold.' He listlessly shook hands with her and descended the hill with long rapid strides.

He would not intentionally have hurt her. He did not realize that he was wounding her. It would have been as difficult for him to revive his passion for her as to bring Everson back to life. Gabriel knew there could be fresh horror added to the situation. Discovery would have added to it; a false accusation would have deepened it. But he never dreamed of the new horror coming as it did, through Tante Elodie, when he found the knife in his pocket. It took a long time to realize what it meant; and then he felt as if he never wanted to see her again. In his mind, her action identified itself with his crime, and made itself a hateful, hideous part of it, which he could not endure to think of, and of which he could not help thinking.

It was the one thing which had saved him, and yet he felt no gratitude. The great love which had prompted the deed did not soften him. He could not believe that any man was worth loving to such length, or worth saving at such a price. She seemed, to his imagination, less a woman than a monster, capable of committing, in cold-blood, deeds, which he himself could only accomplish in blind rage. For the first time, Gabriel wept. He threw himself down upon the ground in the deepening twilight and wept as he never had before in his life. A terrible sense of loss overpowered him; as if someone dearer than a mother had been taken out of the reach of his heart; as if a refuge had gone from him. The last spark of human affection was dead within him. He knew it as he was losing it. He wept at the loss which left him alone with his thoughts.

VII

Tante Elodie was always chilly. It was warm for the last of April, and the women at Madame Nicolas' wedding were all in airy summer attire. All but Tante Elodie, who wore her black silk, her old silk with a white lace fichu, and she held an embroidered handkerchief and a fan in her hand.

Fifine Delonce had been over in the morning to take up the seams in the dress, for, as she expressed herself, it was miles too loose for Tante Elodie's figure. She appeared to be shrivelling away to nothing. She had not again been sick in bed since that little spell in February; but she was plainly wasting and was very feeble. Her eyes, though, were as bright as ever; sometimes they looked as hard as flint. The doctor, whom Madame Nicolas insisted upon her seeing occasionally, gave a name to her disease; it was a Greek name and sounded convincing. She was taking a tonic especially prepared for her, from a large bottle, three times a day.

Fifine was a great gossip. When and how she gathered her news nobody could tell. It was always said she knew ten times more than the weekly paper would dare to print. She often visited Tante Elodie, and she told her news of everyone; among others of Gabriel.

It was she who told that he had abandoned the study of the law. She told Tante Elodie when he started for the city to look for work and when he came back from the fruitless search.

'Did you know that Gabriel is working on the railroad, now? Fireman! Think of it! What a comedown from reading law in Morrison's office. If I were a man, I'd try to have more strength of character than to go to the dogs on account of a girl; an insignificant somebody from Kansas! Even if she is going to marry my brother, I must say it was no way to treat a boy – leading him on, especially a boy like Gabriel, that any girl would have been glad – Well, it's none of my business; only I'm sorry he took it like he did. Drinking himself to death, they say.'

That morning, as she was taking up the seams of the silk dress, there was fresh news of Gabriel. He was tired of the railroad, it seemed. He was down on his father's place herding cattle, breaking in colts, drinking like a fish.

'I wouldn't have such a thing on my conscience! Goodness me!
I couldn't sleep at nights if I was that girl.'

Tante Elodie always listened with a sad, resigned smile. It did
not seem to make any difference whether she had Gabriel or not.
He had broken her heart and he was killing her. It was not his
crime that had broken her heart; it was his indifference to her
love and his turning away from her.

It was whispered about that Tante Elodie had grown indifferent
to her religion. There was no truth in it. She had not been to
confession for two months; but otherwise she followed closely the
demands made upon her; redoubling her zeal in church work and
attending mass each morning.

At the wedding she was holding quite a little reception of her
own in the corner of the gallery. The air was mild and pleasant.
Young people flocked about her and occasionally the radiant
bride came out to see if she were comfortable and if there was
anything she wanted to eat or drink.

A young girl leaning over the railing suddenly exclaimed
'*Tiens!* someone is dead. I didn't know any one was sick.' She was
watching the approach of a man who was coming down the
street, distributing, according to the custom of the country, a
death notice from door to door.

He wore a long black coat and walked with a measured tread.
He was as expressionless as an automaton; handing the little slips
of paper at every door; not missing one. The girl, leaning over the
railing, went to the head of the stairs to receive the notice when
he entered Tante Elodie's gate.

The small, single sheet, which he gave her, was bordered in
black and decorated with an old-fashioned wood cut of a weeping
willow beside a grave. It was an announcement on the part of
Monsieur Justin Lucaze of the death of his only son, Gabriel, who
had been instantly killed, the night before, by a fall from his
horse.

If the automaton had had any sense of decency, he might have
skipped the house of joy, in which there was a wedding feast, in
which there was the sound of laughter, the click of glasses, the
hum of merry voices, and a vision of sweet women with their
thoughts upon love and marriage and earthly bliss. But he had
no sense of decency. He was as indifferent and relentless as
Death, whose messenger he was.

The sad news, passed from lip to lip, cast a shadow as if a cloud had flitted across the sky. Tante Elodie alone stayed in its shadow. She sank deeper down into the rocker, more shrivelled than ever. They all remembered Tante Elodie's romance and respected her grief.

She did not speak any more, or even smile, but wiped her forehead with the old lace handkerchief and sometimes closed her eyes. When she closed her eyes she pictured Gabriel dead, down there on the plantation, with his father watching beside him. He might have betrayed himself had he lived. There was nothing now to betray him. Even the shining gold watch lay deep in a gorged ravine where she had flung it when she once walked through the country alone at dusk.

She thought of her own place down there beside Justin's, all dismantled, with bats beating about the eaves and negroes living under the falling roof.

Tante Elodie did not seem to want go in doors again. The bride and groom went away. The guests went away, one by one, and all the little children. She stayed there alone in the corner, under the deep shadow of the oaks while the stars came out to keep her company.